MW00930528

To Hunt the Hunter

Girls Who Dare, Book 11

By Emma V. Leech

Published by Emma V. Leech.

Copyright (c) Emma V. Leech 2020

Cover Art: Victoria Cooper

ASIN No.: B086SKQ1P9

ISBN No: 9798634605029

Table of Contents

Members of the Peculiar Ladies' Book Club

Prunella Adolphus, Duchess of Bedwin – first peculiar lady and secretly Miss Terry, author of *The Dark History of a Damned Duke.*

Mrs Alice Hunt (née Dowding)–not as shy as she once was. Recently married to Matilda's brother, the notorious Nathanial Hunt, owner of *Hunter's*, the exclusive gambling club.

Lady Aashini Cavendish (Lucia de Feria) – a beauty. A foreigner. Recently happily, and scandalously, married to Silas Anson, Viscount Cavendish.

Mrs Kitty Baxter (née Connolly) – quiet and watchful, until she isn't. Recently eloped to marry childhood sweetheart, Mr Luke Baxter.

Lady Harriet St Clair (née Stanhope) Countess of St Clair – serious, studious, intelligent. Prim. Wearer of spectacles. Finally married to the Earl of St Clair.

Bonnie Cadogan – (née Campbell) still too outspoken and forever in a scrape alongside her husband, Jerome Cadogan.

Ruth Anderson– (née Stone) heiress and daughter of a wealthy merchant living peacefully in Scotland after having tamed a wild Highlander.

Minerva de Beauvoir (née Butler) - Prue's cousin. Clever and resourceful, madly in love with her brilliant husband.

Lady Jemima Rothborn (née Fernside)– happily installed at The Priory, skilfully managing staff and villagers and desperately proud of her heroic husband.

Lady Helena Knight (née Adolphus) – vivacious, managing, unexpected and adventurous, having finally caught her Knight in shining armour.

Matilda Hunt – blonde and lovely and ruined in a scandal that was none of her making.

Chapter 1

Dear Miss Hunt,

I wish you were here with us. Everything is strange. Uncle won't let me out of his sight. I got cross yesterday because he won't tell me anything and I punished him by hiding. By the time he found me, I regretted it very much. He was so frantic he looked like he might be ill. I don't know why we left London so quickly or why uncle is so quiet and worried.

I know I must not ask you to come. Uncle forbade me to do so. He says that you may not be friends with him anymore and that if people thought you liked him, they would be cruel to you and no one would talk to you. I don't understand why that is or why there are such stupid rules. I hate all these rules and the people who make us obey them. When I'm a grown-up, I shan't obey the rules if I don't agree with them and I don't care what anyone says about me for doing it.

I wanted to tell you that we are both your friends still, no matter what stupid people say, even if we can't see you anymore.

I miss you.

—Excerpt of a letter from Miss Phoebe Barrington to Miss Matilda Hunt.

24th April 1815. Beverwyck, London.

Matilda watched with mixed emotions as Helena made her escape with her new husband. The two of them were so obviously desperate to be alone with each other she could not help but smile, yet that was the last of her little chicks married off and settled. As Bonnie had so helpfully pointed out, that only left her. It hadn't been said with any malice; indeed, Bonnie was being kind, wanting desperately to see Matilda as happily settled as the rest of them.

Somehow, that did not make her feel any better.

Besides, she had more important things to worry about than playing along with the idea she was looking for a husband. She had given up pretending there was the slightest chance of her falling in love with someone else, not when Lucian occupied her every waking moment. Perhaps one day, she would feel able to face the prospect, likely when she was too old to be of interest to anyone… but for now she could not deny what her heart was telling her. Lucian was in trouble, though of what variety she did not understand. Phoebe was afraid for him. They both needed her and, if there was something that Matilda wanted above all else, it was to be needed.

It was remarkably easy to slip away from the gathering unnoticed, and by the time she returned home she was relieved to discover that her packing was done, as she'd requested. She changed quickly as her bags were being secured on the carriage and went down the stairs to find her companion, Mrs Bradford, awaiting her, stony faced. Matilda braced herself, ready for what was to come.

"It won't do, Miss Hunt. I know as well as anyone that you're a good girl, and all those wicked rumours were nothing but hot air, but this… this is madness, and you know it."

"Yes," Matilda said, smiling at the woman. She was a stocky, no nonsense sort, and exactly the kind of chaperone she had sought for herself—that being one who was not overly concerned with the duties of chaperoning if she had a glass of champagne and a companion to chat with. "Mrs Bradford, I know you are quite correct, and I am sorry if my decision is causing you any distress."

"Well, it is, Miss Hunt. You have my promise that I shan't breathe a word of your folly, but be a part of it I won't, and that's an end to it."

Matilda nodded, feeling a little relieved if the truth was told. If she must burn her bridges, she'd rather not have an audience for it. Not that she was going out of her way to ruin herself—if all went well, no one would be any the wiser—but still, it *was* madness, there was no getting away from it.

"It's quite all right, Mrs Bradford. Will you go to your sister's, then?"

"I will, and providing you've got a reputation to protect when all's said and done, you may find me there on your return."

"Thank you." Matilda's reply was warm. She knew it was all she could ask for. "And thank you for your discretion. I do appreciate it."

"Ah, well," Mrs Bradford said. "The world is a cruel place for a young woman sometimes, and I know you've a kind heart—too kind, that's the trouble—but you must do as you see fit. Good afternoon to you, Miss Hunt. I wish you well and Godspeed."

Matilda watched as the woman left, and then turned at the sound of footsteps on the stairs.

"Well, good riddance, I say."

Matilda smiled at her maid.

"Oh, Sarah, I can hardly blame the poor woman. I rather feel I have lost my mind, but… well, my heart won't let me rest until I know what is going on."

"I reckon you and Montagu have got unfinished business and that's the truth," Sarah said. "And it's what women do, isn't it? Follow their hearts, even when it leads them into danger. I'll be beside you though, miss, no matter what. You've my promise on that."

Matilda blinked back tears, touched by Sarah's words. She was a sweet, good-hearted girl, and had always staunchly defended any decision Matilda made, never mind how idiotic. She suspected that Sarah was far too romantic and perhaps just a little ambitious, though, hoping underneath it all to one day be lady's maid to a marchioness. Well, there was no hope of that, and Matilda had told her so, but she was not convinced her words had hit home.

"Well, then, we'd best be off, or we won't be there before dark. Are you ready, dear?"

"Ready for anything, I am," Sarah said with a grin. "I'll just go and check all your bags have been packed properly, and I'll be with you."

Matilda nodded. She went and settled herself in the carriage. While she waited, she took out the letter Phoebe had sent her and read it for the fiftieth time.

"I'm coming, Phoebe," she said softly, before folding the letter and putting it away once more. "I'm coming."

***

24th April 1815, Dern, Sevenoaks, Kent.

Bertha Appleton had worked at Dern since she was just a girl. She'd begun as a scullery maid until she'd gained a place in the kitchen, where her talent had been spotted by the cook, a Mrs Drugget. When that fine lady was finally persuaded to enjoy her retirement some fifteen years later, she was quick to recommend Bertha to take her place, a service which Bertha never forgot, and so she always took pains to visit Mrs Drugget in the little cottage on the estate set aside for the purpose. It was one thing you could say for the Barringtons: they always paid their staff well and looked after their needs. Mind you, they had to oftentimes, as loyalty wasn't cheap, and a family with more secrets would be hard to find, and that was a fact.

Bertha, or Pippin as she had become known to the last lot of Barrington children, had seen three marquesses come and go, but there was no question that the present Montagu was her favourite. As a child he'd been bright, lively, and funny, and the cleverest little lad she'd ever come across. Little Lucian. Ah, what a handful he'd been! Of course, that was before the dark days, and nothing had ever been the same since. He certainly had never been the same. It had fair broken her heart to see the change in him, but what was done was done and there was no point crying over spilt milk, no matter how much it grieved you.

It was certainly not her place to do so, but she mothered the fellow and his little niece as best she could, though no doubt she overstepped the mark a time or two. She might get one of the master's cool looks on occasion, but he knew as well as she did that it cut no ice with her, and was all for show. She was as popular with them as they were with her, and that was just fine. So, it was with little surprise that she looked up to see Miss Phoebe had snuck into the kitchens and was beside her in a moment, tugging on her apron.

"And what can I do you for, my little mistress?"

"Nothing," the girl said with a heavy sigh. "I was just feeling sad and I wanted to be with someone cheerful."

"Now, and don't you tell me your uncle isn't full of smiles for you?" Pippin asked, pulling out a chair at the kitchen table and pouring the girl a glass of milk.

"Oh, no. He is, of course, but they're not real smiles at the moment. They're the sort he puts on his face when he's trying to make sure I'm happy, so I don't worry for him."

Pippin sighed inwardly. The trouble was the girl and her uncle were two peas in a pod. She was a sight too perspicacious for her age, or her own good.

"Do you know why we came back, Pippin?"

"As if his lordship confides his business in me!" Pippin exclaimed with a laugh, though she knew all too well, and the truth of it made her sick to her stomach. Poor Lucian. No wonder he'd looked so grey and ill when they'd returned. She didn't blame Phoebe for her concern. She felt it herself, as she had felt the atmosphere the moment he'd stepped through the door, the weight of the past so tangible you could cut it with a knife. The palace was full of secrets and Lucian carried too many of them alone. She had hoped, for a brief time... but no, there was no point in hoping for things that would never come to pass.

Duty.

God, she hated that word, hated the way those little boys had been lectured and bullied into believing their only purpose was to serve the family name, to bring honour and glory and power to the great house of Barrington. It was their solemn duty to achieve more than their forebears, whether through politics or marriage. It didn't much matter which, only that the Barringtons were the greatest family in the country. There was never any talk of happiness or love. Those were concepts the children of a Montagu could not afford, poor little blighters.

"Well, he won't tell me either," Phoebe said with a sigh as Pippin slid a plate of biscuits in front of her.

With a sharp gesture Pippin sent the two kitchen maids away, telling them to find work elsewhere for the moment. All the staff were loyal to Montagu, but there was no sense in giving them things to tattle about if it could be helped.

"I was so looking forward to going to Gunter's and Astley's, and all the places he promised we would go, and I can't even complain, as he looks so wretchedly guilty it makes my tummy feel all squirmy and uncomfortable."

Pippin felt her heart squeezed in her chest. Not for the first time, she cursed herself for her blindness all those years ago, for not having realised sooner what was going on beneath this roof, and under their very noses. She was not a woman who condoned violence—in her opinion there wasn't much that couldn't be resolved with a bit of honesty and a good talk over a cup of tea—but remembering those days brought it all back, and she wanted badly to hurt those responsible. Not her place, though, she'd done as much as possible to protect Lucian. They all had, her and Mr Denton and Mrs Frant, but servants were limited in what they could achieve, and they'd risked all that they'd dared. So now she did what she could once again, as little as it seemed to be.

She pulled out the chair beside Phoebe, and sat down.

"Grownups sometimes have to do things they don't want to do, my lamb, and it might not seem to make the least bit of sense to you, but your uncle is taking care of you as best he can. You trust him, don't you?"

"Oh, of course I do," Phoebe said, wide-eyed at the idea Pippin might think otherwise. "The problem is, I sometimes think he doesn't trust himself. He's always looking at that horrid book, and afterwards he looks so… so pale and determined, like he's persuaded himself to eat a slug."

Despite everything, Pippin felt her lips twitch. Phoebe had quite an imagination, and quite a turn of phrase. Still, she knew what the girl meant and heartily wished she'd burnt the bloody book when she'd had the chance. She hadn't dared at the time, knowing it contained a great deal of knowledge the young marquess would badly need. If she'd known then what else it contained, she'd not have hesitated. Poor Lucian had not required his father's voice bullying him, even from beyond the grave, but it was too late now. The damage was done.

"Do you think he'd marry Miss Hunt if not for that book?"

Pippin stared at Phoebe, a little surprised, though why she had no idea. Two peas in a pod, indeed. You couldn't get anything past either of them.

"It doesn't really matter, does it?" she asked softly. "He won't ever make himself happy if it meant damaging the family name. You know that."

Phoebe face darkened, a familiar thunderstorm entering her eyes, her jaw growing tight, and in that moment she looked so much like the energetic, vibrant little boy Pippin had known that she wanted to cry. Phoebe stood so quickly the chair she'd been sitting on toppled backwards.

"I hate it!" she cried, her slender hands balled into fists. "I hate the horrid name. I don't want to be a Barrington. I should prefer to be a Smith or a Brown or... or *anything* else if it meant he would be happy and... and... Oh, I *hate* it!"

With a strangled sob, Phoebe turned to run, but Pippin stood and caught her, pulling her into a fierce hug and holding her tight while the little girl cried out all her frustration.

Finally, she was quiet and exhausted. Pippin sat down in the chair with Phoebe on her lap, and stroked her hair, remembering another child and another time, many years ago.

Chapter 2

Mr Knight,

It seems I must felicitate you on your recent marriage to Lady Helena. You made an exceptional choice. She is a spirited young lady and I recall how much you enjoy a challenge. I have the greatest admiration for you for getting Bedwin to accept your suit. I am all agog to hear how you achieved such a coup, but after all the man has a deal of good sense and must see it is an apt match, the views of the ton notwithstanding. I wish you both happy, of all men I believe you deserve it.

I thank you for your note regarding Burton. He is indeed becoming a thorn in my side. Sadly, not the only one. I hesitate to make this request in the circumstances, but I have need of your men's particular skills. If you can tear yourself away from your lovely bride for a few moments, please instruct them to find out everything they can concerning my uncle, Theodore Barrington. I want to know where he goes, who he sees and, most particularly, who is funding his stay in London, for I believed I had cut off all but a very modest allowance. Yes, I am a wicked nephew, am I not? I will leave you to speculate as to my motives. Most everyone else has painted me a villain, so I am curious to know what you'll make of this. Naturally, my own sources are investigating the matter too, but he is aware of my methods and, as yours tread a different path, it would be as well to combine forces. As ever, you will find me suitably grateful for your aid in this.

—Excerpt of a letter from The Most Honourable Lucian Barrington, Marquess of Montagu, to Mr Gabriel Knight.

24th April 1815. Dern, Sevenoaks, Kent.

It was dusk when the carriage carried them through the first of Dern Palace's impressive gatehouses. Matilda put a hand to stomach to settle the sudden eruption of butterflies. She drew in a deep breath as her heart sped, wondering if perhaps this had been such a good idea. What on earth was Lucian to think if she arrived on his doorstep at this hour? He'd no doubt think what any man would, that she'd changed her mind and decided to become his mistress. She could hardly blame him for it. Well, she'd have to take her chances. A warm hand covered hers, which was decidedly damp and clammy, and Matilda smiled at her maid.

"Courage, Miss Hunt. We've come this far."

"Indeed we have," Matilda said with a huff of laughter.

Well, she'd gone and done it now. She'd have to see what hand fate would play her from this moment on.

She was helped down from the carriage by an imposing footman, resplendent in Montagu's usual black and silver colours. Mr Denton, the butler, came forward to meet her. Matilda had taken an immediate liking to the Welshman during her brief stay here at the beginning of March, and her opinion was not damaged by his manner.

"Good evening, Miss Hunt. I am afraid we were not expecting a visit," he said, without betraying the least suspicion of judgement.

"I know," she said with a rueful smile. "Indeed, I did not expect to be here, only…."

She hesitated, uncertain of what to say to him.

"Only?"

There was a glint of something in his eyes that might have been hopeful, and so Matilda decided she could do worse than confide in him. If she'd made a terrible mistake, perhaps he would tell her so, and she could turn around and go home with no one any the wiser.

"Oh, Denton. I don't know what I'm doing, truth be told, only I had the… the strangest feeling that Lord Montagu… that he was in trouble, and that he needed someone. A… A friend. Oh, dear, how ludicrous it sounds when you say it out loud, yet it seemed perfectly reasonable back in town."

Matilda had practically convinced herself to turn around and get back into the carriage when Denton did the most extraordinary thing for a butler. He reached out and took her hand. He squeezed her fingers, so briefly she could almost think she'd imagined it, but then he compounded the breach of etiquette by smiling at her.

Good heavens.

"Thank you," he said, and then all at once he was again the grave and distinguished butler she'd met before. "If you would come this way, Miss Hunt. I believe you must be fatigued by your journey. I shall have tea brought to the salon."

Matilda exchanged a glance with Sarah, who was looking quite as stunned as she felt, before they followed Denton indoors. They had barely taken two steps through the door when Matilda saw Phoebe, holding the hand of a plump, older lady with greying hair. With a cry of delight, Phoebe let go of the hand she'd been clutching and flew at Matilda, barrelling into her with such force that Matilda nearly lost her footing.

"Miss Hunt! Miss Hunt!" the girl cried, clinging to Matilda with surprising strength, considering her slender frame, and sobbing her heart out.

"Phoebe!" Matilda said, getting to her knees and hugging her tightly. Whatever misgivings she might have had flew away in an instant as Phoebe clung to her like a limpet. "Come now. There, there, don't cry. It's all right."

"You came," Phoebe sobbed, choked as she wiped her eyes and nose with the back of her hand. "I kn-knew you'd come. Uncle said you couldn't, but I kn-knew...."

"Matilda?"

Her name, spoken as if from a long way off, had her head snapping around, and Matilda felt her breath catch.

Lucian.

She'd never seen him look anything but pristine, and to see him now, wearing only dark trousers, a rumpled shirt with the sleeves pushed up to his elbows and no cravat.... How unfair it was that he looked more beautiful than ever in disarray, where she likely looked a fright after her hasty leave taking and some hours in a jolting carriage.

"Good evening, Lucian," she said, not the least bit surprised her voice quavered, but rather astonished that the words came out at all.

The staff melted away at the briefest tilt of his head, Mr Denton discreetly taking Sarah with him, and the three of them were alone.

"Have you run mad?" he asked, staring at her as though he could not quite believe she was here.

"Of course she's not mad. She came because she knew something was wrong. I told you she would. I *told* you." Phoebe's voice was indignant, and her grasp on Matilda unrelenting.

"Phoebe, you know she can't stay. We discussed this," he began, the confusion in his eyes so evident that Matilda had to suppress the desire to laugh. Poor Lucian. He'd pursued her for so long and, when he finally tried to do the right thing, she landed herself on his doorstep.

"You will stay, won't you?" Phoebe demanded, looking very much as if she would take a pet if Matilda said no.

"Yes," she said, though she looked at Lucian as she said it. "I will stay for a little while, until I am certain that you are both well. That is what friends do, no? Is that not so, my lord?"

Lucian stared at her, his expression unreadable.

"Pippin," he called softly. "You may as well show yourself. I know you're there."

A moment later the older lady who had been holding Phoebe's hand appeared. So this was the beloved cook that Phoebe had spoken of during her last visit. The woman didn't look at all sheepish at having been caught eavesdropping, nor did she seem the least bit impressed by Lucian's cool glare.

"Take Miss Barrington to her governess, if you would, please, and then you may send refreshments to the library."

"My lord," the woman said, bobbing a curtsey before approaching Phoebe. "Now then, my lamb, do as your uncle says."

Phoebe turned imploring eyes upon Matilda. "You won't let him send you away, will you?"

"Phoebe!" Lucian said, clearly exasperated.

Matilda smiled and shook her head. "He's never been able to make me do something I don't want to yet, Phoebe, so no, I won't. I promise."

Phoebe let out a breath of relief and kissed Matilda's cheek. "Goodnight, Miss Hunt, and thank you so much for coming."

Matilda watched until Phoebe disappeared before she could bring herself to face Lucian again.

"Why?" he demanded, a thread of anger behind that one word. "Why have you come?"

"Because you are all alone and I think something is very wrong. I told you I would be your friend, Lucian. I meant it. I don't abandon my friends."

She could read nothing from his eyes and had not the slightest idea what he was thinking, whether he was furious or overjoyed, or both. Neither. Before she could take a guess, he turned on his heel.

"Come, then. You may take tea and explain to me, in comfort, what manner of madness has overcome you."

Matilda followed him, pleased to go to the library which had been one of her favourite rooms when she'd visited before. It was a lavish space, heavy with oak panelling and thick rugs. There were many seating areas, and lamps which cast golden pools of light at inviting intervals, beckoning you to sit and make yourself comfortable with a book. She had noticed this often at Dern. For all its grandeur and pomp, now and then she'd stumbled upon a room which had a different, private feel to it. This was one of those, and she suspected it showed this man's hand at work. He had made a home here among the rooms of this cavernous palace, for himself and for Phoebe, carving out a few spaces in the acres of magnificent splendour where they could be at ease... though ease was not a word to describe the present atmosphere.

Lucian beckoned her to sit and then went to stand at the fireplace, leaning upon the mantel and staring down at the flames. Though she'd spend the entire journey here thinking about what she would say to him, Matilda was at a loss and was beyond relieved when Denton arrived bearing a tea tray.

"We have prepared the yellow suite for Miss Hunt, my lord," he said, deftly arranging cups and saucers and placing a plate with a selection of bite-sized savoury tarts, and another of small pastries before her. The kind of thing to tempt the most reluctant appetite.

Matilda thought she saw a flare of something in Lucian's eyes, but could not guess what it signified and, whatever it was, Denton staunchly ignored it by not meeting his master's frigid gaze.

"Shall I pour the tea, Miss Hunt?"

"Please, don't trouble yourself," Matilda said, intrigued by Lucian's obvious tension and now rather wishing the obliging butler would make himself scarce so she could discover its cause.

"Your maid is unpacking your belongings," Denton continued with blithe calm. "You may rest assured I will see to her comfort too, Miss Hunt."

"Thank you, Denton, you are most kind. Do tell her not to wait up for me. I shall see to myself tonight."

"Very good, miss."

Matilda wondered if she was imagining the warmth in the man's eyes, and decided that it had been such an eventful day, she'd best set no store by it. Her emotions were all out of kilter and, in her present state, she'd no doubt read too much into it.

Soon they were alone once again, and Matilda followed the butler's example by pretending Lucian wasn't there, so she didn't have to meet that uncomfortably searching silver gaze, which she could feel trained upon her.

"Milk?" she asked, not looking up.

"Yes."

"Sugar?"

"No."

His words were clipped and Matilda kept her eyes on the tea until she had made it to her satisfaction, and then dared to lift her gaze with the cup she offered. His scrutiny was everything she had expected, and the cup rattled a little in the saucer until he deigned to take it from her.

To her relief, he did, and sat in the chair to her left rather than beside her on the loveseat.

They sipped their tea in silence for what seemed like an eternity to Matilda, whose stomach was tying itself into a Gordian knot. Finally, he spoke.

"You are too good, Matilda. Foolish beyond measure, forgiving beyond anything any reasonable person would expect, and… and I am touched, but this won't do. You must see. You have impressed upon me time and again the importance of everything you hope for, and now you would throw it all away, and for what? You've not come here to be my lover. I'm not fool enough to believe that. So, you would risk everything and gain nothing?"

"If you need me, as I believe you do, yes, Lucian. I would."

She held his gaze and this time it was Lucian who looked away, unsettled. He rarely let anyone see what he felt, had allowed her only a few brief glimpses of his heart, but his confusion was evident now.

Matilda smiled. "It is what you never understood. You cannot force me to your will with promises of wealth or power, but when you trusted me with a little of your real self, you treated me as a friend, a confidant. For that, I would move mountains if needs be."

He let out a breath and set down his teacup. "I cannot help but think fate is laughing at me."

"How so?"

She watched as he turned to face her. "Do you not understand the temptation you present, even now? Can you truly have no idea of the control it requires to sit here and not beside you, to not take you in my arms and persuade you to be with me for always, and *not* as my friend, Matilda? Not only that, at least. You once told me you were glad I'd not asked you to marry me, to save your reputation, for you'd rather be ruined than married to a man more dead than alive."

Matilda blushed, remembering that particular clash all too vividly.

"Oh, no, don't you dare regret it," he said, his silver eyes flashing. "You were right. I have been cold and dead inside for too many years but, you and Phoebe, you won't leave me be, you won't let me skulk about in the dark where I belong. The pair of you... you're always...."

He stood suddenly, raking a hand through his hair, and Matilda felt her heart clench. He sounded almost angry, certainly frustrated. She knew she had caught him unawares, unprepared to see her. If he had known she was coming, she would never have seen this side of him, he would never have allowed her a glimpse of this dishevelled, less than pristine version of the marquess.

"Always what?" she asked gently.

There was a taut silence. "You make me wish I were different."

"Different how?" Matilda's heart gave an uncomfortable thud in her chest, and she was too aware of the breathlessness of her words.

"If... If my father and Philip had lived, if I had only been the second son—the spare—I might have courted you." He let out a breath of laughter. "My God, what am I saying? Even then Father would have been furious. He would never have allowed it."

Matilda set down her teacup before she dropped it. "Would he have cut you off?"

"Probably."

"But you... you'd have done it, anyway?"

He turned back to her and nodded, holding her gaze. "Yes."

Matilda's breath caught. *Oh.*

He turned away from her then and moved to the door. "Finish your tea, Matilda. I'll have Denton show you to your room. Goodnight."

He didn't look back, just closed the door on her. Matilda hardly knew what to make of what had been said, and they'd never even mentioned his uncle.

Chapter 3

My lord,

I thank you for your kind words and good wishes upon my recent marriage. I confess I wrongly assumed that you of all people would be appalled by my having so lowered Lady Helena in the eyes of society. I am gratified by your comments and estimation of my character. Among the men of higher rank I have dealt with, you have always been the most honourable and truthful – not always a pleasant experience, but at least one knows where one stands.

For the record, I saw your uncle at Baron Fitzwalter's – I believe he was staying there. I have always trusted my gut instinct and mine was one of deep misgiving for the man. I do not believe you wicked, or that you would move against anyone, let alone a family member, without strong motivation. I will do all in my power to seek the information you require.

—Excerpt of a letter from Mr Gabriel Knight to The Most Honourable Lucian Barrington, Marquess of Montagu.

25th April 1815. Dern, Sevenoaks, Kent.

Matilda started awake with the strong conviction she was being watched. With a little shriek she sat up in bed to discover Phoebe sitting cross-legged at the bottom of the mattress.

"You stayed," she said simply, beaming at Matilda.

Letting out a breath of relief, Matilda sagged back against the pillows and closed her eyes.

"I did," she agreed.

Once her heart had settled down, she opened her eyes again and regarded the child. She looked rather adorable in a white cotton nightgown, with her hair all done up with little rag ribbons to make it fall in ringlets.

"Uncle was happy to see you, wasn't he?" Phoebe grinned at her and Matilda cleared her throat, not entirely certain how to answer that. "Well, perhaps he wouldn't say that he was, because he knows you might get into trouble for coming. He gets cross when he's worried, you see."

"Does he?" Matilda asked, watching with amusement as Phoebe crawled up the bed and settled closer to her.

"Oh yes. He never scolds me when I'm naughty, or at least not properly, but if I frighten him, like when I hid, oh… that's different." She was quiet for a moment. "Can we go for a picnic? It's going to be a lovely day today."

"I don't know," Matilda said, trying not to imagine a picnic with Lucian and Phoebe. The image was too tempting to be good for her. With difficulty, she reminded herself why she was here, why she had risked her own future, and it was not to enjoy herself, but to discover what had sent Montagu running from town with Phoebe. "I think perhaps you'd better get washed and dressed before you get into trouble with Miss Peabody. I'll see you at breakfast, and then we can discover what your uncle has in mind."

"All right, then," Phoebe said, climbing off the bed. "But do try to persuade him that a picnic is a good idea. I'm sure he'd say yes if you asked him."

Matilda laughed and watched as Phoebe scurried from the room.

***

"Well, you look a picture and that's a fact, miss, even if I do say it myself," Sarah said with a satisfied sigh as she put the finishing touches to Matilda's hair. "And this room is just sumptuous. Even my room is done up pretty. Imagine living in such a place!"

Matilda sent Sarah a reproving look. "No, Sarah, do not imagine it. Remember what I told you, and don't go getting any romantic ideas. I'm here to be a friend to someone who has no notion of what a friend is, that's all."

Sarah made a disgruntled noise that did not sound as if she approved of this idea, but Matilda was in no mood to labour the point. Besides, she did look rather well. Inspired by the sunny yellow room and the beautiful day that had dawned outside the windows, she had chosen a bright yellow gown with a fine yellow tulle overlay embroidered with tiny black dots. It was lovely, and such a cheerful colour that she hoped it would encourage fortune to smile on her endeavours. Either way, it lifted her spirits, and that was the main thing.

Matilda made her way down the stairs to find Denton waiting to greet her.

"Good morning, Miss Hunt. I do hope everything was to your satisfaction?"

With a little laugh, Matilda nodded. "I would defy a queen to find a single thing not to her satisfaction. It's all beautiful and quite beyond anything I've ever experienced."

Denton nodded his approval. "His lordship likes things just so, Miss Hunt, and we take pains to ensure everything is as he likes it."

"Is he an exacting master, then?" Matilda asked with interest.

"Only in as much as he expects everyone to do their best, miss. The standards he sets for himself are far more exacting than anything he demands of his staff."

Matilda nodded, unsurprised by this. "You've worked here a long time, I think?"

"Five and thirty years, Miss Hunt. I was a footman until Lord Montagu did me the great honour of making me his valet when he was a very young man, but I had always held an ambition to be butler, which his lordship well knew. Thanks to him, I have held the position for almost fifteen years."

Their conversation was curtailed as they'd reached the breakfast parlour, and so Matilda thanked him and went in. Lucian sat at the table reading a letter, looking as pristine and coolly elegant as he always did, the crumpled shirt of last night a distant memory, though one Matilda would never forget. He looked up as she approached, and stared for a moment before getting to his feet, still holding the letter.

"Miss Hunt," he said, never taking his eyes from her.

"My, we're very formal this morning. Are you still angry with me?"

He frowned as though the question puzzled him and then glanced at the letter, his frown deepening. He set it down and cleared his throat. "I was never angry with you... Matilda."

Matilda smiled at the footman who drew out a chair for her to the left of Lucian, who sat at the head of the table. Once seated, she accepted a cup of hot chocolate before glancing up at Lucian. He was still standing, staring at her.

"Is there something wrong?" she asked, a little anxious now.

He shook his head and sat down again.

"No," he said softly. "Not a thing."

She gave him a quizzical look, uncertain of his mood and a little daunted by the intensity with which he looked at her. Self-conscious now, she reached for a fresh baked roll and tore it in half, applying butter before regarding the preserves.

"The cherry jam is exceptional," he said. "We have the most marvellous crop every year. I used to make myself ill as a boy, gorging on them."

Matilda gave him a sideways glance, amused. "I cannot imagine you indulging in anything to excess. You're far too controlled. You don't even drink, do you?"

His brows drew together a little. "I drink, but not a great deal, certainly not to excess. Is it not the mark of a gentleman to control such urges? An excess of anything is unbecoming, is it not?"

"I suppose it depends on how far one carries the theory. Drunkenness and gluttony, or any addiction to vice, is certainly unbecoming in anyone. But too much control can be as damaging as none, if it is exercised too rigidly."

"We must beg to differ," he said, a taut note entering his voice. "If you wish me to behave myself."

Matilda felt the blush creep up her throat, and returned her attention to her breakfast.

"Why did you leave London?"

She dared to look up and saw him lift his hand, a small, silent movement that nonetheless had the servants filing out one after the other and closing the door behind them.

"I don't wish to speak of that now."

"Later then?" she pressed, reminding herself why she had come.

"Perhaps."

"What do you wish to do, then?"

He gave her a long, scrolling look that made her stomach quiver.

"To spend the day enjoying my extraordinarily good fortune in having your company," he said softly.

Matilda licked her lips, failing to settle the sudden burst of nervousness that had her all a-flutter.

"Phoebe suggested a picnic."

She knew she ought not to have said it; it was too beguiling, as though this was a place outside of reality, somewhere they could exist without the world intruding on their idyll. That was a dangerous facade, but one in which she could too easily believe.

"Then we had best not disappoint her. I'm delighted to have an excuse to cancel a meeting with my solicitor. I shall rearrange it for tomorrow morning. I'll have Denton occupy the fellow and keep him out of my hair until then. We would not wish for our day to be interrupted."

Though she tried her best to concentrate on her breakfast, Matilda had become all fingers and thumbs and the knife clattered onto her plate.

"Drat," she exclaimed, embarrassed, and then what little composure she possessed left her in a rush as Lucian reached across the table.

He trailed a fingertip down the back of her hand.

"You're real," he said with a breath of laughter, sounding astonished and as mystified as she felt.

"Of course," she said, a little tart now in her confusion. "I'd hardly be this clumsy otherwise."

"You're everything I dream of, exactly as you are."

"Lucian," she protested, with the strangest feeling in her chest, as though someone had reached in and squeezed her heart.

"It's true."

She closed her eyes for a moment and when she opened them, his hand still rested beside hers on the table, palm up, close but not touching. He wouldn't, she realised. He'd given his word and he wouldn't break it. That brief touch was as much as he would allow himself. Matilda swallowed, knowing she was a fool, but she inched her hand closer. Her heart thudded unevenly, and her conscience screamed *danger,* but she ignored it and lifted her hand, resting her palm upon his. Their fingers twined together, neither of them saying a word, neither of them looking at the other, only at the place their hands met. The moment was unbearably sweet, ridiculously innocent and yet the air between them simmered with everything that was unsaid, everything they could not have.

The door burst open and Matilda snatched her hand back as Phoebe ran into the room.

"She stayed!" she cried, triumphant as she crossed the floor in the space of a second and threw her arms about Lucian's neck. "I told you so. I told you."

"So you did," Lucian said dryly. "And, seeing as you are in such good spirits, do you think you could refrain from strangling me and ruining my cravat? And sit down like a young lady. I'd rather Miss Hunt did not believe you have been raised by wolves."

"Oh, pooh. Miss Hunt doesn't mind. Do you, Miss Hunt? And your cravat is just as perfect as it always is, but I will sit down because I'm famished! Oh, is that cherry jam? Lovely. It's my favourite. Have you tried it, Miss Hunt? Can we call you Matilda, please? I should like it if you called me Phoebe. She can, can't she, Uncle?"

"I doubt it, bearing in mind she cannot get a word in edgewise at present."

27

Phoebe snorted and Lucian raised his eyes to the heavens. Matilda just watched, utterly enchanted, and with a fatalistic sense of panic growing in her chest. She was in deep, *deep* trouble.

***

After breakfast, arrangements were made for their outing. Matilda had been to picnics given by those of the *haute ton* on many occasions. It differed little from eating in a lavish, formal dining room, except that the poor servants had the onerous task of carrying everything outside and setting it up under an awning. So she admitted herself surprised when she met Phoebe and Lucian outside the house to discover a very modest pony and gig, which had an enormous wicker basket strapped on the back. Lucian held the reins, with Phoebe practically bouncing with impatience beside him.

"How charming this is," Matilda exclaimed as a footman handed her up. She settled herself beside Phoebe.

"There's a lovely spot under a great oak tree at the Mast Head, and at the bottom of the hill there's a little stream," Phoebe said, her eyes alight with excitement. She held up a large glass jar with string tied about the neck to make a handle. "You can catch sticklebacks, too, and it's ever so pretty, but it's too far to walk. I suggested the gig. It is a good idea, isn't it?"

"It's perfect," Matilda assured her as Lucian urged the pony into a smart trot.

Lucian glanced over at her. "Did you think me too high in the instep to sit on a blanket and eat with my fingers?"

"Yes," Matilda admitted, earning herself an amused smile.

"What an opinion she has of me, Bee."

"And what would you expect me to think?" Matilda countered.

"Oh, but I told you he's not like people think he is," Phoebe explained. "Not nearly so proud and cold as he seems."

Matilda smiled at Phoebe's earnest assurance. "That's because he loves you best, Phoebe. It's different for the rest of us mere mortals."

"Oh, but not for you, Matilda. I know he feels the same way about you. Don't you, Uncle?" It was an innocent, childish remark, but the impact on Matilda's heart was a devastating one. A blush crept up her throat and she turned her head away, pretending to be engrossed in the passing scenery.

"Not *quite* the same way, child," Lucian replied, though the teasing note Matilda had expected to hear was not in evidence.

"Well, no, of course not. Matilda is a grownup, a lady."

"Indeed."

An uneasy silence settled over them which Phoebe was oblivious to, thank heavens, and the little girl chattered and laughed and soon the atmosphere dissipated. It was impossible to be uneasy with her animated company and the droll things she said.

On the way, Lucian halted the pony so that they might admire the deer which abounded in the vast parkland surrounding Dern Palace.

"The park was first enclosed in the mid-fifteenth century," Lucian said as they viewed dozens of deer peacefully grazing in an open field. "Today there are close to four hundred fallow deer in the park."

"They're wild," Phoebe said with a heavy sigh.

"Phoebe is determined to tame one." Lucian gave his niece a reproachful glance.

"Oh, but they are so pretty," Phoebe retorted. "I just want to stroke one."

"Oh, yes, and feed it cake and tie it up with ribbons, no doubt," Lucian said with the lift of one eyebrow. "What a pitiful fate for such a beautiful creature."

"Oh, pooh," Phoebe scoffed. "I bet it would like cake and ribbons if it had the chance to try them."

Lucian laughed, a proper full-hearted laugh, and Matilda was so astonished that she stared at him, wide-eyed. He caught sight of her shocked expression and stopped abruptly.

"What?"

"Dimples," she said faintly.

Oh lord, she was doomed.

Lucian frowned, glancing between her and Phoebe.

Phoebe snorted. "I told you," she crowed, laughing at her uncle, and bouncing in her seat. "Ha ha! I *told* you so."

Lucian mock glowered at her. "Don't be ridiculous. I do not have dimples."

"He does, doesn't he, Matilda?"

"I'm afraid so. How shocking," Matilda replied, shaking her head as though it was the most scandalous thing she'd ever heard. "Just wait until the *ton* hears about this."

"Now we have something to blackmail him with," Phoebe said with a smug smile. "We can make him do anything we want."

"Two against one. How cruel you women are," he lamented, and Matilda could not look at him, could not withstand the warmth in his eyes. She ought not have come. She knew she ought not have come, yet she could not regret a moment of this day, *would not* regret it.

Lucian turned the pony onto a narrow ferny path that led uphill, winding through hawthorn bushes and thick clumps of yew and hornbeam, and graceful, lofty ash trees. A pheasant lifted from the bracken with an indignant squawk and a flurry of wings, and Lucian soothed the startled pony, who shook his head and huffed before walking on.

"This part of the park hasn't changed since the middle ages," Lucian said. "There are vast areas which have been replanted recently, that's to say two centuries ago. Beech stands and tree-lined avenues. There's the chestnut walk and others of beech and oak. They're very grand, but I rather like it here. It's wilder and terribly ancient. You can sense it, I think. The ancient nature of the place, a connection to an undisturbed earth which is sometimes missing elsewhere. It's peaceful."

Stop it. Matilda wanted to say it out loud. To demand he not speak so, not reveal more of a man about whom she wanted to know everything. She had been attracted to him from the start, though she'd never understood why. His beauty, perhaps, or his damned arrogance, for she had never been able to refuse a challenge. Yet, over the past months, that had changed. *He* had changed. He had allowed her a glimpse of the man, not the marquess, and with each glimpse her interest had grown, her desire for more of him had led her on. She had foolishly offered her friendship, and that she could not take back.

Now, here she was, falling too hard and too fast for a man she could never have, unless she would share him with a wife. How could she love a man and watch him go to another, have a family with another, and call his wife beloved in public? No matter the truth of his feelings… no. *No*. Her heart hurt.

The woodland opened out again and they crested a hill crowned by a single, proud oak tree. It was thick and gnarled, with a vast trunk and a heavy low-hanging green canopy. Lucian drew the pony to a halt and climbed down, moving around to the other side to give Matilda his hand. Matilda took it, avoiding his eye, and releasing her hold the moment she'd stepped down.

"Come along," Phoebe said, grinning at Matilda and holding the jar she'd brought aloft as she jumped down from the gig with a flurry of skirts, before her uncle could lift her down. "I want to show you the stream."

They left Lucian to see to the pony and walked down the hill to where a twining stream glittered and burbled in the spring sunshine, worrying its way around rocks and over glistening pebbles. It was exactly the kind of place Matilda had loved as a child, hiding from her governess and escaping to her own world of small adventures, where she could strip off her stockings and paddle, and search for little creatures under rocks and catch tiny, darting fish. She watched with amusement as Phoebe did just that, hitching up her skirts and splashing into the water as she tried to catch the elusive silver sticklebacks, with their sharp spines and glaring eyes.

Matilda watched for a while, calling encouragement and commiserating when the fish proved too speedy and slippery. Taking her own turn, she very nearly fell in, much to Phoebe's delight, and soaked her gloves. It was a good excuse to take them off, though, as it was growing hot, and the lovely day Phoebe had promised hung warm and golden upon the lush green surroundings. She could not resist an occasional glance up the hill. Lucian had unhitched the pony, who was nosing at the grass and chewing with peaceful content. What a beautiful spot this was. She could see why it was a favourite place for them to visit. She did not see Lucian at first and had to search for him, finding him sitting deep in the shade of the great oak, his back against the trunk.

"You can go back if you like."

Matilda looked around to see Phoebe watching her with a satisfied smile, and she felt a surge of embarrassment for having been caught staring. Phoebe only laughed, grinning broadly.

"Oh, go on," the child urged. "He'll be pleased if you go and talk to him. Can't you tell how happy he is that you've come?"

Yes, Matilda thought desperately. Yes, she could. Despite knowing better, she walked back up the hill, her skirts swishing through the meadow grass, brushing past yellow cowslips and shiny buttercups, bold dandelions and drifts of cow parsley.

"You look like a meadow sprite," Lucian observed as she drew nearer. "Like the embodiment of sunshine in that yellow gown."

"Such pretty compliments. You won't turn my head, you know," Matilda lied, throwing her wet gloves down and trying to keep her voice impassive.

"I wasn't trying to. It's mine that been turned, I assure you."

He'd laid two thick blankets on the ground beside the basket and Matilda sat down, carefully arranging her skirts and not looking at him.

"You're so far away. Am I so untrustworthy? You have Phoebe to satisfy propriety, after all. Surely you do not believe me so depraved as to make love to you with her close by?"

"Of course not!" Matilda exclaimed, flustered.

It wasn't *him* she doubted. It came as something of a shock to discover she did trust him after he'd been so blasé about her becoming his mistress. He knew her feelings and, finally, he seemed to have accepted them. So, she was trusting him with her reputation, her virtue. Everything. He would not betray that trust. She believed that.

"Are you afraid of your uncle?"

The question slipped out, rather balder than she'd intended, but she needed to put some emotional distance between them as badly as she did the space of a picnic blanket.

Remember why you came.

His demeanour changed in an instant, and she regretted her demand, but still, it had to be asked. She was not here to become his mistress. She really had no right to be here at all, not as she was, neither lover nor an acceptable friend, fish nor fowl. It was unfair to Phoebe to allow her to believe that Matilda could be a part of their lives. She must help Lucian resolve whatever trouble he was in—if it was within her power—and then she must leave.

"Yes."

She hadn't expected such an answer and was momentarily too surprised to react. So it had been fear she'd seen in his eyes. How strange. She had thought of Lucian—no, of Montagu, for she was beginning to see that these were two distinct personalities—as being arrogantly confident, fearless, emotionless. Powerful. Yet that rather bumbling, gently smiling man with the sparkling eyes had turned him as white as alabaster and sent him running from town. *Why?*

"Must we talk of him?"

He wasn't looking at her, his blond brows drawing together, his gaze intent and his elegant, long fingers worked at snapping a twig into increasingly tiny pieces and arranging them as if for a small bonfire. A heavy gold signet ring glinted on his little finger, the eagle crest catching her eye.

"It's why I came," she said.

"Is it?"

"*Yes.*"

He swept the small pile of twigs away with the side of his hand, an irritated gesture, and then leant his head back against the tree trunk, closing his eyes.

"Lucian, what happened between you? Your uncle told me you tried to kill him."

"That's true."

Matilda gasped as his eyes flicked open, a flash of silver like the darting of fish in the stream below.

"Fair's fair," he said, his tone mocking. "It was my turn."

Chapter 4

Dearest Aashini,

*I am going away for a few days. I have sent
word to my brother that I am staying with you.
If anyone asks, please confirm this and tell them
I have caught a chill and am indisposed. I know
it is wretched of me to ask this of you, but I do
ask, my dear friend. <u>Please.</u> I assure you I am
quite safe and in my right mind — more or less.
Don't worry for me, though I know you shall all
the same. I will explain all on my return. I
know that you, of all people, understand that we
must sometimes take a risk to defend what is
most important to us. I thank you with all my
heart.*

**—Excerpt of a letter from Miss Matilda
Hunt to Aashini Anson, Countess
Cavendish.**

25th April 1815. Dern, Sevenoaks, Kent.

Matilda stared at him, her stomach roiling. "You can't be serious. Surely? Lucian, tell me, what happened?"

In one fluid movement he was on his feet and stalked to the far side of the oak tree.

"Lucian!" she called, but he did not answer.

Unable to leave it at that and knowing he would turn the subject given the least opportunity, she got up, ducking under a low branch to follow him. She held onto it, as though needing to cling to something solid as reality shifted beneath her feet. She was standing behind him, seeing only the rigid set of his shoulders.

"He tried to hurt you?" she asked.

"No. He *did* hurt me. He *tried* to kill me. He's tried many times."

Matilda stared at his back, her breath suspended.

"Why?" she whispered.

There was a disbelieving huff of laughter. "Think about it, Matilda."

"The title," she said, realising at once how obvious it was. "Oh, my… oh, Lucian. But surely, if you—"

"If I what?"

He turned around to face her, his expression hard, his voice as cool as emotionless as she'd ever heard it, as light as if he spoke of nothing more devastating than the weather.

"If I told someone?" One blond eyebrow lifted. "Oh, I tried that. The first time, I was twelve. My aunt Marguerite slapped my face and told me I was wicked and hateful, a vile liar with a spiteful imagination. I tried again a year later, and faced questions about my sanity, about my emotional stability and whether I was sane enough to take control when I came of age. Bedlam beckoned, much to my uncle's amusement, so once again I was forced to back down. No one ever believed me, Matilda. Well, you've met him. You tell me. Isn't he kind? So very genuine, so concerned for everyone's wellbeing. He's so terribly reasonable, so easy and charming and likeable, and I…. I am not."

Matilda felt her chest constrict. When he was twelve. The first attempt on his life had been when he was *twelve*?

"I think he might have been content with controlling the power through me. It was his intention, I believe. The trouble was, unlike Thomas, I was not the least bit biddable. Uncle Theo tried to destroy everything our father had taught us, tried to discredit him and his ideas. Likely he thought that would be easy to do. It was not hard to see how impatient Father was with us, his barely concealed contempt for Thomas' sickly nature and timidity, and my lack of enthusiasm for blood sports and all the things he believed made a man what he was."

He paused and Matilda did not dare speak, not wanting to halt his explanation and sensing how hard it was for him to speak of such things. So she waited, patiently, as he gathered himself to continue.

"My father despised Theo and ignored us, and so Uncle believed we would turn against his values with ease. What he never understood was that I did not resent such treatment. My father *was* Montagu. No matter what you thought of the man, he held the title and the power and did a deal of good, both for the family and those who depend on it. My brother, Philip, was everything Montagu should be, yet with a warmth of manner none of the rest of us possessed. I knew that and I did not resent him. I admired him, for heaven's sake… hero-worshipped him, if you want the truth. My uncle never understood it. He could not. Not when he resented his own brother so thoroughly."

"How?" Matilda asked, hardly daring to, but she had wanted the truth.

He shrugged. "A riding accident the first time. The girth on my saddle worn through—with a little help. It gave way when I took a jump that my uncle assured me I could manage, though it was higher than anything I'd tackled before. Luckily, I only broke my arm, and uncle was so very contrite, so terribly remorseful. He sacked one of the grooms for that. I think I knew even then, in my gut. No one on the staff could have let something like that happen, but we were still friends then, he was still *Uncle Theo*, despite our disagreements. It wasn't until a year later and the third *unfortunate accident* that the scales fell from my eyes. Finally, I allowed myself to believe that I was living with a monster, but by then it was too late."

There was a such a bleak edge to the words, every one weighted with regret, with guilt.

"Why too late?" she asked, confused, for Lucian was alive and so his uncle had failed.

"He'd found the way to manipulate me. By hurting Thomas."

Her breath caught, the shock of his words, the implications....

"Lucian, I'm so—"

"Don't," he said savagely, turning away from her. He dashed a hand over his eyes and walked farther around the tree, leaning back against the trunk.

Matilda followed him tentatively.

"Don't spare your tender feelings for me, Matilda. It was Thomas who suffered, Thomas who...." He broke off and shook his head. "No more. I won't... I *can't* talk about this anymore."

Matilda nodded, hearing the anguish behind his anger. She did not need him to explain that he'd never spoken of this before. It was too obvious. He watched her warily as she moved closer. Good lord, no wonder he kept everyone at arm's length, when even those nearest to him could not be depended on. How foolish to consider trusting a stranger when your own family would betray you in a heartbeat. She ached for the terrified, lonely boy he must have been, and for the man he'd become, cold and powerful and isolated. But he wasn't cold, that was the problem. He was alone, but not the least bit cold.

How she had the courage she did not know, but she lifted her hand to his cheek, an offer of comfort to someone who needed it so desperately.

"You suffered too, Lucian. He hurt you badly, and I *am* sorry. You ought not have been hurt and alone. I am so very sorry, whether or not you want me to be. You can't stop me, you know. I wish I could make it better."

He watched her, and his expression made something painful unfurl in her chest, as though he did not know how to take her words, as if no one had said such things to him before.

He shook his head, as if asking her to stop, but then he closed his eyes and turned his face into her palm, seeking the comfort she offered him.

"No more questions," he said softly. "Just give me today. Please, Matilda. You must go, we both know it, but I am selfish enough to take this day for myself, if you'll allow it."

Matilda nodded, stroking her thumb over the high cheekbone of a face that could appear so cold and austere, but that was warm beneath her touch.

"Just a day," she murmured, knowing what she would do and feeling her blood thrill in her veins at her own audacity.

She took a step closer to him, their bodies almost touching. His gaze sharpened, suddenly intent. "May I…"

"No."

She had no resistance against him, not if he touched her as he so plainly wanted to. Never knowing what it was to kiss him was too dreadful to consider, but she could risk only this.

"Don't move," she warned.

If he put his hands on her they would both be lost. Matilda took hold of his wrists and pressed his hands to the tree trunk.

"Like this, or not at all."

"But…" he began, and she shook her head.

"Don't touch me. Promise?"

He let out a pained huff of laughter.

"Promise," he said begrudgingly, his tone dark.

Matilda glanced down the hill to see Phoebe was still occupied with catching fish before looking back at Lucian, whose eyes were fixed upon her.

"You said it would be sweeter if I instigated our first kiss. Do you remember?"

A sweep of blond eyelashes shuttered his expression for a moment. "Don't remind me of all I have said and done. I am well aware of how little I deserve this, and yet... I was right, was I not?"

"Let's see," she said, and placed her hands upon his chest.

His heart thundered beneath her palm, which was reassuring as he was outwardly as placid as always, save for the way his eyes had grown dark, the pupils wide and blown. She slid her hands to his shoulders, lifted onto her toes and leaned in, pressing her mouth tentatively against his. Her breath caught and sensation lit her up like a lightning strike as desire lanced through her. Lucian kept his word and did not move to touch her, though his breath was coming fast now. Matilda moved her mouth over his, another soft press of lips, and he uttered a low sound that made her heart skip about. She drew back and he followed, seeking more, but she pressed a finger to his lips, a warning.

"Is this retribution?" he asked, his voice husky. "Will you tease and torture me when I have given you my word not to touch?"

Matilda laughed and almost agreed but decided on honesty instead. "No, this is me daring to pet a tiger. It's self-preservation, Lucian, and you know it."

"Then for God's sake, take what you want. I'm dying here."

So she did, pressing closer, her breasts against his hard chest, her mouth firming over his. He angled his head and she gasped as his tongue traced the seam of her lips, seeking, asking. It was both too much and not enough as his tongue found hers and stroked. Oh, she was lost, this was too sweet, too delicious. He did not move, did not break his word, and yet he was utterly in control, drawing her closer with his kiss, making her want more and more with each press of that sinful, wicked, mouth. She had seen him use words as weapons, seen the cruel set of that mouth when he was at his most austere, and yet now it was so achingly tender, so soft, tempting her down a path she could not take.

Matilda pressed closer still, her body alive with need, the place between her thighs that clamoured for him throbbing and damp. Good Lord, but Phoebe was close by, and she… and she wanted….

Matilda broke away from him and stepped back, breathing hard.

"Matilda."

Her name was a plea. His eyes said *more* and *please* and *don't go.* She couldn't look at him, aware of how close she'd been to asking him to touch her, to do anything he wanted.

"I'm sorry," she said, shaking her head and turning away from him. "I… I should not have—"

"Don't," he commanded, his voice sharp. "Don't regret it, for the love of God. I'll remember this until the day I die, Matilda. You did nothing wrong. Damnation, I want you so badly. I don't know…." He gave a soft laugh, though there was no humour in it. "How do I let you go? Tell me how."

Matilda wanted to cry but she forced herself to smile, though she could not bear to turn and look at him. "You say, *goodbye, Matilda*, and I leave. It's quite simple. But I shan't go until I know what I can do to help you."

He made a sound of disgust. "There is nothing you can do, and I suppose that will save you. It is the one thing that can force my hand and make me send you away. My uncle has consistently failed to put a period to my life, and so he will make me pay instead. He will hurt me through those I love, as he has always done."

"Phoebe," Matilda said in a rush as she turned back to him, her hand covering her heart as it was struck with fear. "That's why you left London. That's why you were afraid, you were scared he would hurt her."

Lucian nodded, his expression grave and regretful. "And you, Matilda. If he had the slightest idea how I feel for you...."

Her breath caught at the look in his eyes. Did he mean...?

"Look!"

Matilda almost jumped out of her skin, not having heard Phoebe approach, too caught up in Lucian and his words.

"I caught one!"

There was a moment of stunned silence before Lucian rescued them.

"I'm not certain that will feed us if you were hoping to supply lunch, Bee."

Matilda looked at him in awe. He had crouched down to inspect Phoebe's catch of a single stickleback, and she was astonished at how calm he sounded, when she was still all a-quiver from their kiss and the implication of his words. Practise, she supposed. He'd had years and years to learn how to disguise his feelings, to hide everything but what he wished people to see of him.

"Don't be silly," Phoebe huffed, rolling her eyes. "We can't eat it, but I am famished. Can we have our picnic now?"

Lucian made a show of inspecting the fish before looking back at his niece.

"You look like you fell in," he observed, taking in her rumpled dress and its sodden, muddy hem. "But it is a very fine fish, and of course you are famished. There is no other state for you, child: I believe you have hollow legs. But yes, I think perhaps we should eat now. Go and unpack our feast."

Phoebe gave a little yip of triumph and hurried back around the thick tree trunk to the other side where they'd set out the picnic. Lucian looked up at Matilda, his expression somewhat rueful.

"What an excellent chaperone she is," he murmured. "And no picnic, no matter how lavish, will satisfy me today, I fear."

Matilda blushed, but held his gaze as he straightened and offered her his hand. She took it and he raised it to his lips, kissing her knuckles, his eyes never leaving hers.

"Come along," he said with a sigh. "Before I steal you away on the pretence of playing least in sight. I am dangerously close to such despicable behaviour, I assure you."

Matilda smiled, deciding it was best not to mention that she was dangerously close to playing along.

Chapter 5

Theo,

I've damn near lost everything, you bloody old fool. Is this the thanks I get for helping you? I want what I was promised. <u>All of it</u>. You'd best find me a way in because if I fail, so do you.

—Excerpt of a letter to Mr Theodore Barrington, from an unknown correspondent.

25ᵗʰ April 1815. Dern, Sevenoaks, Kent.

It was rather like living in a dream, the kind of dream she had never dared allow herself to even glimpse. It was too lovely to be real, too close to everything she'd ever wanted to be good for her. Such dreams only led to dissatisfaction and disappointment when you realised reality could never, ever compare. Yet here she was, picnicking at Dern, surrounded by wildflowers, sitting under the shade of an oak tree on a warm, spring day, with Lucian and Phoebe.

Phoebe was in high spirits. The little girl had confided that Matilda had the honour of being her favourite person in the world—besides Lucian—though Pippin came a very close third. So, to have her two favourite people together had her full of joy and laughter, which was quite infectious and impossible to resist. No matter how hard Matilda tried to guard her heart, it was a hopeless venture. She might have had more luck if Lucian wasn't so irresistible in such a setting.

He was still immaculate, and every inch the marquess, but she realised she was seeing him with a few of his defences lowered. Not all. She caught the guarded look in his eyes on occasion, a wariness that told her she was not the only one risking things here. He'd lost everyone he'd ever cared for, except Phoebe, and Matilda did not doubt he had no desire to be hurt again. The revelations about his uncle were so shocking it only made the dreamlike feel of the day more pronounced, for if this was a dream, that was surely a nightmare. She had so many questions, not one of which she could ask for fear of spoiling the day she had promised to give him.

"I agree, Sidney is a fine name for a stickleback," Lucian said, with every expression of gravity. "But, nonetheless, he must be put back in the stream."

"Oh, but, Uncle!" Phoebe pouted. "Can't I take him home?"

"No. The poor thing will die. Just think how lonely he'll be."

"But I'll keep him company," she protested.

Lucian sent Matilda an appealing look.

"Yes, but you are not a stickleback," Matilda said gently. "And perhaps he has a wife. Children, even. They'll be worried for him."

Phoebe huffed. "Oh, I hadn't thought of that. Very well, but you have to come too."

She tugged at Lucian's arm, and Matilda watched as they walked hand-in-hand down to the stream to set Sidney free. They crouched down by the water, two impossibly blonde heads bent together, the sun turning them to gold, glinting like a field of barley. She drew in a deep breath. One day. Just one perfect day. It must be enough. She smiled as Phoebe waved to her, and waved back, catching her breath as Lucian blew her a kiss once Phoebe had returned her attention to the stream. She laughed and pretended to catch it, making him smile.

A snap of twigs and the indignant squawk of a bird had her glancing away from him towards the woodland they had driven through on the way here, half expecting to see someone walking about in the undergrowth. Matilda squinted into the sunlight but saw nothing moving. Just a deer, no doubt, or perhaps a gamekeeper. She looked back to Lucian, who was holding Phoebe's hand as she waved goodbye to Sidney, and sighed. Gathering herself, Matilda tidied away their picnic before she grew maudlin.

She wasn't about to waste what little time they had with regrets; there would be days enough for those later.

"Here!"

Matilda looked up from fastening the picnic basket as a bunch of wildflowers was thrust in her face. A tangle of buttercups, dandelions, and cow parsley greeted her, and Matilda exclaimed, touched.

"Oh, how beautiful. Thank you, Phoebe. They're quite lovely. I shall ask Mrs Frant if she will have them put in water for me and placed by my bed."

"And when they die, I shall pick you some more," Phoebe said, as Matilda got to her feet. "The roses are lovely, aren't they, Uncle? We could pick a big bunch. I'm sure Matilda would like the pink ones."

"I should love the pink ones," Matilda replied, "but I shall have to go before then, love."

Phoebe's face fell. "Oh, no. You can't go so soon. You've only just come."

"I must, I'm afraid. I ought not be here at all," Matilda said, reaching out and taking her hand. "But it has been so lovely. I shan't ever forget it."

"But you'll come back again."

It wasn't a question, and there was a fierce look in the girl's eyes that Matilda struggled to meet. It would have been easy to lie, to placate her with promises, but that was not fair.

Matilda shook her head and saw Phoebe's lip tremble. She looked helplessly at Lucian, whose expression had been wiped clean of emotion, his jaw set. Before Matilda could find her voice, he swept Phoebe up into his arms and walked away with her. Matilda could hear his low voice, but not what he was saying and her throat grew tight as she saw Phoebe clutching at his neck, her face pressed against his shoulder. Lucian held her tightly, and Matilda could not watch any longer.

By the time they returned, Phoebe was calm, if subdued. She helped Lucian put the pony back in harness, and then climbed up into the gig. She leaned into Matilda, who could do nothing more than put an arm about her.

When they arrived back at Dern, Mrs Frant bore off the untidy posy as if it were the most exotic of bouquets. Miss Peabody exclaimed in horror as she took in her charge's bedraggled appearance, and dragged a disgruntled Phoebe off to be changed into something clean.

Left alone in the great hall, Matilda turned to Lucian.

"I feel like I'm doing more harm than good," she admitted, unable to hide the catch in her voice. "I wanted so much to help, but poor Phoebe… I'm just m-making everything…."

"Matilda, if you don't want me to hold you, for the love of God, don't cry," Lucian protested.

"I do, though," she said helplessly. "I do want you to. Please."

The words were out before she could think better of them, and Lucian did not need another invitation. She closed her eyes, her head on his shoulder as his arms went around her, pulling her against him. *Oh, this*, her heart cried. He smelled of clean linen and shaving soap, a faint, lingering scent of bergamot rising from his skin.

"It is better to have something lovely for a short time, than not at all," Lucian said, his voice soft. "I admit, it has taken me many years to accept the truth of that. It is too easy to lose yourself in hatred and bitterness and regret, too easy to lose what happiness you might find in something fleeting. It is something I struggle to do, but Phoebe is teaching me to be better, as are you."

Matilda swallowed hard, forcing the tears not to fall.

"I have to go," she said, utterly miserable despite his words.

"Yes."

"And you have to get married."

"Yes."

Matilda took a deep breath. "You will not persuade me to be your mistress, then?"

"I cannot," he said, his voice heavy. "It is not what you want at heart. We both know it and I won't persuade you to change your mind. Besides which, Phoebe loves you. One day she would understand what I had done, what I had asked of you. How could I meet her eyes? How could I explain it? I would do anything to keep you with me, Matilda, but I know what you want and, though I do not see it the same way, you are correct. Society *would* judge you. I won't bring illegitimate children into the world if I can help it. It is wrong to force a child to bear the stigma, and you, of all people, you need a family around you." He stepped back a little to look at her, raising her chin with a finger. "It is perfectly obvious to any fool that you will be a wonderful mother, I would be cruel indeed, to take that from you and despite what you might think, despite plenty of evidence to the contrary, I'm not entirely heartless—selfish, yes, too used to getting my own way—but not heartless."

"I would do it," she said suddenly, needing him to know why. "I would stay without a second thought, you would need not even ask me. I could be content, with you and with Phoebe, but... but I can't share you with a wife, Lucian."

48

He stilled, staring at her. She could read nothing from his expression, which she realised now was telling enough. He hid any strong emotion behind that cool mask, likely a habit he could not break after so many years.

"Not even if you alone held my heart?" he asked, and there was the emotion she craved, the longing clear in his voice.

"And what if *I* married, Lucian? Could you bear it, knowing I returned home to my husband, to his bed?"

He swore violently under his breath and turned away from her. He raked his hands through his hair, his shoulders set, every angle of his body taut. For just a moment, the façade of the ice cold marquess, who never raised his voice, never showed anger or impatience, or anything at all, fell away. She supposed she ought to feel some measure of triumph in that, in having gained such a reaction, but she could feel nothing but sadness for them both.

"There, you see," she said softly. "It's impossible."

"Yes." His reply was bitten off, harsh and angry. "And with a few words you have proven I am a heartless bastard after all."

The silence that followed seemed to fill the great hall, pulsing against the magnificent oak panelling, the huge carved coat of arms on the wall reminding her of all the reasons why. Portraits of generations of Barringtons stared down at them, no doubt having seen too many dramas played out beneath them to be impressed by a tragic love story.

"We still have today," she said, trying to lighten her voice and the mood. "And I have seen so little of your splendid home. Will you show me some of it?"

It took a moment before he responded, before he would turn and face her again.

"Of course," he said politely, and held out his arm to her.

Matilda hesitated, uncertain of what he was feeling. "Are you angry with me?"

"With you?" His blond brows drew together, puzzled. "No. Never with you. With circumstance, and fate, and all the things I have no power over, but never with you."

Matilda nodded and went with him as he escorted her through the vast building. Little by little, the simmering tension eased, and he showed her his favourite places, paintings of famous ancestors, and they talked. They talked of everything and nothing and, despite the sorrow in her heart, Matilda found herself laughing and enjoying his company. It was too easy to do, that was the trouble.

"You're not at all how I thought you would be."

He laughed at that. "Am I not? Don't fool yourself. I'm that same man. You just bring out the best—and the worst—in me. I am happy now, happy that you came to me, and so I am behaving myself. The truth is I'm just trying desperately to…." He let out a breath and shook his head. "I ought not open my mouth. You make me reckless, foolish beyond measure. I tell myself I cannot possibly make this situation any worse, but with every moment in your company the idea of letting you leave me becomes harder to bear."

She smiled, finding some comfort in the fact that he felt the same way. "I know, and that is why you are not how I thought. That man would not have let me be his friend. He could not have allowed me to come here and not tried to seduce me. How much of who you really are is Montagu, and how much of him is who your father wanted you to be?"

He didn't answer, only casting her a curious sidelong glance and changing the subject.

"Talk to me about your friends," he said, taking her hand, his fingers twining with hers. It was far too intimate, but it appeared foolish to object now. She had kissed him. The idea seemed impossible. "You were at Lady Helena's wedding?"

Matilda nodded, staring up at him and remembering the feel of his lips beneath hers, wanting it again, and wanting so much more.

"I was. It was a wonderful occasion. They'll be very happy, I think. They're very much in love, certainly."

"Lucky Mr Knight," he said softly.

"You never considered Helena as your bride?"

Why on earth had she said that? She hated herself for it the moment the question left her mouth, but it was too late to take it back.

"Bedwin would never have countenanced the match," he said, shaking his head. "There was little point in adding her to the list."

"The list. Of course there's a list," she said with a bitter huff of laughter, wanting to cry, to scream with frustration.

"Matilda...."

"No, change the subject," she said, determined to move on. How much longer did they have? Hours? She must go, first thing tomorrow, and she'd achieved nothing that she'd wanted to. "What are you going to do about your uncle?"

"You promised me we'd not speak of him today."

"Yes, but me being here is upsetting Phoebe and making everything so difficult for both of us. I must leave tomorrow, you know it as well as I do. So what will you do? You cannot hide here with Phoebe forever."

His face darkened. "I have no intention of doing so. It was an almighty shock to see him in London when I'd believed him in India. I needed time to think, and I feared...I feared he'd already got to Phoebe. I could not give him the chance, and it is far safer here. I dealt with him before, I'll deal with him again."

"By sending him back to India?"

"Yes. He has a measure of freedom there and more comfort than he deserves, but he ought to have been guarded."

She watched something cold and resolute flicker in his eyes, his jaw growing taut.

"Something went wrong. Someone helped him to return here, and I shall discover who. They will be dealt with, as will he. Yet, much as it grieves me to admit it, I am not cold-blooded enough to have a man murdered. In the heat of the moment, I could do it. After Thomas died… I could have killed him then, without a moment's regret. I cannot order an execution, though. I suspect my father could have done it—no doubt he would see my inability to act decisively a failing—but there are some lines I will not cross. I will not become like Theodore. Not even for the family name."

"I'm glad to hear it," she said faintly, wondering at the life he had led, at what it must be like living with the fact your nearest kin meant to put you in the ground. "But why after Thomas died? What happened?"

"You heard of my brother's death?" he asked, his voice dispassionate.

"No, actually. I believe at the time it occurred I had troubles of my own," she said, smiling a little to take the sting from the comment, as she knew now that it had been shortly after their first meeting, the night when her life had changed. She'd lost her father and her reputation in the space of a few hours. "A friend of mine told me about it, though only that he'd died. She did not know of the circumstances."

"She wouldn't," he said darkly. "No one did. It took a great deal of work to conceal the truth."

"Lucian?"

His fingers tightened on her hand. "He died in a gentleman's club. The circumstances were predictably sordid. My uncle might not have forced opium down his throat, or copious amounts of brandy, or whatever the hell else he took to keep his demons quiet, but he gave him the demons that drove him to it. If I had seen him in the days that followed Tommy's death, I *would* have killed him."

"I'm so sorry, Lucian."

He shrugged. "It was inevitable. Thomas was on a road that had one destination and he wanted the journey done as speedily as possible. He achieved his goal."

The words were flat and emotionless, and it would have been easy to assume him callous, to believe he did not care. "It must have hurt that he left you alone."

She watched as he closed his eyes and let out a breath. "How," he said. "How do you always do that? Anyone else would have just murmured a polite word of condolence, but not you. Oh, no. You are brutally honest and unflinchingly kind, and I feel like you can see inside my damn soul. You make me want to tell you all of it. To unburden myself, and yet that's unfair, when I can give you nothing in return."

"But in telling me you are giving me your trust," she said, squeezing his fingers. "And that is more of a gift than I ever hoped for. I know it is not something you give lightly, after all."

He watched her, that wary glint back in his eyes. "It is not a pretty story," he said, shaking his head. Matilda stepped closer to him, taking both of his hands.

"Life is not always pretty, Lucian. If you lived it, I can hear it. I won't break."

A wry smile touched his mouth, one of the dimples she'd noticed making a brief appearance. Matilda's breath caught as he moved closer still, so they were almost touching. "No, you won't break. You look delicate as lace but there is steel at your core, Matilda Hunt. You are the strongest person I have ever met, and the loveliest, inside and out."

"Oh, don't be nice to me," she pleaded, feeling her eyes grow hot. "You'll make me cry again, and then you'll be sorry."

"No, I shan't," he murmured. "If I make you cry, you'll let me hold you again, and I want that more than anything."

"Lucian…." Matilda shook her head, trying to remind herself of the conversation. "You'll tell me everything that happened?"

"I will," he agreed, though his voice had lowered, and his eyes told her he was not thinking of the past right now. "Tonight, once Phoebe is abed, I'll tell you the whole sorry tale."

"Good." She could not look away from him, caught in his gaze like he'd cast a spell. "That's… good."

Her breath hitched and she knew she ought to put distance between them, but she could not, would not.

"I want to kiss you so much."

The words were anguished, and she knew the pain of them acutely, feeling just as he did.

"I know, I want it too, but we mustn't…" she murmured, a half-hearted protest at best.

"Make me stop," he told her, his voice harsh now. "Tell me no."

"I can't."

He let go of her hands, raising his to cradle her face and lifting it towards his.

"I will go mad when you leave," he whispered, and then his lips were on hers, soft at first, tasting, coaxing, a series of delicate touches that blurred to become one endlessly tender kiss. But there had been too much wanting for too long and little time passed before such gentleness burned away, leaving longing and need and desperation.

Matilda slid her arms around his neck, needing more of him. She pressed closer and he groaned against her mouth. One hand left her face to settle at her hip, tugging her flush against his body. A gasp tore from her as she felt his arousal, hard and insistent, urgent against her belly. She knew she ought to be shocked, ought to protest, but that was the last thing she wanted, and instead she plastered herself against him, as though she could never be close enough.

His lips left her mouth, trailing hot kisses along her jaw, down her neck and she wanted to cry with the pleasure of it, with the desire to ask for more, to demand everything he could give her. He moved her then, and Matilda was too dazed to understand why until she became aware of the cool touch of a wall at her back. She leant against it with relief, needing something to steady her when her limbs no longer felt able to support her. The longing to lie down, to take him with her and feel his weight upon her body was a desperate ache inside of her, a low, relentless throb between her legs.

"Lucian," she sobbed, beside herself with wanting him.

"My love," he whispered against her neck. "My dearest love, I have never wanted anything as I want you."

"Nor I, and I tried so hard not to want you."

He laughed a little, standing with his forehead touching hers. "You ought not want me. I'm not worthy of you and I was an utter fool to think otherwise. Anyone who cannot see that is a damned fool, but the world is full of fools and liars."

He took her mouth again and there was nothing left inside of her but needing him. Her body ached and clamoured, the empty sensation deep in her core demanding to be filled and she arched her hips against him, seeking relief. Shifting impatiently, she gasped at the jolt of pleasure she found as she moved against his body.

He made a harsh sound, tearing his mouth from hers. "Oh, Christ, Matilda. If you want to leave here the same way you arrived, don't…."

The words died in his throat as she moved against him again, beyond rational thought, all instinct and desire and longing. This man had always been the one. No matter how she'd fought it, he was her destiny and that fact seemed to override all else.

She stared up at him, entranced by the darkness of his eyes, the black swamping the silver.

"Matilda," he said, his voice soft, reverent. "Matilda, I know I ought not say it, I have no right to, but…."

He paused, muttering a curse, and turned his head towards the door through which they'd entered.

Voices pierced her consciousness, far off yet, but growing closer, and some ragged sense of self-preservation belatedly asserted itself.

"They're looking for us."

Lucian closed his eyes and drew in a rough breath. "Damnation."

With something like defiance, he stole one last kiss before he pushed away from her and stalked to the far side of the room, turning his back on her.

Matilda took a series of shuddering breaths, trying to steady herself as she took a swift inventory of the state of her hair and dress. Satisfied that nothing was too dreadfully dishevelled, she pressed the backs of her hands to her cheeks to cool the flush that had consumed her. It was a hopeless task. She was burning inside, and she knew now just how reckless they had been. Before today, she had wanted him, but she had not known the touch of his lips, the reality of being in his arms. Even their kiss this morning had been a fragile thing, a simple promise of what could be, a match set against a forest fire compared to what had just happened between them. Her imagination had supplied images, conjured an idea of how it might be, but he had burned away those frail suppositions like tissue paper and left in their place the blazing heat of truth. How much harder now to walk away from him, knowing what she did.

"There you are," said a frustrated voice as Phoebe appeared, dragging a reluctant Miss Peabody in her wake. "We've been looking everywhere."

"I'm sorry, dear," Matilda said, relieved that she could speak at all, and for once doing better than Lucian, who was still standing with his back to them. "Your uncle has been showing me around."

Somehow, she said it without blushing, not that it mattered. She could still feel the heat simmering under her skin, so she must be scarlet, anyway. To underline this fact, Miss Peabody was studiously avoiding her eye and looked remarkably uncomfortable. She wondered what the woman thought of her, and decided she didn't care. People had been making assumptions about Matilda's morals for years, at least now she'd done something to earn her reputation. There was some perverse sense of satisfaction in that.

"It's almost dinnertime," Phoebe said, looking at Matilda in surprise. "Aren't you going to get ready?"

"Is it so late?" Matilda said, shocked as she considered how long they must have been wandering the building alone together.

"We keep country hours at Dern," Lucian said, a little apologetically.

Somehow, she forced herself to meet his eyes to discover he was not quite as composed at he usually was, something dark and restless still visible in his eyes, and his hair slightly disarrayed. She must have done that, she realised, and had to look away as a blush threatened, remembering the warm silk of his hair sliding through her fingers.

"Then I had best go and change at once," she said, too brightly. "Can you guide me to my room, Phoebe? Or else I shall be lost for years and miss everything, never mind dinner."

Phoebe laughed and skipped up to her, taking her hand. "Of course. It's not so difficult once you get used to it."

Matilda held back the obvious comment. The girl had recovered her good humour, and she did not wish to dent it again, so she followed Phoebe out of the room and did not look around to see if Lucian watched her go.

She did not need to.

Chapter 6

Dear Prue,

Have you seen Matilda at all? She seemed so distracted at Helena's wedding. No doubt I'm just being silly, but I got the strangest feeling she was in some kind of trouble, or that something was wrong. I'm worrying over nothing, I expect. Only I called upon her, and her butler was most evasive. She's gone away for a few days, but he would not say where and… Oh, ignore me. I'm just being a busybody, no doubt.

How are you feeling? You must be so excited. Not too long now before we all get to meet the newest member of the family.

—Excerpt of a letter from Mrs Minerva de Beauvoir to Prunella Adolphus, Her Grace the Duchess of Bedwin.

25ᵗʰ April 1815. Dern, Sevenoaks, Kent.

Matilda took her time to get ready for dinner. She needed as long as possible to quell the simmering heat thrumming in her veins. It was hopeless though, and there was little point in denying the danger she was in. Tonight, after Phoebe had gone to bed, they would be alone again. The idea filled her with a rush of anticipation, rather than the terror and anxiety she ought to experience. She reassured herself she would not be so reckless as to forget herself entirely and go to his bed. She was not so great a fool as that. Yet, how she wanted to be a fool! Would she ever have another chance to experience such passion? Not with Lucian. At some point this year he would take a wife, and she would not be here to watch him do so. It would break something in her to see him with another. She would go away, perhaps to stay with Ruth in Scotland for the summer, where news of Lucian would be far away, and she could tend the pieces of her heart in private.

It was for the best.

"Are you all right, miss?"

Matilda looked up, realising too late she'd barely spoken a word to Sarah and had been staring into the far distance for some time, though she was ready to go down.

"I beg your pardon, I'm afraid I was wool gathering." Matilda began pulling on her gloves, shaking herself from thoughts of the bleak prospect awaiting her.

"He kissed you, didn't he?" the girl said with a wistful smile. "Was it lovely?"

Matilda didn't even blush this time. She just gave a soft laugh and nodded.

"Yes," she said, realising how ridiculously inadequate the description was. "It was certainly lovely."

Sarah gave a happy sigh and hugged herself, no doubt filling her head with visions of living at Dern and being a lady's maid to a marchioness. Matilda had neither the heart nor the energy to remind her she was living in a dream world. Not when she was there too, right beside her. The only difference was, Matilda knew it was a fantasy, and in the morning, she would have a rude awakening.

She opened the door to find Phoebe waiting for her.

"At last," she said, grinning at Matilda and running to take her hand. "Oh, my. What a beautiful dress. It's the same colour blue as your eyes, you know. You do look pretty."

"Thank you, and I must return the compliment. How lovely you look. You'll be a great beauty one day."

Phoebe nodded. "I know. Uncle said so too. Is it nice, being beautiful?"

Matilda laughed a little at that. "Well, yes. I suppose it is. Though I think you will by far exceed me. Your poor uncle will be beset by your admirers."

Phoebe shrugged, apparently unimpressed with this idea. "Well, it doesn't matter. I shan't marry anyone. Uncle would be so sad if I left him alone. I couldn't bear it."

"Oh, but he won't be alone by the time you're grown up." Somehow, Matilda kept her voice light, though the words threatened to choke her. "He'll get married soon, and then you'll have lots of little cousins to play with. So, you see, he won't be alone."

A belligerent expression settled upon the child's delicate features. Matilda's scolded herself for the surge of pleasure it gave her to know Phoebe wanted *her* here, and not one of the prospective brides on Lucian's list.

"He doesn't want to marry any of those stupid women, and they won't want me here. I'll just be in the way. They'll just end up arguing over me because Uncle will want me to stay and his new wife will want me gone, and with good reason, for I shan't like them. If he marries any one of them, we shall all be miserable."

"Phoebe," Matilda began, knowing she must do something, say something to ease the poor girl's heart.

"No." Phoebe stamped her foot and stared up at Matilda. "I'm not blind. I know he loves you, and you love him, and you should be married to each other. It's so stupid. Who cares about a name? They're all dead! *They're all dead*! Mother and Father are dead, but he's not dead, and neither are you."

Matilda got to her knees and hugged Phoebe tightly, feeling her little frame trembling with emotion. "I'm so sorry, Phoebe. I know it must seem very stupid to you. Indeed, it is stupid. There are so many things about life that are cruel and unfair, but there are lots of lovely things too. Don't make yourself hate someone before you've even met them. I'm sure whoever your uncle marries will be someone you'll like. After all, if he likes her well enough to marry her, you are bound to like her too."

Phoebe made a sound of quiet rage but said nothing. Matilda sighed, wishing this were not so dreadfully hard. She tried again.

"Besides which, your uncle does not love me, not well enough to marry me. We are just friends, good friends. That's all."

Phoebe fumbled for a handkerchief, retrieving one from the sleeve of her dress. She wiped her eyes and blew her nose before sending Matilda a look of such pitying disbelief, Matilda might have laughed if the circumstances were otherwise.

"Come along," Phoebe said, her voice terse, though making it obvious that this conversation was not over.

Matilda followed obediently, wishing Phoebe was a little less perceptive, and hoping fervently that they'd manage the rest of the evening without any further incident.

***

Phoebe simmered all the way through dinner. She suspected her uncle was quite aware of her mood, as he'd dismissed all the staff as soon as the meal had been served. No doubt he didn't want them witnessing a scene. For the moment she was too cross to speak, so she just ate and pretended that she was behaving herself whilst concocting all manner of ways to keep Matilda at Dern. She considered creeping into Matilda's bedroom and painting her with spots so everyone thought she had measles, but reflected that these would wash off too easily and be unconvincing. She thought then about finding something in the medical cupboard to make her sick, or sleepy, but that was obviously far too dangerous. That was a shame, for if it was like in Sleeping Beauty it would be terribly romantic, but life was never like it was in fairy stories and she wasn't such a ninny as to believe it was.

Next, she considered setting all the horses free so there would none to draw Matilda's carriage, but Phoebe would never get past all the grooms without someone seeing her, so that was no good. The best idea she had was to lock Matilda in her room and hide the key. The doors were solid oak and the locks very strong indeed. It would take some time to set her free. That was only a short term solution, though, and one that would get her into a lot of trouble, but it was the best she had at present, and it would give her time to think.

"What are you plotting, miss?"

Phoebe looked up and found her uncle watching her. Drat. He always knew when she was up to mischief. He had the kind of impenetrable gaze that made you want to squirm in your seat, like he knew exactly what you were thinking. She'd had plenty of practise at meeting it, however, and though she never lied to him, she did not think she needed to tell him her every thought.

"How to make you see sense," she muttered under her breath.

"I beg your pardon. How to what?" he asked, as she'd deliberately spoken too quietly for him to hear. She was surprised he'd heard that much.

"Nothing." She glowered at the bowl of syllabub in front of her, wondering if she should push it away in protest at his stupidity, but she did love syllabub, and it wouldn't stop him being stupid, so that was a waste. Huffing, she picked up her spoon and took a defiant mouthful.

"You'll get indigestion if you scowl at your food like that," he observed.

"I don't care."

"You might if you curdle the cream."

Phoebe snorted in disgust. "You can't curdle the cream with a look, no more than you can pretend you're not in love with Matilda. Both things are so obvious it's ridiculous!"

There was the kind of silence that made the hairs on the back of her neck stand on end and her cheeks grow hot, but she wouldn't apologise. Instead she snatched up her bowl and spoon and ran from the room, slamming the door behind her.

***

Matilda swallowed, not knowing quite what to do or say.

"Perhaps I'd best go after her."

She got to her feet, but Lucian reached out and took her hand.

"No," he said. "No, let her go. She'll find Pippin. Our cook is a wonderful source of comfort. Not to mention fresh biscuits."

"She was here when you were a boy, I believe?" Matilda said, hoping to steer the conversation to safer ground as she sat down again.

Lucian nodded. "I'm not sure how I'd have survived if not for Pippin. Mrs Frant and Denton too, actually. They are far more loyal than I deserve, I'm sure."

"I doubt that's true. If people are loyal, it is because they wish to be, because you've earned their trust, and their respect."

"Or because they are too kind to be anything else." He smiled at her, releasing her hand and she let out a breath.

"She's afraid your—" Matilda had to pause for a moment, to take a breath and start over, well aware she overstepping the mark. "She is afraid that when you marry, your wife will not want her here, that she will be the cause of resentment or antagonism."

His face darkened. "This is Phoebe's home and I am her guardian. There is no question of her ever being anywhere else. It will not be a cause for argument, for it is not something I will negotiate over."

Matilda could not help but smile a little. There spoke the marquess.

"What?"

She shook her head, knowing it was not her place to interfere. Too much had been said already.

"No," he insisted. "You have an opinion, speak it."

Why was she doing this to herself? She would have wondered, except it was not for her, it was for Phoebe.

"Lucian, no matter how big this house is, your wife will become a part of your family, of your and Phoebe's lives. She will be with you at mealtimes. It would be natural for her to involve herself in Phoebe's world, perhaps to choose her clothes, or take her on outings."

"And so?"

"And so, if Phoebe is correct and your wife resents her, how many opportunities to make the poor girl's life unpleasant will present themselves during the day? Conversely, if Phoebe takes your new wife in dislike, as she seems determined to do, she will make the poor woman's life a misery."

Lucian frowned at his wine glass, twisting the stem back and forth between his fingers. "And what would you have me do about it?"

Matilda laughed. "I have not the slightest idea, but you must choose carefully. It is all very well to say your marriage will be for power and land and breeding, and whatever other lofty ideals your title demands, but just remember Phoebe is caught up in the mix too, and that your decision will affect her, whether or not you mean it to."

She knew the words were edged with bitterness, but she could not help that. The last thing she wanted was to speak of his marriage, but she would endure it for Phoebe's sake.

An uncomfortable silence settled between them. Lucian did not speak, his brow furrowed with displeasure. She wondered if he was angry with her for having spoken of things that did not concern her.

"I'm sorry. I ought not have said anything. It is none of my affair."

She did her best not to sound brittle and defensive, but suspected she failed.

Lucian slid her a glance from under his lashes. "No. You're not the least bit sorry, and neither should you be. I asked for your opinion, and it is duly noted."

Matilda let out a breath, hoping they could change the subject, though she knew he would be reluctant to keep his promise to her. "You said you would tell me about your uncle, about Thomas."

He sighed, swirling the remaining wine in his glass, and staring despondently down into it. She knew what he was thinking, for she was thinking the exact same thing. There were far more pleasant ways in which they could spend their evening, their *only* evening together. Talking of things which Lucian would likely find painful was hardly something he would wish for instead.

Yet he had promised, and Matilda felt he needed to speak of it. Whenever her friends had unburdened themselves of their troubles, they had always felt better for it. Solutions had become easier to see once the problem had been aired and shared with someone who had their best interests at heart. That at least she could give him. It was why she had come.

"Lucian?"

He closed his eyes for a moment.

"Very well," he said, but with such reluctance she felt wretched for insisting. "Come along, then. We'll retire to the library."

Matilda set aside her napkin and stood when Lucian pulled out her chair for her. As they retired, Lucian instructed Denton that they were not to be disturbed and that the staff could retire once their work was done. Matilda suppressed a thrill of anticipation, reminding herself sternly that it was only because they must speak of private matters.

"I still don't remember which way it is," she said, trying to lighten the mood a little as she took his arm.

"The place is a maze," he admitted. "And heaven help you if you set something down and don't remember where it was."

"Marvellous for playing least in sight, though." She squeezed his arm, smiling up at him.

"You might think so," he said wryly. "However, it is possible to hide indefinitely in a house like this. It is full of secret rooms and hidden passageways. It can be tiresome if you're not found after half an hour or so. Here you could wait an eternity, and if you can't find your way back out… you might not have a choice."

Matilda shuddered. "Very well, have it your way. I've quite gone off the idea now."

He chuckled, and she was pleased his good humour had been somewhat restored.

Lucian opened the door to the library and gestured for Matilda to go through. She stepped into the room, smiling with pleasure to be back in the lovely space.

"I think this is one of my favourite rooms," she said, turning back to him, her breath catching in disbelief as a dark shape detached itself from the shadows behind the open door.

Matilda screamed.

Chapter 7

I warned you my nephew was not to be underestimated, though if the conditions in your mills were as vile as reported, you're a fool. It was bound to come to light. There are always do-gooders wanting to meddle in private affairs.

The attached plan will give you what you need. It is my nephew's habit to retire to the library after dinner. He does not know I am aware of this tunnel, a secret his father guarded closely. Providing you can evade the staff and get to it unseen, you'll take him completely unawares. The rest is up to you.

—Excerpt of a letter from Mr Theodore Barrington to Mr David Burton.

25ᵗʰ April 1815. Dern, Sevenoaks, Kent.

Lucian spun around to face the threat as it resolved itself into the figure of a man in a black cloak. Matilda felt her heart racing, a cold, sick sensation rolling over her as she saw the glint of a knife in the lamplight.

"*You,*" Lucian said, his expression one of disgust.

There was a dark laugh, and the man threw back the hood of the cloak.

Matilda grabbed hold of the nearest piece of furniture as her knees threatened to give out. David Burton stood before them, all trace of the amiable, polite man she'd once considered marrying wiped from his features. This creature was something else entirely. He sneered as he turned his head and looked at her.

"What a surprise to find you here. I always knew it was him you wanted. You'd rather be a slut for a titled fool than married to a decent man."

"You dare come onto my property and slander my guests?" Lucian said before Matilda could speak.

He seemed utterly indifferent to the fact there was a deadly looking blade pointed at his heart.

"Mr Burton has a strange notion of what makes a man decent," Matilda said, trying to deflect Burton's attention from Lucian, as it was all too clear why he had come here.

She wondered if there was a chance the staff had heard her scream, but Lucian had dismissed them all and the walls of Dern were thick and ancient. No one would come.

"A guest, is she?" Burton said with a laugh. "That's rich, and yes, I dare. You destroyed my life, so a little trespass seems the least I can do, though I'm afraid I shall have to cut your throat before I leave."

He said it lightly, his conversational tone making the threat even more chilling.

"Lucian did not ruin you," Matilda said with fury, desperate to figure out a way to give Lucian a chance. He had the wall at his back and nowhere to move, no weapon in sight. "You did it to yourself, the moment you treated those poor people with less respect than any decent person would give an animal."

Mr Burton frowned a little. "Oh, you think that's why I'm here? For revenge? Well, yes, there is satisfaction in killing him for that. I'll admit it pleases me to repay him for everything I've lost. However, all will be restored to me once I am done, and this was always a part of the plan."

"The plan?" Matilda echoed, wondering what on earth he was speaking about. She saw him flash a cocky grin at Lucian.

"Will you explain, or shall I? I don't doubt you've worked it out by now."

Lucian returned a look of sheer contempt and Burton chuckled. "Rather amusing really, when you think of it. If not for your interest in this pretty bit of goods, your uncle would never have contacted me. The scandal rags were full of it, though, and you know how your uncle loves gossip. He had them sent to India, where he read how the lowborn mushroom from up north and the marquess were vying for the same female. He took an interest in the story and lent me a helping hand. When he learned more about the man I was, he was pleased to find one ruthless enough to take what he wants."

"Yes, and one about as trustworthy as he is, by my reckoning," Lucian remarked, leaning back against the wall and crossing his arms. He looked perfectly at ease, only the dangerous glint in his eyes betraying any emotion. "Let me see if I have this straight. My uncle told you how to get into Dern unseen, about the hidden tunnel to the library. I admit, I did not believe he knew about that one. My father kept such things between himself and his sons, but somehow he discovered it, and drew you a pretty map so you can put a period to my life. Happy Theodore then inherits the title. In return for this service, he has promised to restore your fortunes and your reputation, to help elevate you among the nobility. He'll introduce you to the right people and get you into all the right places, even help you find a worthy bride, now Miss Hunt has seen sense and refused to have you. Do stop me if I'm wrong."

"No, no, carry on," Burton said with a smile that made Matilda's heart stutter with fear. She could not believe the two of them were standing about discussing Lucian's death in such a bloodless manner.

Lucian made a low sound of amusement. "There is a minor flaw in that plan, I'm afraid."

"Oh?" Burton said, raising one dark eyebrow.

"Yes," Lucian said, the faintest trace of a smile touching his lips. "My uncle is a liar."

"Oh, don't you worry about that, my lord, I'll see he keeps his word."

Matilda shivered at the laughter in his voice, but Lucian just stared at him, that not-quite-smile still at his lips.

"You don't have the slightest idea what you've gotten mixed up in, you poor fool. You're just a pawn. Expendable. If you succeed, he'll have you hanged for my murder, and his sincere outpouring of grief will be worthy of a Greek tragedy. You'll not get out of this alive, I promise you. Unless you leave now. Do that, and I'll even give you a five minute head start before I raise the alarm. My word as a gentleman."

"Sorry, old man," Burton said, mocking Lucian's accent. "I'm afraid I can't do it."

"No," Lucian said, his voice growing colder, dripping condescension. "You long to be one of us, don't you? Yet you don't have the first idea of what it means to be a gentleman because you're an ignorant pleb. You'll cut my throat because you are too paltry a human being to act like a man. A gentleman would duel with honour, the better man left standing. *You....*" he said, a world of disgust and generations of breeding loading that one word with unutterable scorn. "You don't have the guts for it, you white-livered scum."

Matilda watched with her heart in her throat, wondering what on earth Lucian was playing at, goading him so savagely. She expected at any moment that Burton would lash out and kill him where he stood, except that she saw now that Lucian's words had been calculated with vicious precision, to give himself the only chance he had. He was taunting Burton on purpose with the thing most likely to rile him, his lack of breeding.

"Pistols at dawn?" Burton said, shaking his head, though the desire for retribution shone in his eyes. "Oh, no. Any fool can get lucky with a bullet."

Lucian waved a negligent hand, as if this was a mere detail. "Swords then, as in the days of my forebears."

"You think you can beat me, with your prancing about at Angelo's?" Burton waved the knife at Lucian as Matilda felt a cold bead of sweat slither down her spine. "You don't know what a fight is, milk-sop. Where I grew up, we had to fight for our bloody lives, not mince around with sharp little sticks, poking holes in each other in some fancy club. And don't go assuming I don't know how to hold a sword, for you'll not have time to be sorry for it. You wouldn't last five minutes in a proper fight."

"Then you'll walk away with honour and not a scratch upon your person," Lucian said easily. "Prove to me how worthy you are. Teach me to respect you at the tip of a sword. Make the Marquess of Montagu kneel to the better man. *I dare you.*"

Matilda closed her eyes. She had heard the phrase so often over the past years, and no matter how shocking and risky the dares had been, no one had ever been in serious danger. Hearing those words now, in this context, she felt sick to her stomach. This was not a dare to kiss a stranger, to dance under the moonlight in a garden. This was life or death, yet it was the only chance Lucian had to escape this madman's plans.

She wondered with terror what Lucian's chances were. Mr Burton seemed transformed into something rough and brutal, a man who would kill without a moment's remorse. Lucian was a touch taller but not so heavily built, and so Burton seemed to be the obvious choice to come out the victor. Lucian was sophisticated and elegant, too well bred for this manner of confrontation. Wildly she looked about the room, searching for something she might use as a weapon.

A bronze figurine about ten inches high caught her attention. It had a heavy marble base. Breathing hard, she inched backwards, but she'd barely made it a foot before Mr Burton noticed. He swung around and grabbed hold of her wrist, pulling her to him and pressing the knife to the delicate skin of her neck. A scream died in her throat, her fear so overwhelming she was too terrified to even breathe.

"*No!*" Lucian shouted, holding his hands out. "It's me you want, me you came for. Miss Hunt is innocent in this. She never betrayed you. She is not here for me but for my niece, Phoebe. Miss Hunt loves the child and wanted to assure herself of her wellbeing. She won't have me, Burton. She won't be my mistress, though I've tried my damndest to entice her, I assure you. She's too good for either of us."

"That true?" Mr Burton demanded, his voice in her ear soft, almost gentle.

Matilda stared at Lucian. She was trembling hard, her breathing erratic, and she knew what she ought to do. Lucian's eyes begged her to say the right thing, but she did not believe Mr Burton meant to leave her alive or, if he did, he would realise soon enough he could not afford to take the risk. He could have no witnesses to his crime. She was a liability, and no matter if he still wanted her, he could not risk letting her speak of what she'd seen.

If they would die anyway, she'd have Lucian know the truth.

"No," she said, the word barely more than a whisper. "I came for both of them. I love Phoebe, but I love Lucian too, with all my heart."

For perhaps the first time she saw genuine emotion shimmering in Lucian's eyes: triumph, joy, and such pain that she felt it echoed in her own heart. Mr Burton was not about to give them any more time to reflect on her words, though.

"Dirty whore," he growled. "I would have married you. I would have treated you with respect, like a queen, given you anything you desired, but you'd rather debase yourself, disgrace yourself with *him*."

"Yes," Matilda said simply, feeling a tear slide down her cheek.

Lucian closed his eyes, and she saw him gather himself. It was almost imperceptible, invisible to anyone who did not know him well, who did not understand the monumental control he exercised over himself and his emotions.

"So, Mr Burton," he said, his voice cold, a dangerous glitter in his eyes. "Come and slit my throat, as that is what you've come to do. I won't be the first nobleman to die at the hand of a lowborn upstart with pretensions of gentility. There is no honour to be found among such men as you. You are a breed of cowardly curs who would rather strike down their betters than be better themselves, despite all your posturing and aping the part of a gentleman."

"You're no better than me," Burton sneered, and Matilda felt indignation stiffen his body, felt the heavy muscle in his arm tense.

The hand that held her wrist tightened with fury, grinding bone, and her breath caught at the pain, but she did nothing, only breathed shallowly, trying to hold onto some semblance of calm.

"So you say," Lucian drawled, looking as though he was bored to death by the entire exchange. "Yet you are too craven to prove it. So, you'd best get on and murder me. That *is* what you came for, I believe? As edifying as this little chat has been."

"*Fine*." The word was gritted out through clenched teeth and Mr Burton's anger was palpable now, filling the room, a rank, sour stench that she could almost taste over her own fear. "If you're so keen to be humiliated as well as cut down, I can indulge you, I suppose. Then Miss Hunt can see who the better man really was."

"As you say," Lucian replied, dry as dust. "I sometimes practise in the ballroom, as it offers plenty of space. I have a fine set of duelling rapiers, if you dare. They belonged to my grandfather. Or do you prefer the foil? You do understand the difference?"

Mocking now, Lucian arched an imperious eyebrow.

"Rapier, then," Burton replied tersely.

Having seen her brother practise as a young man, Matilda knew a blunt foil was generally used for practising. A true foil was only sharp at the tip. A rapier, however, had a razor-sharp blade on both sides.

"Excellent," Lucian replied. "Shall we?"

He gestured to the door and Burton jerked his head.

"Miss Hunt and I will follow. We shouldn't want anyone to raise the alarm, after all."

Lucian's jaw tightened as he saw that Burton had moved the blade from her throat to low at her side, hidden from immediate view. The implication was clear enough. If either of them tried to raise help, Matilda would suffer for it.

Lucian opened the study door, and Matilda's heart seemed jammed in her throat as she saw Phoebe, her hand raised as if to knock. She was in her nightgown, her little feet bare, and she looked absurdly young and fragile.

"Phoebe."

She could hear the terror in Lucian's voice, the effort it took for him to steady it. The child could not see Mr Burton, who had dug the knife at Matilda's side in a touch deeper. She felt the sting as it pressed into tender flesh.

"What are you doing out of bed?"

"I came to say sorry," Phoebe said, her voice dull. "I... I don't want you both to be angry with me. It's only—"

"I know," Lucian said quickly, reaching out to touch her cheek. "And neither of us is angry. I promise, sweetheart. You were quite right, Phoebe, everything you said, and I *am* sorry for it, but now you must listen. Do you remember the other day when we spoke about… about bad dreams? What you should do if the *nightmare* came back?"

Matilda saw the girl stare at her uncle for a moment and then her eyes grew wide, her face draining of colour, but she nodded, a barely perceptible bob of her head.

"Good girl," Lucian said. "Go. *Now*."

Phoebe stared at him and Lucian nodded. Phoebe turned and ran. Matilda let out a ragged breath, closing her eyes and thanking God.

"What was that about?" Burton asked, suspicious.

"Miss Barrington was scolded earlier for not going to bed nicely. She pretends bad dreams in order to stay up late," Lucian said lightly. "It was just a reminder she would be in trouble if she did not return to her room at once."

Burton gave Matilda a little push. "Go on, then."

Matilda thought it typical that a place the size of Dern Palace, which was run by a vast army of staff, could not conjure up one solitary footman in the time it took them to cross the not inconsiderable distance from Lucian's study to the massive ballroom. That was the way of it, though, and so no one was any the wiser. There was no one to sound the alarm, unless the cryptic message that had made Phoebe's eyes grow round had included instruction to get help. Mr Burton had helpfully yanked a yard of silken rope off a curtain as he passed, and now tied Matilda's arms tight behind her back.

"Don't even think about trying to run," he warned her, waving the knife he held in her face by way of illustration.

"You're a vile excuse for a human being," she said, wondering how she dared speak and hardly having breath enough to get the words out. "Even if you kill us both, you'll not get away with it. Lucian is right, his uncle is far cleverer than you, and far more dangerous. You're doing his dirty work and you'll be caught, and hanged for it too."

"Shut up."

He slapped her, a negligent swipe of his hand that knocked the remaining air from her lungs with the shock of it. It hadn't even been a particularly hard blow, though it stung like blazes, but no one had ever touched her in anger before and the casual violence of it was stunning.

"Touch her again and I'll dismember you, one piece at a time."

The frosty voice drew her attention back to Lucian, and she forced a smile.

"I'm all right. Please be careful, Lucian."

He was holding a large, narrow leather box, his eyes on Burton as icy as she had ever seen them. Lucian set the box down, flicked back the clasps and opened it. Two elegant swords lay on a bed of blue silk. Lucian reached for one and lifted a long, wickedly glinting blade with an ornate, engraved hand guard. With the toe of his gleaming boot and a contemptuous gesture, he kicked the box so it slid across the floor to Mr Burton.

Matilda watched, disbelieving, as Burton took up his own sword, the knife he held transferred to his left hand. Surely this was a bad dream. Things like this did not happen any longer. The world was a different place from the time of their grandfathers, when men duelled to the death or maimed each other with these deadly blades. Yes, gentlemen still duelled for honour occasionally, but rarely, and with pistols, where there was a far greater chance of walking away unscathed. This... This was madness.

Yet the two men were preparing, stripping off coats and waistcoats and untying their cravats so nothing would impede their movements. They took up the swords again, Mr Burton taking up the knife in his left hand too, and moved to the centre of the ballroom, circling one another.

Matilda gasped in horror as the two men came together in a flurry of movement, the shriek of steel against steel a sound she had never heard in such a violent context. Mr Burton laughed and surged forward, wielding the blade with brute strength. In that instant, Matilda was certain Lucian would die. They were both powerful men, but Mr Burton was filled with rage and violence and it seemed impossible that Lucian, bred to be a marquess, could survive such an onslaught. Did anyone even dare challenge him at Angelo's, or was he allowed to win because no one had the nerve to beat him?

Yet, Lucian withstood the assault and, as the two men disengaged, he was very much alive and didn't have a scratch on him. Mr Burton renewed his attack with equal violence, such force behind each strike that, if even one had made contact, Lucian would surely have been cleaved to the bone. Up and down the ballroom they went, with Lucian always in retreat, Mr Burton grunting with effort, the full force of his body behind every swing of the lethal blade. Again and again Burton attacked, furious and ferocious, until he was breathing hard, his hair damp against his head, sweat trickling down his forehead. As they disengaged once more, Lucian watched him with unnerving calm, his breathing undisturbed, silver eyes cool. It was a calculating look, utterly bloodless, and Matilda realised in that moment that she had underestimated Lucian as much as Mr Burton had. He was weighing Burton up, judging the quality of his opponent. He had not been retreating, had not been forced into a submissive stance, but had allowed his opponent to expend all the energy he wanted to without exerting himself the smallest amount.

Before that thought had really sunk in, Lucian moved, lunging forward, blade outstretched. Burton parried, knocking the blade back with a hard strike that clashed with a ringing bell of sound in the space, but Lucian turned as he passed, the sword moving effortlessly as he swiped it behind his back, spinning past in a move almost too fast to track. When he stepped away, Mr Burton had a bloody slash across his shirt front, the fabric gaping to reveal a bright line of red.

Burton looked down at it, as if he too was uncertain of how or when it had occurred. Snarling, he went back on the offensive, charging at Lucian with all the ferocity of a wounded animal. Now, however—now that she could see Lucian was not about to be cut down before her—Matilda watched in silent awe. Each one of those savage, unrelenting cut and thrust attacks was turned easily aside with an effortless flick of Lucian's wrist. Repeatedly, Burton attacked, his sword crashing down with killing force, and each time Lucian's blade turned it back with negligent ease.

Indeed, Lucian had the gall to look as though he was bored to death, an expression nicely calculated to make Mr Burton lose his damned mind. It worked admirably.

Burton lunged at him with a roar of frustration. Lucian parried, turning the attack to one side, and lunged, forcing his opponent back and back again. Burton met the threat and struck out. His sword missed its target, but the impetus carried the stroke on, too much power in it to be halted quickly enough. Lucian slashed his undefended right side, slicing through his upper arm. Burton shouted with rage and pain and clutched at the wound, almost dropping the knife in his left hand and taking a few wary steps back, reassessing the threat.

The two men engaged once more and now Matilda watched, still with her heart in her mouth, yet with the growing realisation that it was not Lucian being taught a lesson here, but Mr Burton. Lucian Barrington, the Marquess of Montagu, was not some idle, preening aristocrat who wasted his days on indulgence and pleasure seeking. The amount of skill being displayed here took years and years of practise, a single-minded dedication that must have begun decades ago, and no amount of brute strength could turn aside such exquisite dexterity. The next time the men disengaged there was a raw, red line down Burton's cheek, and that insolent not-quite-smile touched Lucian's mouth. All traces of boredom had vanished from the silver eyes now, nothing but a dangerous calm to be seen in the glittering gaze levelled upon Mr Burton.

Up and back down the ballroom they went, but this time it was Lucian pushing Mr Burton back, and back and back. Burton was swinging wildly now, stabbing with the knife whenever he could get close enough, his face a feral snarl of rage. By the time Lucian had turned him twice about the vast ballroom, it was clear Mr Burton was tiring. Lucian too was breathing harder now, a flush upon his cheeks and his pale blond hair darkening with sweat, but there was not a mark on him. Conversely, Burton's shirt had been cut to ribbons, ominous red patches blooming like strange, bloody roses beneath the fine linen.

"I thought you meant to teach me a lesson?" Lucian remarked, taunting him. "If it was a lesson in wasting my time, you're doing admirably. However, I had the impression you meant to kill me. Do let me know when you mean to start. I should not like to miss it."

Matilda could have kicked the reckless fiend as his words pricked at Mr Burton's temper and seemed to give him a second wind. He flew at Lucian, the strikes more calculated this time, his concentration absolute. It made not a whit of difference. Lucian met his every blow and turned each one aside, and Mr Burton backed off with a hiss of pain and a new red stripe across his side.

"Devil!" Burton growled at him.

"Oh, you have no idea," Lucian replied with a grim smile, and now, at last, Matilda could see the anger in his eyes. It was cold and hard, the kind that would burn for years and decades and lifetimes. "You've been supping with the devil all this time, you poor fool, and you forgot to bring a long enough spoon. I'm only his nephew, a mere pretender, though he taught me well enough. He'll eviscerate you. I really ought to kill you outright. It would be kinder. Would you like me to be merciful, Mr Burton? Shall I end it now?"

"Try it," Burton sneered, despite bleeding from a half dozen slashes.

"Oh, I don't think so," Lucian replied, his smile a terrible expression. "Dear Uncle Theo would call me a murderer and tell the world how he always suspected I was not quite sane. I'm sure he's armed with a litany of telling little anecdotes that would paint me in the colours of a madman, capable of cold-blooded murder. No, no, Mr Burton. You run along home and tell him all about it. Tell him how you failed to do his bidding, I should pay to be a fly on that particular wall."

"Oh, we're not done yet," Burton snarled. "Not by a long chalk."

"Very well, if you are so keen for me to slice you up, one piece at a time, I am happy to oblige."

The sound of metal on metal rang out once more, and this time Lucian snatched the sword from Burton's hand with the tip of his own blade and sent the weapon skittering across the floor. Matilda could not fathom exactly how it had been done, and from the disbelieving look in his eyes, neither could Mr Burton.

Lucian's sword point rested upon his chest, over his heart.

"You're dead," he said softly.

Burton glared at him with utter hatred as Matilda breathed a sigh of relief. It was over.

"Pick it up."

She jolted at the sound of Lucian's voice, dripping contempt. Surely he hadn't…?

With disbelief, she watched as Lucian allowed his opponent to retrieve his sword, and the clash of metal rang out once more. She wanted to scream with frustration until once again Lucian flicked the sword from Burton's hand, sending it sailing away from him. His sword tip trailed across Burton's throat, leaving a delicate red scratch.

"Dead again, Mr Burton."

"Lucian!" she shouted across the floor, but the wretched man was beyond hearing her, the look in his eyes quite terrifying.

"Pick it up," he said, the words precise and bitten off.

Burton stalked across to his sword, never taking his eyes from Lucian. His expression was no less daunting, the passionate fury that came from humiliation, from the desire for retribution. When they came together this time, there was a new recklessness to Burton's attacks, born of desperation. The cool insouciance Lucian had begun with had vanished now, a murderous glint in his eyes that Burton would have done well to heed. But Mr Burton was in the grip of the same bloodlust, and when the savage attack he let fly was turned back like all the others, his fury filled the room. He let out a bellow of rage and kicked out at Lucian, who danced back out of the way with a laugh.

Burton stood, seething, his chest heaving with effort, his face a savage mask as he reached back and flung the knife at Lucian. Matilda screamed as it arced through the air, falling to her knees with a sob as Lucian's sword hit it with a crash, sending it clattering to the floor.

Oh God. Oh God.

Would this never end?

Burton flew at Lucian, smashing his sword down hard, and barrelling into Lucian's side with his shoulder, sending him to the floor. Lucian rolled, and the flickering glint of a blade caught the light, a glimmer dancing across the edge as it struck out and slashed across Mr Burton's thigh. The man dropped his sword and fell with a cry of agony as blood poured from the wound.

Lucian stood, staring down at Mr Burton before moving forward and kicking his sword out of reach.

"I believe you've had enough, sir," he said coldly. "I will have a physician dispatched to tend your wounds, but I hope you'll forgive me if I have you sent elsewhere for the treatment."

He stepped back, breathing hard, and then turned to Matilda, his face clearing as he saw her, as though he'd been somewhere else entirely and was emerging from a thick fog into the light.

"Matilda," he said, letting out a breath.

"My lord!"

They both turned as Denton and a dozen footmen hurried into the ballroom.

"Have someone fetch a doctor, Denton, and get this wretched fellow out of my home."

"At once, my lord."

Lucian turned back to Matilda and smiled, moving quickly towards her, but a flurry of movement behind him caught her eye. Mr Burton reaching for something in his boot, something that he clasped in his hand and raised.

"*Lucian!*"

The sound was so loud in the great expanse of the ballroom, it seemed to suspend time. It was a moment before she realised what it had been.

A gunshot.

Denton and the footmen shouted, all of them rushing towards Mr Burton as Lucian staggered.

No. No.

No, no, no.

"Lucian!" she screamed, struggling to her feet, hindered by the ties binding her wrists together. "Lucian!"

She ran towards him as a red rose bloomed at his left shoulder, staining the pristine white of his shirt. He put his hand to it, staring in surprise as his fingers came away dripping blood, and laughed softly.

"Honour be damned," he said, and fell to his knees.

Chapter 8

I don't know if I shall ever send this. If I will ever tell you all that is in my heart. I don't know if it would be a comfort to you or a curse and I would not bring you pain for all the world, though I do not expect you to believe that. When did it happen, this thing that has taken me over, invaded my heart and mind, my every waking moment and my dreams? This is something I still cannot answer. Yet the why of it is obvious enough.

I have been too used to having my character assassinated to pay any heed to harsh words. They lost their sting too long ago to penetrate my callous hide, and it has been decades since a barbed comment could hurt me. Your words of condemnation were different. Why did I care so much what you thought of me? Perhaps because your goodness shines from you, because everyone who is taken under your wing is protected and cared for and loved, no matter what it costs you to do so. I envied your friends so much I was sick with it. I wanted to be one of the chosen ones, those whose lives were gilded by your care and attention. There are so many things I regret in my life, Matilda. There have been so many terrible decisions, so many missteps. Yet despite the pain it brings me, I shall never regret loving you. I do love you, you see, so much it terrifies me. You make me want to be better, to be a man you might have looked upon with pride. A man you could have loved, if things had been different.

—Excerpt of a letter from the Most Honourable Lucian Barrington, Marquess of Montagu to Miss Matilda Hunt—Never sent.

25ᵗʰ April 1815. Dern, Sevenoaks, Kent.

Finally someone freed her wrists of their bindings, and Matilda sank down beside Lucian.

"Fetch a doctor!" she screamed, to which the infuriating man shook his head.

"No. Denton, fetch Pippin."

"Pippin!" Matilda exclaimed, beside herself with terror. Blood was welling from the wound, dripping between his fingers where he'd pressed his hand against it. "You've been shot, you impossible man. You need a physician, not a cook!"

He smiled at her, though the expression was a little strained. "Pippin is from a lengthy line of wise women, my love. She's a skilled healer, and I'd rather have her tend me than any blasted quack. Denton, I take it Mr Edwards remained to attend our meeting in the morning? Good. Fetch him. I need him here at once."

"Is Mr Edwards a physician?" Matilda asked hopefully, still a little dubious how a cook could double up as a competent physician.

Lucian frowned.

"No, my solicitor," he said, before returning to issuing orders about what must be done with Mr Burton and who must be sent for.

Deciding that the ridiculous man was too busy to care that his lifeblood was exiting his body at a terrifying rate, Matilda yanked up her skirts to expose her petticoats and tore at the seam.

Lucian fell silent, his gaze falling to her ankles.

"Oh, now I have your attention, do I?" she said tartly, wadding up the material before taking his hand from the wound and pressing the cloth hard against it.

Lucian blanched, sucking in a breath.

"Oh, I'm sorry. I'm so sorry." Contrite, she burst into tears, and Lucian lifted a hand to her face, only to pause as he realised it was red with his own blood.

Matilda snatched it up and held it to her face, not caring about anything but that he should know he was loved.

"You must find Phoebe, sweetheart," he said softly. "She's hiding. She'll be frightened."

"Oh, yes, I will," She said, though the thought of leaving him for a moment tore at her heart. "But—"

"I'll be fine. Go and get her and put her to bed. Tell her not to worry."

"Oh, h-how can I?" she demanded, her eyes drawn to the wad of material that was growing dark with his blood.

"My lord? Someone said you'd been hurt…. Oh, my stars!"

They both looked up as Mrs Appleton hurried towards them.

"Pippin," Lucian said, his relief palpable. "I'm very glad to see you."

"Oh!" The woman said, pressing her hand to her mouth, her eyes filling with tears. "Oh, my boy. What has that wicked man done now?"

"Now, now, Pippin. No histrionics, I beg you."

Pippin sniffed, blinking hard, and brought herself firmly under control, her shoulders stiffening. She nodded, her expression brisk.

"Histrionics indeed," she said indignantly. "I should think not. Now mind out of the way, if you please, Miss Hunt, and let me see what's to be done."

"Phoebe," he said, pleading in his eyes now as he looked to Matilda.

"Of course." She nodded, unable to refuse him, though she did not want to leave. "Where will she be?"

"Can you find your way to the Long Gallery?"

"I think so."

"Stand by my portrait, the one by Lawrence. Call out to her. She'll come."

His voice was strained, breathless, and his face was a ghastly shade, too pale. Matilda stared at him, not wanting to leave.

"*Please.*"

He closed his eyes.

"Very well."

Matilda got to her knees again, swiftly now, leaning in and pressing her mouth to his, not caring a damn that Mrs Appleton and whoever else was in the room could see.

Lucian sighed, a slight smile lingering at his lips.

"I needed that," he said, as she drew back, a glimmer of amusement in his eyes.

"I'll be as quick as I can," she promised, and squeezed his hand tightly before running to find Phoebe.

***

To Matilda's frustration, she took two wrong turns before she finally stumbled upon the Long Gallery. She stood before the disdainful regard of generations of Barringtons and held the lamp aloft. Lucian's cool silver eyes glinted down at her from his portrait.

"Phoebe!" she called into the darkness beyond the pool of lamplight. "Phoebe, love, it's Matilda. It's all right. You can come out now."

There was a long silence and Matilda waited for a while before calling again.

"Phoebe!" A scratching sound made her pause, lamp aloft, holding her breath. "Phoebe?"

Matilda watched in astonishment as the huge portrait and the panelled wall it was fixed to swung open on silent hinges, and a pale, frightened face peered out.

"Matilda?"

She set down the lamp and hurried to the girl.

"Phoebe! Oh, thank goodness."

Phoebe ran into her arms with a sob. "Is he all right? Is Uncle Theodore here? Did he hurt him?"

Matilda's heart clenched, and she held Phoebe tightly. "No, he is not here, love. You're quite safe."

Phoebe looked up at once.

"B-But Uncle Monty…." Her expression changed, horror in her eyes as she touched a finger to Matilda's cheek. "Th-That's b-blood."

Matilda hesitated, wanting to pretend everything was fine but knowing how much store Lucian set by the truth, and how much Phoebe appreciated him for it.

"Yes. He's hurt, love, but he will be all right," she said, praying she was telling the truth about that. She could not bear to think about the alternative.

"Hurt? Who hurt him? Oh, no… what happened? I must go to him—"

"Phoebe, no, love. Not now… I don't think…."

But Phoebe had torn herself from Matilda's arms and Matilda could do nothing but snatch up the lamp once more and hurry after her. To her immense relief, they saw Denton coming up the stairs just as Phoebe was about to run down them.

"Where is he?" the child cried, tears running down her little face. "Where is my uncle?"

"There, there, now, Miss Barrington. His lordship has been taken to his room and Pippin is with him. You trust Pippin to look after him, don't you?"

"Y-Yes," Phoebe stammered, trembling hard. "B-But I w-want to see him."

"And so you shall," the butler said kindly, taking her hand. "Come along, but you must wait until Pippin says you can go in. Do you promise?"

Phoebe nodded and then paused, holding out her other hand to Matilda, who hurried forward to take it, feeling she needed the reassurance just as much as Phoebe did.

It seemed an eternity that they lingered in the dim hallway, a clock somewhere ticking the minutes away as Matilda's heartbeat measured them out with dull, aching thuds. Phoebe clung to her and Matilda held her tightly, knowing they were both living in the same nightmarish place where neither of them dared breathe in case the world shattered around them.

They looked up as the door opened and a small, thin man with a serious face and spectacles came out, clutching a sheaf of papers.

"What is he doing with Uncle?" Phoebe demanded, her voice shrill with anxiety.

The man frowned at Phoebe as he closed the door quietly behind him. "His lordship had some business he needed taken care of. Nothing to trouble yourself over, child."

Phoebe turned to Matilda, her eyes reflecting all the terror that Matilda was feeling as Phoebe voiced the question she'd not let herself consider. "What business does he need to do at such a moment, if he's hurt? What are those papers?"

Before Matilda or anyone else could halt her, Phoebe darted past the man and yanked open the door, running into her uncle's bedroom. Matilda knew damn well she ought not follow, but her reputation was likely past saving, and she cared little for it in this moment. Lucian was all that mattered. She followed Phoebe in, watching as the girl threw herself upon the bed, making Lucian suck in a sharp breath.

"Uncle!" she cried as Lucian held out the arm on his uninjured side.

"It's all right, sweetheart," he said, though he looked horribly pale and sounded exhausted. "Don't fret. Pippin is taking excellent care of me."

"B-But what happened? What is that bandage for?"

"I fought a duel," Lucian said solemnly, watching with amusement as Phoebe's expression lit up with awe.

"With pistols?" she asked, frowning.

Lucian shook his head. "A sword fight."

"Then why are you hurt?" she demanded, clearly knowing her uncle's skill, for her scorn at him being injured in such a way was evident.

"No, love. I won the duel, but the blackguard shot me in the back. Got me in the shoulder."

"The scoundrel!" Phoebe cried in fury. "But if you knew he was a blackguard, why on earth did you turn your back on him? That was very silly of you!"

Lucian hugged her tighter.

"I know, Phoebe," he said, his voice catching. "It was. Extremely silly, and I'm sorry for it."

Matilda looked away, afraid she would cry herself, and instead moved towards Mrs Appleton.

"Will he be all right?"

The woman's face was set, her voice firm. "The wound is clean, the bullet went straight though and didn't hit bone, praise be. He's weary now from the blood loss, but it's the infection that we've to worry about. I'll give him a tot of laudanum, though he'll kick up about it, I've no doubt. Makes him sick, but he's in a lot of pain. Not that he'd let you know it." Mrs Appleton gave her a direct look, full of curiosity. "He'll need a deal of nursing. Likely you'll want to get off back home, as he won't be fit for entertaining guests for some weeks by my reckoning."

Matilda stiffened, wondering if Mrs Appleton thought to send her packing. Over her dead body. "No. He needs to be taken care of. He needs *me* and I'm going nowhere," Matilda said, glaring at her. "Not until he's well enough to tell me to go himself, at any rate."

To Matilda's surprise, the cook's face softened at once, approval warming her eyes.

"Aye, thought I had you pegged right. Well, you need not worry that anyone will find out about it. We know how to keep secrets at Dern, Miss Hunt."

Matilda gave a rueful smile, touched by the woman's support. "I suspect Mr Burton will take care of that."

"Oh, I wouldn't bank on it, miss. The staff here are loyal and they're none too pleased at tonight's piece of work. I reckon if Mr Burton wants to see that doctor his lordship sent for, he'll have to agree to keep his damn mouth shut."

Matilda stared in astonishment, and Mrs Appleton laughed.

"Oh, we know his lordship's reputation, and it's not all talk. A right devil he can be when he puts his mind to it, but there's a good heart in there, which is a miraculous thing after all he's endured. He treats all the staff fairly, the pay's good and most of them enjoy his reputation. Adds a touch of swagger to their own lives, I reckon. Anyway, he's our devil and this attack in his own home… well, they're ready to lynch someone, I can tell you."

"They wouldn't…." Matilda began, alarmed even though she cared little what befell Mr Burton now.

"No," Mrs Appleton said grimly. "But only because he forbade it. The fiend is to be taken to the nearest inn, and a doctor provided at his lordship's expense. Honour must be served, Miss Hunt."

Her dry tone and the look in the woman's eyes told Matilda that her thoughts on the male code of honour were many and varied, but she said nothing more.

"Pippin."

They both looked around as Lucian called out wearily.

"Phoebe needs to go to bed now," he said, though Phoebe's arms tightened around his neck at his words. "Send for Miss Peabody."

Matilda watched as the woman hurried to the door and stuck her head outside to talk in a hushed voice to Denton, who must have been standing sentry.

"I don't want to go."

Phoebe's muffled voice emerged from Lucian's neck and he stroked her hair. His face was white and taut with pain, and Matilda realised it must be costing him dearly to keep up a brave face in front of the child.

"I know, sweetheart, but we both need some rest now."

The child let out a sob.

"Don't die," she pleaded. "Please, please… don't die. Don't leave me by myself. Promise me."

Lucian closed his eyes and held the girl to him, his grip on her tightening. "I promise to do my very best to grow to be a very old man. It will take me that long to make you into a well-behaved lady, after all."

Phoebe sobbed harder and Matilda's heart ached, a lump in her throat so large she could barely swallow. Lucian looked up at her, his breathing shallow now, a fine sheen of perspiration across his forehead. Forcing herself to remain calm, she moved to the bed and put her hands on Phoebe's shoulders.

"Come along now, darling," she said gently. "Your uncle needs his rest if he's to get well, and you must be worn out too. Everyone needs a good night's sleep to get over all the upset. I promise you I shall take very good care of him while you're sleeping."

Phoebe turned her head, staring up at Matilda, her blonde eyelashes spangled with tears. "You'll stay and look after him? Until he's well again?"

"Matilda," Lucian began, his voice faint but full of protest. "You know you can't—"

"Yes," Matilda said firmly. "I will stay until he's well again. I promise."

Phoebe let out a ragged breath.

"Well, if you will be with him as well as Pippin," she said, still reluctant, "I suppose I could go to sleep for a little while. I know you'll not let anything bad happen to him."

Matilda smiled, too choked to reply as Phoebe kissed her uncle's cheek. "Good night. Get better quickly, please."

"Good night, sweetheart."

Matilda helped Phoebe off the bed and took her to the door to discover Miss Peabody waiting for her. Matilda hugged Phoebe, promised again that she would look after her uncle, and watched the child follow her governess back down the hall.

Upon returning to the room, she discovered Mrs Appleton scowling down at Lucian.

"You'll take your medicine, my lord, if I have to prise your jaws open and tip it down myself."

Lucian glared at the woman and Matilda discovered herself relieved to see his iron will had not left him. That was a comfort.

"I'm no longer five years old, Pippin, much as you might like to think it. I can manage quite well without…."

His breath caught and his lips clamped shut, his body growing taut as he succumbed to the obvious pain he was in.

"You were saying?" Mrs Appleton said, with an imperious lift of one eyebrow he could not have bettered himself.

"Damn you, you interfering old—"

"And you'll keep a civil tongue in your head, marquess or no, and in front of Miss Hunt too. What will she think of you, arguing with me like a sulky boy and not taking your medicine when you know I'm doing what's best for you?"

Lucian returned an arctic glare, but held his tongue as Mrs Appleton measured out a dose of laudanum.

"Wait," he said, huffing as Mrs Appleton gave him a warning glare. "I wish to speak to Miss Hunt in private before you dose me, you blasted tyrant. *If* I may?" he added tersely.

"Five minutes," the woman replied, giving him a stern wag of her finger. She moved towards Matilda on her way out, speaking in an undertone. "Don't let him talk too long. He's fighting the pain, but he's wearing himself out. He must rest."

Matilda nodded and waited until she'd gone to sit beside Lucian, taking his hand in hers. He sighed, gazing at her under heavy-lidded eyes, exhaustion catching up with him.

"Matilda," he said, her name little more than a breath of sound.

"I'm here."

He laughed softly. "I'm still having difficulty with that idea. Am I delirious with fever already? Did I dream you?"

"No." She raised his hand to her lips and pressed her mouth to his palm. "No," she repeated against his skin, her voice cracking with emotion.

"Say it again," he said, his silver eyes intent, though a little too bright.

She knew what he meant and laughed this time, or perhaps it had been a sob, a strange hiccoughing sound that caught in her throat. "I ought not."

"I know. Say it anyway."

She stared down at him and reached out with her free hand, cupping his face and stroking his cheek. "I love you."

He stared at her, happiness and bemusement tangled in his expression. "Why?"

"Don't," she said as tears welled in her eyes. She shook her head. "I'll tell you when you're well."

He made a disgruntled sound and she kissed his palm again.

"I've had papers drawn up," he said, the turn in the conversation making her start. "If… If anything happens to me…."

Matilda shook her head vehemently. She could not think of that.

He smiled a little and squeezed the hand that held his.

"I'm not so feeble as that, and I have no intention of going anywhere just yet, I assure you, but… but things happen. Life is… *uncertain*, and… he'll try again, Matilda."

Matilda gave a sob and covered her mouth.

"Don't cry," he said, tugging at her hand, drawing her down to lie beside him. She went, moving carefully, snuggling into his good side. "I need to tell you this, and Pippin will be back insisting on making me swallow that vile stuff, though it will make me sick as a dog. Please don't stay to witness that, I beg of you."

Matilda shook her head. "I promised Phoebe. I don't break promises, and I've nursed my father and Nate too, occasionally. Your sickbed holds no horrors I've not witnessed."

"You were not in love with them," he said curtly. "Leave a man a little dignity."

Matilda propped herself on her elbow. "Not *in* love with them, no. But I loved them. That's what you do when you love someone: you stick with them, no matter what, through thick and thin, whether it's pretty or not."

He frowned and she stared down at him, feeling her love for him as a weight in her chest, expanding and filling her up.

"It won't change how I feel about you."

"Oh, yes," he muttered. "I'm sure you'll have many passionately romantic thoughts of me once you've seen me cast up my accounts."

Despite everything, she laughed at his indignation. "Oh, Lucian. My feelings are not so superficial as that. You've really no idea what it is to be loved, if you think such a thing could make the smallest change to my feelings."

"Perhaps I don't," he said with a sigh, his voice growing soft. "But I think I know what it is to love, or at least, I'm learning."

Matilda's breath caught, but he stiffened, his face taut with pain.

"Lucian, you need to take the laudanum."

"Not yet," he gritted out. His breathing picked up, and he stared up at her, his eyes full of fear, glinting with a febrile intensity that frightened her. "Listen to me. I've made you Phoebe's legal guardian. If… if anything happens to me, keep her away from my uncle, *no matter what*. Promise me, Matilda. I know it's a great deal to ask, too much, but I do ask it. She's all I've got, and I swore to protect her. Please, please, my love…."

"Yes. Yes, of course," Matilda said, alarmed at the sudden urgency with which he spoke and needing to calm him. "It would be an honour, Lucian, but I tell you now, you're going nowhere. I shall never forgive you if you leave me in such a way. You can't die. I *won't* let you die, I-I w-won't." Her voice broke and Lucian held her to him, hushing her softly.

"Thank you." The tension left his body all at once. "Thank you so much. You have no idea—"

"Yes, I do," she sobbed. "I know how much you love her, like she was your own daughter, and I shall love her like my own too. I do already, you foolish man. Surely you know that?"

"Yes," he said, and she heard the smile in his voice. "And this is how you ruined yourself all those years ago, by acting selflessly, by plunging ahead to grant the wishes of those you loved, heedless of the cost to yourself."

"Sometimes that is the price love commands, Lucian. If you are not prepared to pay it, it is not love at all."

"My God, you are brave." He stared up at her in wonder. "I've never met anyone else like you in all my life."

"How lucky you've been," she said, trying to smile at him, but he was closing his eyes now, his breathing uneven and a fine tremor running through his body. "Lucian?"

He didn't answer, and the shivering persisted. Afraid now, Matilda slid from the bed.

"Mrs Appleton!" she called, relieved when the woman opened the door at once and hurried to his bedside. "Is it fever?" she asked anxiously as the woman laid her hand upon Lucian's forehead.

"No, not yet," the woman replied, her voice soothing. "That will take a while to set in. This is his body protesting all that's been done to it." She reached for the small glass into which she'd measured a dose of laudanum and sat beside Lucian, sliding her arm beneath his neck and raising his head a little. "Come now, my boy. Take this and get some rest."

"Pippin," he protested, her name spoken fretfully.

"Ah, do as you're told now, Lucian, for your old Pippin, there's a good lad."

He huffed, but swallowed the mixture with a grimace and a muttered curse. "Matilda."

"She's here," Mrs Appleton assured him, settling him back against the pillows. "Lucky fellow, aren't you, to have such a pretty nurse?"

"She ought not...." he said, his breathing picking up.

Mrs Appleton gave a soft laugh. "I don't think she's the sort you can order about, my lord. Reckon she'll just dig her heels in all the harder. I like her," she added, patting his hand. "Now get some sleep and stop fretting. There's nothing for you to worry about. Phoebe is safe and Miss Hunt is here. All is well."

Matilda watched as Lucian subsided, sliding into unconsciousness.

"Well, then," Mrs Appleton said with a sigh. "If I were you, I'd go and get washed and have a couple of hours sleep, at least. It will likely be a long few days if you mean to stay by him."

"Oh, but Mrs Appleton...." Matilda protested, hating the idea of leaving him at all.

"Away with you," she said sharply. "If you mean to be of any help to me, you must be well rested, and you've had a nasty shock too. I'll stay by him, but he'll sleep peacefully now, so you do the same. I'll fetch you if there's any change. My word upon it."

"You promise?" Matilda said reluctantly.

"I do, and none of this 'Mrs Appleton' business. It's Pippin to the family, and it seems you're a part of it now."

Matilda blinked hard and swallowed, uncertain of what to say.

"There, there," Pippin said softly, moving to Matilda and giving her a hug. "He'll be fine, my word upon it. We can only hope such a close shave to the almighty makes him realise the living are who we must live our lives with; the dead have had their turn." She gave Matilda an approving look. "He could do with a woman like you at his side, but hopefully he'll come to that in his own time. He never could be told anything, that's for certain. Stubborn devil."

She laughed at the astonishment in Matilda's eyes and took her arm, guiding her to the door. "Yes, I know. I'm a deal too free with my opinions. Believe me, you're not the first to have remarked it, nor will you be the last. Now, run along and get some rest. I shall expect you to take over in the morning."

Dismissed, Matilda found herself standing on the other side of Lucian's door. Too numb to do otherwise, she moved along the corridor, noting for the first time how close her room was to his. She went inside to find Sarah waiting for her. The maid ran at her and flung her arms about her, and Matilda just stood there clutching her in return.

"Oh, miss. Is it true? His lordship's been shot?"

Matilda let Sarah go and stepped back, and Sarah gave a little shriek as she saw Matilda's hands. Lifting them to her face, she saw that they were still covered with Lucian's blood, her blue gown stained with it. The sob caught in her throat and Sarah hugged her again, tighter and tighter as Matilda broke down.

Dimly, she was aware of Sarah undressing her, helping her wash the blood from her hands and face, and guiding her into bed. Despite her fatigue and the exhaustion that tugged at her mind, it took her a long while to find sleep and, when she did, dreams of glittering swords and villains plagued her through the darkness.

Chapter 9

My dear Charles,

I thank you most kindly for your hospitality these past months. It is good to know my old friends have not deserted me. You were right, of course. It was most foolish of me to seek a reconciliation with Lucian in public, or indeed at all. But there is no fool like an old fool and my heart was so overjoyed to see him again, I forgot our enmity and allowed my feelings to get the better of me.

I am sorry I could not wait to speak with you in person before my abrupt leave taking, but I did not wish to intrude on your family celebrations after the happy marriage of your lovely niece. I'm afraid I have this morning received dire news indeed, however. News that leads me to believe that my nephew is, as I have always feared, not entirely sane. I must away to Kent, to discover the truth of what has transpired, though I confess I am afraid to go. I only hope he does not discover my presence close to Dern, for I believe I must fear for my life.

It appears Mr Burton has been mortally wounded by my nephew, who attacked him without provocation. I spoke to the man – who has been most grievously ill-used by my nephew – before he left for Dern. He wished to plead with Montagu to leave him be, for it seems Mr Burton has been defamed most unjustly, and all for my nephew's wicked desires for the woman Burton aspired to marry. I warned him of the dangers, but the poor deluded creature believed he could appeal to my nephew's better nature. Sadly, as I know to my cost, he does not possess one. In normal circumstances I would ask you to keep the news to yourself, to save the family name, but the gossip will begin soon enough, I'm afraid, so there is little point in secrecy. Whatever am I to do? Do you think Bedwin would step in and help me? I am at my wits' end.

—Excerpt of a letter from Mr Theodore Barrington to Charles Adolphus, Baron Fitzwalter.

26ᵗʰ April 1815. Dern, Sevenoaks, Kent.

Lucian woke to a world of nausea and pain. Disorientated, he tried to open his eyes and groaned as light seared through his tender brain. God, he was cold. Why was he so bloody cold? Yet the sheets seemed to stick to his skin, his body damp with sweat. He shifted on the bed and pain lanced through him, stealing his breath and making his stomach roil. *Oh, God.* Though the agony of it almost made his mind grow black, he turned on his side and retched, vomiting helplessly.

Dimly, he registered a voice calling for the curtains to be closed, and that someone had mercifully provided a bowl to catch the vile mixture he'd heaved up. A glass was lifted to his mouth, and he drank gratefully, wanting more, and protesting as the sweet water was taken away.

"Slowly," said a soft voice. "Only sips."

He tried once again to open his eyes, but found nothing but blurry shapes as a warm cloth wiped over his face. He shivered.

"Cold," he murmured.

"I know," said the voice. Such a lovely voice. He wanted to hear it again.

"Cold."

"Poor Lucian, I'm so sorry, my love."

My love. My love. His mind snagged on the words and held on tight. *My love. Matilda.*

"Matilda?"

"Yes, darling, I'm here."

Relief flooded him. Matilda was here. She was here. Matilda loved him. Yet, if Matilda was here, then…. Shame rose, the heat of humiliation battling the chill in his bones as he realised *she* was tending him. She had held the bowl…. *Oh God, no.* He shook his head.

"No," he said. "*No.* Not like this…."

"Don't be cross," she soothed him. "I will not leave, so you'll just have to put up with it."

He made a harsh sound of mingled rage and frustration. He didn't want her to go, couldn't bear her to leave, but to see him… like *this*…. It was intolerable.

"Lucian, calm down. I promise you I'm not the least bit revolted. Indeed, you look ridiculously handsome in the circumstances, so do stop fretting."

He groaned, a little outraged yet relieved too. She wouldn't leave him. Despite the fact he was bedbound, sweating, vomiting, and out of his head with pain, she would stay by him. He had no right to it, this loving devotion, his mind lucid enough to comprehend that truth down to his bones. Yet he wanted it, needed it so badly, and he loved her. Oh, God help him, he loved her so much he feared the emotion would swallow him whole, like the whale had swallowed Jonah. Yet, he could not have her. Even if he dared to consider defying generations of Barringtons, hundreds and hundreds of years of breeding, of grasping at power....

He could feel his father's fury and scorn burning him from wherever he was in the hereafter at the mere idea. Even then, though, even if he could defy everything he'd been raised to believe in and cast aside his chance to increase the power and wealth of the family as was his duty... it was too dangerous while his uncle lived. Everyone he'd ever cared for had been taken from him, whether by accident or design. Only Lucian had been so dreadfully hard to kill, as though some benign spell had been cast on him, making him untouchable.

Almost....

He felt a gentle finger trace over the scar on his wrist and his breathing hitched. His uncle *had* nearly succeeded. Once. And he'd not had to lift a finger himself. Lucian had been too weak and too lonely to fight him any longer. Shame rose again and he tugged his hand free of the anchor that held him, sliding it under the covers. Matilda must leave. If Theodore discovered her here, if he realised it was more than desire that Lucian felt for her....

Oh, God.

"You... *must* go." He forced the words out, though his heart protested vehemently. "Dangerous, too dangerous."

"I'm not going anywhere, my love, and if you want to throw me out, you must get well so you can do it yourself."

Frustrated, Lucian tried to open his eyes, to focus. Damnation, Pippin must have dosed him again, for it was like swimming through treacle. A sudden memory snatched at his mind, dragging him off course, down into the darkness. His lungs were burning, his mind closing down, the pressure of the water smothering him as he drowned. Drugged. He'd been drugged. It had felt like this, heavy... disorientating. Had the lemonade tasted odd?

"Let's go for a picnic at the lake, boys. We can go swimming and cool off."

His uncle's jovial face was full of pleasure at the idea, him and Thomas laughing with excitement.

Lucian's breath caught in his throat.

"*Thomas!*" he said, trying to shout but the water rushed in, taking his cry and sinking it, down into the green depths.

He saw his little brother splashing merrily at the edge of the lake as Lucian flailed, in too deep. His limbs felt like lead. He was so tired, and it would be so easy to sink to the bottom. Uncle Theo was standing by the lake and Lucian tried once more to shout, to make him see, but then came clarity. That dreadful moment when he could no longer fail to acknowledge the truth. Theo *could* see. He was watching him drown. It all became obvious in an instant. He was supposed to die here, like this, a tragic accident that was no accident at all.

Rage had burned through the drug, giving him a last burst of energy, enough to struggle his way back to where he could touch the bottom. He staggered and collapsed in the mud at the edge of the water, Thomas running to his side, shouting, and suddenly he was being carried back to the house.

Lucian thrashed helplessly, the vile touch of the monster's hands on him, his sweet, jovial voice scolding him gently before the staff and Great-Aunt Marguerite.

"Naughty scamp must have been nipping at my flask of brandy," Theo said, tutting a little, an indulgent uncle not wanting to scold his wayward nephew. "Half drowned himself, the foolish lad."

"Oh, Lucian, whatever next?" Marguerite was as disgusted as always.

Mouldy Marguerite, chanted Phoebe's voice.

"Yes, mouldy," he agreed with Phoebe, who was sitting on his knee, eating biscuits.

Marguerite was a wretched old woman, and he hated her.

"Ah, don't scold him, Marguerite. Boys will be boys and he's learned his lesson. He just had a tot too much. He won't do it again."

"*No!*" Lucian forced the word out, tried to tell them. "No, it wasn't me, it was him. It was *him!*"

But he could see their smiles, see that they believed his uncle and they would not believe him. Only Pippin scowled. Pippin, who came to his bedside though she was not his nurse. Pippin, who wouldn't let him be alone….

"Lucian, hush now, love. Calm down. Your uncle is not here. Everyone is safe."

"*Phoebe!*" he cried, terror clutching at him. Phoebe must not be dragged into dark places, not into the lake, not shut in the tunnels, not tortured with lies and benign smiles that hid razor sharp teeth. She would not live in the nightmares. "Don't leave her… she must not… not alone."

"She's not alone. I promise. Miss Peabody is with her and there are footmen outside her door. Denton arranged it all. There are extra staff in the grounds, too. I will keep her safe for you, darling."

Lucian subsided. His heart was thudding, too fast, too slow, too… *something*…. Everything hurt. He felt strange. Cold. Cold and dead, like Thomas had been. Dead and gone with that strange smile upon his face. *No*…. He shook his head, not wanting that memory to surface, fighting it, but Thomas was there, waiting.

"So sorry, Lucie. I didn't understand what he was until it was too late, I didn't see it. Made amends, though…couldn't live with it… with what I did. Couldn't taint my little girl with it. It was my fault. All my fault, not yours…. So sorry…."

"No, Thomas, don't… *don't*… it wasn't you. Don't go… don't leave me…. We can fight him together this time."

It was not Thomas who answered, though.

"I won't leave you, darling."

Lucian snatched at the lovely voice again, trying to haul himself free of the nightmare, away from the ghostly, ghastly face of his brother the night he'd found him, dead, all alone in the bedroom of a gentlemen's club.

Lucian remembered the room, the club. One of the fashionable gaming halls, full of darkness and vice and all kinds of debauchery on offer. Thomas had died there, alone and eaten alive with guilt, eaten alive by the demons that drove him. A sob tore at his throat and he tried to turn his face away from the scene in that sordid room that stank of opium and despair and death. He turned his head and Matilda was there. *She was there*, too lovely and innocent to be there, in that dreadful place. She was incongruous, like a mirage, a dreadful temptation, the most dangerous desire of all….

"Hush, Lucian."

Warm fingers curled about his, holding on tight, anchoring him.

"Matilda. You shouldn't have been there… Shouldn't have…Shouldn't be… *here*."

"Yes, I should. I am here. I'm not going anywhere. Rest now, my love."

He slept.

***

30th April 1815. Dern, Sevenoaks, Kent.

"Miss Hunt. Wakey, wakey."

Matilda blinked. Her head hurt and her mouth was dry, her eyes all scratchy. She jolted up with a lurch as panic struck her heart.

"Lucian!"

"He's all right, don't get yourself in a lather. I just brought you a nice cup of tea."

Matilda rubbed at her gritty eyes, a little disorientated but relieved to discover Pippin was right. Lucian had been fretful and restless ever since the fever set in, but he was relatively peaceful now. A flush seared his high cheekbones and he'd thrashed the sheet off again at some point, exposing a beautifully sculpted chest and muscular arms. Matilda blushed as she realised Pippin was watching her admire him. She twitched the sheet back up, covering him. She ought to be inured to the sight now, after tending him so personally these past days... but apparently not.

"I'm sorry to wake you, but you've barely eaten a morsel, nor drunk a drop all day, and I've not the time to nurse you too, so that won't do."

Matilda nodded and took the teacup from her hand, sipping at it gratefully. It was only now she realised how thirsty she was.

"There's a nice big piece of fruitcake there, too, so make sure you eat it. It'll perk you up."

"Thank you," Matilda said, her gaze drifting back to Lucian.

"He'll be all right." Pippin soothed her. "You've seen how fit and strong he is and, more than that, he's determined to protect those he cares about. He's not going anywhere."

Matilda sighed, comforted by this woman's assurances. She had been impressed and relieved to discover that Lucian's trust in Pippin was well founded. How many days had it been since he'd been hurt? Three? Four, perhaps? She'd lost track of time. They'd taken shifts, nursing him between them, only allowing his valet to do the things Lucian would have died of mortification rather than have them do. Though Matilda had been more than a little anxious to discover Pippin meant to treat the bullet wound with nothing more powerful than honey and herbs, the results spoke for themselves. Fever had set in, but the infection was under control. It had not grown worse, at least.

"Lucian said your ancestors were wise women."

Pippin looked up at her and smiled wryly, her expression placid. "Yes. Two hundred and forty years ago, one of my maternal grandmothers was hanged as a witch. Men have always feared women with knowledge. Makes us dangerous, you see, powerful in ways they don't like nor understand. Happily, such nonsense is forgotten now, but I was taught the same as she was. I by my mother, as her mother was taught before her, and so on. Lucian—his lordship—came to appreciate my skills as a boy. He needed them, too, more often than I care to remember."

"Because of his uncle?"

Pippin nodded. "He told you."

"Only a little. That Mr Barrington had tried to kill him."

Pippin made a disdainful noise. "Oh, no. He did worse than that. He tried to destroy him, and is still trying. That horrible man won with poor Thomas, twisted and tortured that poor boy into such knots...." She shook her head, clamping her lips together against what was obviously strong emotion. "Thomas was so young, fragile too. He didn't stand a chance against a vile creature like Theodore Barrington. That man told such lies. He made Thomas hate Lucian, and it was years before Thomas realised how he'd been manipulated. When he did, when he understood he'd turned against his own brother and it had all been lies, it destroyed him. Theodore might have got my Lucian too, sent him down the same path, only I saw what he was. Not as quick as I ought to have done, but I saw, and I made sure Lucian knew I'd seen. That I believed him. I made sure he was protected after that. The best I could, anyway."

"Was it very bad?" Matilda felt sick as she saw the look in Pippin's eyes.

"Worse than you can imagine."

Matilda hesitated, not wanting to pry, but….

"There's a scar… on his wrist."

Pippin's gentle features darkened, something that promised retribution glinting in eyes that were usually warm and filled with kindness and compassion.

"He was just a child, all alone, and no one believed him. They thought the loss of his parents had unbalanced his mind, for everyone saw how his uncle doted on him. But once you knew the truth, you heard the threat in every assurance that his Uncle Theo spoke when he said he wouldn't *ever* let Lucian be alone again. All those loving words that he used before everyone, those that made him sound so kind, they always had another meaning. That was the wickedness of it. To Lucian, he was being threatened in plain sight, but no one could see it but him."

Matilda stared at her in silent horror, understanding Pippin's need to gather herself as her voice quavered and she turned away. The woman moved to the bed and stroked the hair from Lucian's forehead. When she spoke again, the words were quiet but still full of rage.

"That man infested this family like a cancer, and he killed it a bit at a time. He tried to destroy Lucian, and he nearly succeeded, but I wouldn't let the devil have him. I knew he was on the edge and so I kept a close eye on him. I found him, before…." Her voice caught. "He was only fifteen. His brother had deserted him, wanted nothing more to do with him. Thomas had said many terrible things to him because of his uncle's lies. Lucian was so isolated, fighting on all sides, and everyone thought Theodore was such a lovely man. I hid what Lucian had done. Bandaged him up and pretended he'd got influenza and needed to rest, or they'd have had him sent to an asylum. His uncle would have relished it. He might not have gained the title, but he'd have had control of everything."

"Oh, God." Matilda covered her hand with her mouth, remembering the way Lucian sometimes tugged at his cuffs, an unconscious gesture she now understood.

She felt sick with grief, with rage, with the need to punish Theodore Barrington with the fires of hell, and never let him near Lucian or Phoebe ever again.

"There's only Lucian left now," Pippin said. "He's all that stands between that wicked man and the blasted title he covets, but that monster won't have him. I won't let him. *We* won't let him, will we, Miss Hunt?"

"Over my dead body, Pippin."

Pippin returned a grim smile. "Oh, no. Not yours, miss. It won't be yours."

Chapter 10

Dear Aashini,

I am worried that Matilda is no better. What does the doctor say? Can we not visit? I beg you to keep the dreadful gossip about Montagu from her. It can only bring her grief. Uncle Charles says he is insane, but I find that hard to believe. The stories are all so wild, but… I hardly know what to think.

—Excerpt of a letter from Her Grace Prunella Adolphus, Duchess of Bedwin, to Aashini Anson, Countess of Cavendish.

2nd May 1815. Dern, Sevenoaks, Kent.

"Why doesn't he wake up?"

Phoebe clutched at Matilda's hand and she squeezed it to reassure the child.

"Because it has taken a great deal of energy to fight the fever in his body, and so he must sleep to regain his strength."

"But he *will* wake up?" she asked, glancing up at Matilda, her eyes wide with fear.

"Yes," Matilda replied, with far more confidence than she might have had a few days ago.

His fever had finally broken as the sun had risen, and though he'd been sweating and fractious throughout the night, he was sleeping now and the hectic flush in his cheeks had subsided.

Phoebe turned into Matilda and hugged her, burying her face against her.

"I was so frightened," she said, her voice muffled.

Matilda got to her knees and pulled the child into a proper hug, holding her tightly. "So was I, but Pippin is terribly clever and knew just what to do."

"And you stayed," Phoebe said, the words thick. "You promised to stay, and you did."

"Of course. I would never break a promise, Phoebe."

"And you do love him, don't you?"

Matilda opened her mouth, knowing she ought to tell the girl some lie to make her accept the future would not change, but the terror she'd felt these past days had worn her down and she could not think of a way to sidestep the truth.

"Yes," she said helplessly, for what else could she say. "Yes, I do."

"I wish you were my mother."

Matilda gasped, the words darting into her heart with the precision of an arrow shaft. "Oh. Oh, Phoebe, love."

"I dream of it sometimes," she said, still clinging to Matilda. "I don't remember my real mother, and I never knew my father at all. When I dream of having a mother and father they look like you and my uncle."

Matilda tried to speak, but she could not. She took a deep breath and forced herself to answer, to blink back the tears. "That sounds like a lovely dream, Phoebe, but sometimes dreams are only that, pretty imaginings that disappear like smoke if we try to hold on to them. Real life isn't as simple, and sometimes the things we want most are the things that are furthest from us."

"But you ought to fight for them," Phoebe said stubbornly. "Uncle says, if you know something is right, you must stand up and say so. He says dreadful things happen when people pretend not to see something bad or unjust because it's easier to ignore it."

Matilda nodded, hearing Lucian's voice, and knowing now why he said such things, why the truth was so dreadfully important to him, and why he did not shield Phoebe from reality with pretty lies, but gently told her what she must expect of the world.

"Yes, that's true, love, but sometimes the world is too big and too powerful, and you know you can't win."

The mutinous expression glinting in Phoebe's eyes as she looked up was not encouraging.

"All the more reason to stand up to it," she said, stubborn to the last. "I hate bullies. Great-Uncle Theodore is a bully, and I hate him too."

Matilda admitted herself thankful when a soft knock at the door brought Denton to fetch Miss Barrington for her French lesson. The little girl went reluctantly, and Matilda returned to Lucian's bedside.

A thick lock of pale blond hair had fallen over his forehead and Matilda brushed it back, relieved to discover the terrifying, burning heat was no longer blazing like a furnace lived beneath his skin. He stirred beneath her touch, turning his head towards her, and she could not resist the desire to stroke his face. The prickle of his beard was a secret delight, something she'd never imagined she'd experience. She smiled, entranced by the feel of it, sharp and soft all at once, and then her breath caught as his eyes flicked open.

They were lucid this time, clear if weary.

"Stubborn girl," he murmured. "Ought to have gone."

"You know very well I'll never do something if you order me to do it," she retorted, trying very hard not to throw herself upon his chest and weep with relief.

Somehow, her voice was reasonably calm, only the faintest tremor betraying her emotion.

He sighed, closing his eyes again.

"Thirsty."

"Oh, of course. Here."

She poured him a fresh glass of water and sat beside him, sliding her arm beneath his neck to help him raise his head. He drank, draining the glass.

"More," he demanded, before adding, "*Please.*"

Matilda hid a smile. "I think you'd best wait a moment and see how that settles first. Your poor stomach is empty."

As if on cue, his stomach made a vociferous sound of protest and Matilda laughed.

"How unbecoming," he said with a sigh. "You are determined to leave me no dignity whatsoever, aren't you?"

Matilda began to make some comment to placate him and soothe his wounded male pride, but instead a sob rose to her throat, and all the fear she'd been holding in check so furiously rose in a wave. She put a hand to her mouth, trying to hold it back, but it was no good and the dam burst.

"I was s-so a-afraid," she said through her tears.

There had been so many times she'd wanted to weep, for her own terror, for the danger he was in, for the danger he had always been in and for all the wrongs that had been done him. So, she wept now, for him, for the past days of worry and the sleepless nights.

"Matilda!"

He reached for her with his good arm and she went to him, weeping into his chest.

"Don't cry, my love. I beg of you. I can't... I can't bear it. Oh, Lord, has Phoebe taught you she can wrap me around her thumb if she cries, the dreadful creature?"

"N-No," Matilda sobbed unsteadily. "B-But I can well believe it."

She made a heroic effort to calm herself and settled against him, sniffling a little. It was so lovely to be here, with her head on his chest, hearing his heartbeat thud at a steady pace, strong and even. The sound was reassuring and wonderful after seeing him brought so low. With a sigh of relief, she listened to it and closed her eyes.

***

Lucian looked up, stiffening as the bedroom door opened. Matilda had fallen asleep next to him and he'd had neither the heart nor the will to wake her. She was exhausted, dark shadows beneath her beautiful eyes, and she fit beside him so perfectly. He never wanted her to be anywhere else. Yet, she was an unmarried woman with a damaged reputation and something like this, if it got out... it would ruin her utterly. No amount of influence from her brother or her friends could save her.

With relief, he saw Pippin come in. She paused for a moment, surveying the scene without comment, though Lucian was certain that was a gleam of approval in her eyes. Hardly surprising that she'd approve of Matilda. He'd known she would. They were alike in an odd way, braver and more resilient than anyone could ever imagine.

"Well, you're awake, then," Pippin said, moving to the bed and giving him a critical once over.

"You make it sound as if I've been malingering," he replied a touch reproachfully.

Pippin snorted.

"Don't be daft, but you've had us all sat upon thorns and no mistake." She nodded at Matilda. "She's a Trojan, that one. Wouldn't have left your side for a moment, had I not thrown her out a time or two."

Lucian felt his throat grow tight.

"She can't stay, Pippin. You know she can't."

To his surprise, Pippin scowled at him. "You tell her that, for I shan't. She's no child to be protected, but a woman grown with a strong heart and a mind of her own."

"But Theo—"

"Damn that man," Pippin said, shocking him. "We shan't let him ruin any more lives."

Lucian laughed, a bitter sound he was well used to. "I tried, Pippin. I thought I'd built the monster a cage that would hold him. I thought we might be safe."

"No, you didn't," Pippin said, not unkindly. "You know as well as I do some evil has to be vanquished absolutely. You can't turn your back on it. Not for a moment. Even Phoebe knew it, and that's because you taught her. I don't know what you were thinking, taking your eyes off that Burton creature."

He snorted. "I wasn't thinking. I was looking at Matilda."

She smiled at him and shook her head. "*Men.* Too easily distracted."

"You think I ought to have killed him. Theo, I mean, not that pathetic excuse for a man who came here to do his bidding."

It wasn't a question and Pippin looked at him, one of those penetrating stares that made you wonder if she could read your mind. Her expression remained thoughtful.

"No. No, I don't think that. You don't need such a stain on your soul. You've dealt with enough for one lifetime. I do believe he needs to die, though."

"Then who?" he demanded. "Who else will deal with him, if not me?"

Pippin shrugged. "Sometimes the world sets things to rights by itself, and I think it's past time he paid for his sins. His game isn't over just yet, but we've not finished playing either. Don't you trouble your head about it, though. Not yet. It will become clear. The goddess will provide. She always does."

Despite himself, a prickle ran up the back of his neck. Not that Lucian was about to ask her what she meant by that. To begin with, he was too tired to figure her out, not that there was any figuring Pippin out when she got all mystical.

"If you're going to invoke the goddess and cast spells, you can just do it elsewhere, you mad old witch," he murmured, though with such obvious affection she only smiled at him.

"Ah, one day I'll convince you."

"Not today," he said with a sigh, closing his eyes.

"That's all right," Pippin said, her voice soothing now. "She looks after you all the same, whether or not you believe. She always has."

"That's nice."

He was exhausted, and Matilda was a warm weight by his side. In some far off place, he could hear Pippin speaking still, the words too far away and sounding oddly foreign, but it sounded like a blessing. Lord, but she was a curious old sorceress, with her heathen ways. His father would have dismissed her on the spot had he known. Luckily for Pippin his father paid his staff little mind. Lucian loved her dearly for all she had done for him, though. He didn't give a damn if she practised magic in the kitchen after dark or wanted to dance naked around a bonfire, so long as he didn't have to watch it. She had protected him when no one else would, she had seen what everyone else refused to see, but she was simply a flesh and blood woman with a good heart, and a knowledge of herbs, no witch. He chuckled at the idea of Pippin in flowing white robes, worshiping her pagan idols under his father's nose, and drifted into sleep, pleased with the image.

Chapter 11

Dearest Aashini,

I write in haste only to say I am well, and you must not worry for me. So much has happened I cannot possibly explain. I can only tell you I am where I want to be, where I am needed more than I could have imagined. I know I am stretching our friendship badly in asking you to lie for me, but please, please... give me a little longer if you can.

P.S. I enclose a letter which I would ask you to forward to Nate and Alice for me.

—Excerpt of a letter from Miss Matilda Hunt to Aashini Anson, Countess of Cavendish.

4th May 1815. Dern, Sevenoaks, Kent.

"If I have to look at these four walls for another minute, I shan't be responsible for the consequences."

Matilda sighed, noting the implacable glare in Lucian's eyes with misgiving. He clearly was not a man who fared well sitting about with nothing to do. Lucian had been too tired to protest too vociferously until today, but now he was getting fractious. He'd already scared the rest of the staff off, which Matilda was wicked enough to be pleased about. She wanted him all to herself.

"One more day," she countered, keeping her voice conciliatory. "For me. That's not so much to ask, is it?"

He glowered at her and huffed, folding his arms across his chest. "Damn you, that's not fair."

"How so?" she demanded, biting back a laugh at the frustration in his eyes.

"You know very well I can deny you nothing, not after... after everything."

"Oh, Lucian." She laughed, shaking her head. "Don't look so mortified. I was more than happy to do it, and it wasn't like it was me alone. Pippin is a marvel. You're very lucky to have her. She loves you like a son, you do realise that?"

Matilda watched him, amused by his discomfort.

"Lord knows why," he muttered. "This family has brought her nothing but trouble, I'm sure. It's a wonder she doesn't despise the lot of us." He sent her a sideways glance, his silver eyes glinting with curiosity. "What do you think of her?"

"I just told you," she said with a laugh. "She's a marvel."

Matilda noted the way he was studying her, and considered the question. There was something remarkably reassuring about Pippin—calming.

"She's a tremendously strong woman, confident and capable. I like her very much. She's... warm. Motherly."

Lucian nodded, apparently satisfied.

"Shall I read to you?"

He cast one longing look at the sunshine outside the windows and sighed. "No. Thank you."

Matilda bit her lip, a little amused. She'd begun reading *Pride and Prejudice* to him, which he'd seemed to enjoy at first, but he'd become tense and discomfited from the moment Elizabeth Bennet had given Mr Darcy her stinging refusal to his marriage proposal. Matilda sat down on the bed beside him and took his hand, linking their fingers together.

"You ought not be here." His voice was taut now and he turned to look at her, concern in his eyes. "What is the gossip among the *ton*? Have you heard? He'll be working to discredit me, you know that. There will be some story doing the rounds painting me as a villain or a madman, or both."

"Not today, Lucian," she said.

Pippin had warned her not to let a scandal sheet near him, not until he was stronger. Not that Matilda knew either. She was too afraid to look, and Pippin seemed to think it could wait. He let out a frustrated sigh and turned his head away again, laying back against the pillows and staring at the window.

"Tell me about Thomas."

He didn't answer at first, and for such a long time that she thought perhaps he'd fallen asleep.

"Thomas loved me. Father only had time for Philip, and Mother doted on Thomas because he was such a sickly child and needed her, but Thomas loved me. He followed me everywhere, and he called me Lucie." Lucian turned back to her, sending her a warning glance that promised retribution. "I'll never speak to you again if you repeat that," he said tersely. "And I'd have murdered anyone else for calling me that too, but I didn't mind when he said it. *My little shadow*, that's what Pippin said of him."

Matilda squeezed his hand, encouraging him. "That's sweet."

"He was sweet, the sweetest-natured child you ever saw. Never cross with anyone, always smiling. Hated arguments or disputes and, if Father shouted at us, he'd hide behind me, which only made Father crosser still. Thomas was afraid of our tutor and not very good at schoolwork, so I taught him his letters. He said he understood better when I taught him things."

"I wish I could have met him," Matilda said.

Lucian laughed, turning back to her. "Oh, he'd have adored you, and you him. He was tremendously funny and charming. Everyone loved him. I'd have been horribly jealous, no doubt, but he loved pretty things. Pretty things and everyone happy, everyone smiling...." He gave a wistful sigh. "Poor Thomas."

"Did… Did he kill himself?"

Lucian shrugged. "Yes. Perhaps not intentionally, not on the night he died, but that was his goal. It was going to happen, no matter what I did. I'd come to town a week earlier, looking for him. I was worried. Pippin would have you believe it was some sixth sense, and perhaps there is truth in that. I don't know. I just knew I had to find him."

"You couldn't?"

Lucian shook his head. "We did not mix in the same circles. Thomas had turned his back on respectable society years earlier. I barely saw him, no matter how I pleaded with him to come home. He believed he was beyond redemption, tainted by his sins and unworthy of my forgiveness. Strangely, that night, he'd gone to his club, though, not that it was any less a den of iniquity, just a fashionable one for the wealthy to entertain their vices in comfort. He hadn't been there in months, but I had paid the staff to send me word if he appeared."

"You went after him."

"Too late."

Matilda shifted closer, sensing his tension, though his voice remained calm.

"I'd been looking in lower hells, his usual haunts. No doubt he hoped, by going to such dreadful places, someone would do the job he was trying to accomplish and murder him."

"I'm so sorry, Lucian."

"He looked rather peaceful. There was this strange smile on his face, like he'd discovered the answer to a fine joke. I've never been able to shake the image from my mind."

Matilda lay down beside him, holding him as best she could. She felt the warm weight of his arm go about her, resting on her hip.

"You were there. That night."

Matilda looked up. "What?"

"It took a great deal of money and organising to hush it up. There were still whispers about his death, naturally, but I took his body home with me. I waited as long as I dared, almost a week, and then put it about that it was a riding accident at Dern. But that night, the night I found him, I had sent for men who worked for me, men I trusted implicitly, to come to the club and get him, to take him home. I intended to wait until the place was closed and then have Thomas taken out the back. As I was waiting in one of the private rooms… you came in."

"*That* was the night?" Matilda repeated, hardly able to believe it, and yet she remembered.

She remembered walking into that room and not knowing he was there because it was so terribly quiet, and then she had turned. She had almost screamed, uncertain if he was real. He was so still, unearthly, standing by the window in the moonlight. The most beautiful man she'd ever seen, like a fallen angel. She'd known something was wrong, though. It was as though he wasn't there at all, as though something was missing, some evidence of life. In the nights that had followed she'd ascribed it to cruelty and indifference, a callous nature that didn't give a damn for lesser mortals. She had not even considered….

"I'm sorry for how I behaved." His expression was unreadable, but his words were sincere, heavy with remorse. "I… I simply couldn't think. I was so consumed with Thomas, with sorrow, with how to keep my brother's name from being dragged into some sordid scandal and… I couldn't *think*, Matilda, about anything, and… I'm ashamed to say I didn't care."

"It's all right," she said unsteadily, hearing the anguish in his voice.

"*No.*" He shook his head, his anger palpable. "It is not all right. It's hard to understand it myself now, but I… I blamed you. Your scandal put me at that bloody club when I needed to keep everything quiet. It made it so much harder to cover up the truth and I was furious with you. I hated you for that, and… I wanted to punish you for your own stupidity in being there at all."

He took a deep breath and Matilda tried to do the same, but her lungs did not seem to be cooperating.

"I'm not proud of what I did, Matilda. The truth is I'm sick with shame, and I would not blame you if you could not forgive me. I don't even know why… it makes no sense why I hated you so much. Only that… that you were so damned beautiful, so innocent in… in the place where my brother had died."

His voice broke and he closed his eyes.

"Lucian," she said softly. "Lucian, it's all right. I had already forgiven you, and this… this makes it so much easier to understand. You were grieving for your brother. How were you to think of anything else?"

He turned onto his good side, moving carefully and wincing, but pulling her into his arms. "You are too good, too forgiving. I believe you could forgive the devil himself."

"No," she said at once, furious at the idea. She pulled back a little so she could look at him. "That I could not do. Pippin has told me, in part at least, about your uncle, about what he did to you, and to Thomas. I have never known what it is to hate someone before, not really. I believed I hated you for a long time, but it was nothing to what I feel for him. He won't hurt you again, I won't let him."

She watched the astonishment grow in his eyes as she spoke. He reached out a hand and stroked her face.

"You would protect me?"

There was amusement in his expression, sorrow too.

"Yes."

He smiled at that, his silver eyes as warm as she had ever seen them, yet she knew he thought it impossible. He believed she was the one who needed protecting.

"You won't even protect yourself, my love, which means I must do it for you. You cannot stay here. I can only imagine what is being said about me, but I do know it will not be flattering. If you are discovered here—"

"I'll be ruined. Yes. Yes, I know that."

"Then, for the love of God, pack your things and go, before it is too late."

Matilda stared up at him, wondering how she could ever do that. It had been hard enough before, when she'd not known the truth and believed only that he was wealthy, powerful, and titled, and needed to get his heirs with a woman equal in rank. Now, though…. How could she leave him alone, this man who had always been alone, and wanted so badly for her to stay, though he would no longer tell her so?

"Is that what you want?" she asked, blinking back tears, wondering if he would lie to make her leave.

"What I *want*?" he demanded incredulously. "When in the name of God did it ever matter what *I* wanted?"

She jumped at the fury in his voice and he cursed, holding her closer to him, burying his face against her hair.

"Sorry. I'm sorry. Forgive me."

"It's all right," she said, trying not to cry, clinging to him.

He groaned, such misery and frustration in the sound that not crying was nigh on impossible. She didn't want him to feel that way, not when she was with him. If she could do nothing else for him, surely she could make him happy. Not knowing what to do, she turned her face towards him and nuzzled against his neck, pressing kisses to his skin.

He stilled utterly, his breath hitching. Encouraged, Matilda carried on, kissing the tender spot beneath his ear, rubbing her lips over his jaw, intrigued by the feel of his beard under her mouth. Her hand, which had settled on his arm, avoiding his injured shoulder, moved of its own volition, or so it seemed. Much to Matilda's chagrin, in the past two days—now he was well enough to sit up and move about a little—his valet had been dressing him in a nightshirt The desire to touch him, though, to touch that beautiful body she'd seen so exposed when he was unconscious and out of his mind with pain, was a temptation beyond bearing. She hadn't dared before. It had seemed a violation of trust when he was so vulnerable, but now….

She tugged at the tie holding the shirt together, and slid her hand beneath the fabric. Wondering how she dared, she moved back a little so she could look up and see his face.

He was staring down at her, his eyes dark.

"Dangerous," he said, his voice husky.

"I don't care."

His mouth found hers a moment later, urgent and hot, demanding, and Matilda sighed with relief. *Yes. Yes. This, oh, please*…. Her body seemed to sing the words out loud. Could he hear it as clearly as she could? She undid another tie, giving herself better access, and he made a low sound of contentment as her questing fingers discovered the flat disc of a nipple, which tightened into a tiny nub under her touch.

"Take it off," she demanded, tugging at the material.

"Oh, God, Matilda," he groaned. "Why did you work so hard to save me if you're only going to kill me now?"

"Don't be so dramatic."

She laughed at him, but the look in his eyes suggested he wasn't joking.

"You don't want to be my mistress," he reminded her, a little tersely. "Remember? You said you deserved better than that, and you were right, but I'm not a saint, love. You're alone with me, in my bed. Don't ask me to be the arbiter of good behaviour here. I'm not cut out for the job."

Matilda looked up at him, considering his words.

"Yes," she said. "Yes, you are. I trust you."

She did. He would not take advantage. She suspected he wouldn't, even if she begged him to, which was becoming increasingly likely with every moment longer in his company.

He closed his eyes with a mutter of exasperation, throwing himself back against the pillows. "That's so bloody unfair."

"That's what you get for being so honourable," she teased him, sitting up and kneeling beside him. She tugged at his shirt again. "Take it off. I've been dying to touch you for days, and I will not miss my chance now."

Her only chance. She didn't say it, though when she was thinking of leaving, she couldn't imagine. She wasn't thinking of it at all. She refused to. Good sense had been suspended, thrown out of the window along with caution, self-preservation, and any notion of propriety. She didn't miss any of them.

"Lucian!" she protested when he didn't move.

"*Matilda*," he said, pleading in his eyes.

She tugged at his shirt again and he sighed, sliding his good arm free before she helped him ease it over his wound. He sucked in a sharp breath, his lips compressing into a taut line for a moment as the movement jostled his shoulder, and then the shirt was gone, tossed to the floor.

The bedsheet had fallen to his hips and, except for the bandage over his shoulder, she was free to look her fill, and to touch. His expression was wary now, watching her with caution as she took him in. God, he was perfect. His high cheekbones were a little more accentuated than usual, and there were shadows under his eyes. The morning sunlight caught him, gilding the hair on his chest and his beard, which was a darker gold than the pale gilt of his hair.

"Come here," he said, a measure of his usual cool control infusing his voice.

Matilda shivered. She moved as directed, straddling his lap, though she hardly knew how she dared, but she wanted to be close to him too much to pretend a coyness she did not feel.

"You wanted to touch me," he said, and there was a break in the insouciant remark that told her he was far from calm about it.

"Yes." She looked him over, noting the rapid rise and fall of his chest. "I've thought about you so often, about kissing you, touching you. I once thought the only safe way to do it was when you'd been dosed with laudanum, but I never took advantage of it."

"Foolish of you," he said, his voice growing darker.

"Yes, wasn't it?"

She reached out and put a hand to his cheek, stroking the soft, prickly stubble, moving her thumb over his bottom lip. He nipped at it, catching at the skin with his teeth and making her gasp. She laughed, and carried on her perusal, leisurely, though the body beneath her touch was fiercely taut, alive with tension. He was holding himself still, allowing this. She slid her hands down his arms, over the curve of defined muscle and back up again, and then down over his chest. His stomach muscles flickered and contracted beneath her fingers, and she smiled. Moving her hands back up, she trailed through the scattering of hair at his chest, then followed the path down that slid beneath the sheet. Only that sheet stood between them, she realised too late. He was naked beneath it, not that she cared. Or, at least, she cared, but not in the way she ought to.

"Enough," he said, reaching for her, pulling her close. She tumbled forward, only just saving him from steadying herself against his injured shoulder. She was braced on her arms, looking down at him, still sat up on her knees. He tugged at her hips, and she sat, discovering him hard beneath her, and how intimately he pressed against her. She gasped as a jolt of pleasure surged through her.

"Oh!"

His hand slid into her hair and tugged her head down, his mouth finding hers. Then both hands settled at her hips, pressing her firmly against him as he arched his body and the pleasure spiked again. Desire burst through her, the aching need to be closer to him—to be as close as two people could get—eating her alive. She wanted his skin against hers, for him to fill the hollow sensation that clawed inside her. She was hungry for him, wanted him with such fervour. The kiss grew hotter and his hands moved to the fastenings at the back of her dress. Good heavens, he was better than any lady's maid, she thought with chagrin, as she found herself coming undone with startling speed. Dress, stays, and chemise all fell to beneath his nimble fingers. His mouth left a fiery trail of kisses down her neck as he pushed the sleeves of her gown down her arms until....

She'd hardly had a moment to realise she was exposed to his view from the waist up before his mouth was on her, hot and wet, consuming her. He suckled at her breast and pleasure rolled through her with such force she could not halt the cry that left her mouth. *Good lord.* Thank heavens the walls of Dern were good and thick. She pressed against him, tilting her hips to find that exquisite burst of pleasure again, and this time he moaned, a wicked sound that thrilled her to her core. His head tipped back, eyes closed, and she stared down at him, entranced by the look of him beneath her, like some pagan god of pleasure, pure wickedness, unadulterated sin. His eyes flicked open, almost black with wanting, a narrow rim of sliver glinting.

"More," he said, the word rough.

His hands yanked at her skirts, tugging them from beneath her, bunching them until only the linen sheet separated their bodies. She could feel the fierce heat of his arousal through the fabric, the shape and the strength of him. The desire to tear the sheet aside was so ferocious that she felt she might die with wanting him, but then he moved, and any thoughts of any kind were obliterated. *More, more...* her body sang the same song and she moved against him, again and again, until they were both breathless, mindless with pleasure. His hands stroked the exposed skin above her stocking tops, then slid around to caress her bottom and pull her harder against him until she was giddy with it. She rocked her hips harder, seeking more as the world began to glitter and white out.

"Holy Christ, stop... *stop*," he said, the words gritted out.

"No...! Oh, Lucian, please... *please*...."

"Wait, love... wait...." He sounded desperate now.

Matilda could do little more than whimper as his hands stayed her movements, but she did as he asked, though she was trembling and beside herself.

"Let me touch you," he whispered, and Matilda stifled a hysterical giggle at his request.

Silly man, did he seriously think she would refuse him?

The impulse to laugh fled as he touched her. Matilda gasped as his fingers trailed through the curls between her legs, sliding between the delicate layers of skin to the aching heat beneath.

"Oh, God, love. I have wanted you so badly, for so long...." His voice cracked, everything she had ever wanted to hear from him so blatant with every word. "I dream of you. You fill my days and my nights with thoughts of you. I never want you to leave. I want you here with me… always…."

She wondered if he knew what he was saying or if it was just desire talking, but his clever fingers were seeking, sliding inside her, caressing and teasing until she could hardly comprehend words at all, too lost in his touch, in the overwhelming heat that was burning her from the inside out.

"Yes," she whispered, writhing beneath his fingers, the pleasure becoming so intense she was torn between retreating from it, wanting to escape, and begging for more. "Yes. Oh… oh, I can't… oh, yes, please… *please*…."

His free hand held her in place, not allowing her to run from him, not that she wanted to. She was too greedy for that. She wanted all of it, everything he would give her, everything he had.

"Come here. Come to me…."

She moved closer at his insistence, leaning down over him as he nuzzled her breasts, rubbing his cheek against the silky skin, kissing and trailing his tongue over her until he sought and found a rosy nipple and closed his mouth over her. The sound that tore from her throat was shocking—the sound of a wanton, abandoned woman—and she didn't care. Not one bit.

"Kiss me," he demanded, sounding as crazed and out of control as she felt.

She did, pressing her breasts against his chest, finding his mouth and kissing him with fierce passion, with all the frustration and longing that she'd held inside herself for so long. Matilda broke away with another cry, frenzied now as his fingers slid over her, caressing and circling before easing back inside. She buried her face in his neck, hardly able to stand it.

"Look at me," he commanded.

It was the hardest thing to raise her head, to meet his eyes, but she did as he wanted.

"Matilda." He spoke her name on a sigh, his eyes dark and blazing with raw emotion. "My beautiful girl. I love you... I love you so much... let me see your pleasure."

The shock of his words tangled with a burst of sensation so intense she could do nothing but clutch at his arms as her body moved beyond her control. She shuddered and trembled and cried out his name as it tore through her with such force she felt she had left the confines of her own body. Over and over it rippled through her, in never-ending waves of joy. Lucian gentled his touch, wringing every last precious jolt of pleasure from her tender skin before he drew her back down. She lay sprawled over him, too stunned and sated to care how she must appear in her tumbled gown, her hair all awry. Her bones seemed to be saturated with honey, sweet and heavy, and she was blissfully tired.

Dimly, she became aware of Lucian, of his hand stroking her hair, of his hard body beneath hers, still rigid with unspent desire. That hardly seemed fair.

"Lucian," she tried, but it was too great an endeavour and she closed her eyes.

***

Lucian tried to breathe. It seemed a tremendous effort. His lungs were tight, his body achingly sensitive and hard as iron. *Breathe in, breathe out,* he told himself severely, but his head was filled with the scent of her, the faint trace of orange blossom and the warm, heady perfume of her arousal making him tremble with the force of his desire. He would *not* take her innocence, not when she'd already given him so much, too much. *Just breathe....* He could do this. He wasn't a mindless beast who had to slake his lust no matter what, but a man. A man who felt as if he was about to lose his mind, admittedly, but still a man.

He glanced sideways at Matilda and stifled an outraged laugh as he saw she'd fallen asleep. *Well, damn.* Wasn't that his job? She shifted a little, sighing against his neck. Her warm breath slid over his oversensitive skin like a caress, making him shiver, and then she moved on top of him. He sucked in a tortured breath, smothering a groan as she fidgeted in her sleep, shifting her body so it fitted his perfectly, his cock cradled intimately against her sex.

"*Breathe*," he muttered fiercely, squeezing his eyes closed. "Don't think about it. Do. Not. Think about it."

Naturally, he could think about nothing else. He was so close to where he wanted to be, and they fit together so perfectly. Desperately, he tried to concentrate on the pain in his shoulder, which was throbbing in concert with the rest of body. It didn't help at all. *Oh, God.* It was *not* possible to die from unfulfilled desire, he assured himself, though he remained entirely unconvinced. It felt like an absolute certainty. She would kill him. Well, he'd rather it this way than any of his other near misses with the reaper.

With no relief in sight, he allowed himself to remember the last moments, the sounds of her pleasure, the feel of her hot, sweet body. She had been so ready for him, wet and wanting him so fiercely, and he'd wanted to be inside her so badly he was ready to weep with frustration. Yet this was more than he'd dared to hope for of late, to indulge in the wicked pleasure of having his love with him here, in his bed. It *was* wickedness, he reflected, and that knowledge killed his own desire more effectively than anything else could. Guilt bloomed inside him.

This beautiful woman deserved so much more. She wanted the safety and security of marriage, to be a wife to a man she could love and be proud of, and a mother to a noisy, happy family that she would love and protect with the heart of a lioness. Instead, she was here, with him, risking her virtue, her reputation, even her life, because she was too loving, too generous to do what she should and run from him. She'd never run from him, not from the start, not when she had hated him and ought to have feared him, and not now, when she loved him and ought to be as far from him as it was possible to get.

It seemed impossible to remember a time when he had hated her, resented her for being there that dreadful night. He'd retreated from society for a long time after Thomas had died, doing his imperfect best to care for Phoebe, to make a home for her where she was safe. When he'd returned, he'd assumed Matilda would have disappeared from the *ton*, but she had not. Far from it. She had been there, defiant and proud, her head held high. Little by little his hatred had turned to admiration, and then to fascination. When he'd finally spoken to her and received an accurate and stinging set down that had shredded his character with precision, he'd felt nothing but pride in her for standing up to him so fiercely.

The rest had been beyond his control.

He tried to imagine his life once she was gone, but his heart rebelled against the image. The bleak years that beckoned him without Matilda in his life made his chest tight with fear. He wasn't at all sure he could survive it.

Yet, no matter how many times he went through it, how many times he tried to justify everything he wanted, the answer never changed. It was too dangerous to keep her close while his uncle lived, and even if the monster died today…. He had a duty to the family, to his father and his brothers and the title. The idea of turning his back on generations of ambition, of letting them all down, made him feel hot and sick. He could hear his father berating him with disgusted fury, even though his voice had not been heard in this house for over twenty years.

Lucian shivered with foreboding. Yet, no matter how much time he spent listing all the reasons why they must not be together, why Matilda *must* leave… his heart told him otherwise, and promised him he could not do it. It would destroy him in a way his uncle had never quite managed.

Matilda murmured in her sleep, and Lucian shifted onto his side to look at her though his shoulder protested with vehemence, the pain of moving making his breath catch. He forced it further, enduring the pain and lifting his arm so he could touch her face, touch the silky skin, trace the line of her beautiful mouth.

Tenderness welled in his heart. What had they done to him, these women? From the moment he'd set eyes on her, Phoebe had made him reconsider the kind of man he wanted to be, might have been, given half a chance. He had shut up his heart for so many years, it was so much safer that way, but then that child had come into his life and prised it open again with ease. He'd tried to repair the damage, but it had been too late, and little by little he'd discovered Matilda had found the breach too, and he'd been lost.

"Don't look so fierce."

He glanced up to find Matilda's lovely blue eyes fixed upon him. She reached out and touched the space between his eyebrows, smoothing out the furrow.

"I thought you were asleep," he said, with just a touch of reproach.

"Hmmm," she said with an indulgent sigh. "Just a little bit. I was so sleepy."

"So I noticed."

She smiled at him, a mischievous light in her eyes. "Poor Lucian. Is there something I can help you with?"

His breath caught as she moved against him, his arousal surging back to life with a vengeance.

"Don't," he cursed. "Damn it, Matilda. Stop that. It's not fair."

"What's not fair about it?" she murmured, pressing closer, trailing small, open-mouthed kisses across his collar bone.

She paused at the hollow of his throat before taking an experimental lick.

He closed his eyes, trying to hold on to sanity.

"Stop."

She did stop then, and he could feel her confusion, feel the weight of her gaze. He opened his eyes, his heart squeezing at the uncertainty in her expression.

"We can't, Matilda," he said, willing her not to test him. His resolve already felt about as substantial as smoke, and it would drift away into nothingness if she pressed him.

"But you brought me pleasure," she said, frowning at him. "And I'm still a virgin—technically, anyway. I'm sure there must be things I can do...."

"Christ! No."

She jolted in surprise and he cursed himself.

"Don't make me any more of a devil than I already am, love," he begged her.

He felt a little affronted by the laughter that comment received.

"Oh, I'm sorry, darling," she said, noting his indignation, and looking not even a bit chastened. "But I spent many months believing you the devil and, I'm sorry to say, you've ruined all your hard work these past weeks. You're nothing of the sort."

He glowered up at her.

"Might I remind you," he said, somewhat tersely. "That you are unmarried, in my bed, and half naked?"

"I know," she said serenely. "Isn't it lovely?"

"Hell's bells, woman! What am I to do with you?"

"I'm sure you'll think of something."

Lucian groaned.

"It's nearly midday," he grumbled. "Denton will be bringing me some foul concoction of Pippin's at any moment, so unless you want to put the poor fellow quite out of countenance, you'd best get yourself dressed. You look very much like you've been ravished."

That, thank God, got her moving, though she still took the opportunity to give him one last, lingering kiss before she deigned to leave the bed. Lucian sighed, watching with deep regret as she shimmied back into her clothes, securing her lovely breasts into corsets and chemise and all the other layers he'd so enjoyed undoing. That he might never have another chance to touch her in such a way made his heart hurt. *For the best*, he told himself. It was for the best. The best for her, at least. It felt as if it might kill him.

Chapter 12

Tilda,

Why haven't you replied to my letter? I do hope you are feeling better and that all this vile gossip about Montagu isn't upsetting you. Surely you cannot be surprised by it. We always knew what manner of man he was. It has been clear from the start and it's about time he was brought to heel. I don't know what kind of hold he has over your heart, but surely even you cannot love a man who is so thoroughly wicked.

I will be in town in a few days and so I will call in and see you – if you can spare the time for your beastly brother.

—Excerpt of a letter from Mr Nathanial Hunt to Miss Matilda Hunt.

5th May 1815. Dern, Sevenoaks, Kent.

"Take your time!" Matilda scolded, as Lucian stopped dead and closed his eyes.

His left arm was in a sling—much to his disgust—his right arm draped about her shoulders for support, and he'd only succumbed that far when he was a third of the way down the stairs. His face had gone the colour of a milk pudding, and she was certain he ought not be up at all, but he'd been properly dressed and shaved, and as elegant as always, when she'd gone to see him this morning. The effort had clearly made him ill, and she knew full well he'd done it because he didn't trust himself to be alone with her in his bed. Foolish man. He would have his own way, though, and so here he was, heading downstairs. It had taken her half an hour to get him to agree to the sling, which his valet had made up and which Lucian had initially tossed to one side in irritation.

Phoebe had been beside herself with excitement at seeing him up and about, but now she stood at the bottom of the stairs. Her grey-blue eyes stared up, grave with concern as Lucian breathed through the pain.

"Uncle?"

"I'm all right," he said, forcing a smile. "Just a little... dizzy."

"That's why you ought to have stayed in bed," Matilda muttered crossly.

He shot her a rueful glance.

"Hmmm, so you could have the pleasure of driving me out of my head?" he mused, his tone low and wicked.

Matilda flushed, whispering in return. "That was your own silly fault, so don't go playing the martyr now."

"Cruel," he murmured, moving slowly down the steps. "So dreadfully cruel."

"What are you talking about?" Phoebe demanded, folding her arms. "Why is Matilda all red?"

"Because I'm making her cross," Lucian said easily, pausing again as the sound of raised voices made themselves known.

"I don't give a damn if he's not *at home*," came an imposing and irritated voice. "He'll bloody well see me. It's for his own good."

"Matilda," Lucian said, stiffening at once. "Go. Go quickly."

Even if she'd wanted to accede to his wishes, there was no time as Gabriel Knight burst through the doors with Helena in tow. They stopped in their tracks as they looked up the stairs to see Lucian and Matilda together, his arm about her shoulders.

"Matilda!" Helena's shock was palpable, her eyes growing wide. "You're... *here*."

"So I am," Matilda said placidly.

"Not a word," Lucian said, his voice as cold and autocratic as she'd ever heard it. "If either of you—"

"If the next word out of your mouth threatens my wife, there will be consequences," Mr Knight growled, his eyes growing dark. "But no one will hear a word against Matilda from us."

"Never!" Helena said staunchly.

Matilda smiled and laid a hand on Lucian's chest.

"Helena is my friend," she reminded him gently, feeling the rabbit-fast beat of his heart beneath her palm. "They won't say anything."

He nodded, his face taut with strain.

"Perhaps you should go back to bed," she said quietly.

He sent her a fierce look which made her clamp her mouth shut, and she resolved not to mention the idea again. Not in front of Mr Knight, at least. Men and their bloody pride.

"What's wrong?" Mr Knight demanded, eyeing the sling and walking closer.

"He was shot," Matilda said, seeing from the horrified looks on their faces, this part of the story had not made it into the gossip sheets.

"Shot?" Helene squeaked in alarm.

"By that horrid Mr Burton," Phoebe said, taking Helena's hand, her little face furious. "They had a duel and uncle beat him fair and square, and then the scoundrel shot him when his back was turned. Isn't that vile?"

"Christ," Mr Knight said before hurrying to Lucian and easing Matilda aside. "Here, lean on me."

"I'm not a blasted invalid," Lucian snapped, subsiding with a frustrated huff as no one seemed to take a blind bit of notice, least of all Mr Knight.

They made it into the library and Matilda settled him in a chair with cushions to support his injured shoulder, while Lucian protested that she must stop fussing. Much to the child's indignation, Phoebe was sent away so the grown-ups could talk, and was only mollified by a promise from Helena to visit her before she left. Once Lucian was comfortable, his sharp silver gaze descended upon his guests.

"Well," he said. "I imagine you've got some interesting story about what I've been up to of late. You'd best share it. I don't doubt it is salacious."

Matilda watched with misgiving as Helena exchanged a glance with her husband.

"Yes, that's why we're here," Mr Knight said, staring at Lucian. "And, for the record, I didn't believe it."

Lucian snorted. "I rather suspect you're in the minority."

Mr Knight nodded. "Much as I'd like to bring you good news—after all, I feel responsible for letting the wretch slip through my fingers—well, the word is that you set the whole thing up. That the reports about the state of the mills in Derbyshire was pure fabrication. The story goes that you slandered Burton because of his interest in Miss Hunt here, and… and that when he came to plead with you to leave him be…."

"I cut him down in cold blood, no doubt?"

Matilda's heart clenched at his icy tone. Here was Montagu in full panoply. She could see the mask slide into place, the change in him sharp edged and vivid. He seemed utterly indifferent to the news they'd brought him when she knew it must hurt him deeply.

Mr Knight nodded. "They say he's crippled after your little run-in. I don't know if that's true, or more wishful thinking by the gossip mill. After all, we heard he was dead two days ago, but that rumour seems to have been scotched, at least."

"What did happen?" Helena asked, looking to Matilda, not Lucian. "Were you here?"

Matilda nodded and reached out to Lucian, wanting to take his hand, but he moved it away. She sighed, knowing why he did it. Not to be thwarted, she reached farther across and took it anyway, twining their fingers together. Lucian glared at her and then sighed, closing his eyes, holding on tight.

"I knew something was very wrong, that Lucian's uncle was up to something, and so I came here, to Dern, to discover the truth."

"Foolish creature," Lucian muttered, but with affection this time.

Helena looked between them, her expression one of rapt fascination. Matilda blushed, but carried on.

"His uncle is a monster," she said bluntly, and with such force they could not dispute her feeling on the matter. "I cannot tell Lucian's story for him, but he has been greatly wronged by that dreadful, wicked man. Theodore Barrington sent Mr Burton here to murder his nephew so he could claim the title. It was not his uncle's first attempt, I might add. It was only Lucian's cleverness and skill that saved us both from having our throats cut, and he nearly died anyway, because that vile man hasn't a scrap of honour."

Her voice trembled and she took a breath, trying to compose herself. She looked up to find Lucian's eyes upon her, shining with adoration, and could not help but smile. He raised her hand to his lips and kissed it.

Matilda glanced back at Helena and her husband to find both of them gawking in astonishment. Mr Knight gathered himself first.

"Well," he said, clearing his throat. "I came to see what we could do. The thing is, the story being circulated is that the vile conditions in Burton's mills was nothing but a fabrication. Now, that in itself should be easy enough to prove. We need only send some representatives of the press to interview those involved…."

"*We*?" Lucian said, staring at Mr Knight with suspicion. "Why would you involve yourself in this?"

Mr Knight frowned, nonplussed. "Because it isn't true. You've been slandered and I know it."

"And so?" Lucian pressed, looking truly bewildered.

"And so," Mr Knight said cautiously, "I shall help you clear your name."

Matilda watched as Lucian's face cleared. He nodded.

"I see. The usual terms, I suppose?"

Mr Knight frowned. "Terms? No… *No*. I… I don't want anything. There will be no debt, no payment."

Lucian looked more bewildered than ever, and rather suspicious. "Why not?"

"Oh, Lucian," Matilda said helplessly. "He wants to help you, love, because it's the right thing to do. Because he'd be your friend, if you'd let him."

Lucian stared at Matilda, then Mr Knight, and then looked away, still frowning and uncertain.

"We can trust them, Lucian."

His grip on her hand tightened, but he said nothing. How impossible it must be to accept that someone was on his side after so many years of being isolated by his uncle, trusting no one whilst he was painted as a cold-hearted devil. She wondered how he had survived, how his heart hadn't shrivelled and died when he'd had no friends, no one to trust beyond Pippin and Denton and Mrs Frant. Thank God Phoebe had arrived in his life.

Mr Knight cleared his throat. "I had been thinking the ideal thing would be for you to go to Derbyshire yourself to speak with the press in person. I have contacts with several men who'd kill for the story. You did an admirable job of hiding your light under a bushel, but modesty is doing you no favours now. People need to know of everything you did there to help those who were injured, and to put things to rights. Of course, I didn't know that you'd been shot, so that rather puts paid to that idea."

"No," Lucian said, shaking his head. "It doesn't. You're right. I must go."

"Oh, Lucian, how can you think it?" Matilda protested. "That's at least three days travel on bad roads. You barely made it down the stairs!"

He stiffened and Matilda's temper overrode good sense.

"Oh, damn your pride! Blast you, Lucian! Mr Knight does not think you any less a man for being injured by a bloody bullet! Will you undo all mine and Pippin's work in nursing you, you obstinate creature?"

There was a long, crackling silence, during which Mr Knight and Helena stared between them, wide-eyed, and Lucian was very still. Then he slid Matilda a wary glance.

"Forgive me," he said, a little uncertainly. "I do not mean to… to worry you, but I must go, Matilda. You would not wish me to let my uncle succeed in destroying my name?"

"Of course not," she said at once, knowing it must be strange for him to have to explain himself at all, let alone take anyone's else's feelings into account. "But could you not wait a day or two?"

Lucian turned back to Mr Knight. "I suspect that is not going to be possible."

Matilda looked to him too, and the man spread his hands in a helpless gesture, clearly wishing he could tell her otherwise.

"Then I shall go with you," she said, folding her arms.

"That you won't!" Lucian retorted, sitting up so fast he had to grab at his shoulder, what little colour had returned to his face leaving it all in a rush. He gritted the next words out between clenched teeth. "You will go home with Mr Knight and Lady Helena and, with luck, no one will be any the wiser about you having been here. God alone knows how the story hasn't got about by now. You ought to have left days ago."

"I'm not leaving you." Matilda folded her arms tighter, mostly so he couldn't see her hands were shaking at the idea of leaving him at all. She glared at his stony face, knowing he was only so cross because he wanted to protect her. "If you don't take me with you, I shall just follow on by myself and then see what a scandal you shall make of me, forcing me to chase you across country."

"Matilda!" Lucian said, outraged, but Matilda just quirked an eyebrow at him.

"Do you think I wouldn't do it?"

Lucian muttered a curse under his breath and turned to Mr Knight, who held up his hands in defeat.

"Don't look to me for help," he said, shaking his head. "She's one of the Peculiar Ladies. If she's anything like this one—or the others, come to that—you've not a hope in hell."

Helena snorted.

"She's not just *one* of us," she said, amused by the men's frustration. "She's the best of us, our leader and self-appointed mother hen. We'd be a deal less adventurous and strong without her."

"That I believe."

Matilda smiled at Lucian's exasperated comment, and she felt her heart swell with gratitude as Helena winked at her.

Lucian was quiet for a long moment before he spoke again.

"My uncle is no fool, quite the reverse, and we underestimate him at our peril. He knows as well as we do that we can prove his words to be lies, and he knows how we should best go about it. He will have planned this as my next move if Mr Burton failed to kill me."

Everyone stared at him in horror.

"Christ," Mr Knight said. "He's a cold-blooded devil, isn't he?"

Lucian returned a grim smile. "I learned from the best, I assure you."

"Lucian," Matilda protested, but he hushed her, shaking his head.

"I hope I am not the kind of man he is. I have tried not to be, but it is pointless to paint me as an innocent party. This game has been in progress for most of my life, and once I decided I had no desire to remain a pawn, to be moved about as he saw fit, I played it too. I know how his mind works, and I know what I would do if I were him."

"So, what do you think he is planning?" Mr Knight asked.

Lucian shrugged as if the answer were obvious. "To get me to leave Dern, where I am less vulnerable, and ambush me on the road. There are fewer highwaymen around these days, but it could be arranged to look like a robbery gone wrong, I'm sure."

Matilda felt her blood run cold.

"So, you see, love," he said, turning back to Matilda and taking her hand once again, "I don't want you in danger."

"And what if I would be in more danger without you?" Matilda countered. "I would be alone and unprotected. What if he took advantage of that fact—"

"I know how we could all go, and no one be any the wiser. Then we would all be safe," piped up a small voice.

"Phoebe!" Lucian said in outrage as the girl appeared from a hidden panel in the walls. "You little wretch. How long have you been eavesdropping?"

"Well, it's not fair that you leave me out of it," she protested, moving to stand beside her uncle and staring at him, quite unfazed by his fierce look of irritation. "That horrid man came here to hurt you, and he still wants to, and now people are saying dreadful things about you again and it's not fair."

She stamped her foot, her eyes filling, and folded her slender arms tightly across her chest.

"It's not *fair*!" she said again, as a fat tear rolled down her cheek. "Not when Uncle Theodore is so villainous and you're nothing like they say you are."

"Ah, Phoebe, sweetheart, don't cry," Lucian said helplessly, holding out his good arm to her.

Phoebe gave a sob and scrambled into his lap.

"I'm frightened he'll hurt you again, and I don't like all those people saying awful things about you," she said, clutching at his coat so hard it would ruin the lapel.

Lucian didn't seem to care. He pulled her close and kissed the top of her head.

"It doesn't matter what anyone else says, Bee. If you know the truth, I don't care about the rest of the world."

"Yes, you do. You care what Matilda thinks."

Lucian smiled. "Yes. I do care what Matilda thinks, very much, and perhaps Mr Knight and Lady Helena too, but the rest of the world can go to the devil."

"They won't, though, will they?" she said. "They'll come here. They'll say you did terrible things and they'll spoil everything. Great-Uncle Theodore will come, and he'll take you away from me."

Her breathing became rapid, terror making her little face stark white and fearful.

"*No*," Lucian said, his voice firm. He put his hand to her cheek. "No. He won't hurt you or me. He won't hurt anyone I care for ever again. I *shall* stop him this time. One way or another."

He stared at Phoebe, and the little girl studied his face with an intense frown, perhaps reassuring herself of his resolve. Finally, she relaxed and nodded.

"You said you knew how they could travel with no one knowing, Phoebe," Helena said, her voice gentle. "What is your plan, love?"

"Oh," Phoebe replied, brightening and wiping her eyes on her sleeve. "That's easy. We shall go in disguise."

Chapter 13

My dear Kitty,

I don't know whether you will have heard about the dreadful scandal that is flying about the ton when you are all the way over in Ireland. I only discovered it myself today, as we had a visitor arrive from London who could speak of nothing else.

They say that Montagu has gone mad and tried to murder Mr Burton, whose life hangs in the balance. Now poor Matilda's name is being dragged through the mud too, as the gossips say she is the cause of the conflict, that Montagu is obsessed with her and Mr Burton in love with her. It's all horrid and Matilda will need us to get through it. I am getting ready to leave this minute and I know the rest of the Peculiar Ladies will be there for her too, so that is a comfort. I thought I should let you know, in case you had not yet heard and could come and offer your support. What we can do, I don't know, but whatever the truth of the matter, Matilda must know that the Peculiar Ladies will rally around her, we will not desert her. No matter what.

—Excerpt of a letter from Mrs Ruth Anderson to Mrs Kitty Baxter.

5th May 1815. Dern, Sevenoaks, Kent.

Though Matilda, Lady Helena and even Mr Knight, thought Phoebe's plan an excellent one, it took a great deal more persuasion to get Lucian to agree to it. In the end, the only argument that worked was that while he was away from Phoebe and Matilda, they would be unprotected and were likely targets for his uncle. If the man got hold of either of them, Lucian's hands would be tied. Therefore it was better they were all together and travelling incognito was the safest way to do that.

Mr Knight and Lady Helena stayed for dinner but refused an invitation to stay the night, preferring to return to London and see what could be done to salvage Lucian's reputation and to ensure the true story of what had occurred was being put about. For this, Helena needed their friends, and Mr Knight—or Gabe, as he had insisted they address him—would see what information he could turn up regarding the whereabouts of Theodore Barrington.

Lucian was quiet once their guests had departed, though Matilda knew he was touched that they had hurried down here on his behalf.

"He likes you," she said, moving to stand beside him.

He was standing before the large study windows, staring outside, though she doubted he saw the landscape. He tugged at his shirt cuffs, first one, then the other, and her heart clenched.

"Knight is doing it for Lady Helena, who is doing it for you," he said, not looking at her.

Matilda sighed and took his hand. "I know this is hard to believe, my darling, but there are people in the world who would stand by you, if you would let them."

He made a low sound of amusement and turned to look at her. "If there are, it's because of you. Don't deny it, love. You know it's true."

Matilda sighed. "Perhaps, but that's only because I know you and they don't. My friends trust me. If I tell them the truth of what you've been through, they will believe me."

To her frustration, Lucian shook his head. "They will believe I have convinced you. That is not at all the same thing."

"Mr Knight and Helena believed you. They didn't know I was here. They came for you alone."

Lucian shrugged. "I suppose so, but I have had dealings with Mr Knight these past years. We've worked well together, and we have come to trust one another. That counts for something."

"It counts for a great deal. Just think how many other people might take your side if they knew the truth?"

He laughed, a weary sound of defeat that made Matilda's heart hurt. "I tried that. No one believes me. My uncle is too charming, too likable. How much easier to believe a man that smiles and flatters and makes you laugh, than one like me."

"My friends would believe you. If you stood beside me and told them what had happened to you, they would believe you."

She did not know what he might have said in response, for then the study door flew open and an elderly woman swept through it. She was dressed in heavy layers of black bombazine in the style of the last century, and the fabric rustled furiously as she moved. Whoever she was, she was not a tall woman, and was as thin as a whippet, with icy grey eyes and white hair drawn up into a severe style that highlighted high cheekbones and an austerely beautiful face. Lucian had dropped Matilda's hand and stepped away the moment the door had been flung open, but now the woman's frigid gaze moved from him to Matilda without a flicker of surprise, though there was a contemptuous curve to her narrow lips.

"*Miss* Hunt, I collect," she said, her voice hard and the words clipped and precise. "I see you finally persuaded her to be your mistress, Montagu. That is one less thing to worry about, at least. Perhaps now you have satisfied your baser instincts, you can concentrate on matters of importance?"

Lucian stiffened, his face devoid of emotion.

"Miss Hunt is *not* my mistress, Aunt Marguerite," he said coldly. "And you will apologise for speaking to her so. She is a guest in my home and deserves to be spoken to with courtesy."

So, this was Lady Astley, his Aunt Marguerite.

The woman snorted. "Dress it up how you like, but she's here with you alone, no chaperone in sight. I'm no fool, my lord, and I've seen it all before, so don't think to pull the wool over my eyes."

"Damn your impudence! I believe you forget to whom you speak," Lucian said, and though he did not raise his voice, there was such intense fury in his words that his aunt's eyes grew wide.

From her reaction, Matilda knew he'd never spoken to her so before.

Marguerite's eyes narrowed as she looked from Lucian to Matilda and back again. "Forgive me, my lord, Miss Hunt," she said, inclining her head a little, though there was no apology in her eyes.

"Why are you here?" Lucian demanded.

Matilda wanted to go to him, to take his hand. She could feel the tension rolling off him in waves. This was the woman who had slapped his face as a child and called him a vile liar when he'd tried to explain that his Uncle Theodore, her favourite nephew, had tried to kill him. This was the woman who had supported Theodore when his doctors—paid nicely for the diagnoses, no doubt—suggested Lucian was unstable when he persisted in trying to make someone, *anyone*, believe him. She had always favoured Theodore over Lucian, had never believed what he'd tried to tell her, and yet surely this woman could not be so blind?

"I had no alternative. The *ton* is alight with scandal, all of it revolving around this creature." She gestured to Matilda as if she was something unpleasant that ought not be spoken of. "And some jumped up mushroom called Mr Burton. I take it you are aware of the gossip. Apparently, you attacked him and left him a cripple."

"And no doubt you believed every word," Matilda retorted as the anger that had burned inside of her erupted. "As you have not offered a word of concern, asked for the truth of what happened or if Lucian is well, bearing in mind you can see he's been injured. I suppose you'll still deny the fact Theodore Barrington is at the heart of it all. Do you really not know the truth, that your nephew sent Mr Burton here to murder Lucian? Or perhaps you are in on the scheme? Would you prefer it if Theodore were Montagu? Would that suit you better?"

His aunt blanched, her complexion becoming that of fine old parchment before a rush of colour stained her high cheekbones.

"I don't know what you are speaking of," she said, though her previously icy tone sounded a touch breathless now. "Montagu, what does she mean by this wild accusation?"

Lucian stared at her for a long moment and then made a sound of disgust.

"Damn you," he said, and turned his back.

"I will have an answer!" The old woman's imperious tone rang out through the study. "I came here to save the family from disaster, to save our name from being dragged through the dirt. Your poor father and brother must be spinning in their graves. How disappointed they would be in you. The only answer is that you marry, and at once. If the *ton* has a wedding to focus upon, they will be less inclined to tear you to pieces. With that in mind, I have invited Lady Constance to Dern. She will arrive the day after tomorrow."

155

"You'd just ignore it," Matilda said in wonder, staring at her in disbelief. "His uncle is trying to kill him, has been trying since he was a small boy, and you'd still just brush it aside and pretend it isn't happening. You'd still make out as though it were all his fault. You wicked old harridan."

"Lucian! Get this creature out of here at once. How I am supposed to carry on a sensible conversation with—"

"With what, Aunt?" Lucian demanded, turning now to face her. "With the truth staring you in the face, do you mean? You'll forgive me if I am inclined to stand beside Miss Hunt, as she has never betrayed my trust, even when I had no right whatsoever to expect it of her. She came here, risking everything, because she was afraid for me, because she could see there was something terribly wrong. *You...* You, who ought to have looked to the safety and happiness of your own flesh and blood, did not wish to look beyond the facade, and now Thomas is dead and I hope the knowledge that it is in no small part your fault follows you to the grave. Should you prefer me to join him and save you any further unpleasantness?"

"Montagu!" she said, one hand going to her slender throat. "This melodrama is quite unbecoming—"

"Answer the damn question!"

Matilda and Marguerite both leapt in shock as his fury rang out through the room. Matilda suspected he'd never raised his voice in such a way in his entire life. The impact was clearly too much for Marguerite, who swooned and crumpled to the ground.

"Good lord!" Matilda cried, and ran to pull the cord for a servant before falling to her knees beside the old woman and taking her hand, chafing it to revive her.

"Is she dead?"

If Matilda hadn't known him so well by now, she would have thought he didn't give a damn, so cold was the enquiry. She did know him, though, and knew just how profoundly he must be hurting to realise that, even in light of everything that had happened, his aunt still did not believe him. Even now, she would believe Theodore over Lucian. She had come only to blame Lucian for the horrid scandal and make him feel wretched, even invoking his father's and brother's names to pile the guilt higher.

"No, sadly," Matilda replied, seeing no reason not to wish the miserable old cow six feet under.

She looked up as Lucian gave a startled laugh. He was staring at her with such adoration that her breath caught.

"I love you," he said.

Matilda smiled, though her heart was breaking.

"I know," she said softly. "I love you too."

They could say no more, as Denton appeared and helped get Marguerite into a chair. Another servant was sent running for hartshorn and water. Matilda looked up as Lucian watched the proceedings with a detached expression.

"Go and see Phoebe," she said, not wanting this wicked old woman to hurt him anymore than she already had. "She'll be wanting to see you before bedtime, and will cheer you up. I can deal with your aunt, I assure you."

"Oh, I can see that," he said, a thread of amusement in his voice. "I see no reason why you ought, though."

"Because someone other than you ought to," Matilda said, her voice gentle. "Someone ought to have done it when you were a boy, and it is a crime that no one did, but I am here, and I will stand beside you for as long as I am able to."

She did not acknowledge the fact that it would only be until he married. It did not need saying aloud, they both knew it. Marguerite was right about one thing, the public announcement of his engagement to some pristine lady of the *ton* would go a long way to repairing the damage his uncle had wrought. They both knew it. As hard as it would be after everything that had passed between them, after hearing him say the words she had never dreamed he would give her, one fact had not changed. She could not be with him if he married another. That was the road to misery and madness. She would never love another man, she knew that and accepted it. Therefore, she would not marry, not have the family she had longed for, but she would have this time with Lucian, no matter how short that was. She was resolved to embrace it, to both the joy of giving herself to him entirely, and the devastation of walking away from him. Her decision had been made and she was, if not at peace with that, then at least accepting of it.

"Lucian," Matilda said again, holding out her hand to him.

He came to her and bent over it, kissing her fingers tenderly, such a courtly, old-fashioned gesture that her eyes filled.

"Now run along and see that dreadful niece of yours. She's bound to be up to mischief by now and she'll have something to say about *Mouldy* Marguerite that will make you smile, I don't doubt."

Lucian held her hand for a long moment, watching her, his expression unreadable. "Thank you."

"I'll let you make it up to me," Matilda whispered, earning herself a flickering smile and the glimmer of a dimple.

She watched him leave as a servant hurried in with the hartshorn. Marguerite was stirring now, one bejewelled hand going to her temples as she groaned and her eyelids fluttered.

Matilda helped her to sit up, handed her water and hartshorn and prepared her a cup of tea once she had revived sufficiently to take the cup between trembling hands. The old woman said not a word during this, not that Matilda had expected her to. Not yet. She would say her piece once she was composed enough to do so, and then Matilda would return the favour. With a bit of luck, she might give the wicked creature a heart attack.

"He'll never make you his marchioness. No matter what he wants for himself. Your father was a bankrupt, your brother runs a gambling club, and you have a damaged reputation. You'd be lucky to marry a man like that jumped up mushroom Mr Burton, and you ought to have snapped his hand off instead of causing all this trouble, leading my idiot nephew about by the nose. How you have the temerity to consider you could be the next Marchioness of Montagu is beyond me. For all his failings, he'd never disgrace the family like that. You'd make him a laughingstock. So you can put the idea out of your pretty head. He'll not marry you."

Matilda sipped at her own tea with every outward sign of serenity, having anticipated the attack. Inwardly she was vibrating with indignation and fury, but she'd rather stick pins in her own eyes than allow the dreadful woman to see that.

"I never expected him to," she said, accompanying the calm reply with a placid smile.

"And yet you deny you are his mistress," the old woman sneered.

Matilda considered this.

"No," she said. "At least, I am not his mistress now, but I will be for a brief time. Until he marries. I love him too much to share him."

"You don't love him enough to share him, you mean," Marguerite sneered.

"Do you believe that?" Matilda asked her, frowning as she considered whether that could be true. "I suppose I can see why you would think it, but I'm afraid I am not the kind of female who can turn a blind eye to the truth. Unlike some. I would make him miserable, for he could never show affection towards his wife without making me wild with jealousy. It would make us all wretched. I love him too much to force him to endure that. He would never have a moment's peace, forever torn between the two of us. That is most unfair to him, and to whomever he marries."

Matilda took a sip of her tea, exerting a supreme effort to keep her hand from trembling, her voice steady. "He should at least try to find happiness, find someone he can be comfortable with, if not love. I am selfish enough to hope he cannot love her as he does me, but they must find contentment of a sort. Otherwise his children will be unhappy too, and that I could not endure, no more than I could stand to see another woman bear them. I believe I would go mad."

"You're honest for a trollop, I'll give you that."

"Unlike you," Matilda replied sweetly. "I doubt you've ever spoken an honest word to him in your life."

The old woman was silent for a long moment. "I *cannot* believe it," she said, and her voice was cracked with emotion, her face screwed up with pain. "Not Theodore, he... he wouldn't. He *could* not...."

"Yes, he could," Matilda said, infusing her voice with all the icy contempt she felt for such an outrageous statement.

She was aware of the old woman's anguish, but felt no empathy, not now, not knowing how many years Lucian had suffered as a child when no one believed in him. Perhaps Marguerite had not been complicit, but she'd been wilfully blind to the truth and had not troubled herself to investigate further. Matilda could feel no sympathy for her now, knowing how methodically Thomas had been destroyed in order to hurt Lucian as deeply as it was possible to be hurt.

"He could and he did, and he is still doing it. For once in your life, I suggest you choose whose side you are on, because I tell you now, if you mean Lucian harm, you have made an enemy of me, and I shall not rest until I know he is safe from all of you."

Marguerite studied her, eyes narrowed. "It's a pity you're so tainted. You'd have made a fine marchioness."

"What are you going to do about Theodore Barrington?" Matilda demanded, ignoring that observation.

"Do?" Marguerite echoed. "What do you imagine I *can* do?"

Matilda held onto her temper by a thread. "Lucian says you wield a great deal of influence. If you tell your cronies it is he who has run mad, that all that comes out of his mouth is a lie, you might go some way to restoring Lucian's reputation."

"More scandal." Marguerite's face screwed up in disgust.

"You cannot escape that now," Matilda snapped, wanting to ring the horrid woman's scrawny neck for her lack of compassion.

This woman didn't give a damn for Lucian's happiness. All she cared about was the bloody title and its pristine reputation. Had the entire family felt this way?

"Your only choice is who the scandal falls upon. Do you wish to sacrifice Lucian or Theodore? *Choose.* But know this: if you choose to save Theodore Barrington you are condemning Lucian. If Theodore succeeds, you can kiss goodbye to the continuation of the Montagu line. He's an old man, too old to sire healthy sons. You just think on that."

She was thinking on it, Matilda could tell, and she knew too that it was the only argument that could hold any real power over a woman like this. She had met such creatures before, ones whose pride in their own bloodline and superiority over other people was their only source of contentment. How foolish. Matilda wondered how much comfort that knowledge would give the old woman when she died alone, with no one to mourn her. Matilda would rather have her children and grandchildren about her, knowing that they would grieve her passing and keep her memory alive in their hearts, than any grand title. With a sharp stab of fear, she realised she was about to turn her back on that possibility herself, but she could not think of that now.

"I will make arrangements for a ball," Marguerite said at length, and Matilda supposed that was all the answer she would get. "Lucian must announce his betrothal as soon as is possible. I shall arrange it for the nineteenth of the month. Two weeks is little enough time to arrange such a lavish affair as it must be, but once everyone knows the object of the event, there will be no refusals."

The old woman looked smug and vindictive, and Matilda steeled her heart against the realisation that two weeks was all she had. She did not doubt that this woman would make the announcement for him if Lucian failed to do so, and damn the consequences.

"I think you should go now," Matilda said, holding onto her composure by a thread. "You'll find the accommodation at The Royal Oak quite adequate."

Marguerite turned glinting grey eyes upon her. "You dare to throw me out of the house, you arrogant chit?"

"I do." Matilda levelled her gaze at the woman.

She was remarkably unmoved by her and her spiteful comments. She hated her so deeply for all the harm she'd done to Lucian and his brother that it was impossible to fear her, or care for the insults she tossed out with such ease. Besides, Matilda had heard it all before.

"You'd be surprised what I'd dare," she said, a hard smile upon her lips. "For example, I dare to tell you that I shall do all in my power to destroy you if you don't do everything you can to protect Lucian. You've failed him his entire life. Fail him again, and I will make sure you suffer for it. There are benefits to having lost your reputation—there is nothing left to fear, you see—and I have powerful friends. You ought to remember that."

Matilda stood and strode to the door, pausing to give Lady Astley one last look of contempt.

"I'll have Denton see you out," she said, as coolly as if she *were* Lucian's marchioness, knowing how deeply it would stick in *Mouldy* Marguerite's throat. "Do not hurry back. You are no longer welcome at Dern."

With that, she swept out, feeling a deep surge of satisfaction at her last look upon Marguerite's grim-faced fury, which she had the pleasure of closing the door on.

Chapter 14

We are going on an adventure! I feel like we are on our way to slay a dragon and I know that we will prevail. <u>We must.</u> And like all the best stories, there must be a happy ending. Except that is the bit that worries me most. How do I make that happen? I know if I leave them to their own devices, my uncle and Matilda will do as the stupid rules tell them they ought to, even though it will make everyone miserable. Somehow, I must make them brave enough to break all the rules.

Every last one.

I would if I were them.

—Excerpt of an entry by Miss Phoebe Barrington to her diary.

6th May 1815. Dern, Sevenoaks, Kent.

By the time Matilda had calmed down, and the urge to smash things had dissipated, she discovered that Lucian had retired for the night. The coward. She knew damn well why he'd done it, and frustration gnawed at her. They had so little time together, and she wanted him so very badly. At the least, she had wanted to sleep in his arms, but he'd gone and got all honourable and conscientious on her at the moment she least required it of him.

She remembered a lavish dinner she'd attended last summer, cursing her bad luck to discover she was seated next to him. He'd tormented her with little more than a fingertip touching her hand, leaving her giddy and muddled, desire singing in her blood. He'd warned her not to be foolish enough to suppose he had a heart lurking beneath his icy facade, and that she was foolish indeed if she believed what was between them could end up anywhere but in his bed. Well, he'd been wrong. He had a heart, one that no one had ever taken the trouble to protect, one that he had hidden beneath that layer of ice rather than allow anyone else to hurt him. He'd been right, too. She would go to his bed, if he would let her.

She let out an incredulous breath of laughter. After all those months of refusing his advances and dancing around the flames of their attraction, and now... *now,* when she was ready to fling herself into his arms with abandon and no regrets, the devil was playing hard to get.

Honestly.

Life was so unfair. The urge to throw things returned with a vengeance.

So it was that the next morning Matilda readied herself for their journey with a headache and gritty eyes, having spent a restless night. By two in the morning, she'd been so close to going to his room and demanding he make love to her that she'd ended up weeping with frustration. No, she'd decided. It was not in her nature to beg. He wanted her badly. He'd made no secret of it and, as they were travelling under the guise of a married couple with their daughter—to Phoebe's incandescent delight—they would share a room. No doubt he'd try to make other arrangements, but Matilda would thwart them. She might have to give him up for the future of his illustrious family, but she would not do so until he announced his betrothal. Until then, he was hers, and she was his, and that was all there was to it.

As they were to leave before dawn, in case Theodore had anyone watching the road out of Dern, Matilda had simply taken a cup of chocolate and some toast in her room while she was getting ready. Now, she turned this way and that in front of the full-length mirror as she inspected her disguise by candlelight. It was a plain but well-made green pelisse with a chip bonnet. The dress beneath was of the same colour as the pelisse, and Matilda wouldn't have been seen dead in it in other circumstances, as it was last year's style and nothing like as elegantly made as she was used to. As it was, it did the job very nicely. Sarah had dressed her hair plainly, too, in the hope she would not draw attention. Her maid was most put out that she was not coming with them, but mollified a little at the idea of staying at Dern and having some free time to explore the place.

They were travelling under the name of Mr and Mrs Bennet— Matilda's suggestion—and would, at a glance, appear to be of the gentry. The one thing that was brightening Matilda's morning— especially as she was vexed with him—was the prospect of seeing Lucian Barrington, Marquess of Montagu forced to play the part of a mere *mister*. She suspected he'd need to be kept out of sight as much as possible, for no one in their right mind would ever take him for anything other than a nobleman.

This supposition was confirmed the moment she stepped outside, where the plain, old-fashioned travelling carriages awaited, instead of Lucian's usual luxurious equipage emblazoned with his crest.

"What on earth are you doing?" Lucian was demanding of Denton, Mrs Frant, and Pippin, who seemed to be loading their own luggage into a second carriage.

Matilda stared at him and felt her lips twitch, even though his inability to blend in was likely to cause them trouble. You couldn't make a silk purse out of a sow's ear, and it appeared you could dress Lucian in a sack and still have no doubt whatsoever of who and what he was. The first glimmer of dawn was not yet lighting the horizon, but the carriage lamps turned Lucian's pale hair the colour of old gold, and highlighted his high cheekbones and that aristocratic profile. His clothes might be of inferior quality, but nothing else about him was.

Denton drew himself up and moved towards his master. He looked anxious but determined.

"We are coming with you, my lord."

"The devil you are," Lucian replied.

"You need us," Pippin said, folding her arms and moving to stand beside Denton with the air of a woman settling in for a fight. "You've no maid for Miss Hunt, and no governess for Miss Barrington neither, as that feeble-minded Miss Peagoose is too afraid of her own shadow to come with you. Even old Nanny Johnson had more backbone than that silly creature. Besides which, Denton's been your valet before and he's content to do so again, seeing as you will need the help, as you've but one arm and have never dressed yourself a day in your life."

Lucian glowered. "I'm supposed to be a very ordinary Mr Bennet, travelling with my wife and daughter. I can't be trailing valets and maids and… what the devil is Mrs Frant supposed to be?" he demanded, clearly impatient to be on his way.

"You aren't. I am your darling mother, my boy," Pippin retorted with a mischievous gleam in her eyes. "And this is Mr and Mrs West, your in-laws."

"Mama!" Matilda said with a wicked grin as she held her arms out to Mrs Frant, for the pure delight of seeing Lucian's outraged expression. "How delightful to have you travelling with us, dearest."

"Matilda!" he said, the exasperation in his voice clear, but before he could launch into his many objections, Denton spoke again.

"My lord," he said, his voice grave. "We've failed to keep that man from causing you harm these many years, though I swear we've tried our best. Let us come with you and do what we may to keep you safe, for I wouldn't stay at Dern another minute if anything befell your lordship, and I know I speak for Pippin and Mrs Frant too. Let us help you. There is safety in numbers and at least, if the truth was ever discovered, we might do what we can to mitigate the damage to Miss Hunt's reputation."

Lucian stared at Denton. His expression was hard to read but his eyes glittered in the lamplight. He gave a taut nod and turned away.

Denton let out a breath.

Matilda smiled and reached out, squeezing the butler's hand. "Thank you."

"It's an honour to serve him," he said, standing a little straighter. "And you, *Lizzie*," he added, giving her a wink.

"Why thank you, Papa," Matilda returned as he handed her into the carriage.

Matilda had just settled herself down when Phoebe came tearing down the steps. She scrambled up into the carriage and threw herself down on the seat opposite, fizzing with excitement.

"Well, someone is bright-eyed and bushy-tailed this morning," Matilda said with a smile.

"I am, and you look splendid, *Mama,* and you too, *Papa!*" Phoebe said as Lucian appeared in the open doorway, and then she crowed with laughter.

Lucian caught Matilda's eye and shook his head.

"All that effort my uncle took to have me sent to Bedlam, and I'm fairly certain I'll be certifiable before the end of the day," he muttered before climbing in beside her.

"Don't be cross, Mr Bennet," Matilda said, winking at Phoebe, who grinned with delight. "Or I shall make you travel with Mama and Papa."

Lucian groaned, tipped his hat over his eyes, and pretended to go to sleep.

Though Phoebe's disappointment was eloquent, they had no need to use their disguises during the course of their first day. Pippin—or Grandmama, as Phoebe insisted on addressing her—had provided a sumptuous picnic, which they ate in the carriage. Lucian was silent, his complexion ashen, and Matilda was in little doubt that the jolting over bad roads was giving him a deal of discomfort. She also knew that the stubborn man would endure the fires of Hades before he'd admit as much. So, she did the best she could to keep Phoebe entertained and quiet, so as not to aggravate his nerves on top of whatever he was suffering.

By the time they reached The White Hart in Saint Albans, everyone was tired and fractious. Lucian's irritation climbed perceptibly the moment it dawned on him that he could not order the entire staff of The White Hart to jump, and wait for them to ask *how high, my lord?* He was Mr Bennet, and Mr Bennet had to wait his turn, and would not get the best room nor the best treatment and, if he got impatient, he could damn well lump it.

Surprisingly, Denton seemed to be taking the blow to his pride in even worse heart than Lucian. His indignation was palpable on his employer's behalf and Matilda thought the entire affair doomed to failure when, finally, the private parlour was made ready for them and dinner appeared promptly thereafter.

Dinner was a tense affair. Denton and Mrs Frant appeared to be sat upon thorns to be dining with the marquess. Lucian picked at his food, eating next to nothing despite Matilda's encouragement that he must keep his strength up. Pippin, whilst quite at her ease, lamented the lack of seasoning in the rabbit stew—not to mention the lack of rabbit—and the fact the vegetables had been boiled to a grey-green paste, and expressed vigorous disappointment with the suet pudding, which in her opinion was fit merely for use as a doorstop. Only Phoebe seemed undaunted, inhaling her dinner with no complaints, and chatting merrily to her companions without batting an eyelid at the strange circumstances in which they found themselves.

When *Mr and Mrs West* excused themselves and retired for the night, with Mrs Frant blushing like a newlywed, Lucian watched them go before turning to Pippin and lifting a pale blond brow in enquiry.

Pippin returned a smug grin.

"What you don't know don't hurt you none, my lord," she said, before her expression turned stiff. "And you'll not punish them none for it, neither, I hope. It's about time they got themselves sorted. Best part of twenty years she's been pining for him and him none the wiser. Took her nearly as long to ask for my help too. Still, I sorted them out. They'd marry if it didn't mean losing their positions."

She gave him a pointed look, and Matilda watched as Lucian returned her expression with a frown.

"Oh, was it a love potion, Pippin?"

Lucian scowled harder as he looked around, remembering too late that Phoebe was listening in and that the child was far too perceptive not to have figured out the gist of the conversation.

"Of course it wasn't a love potion," Lucian said in exasperation. "There are no such things, Phoebe."

Pippin pursed her lips but said nothing. Instead, she turned to Phoebe. "Come along then, my lamb. You can sleep with your grandmama tonight. I don't doubt they've not aired the bed properly, and you'll make a fine bedwarmer."

"Wait. What?" Lucian said, sitting up. "No. There is a bed made up in our room for Phoebe."

"Oh, but you'll not be wanting her chatter all evening, talking your ear off, not when you've had her all day. Besides, I've missed my little Mistress Barrington, and it will be nice to have some company for a change."

"No, Pippin...." he said, his voice stern.

Matilda saw, as Lucian could not see, the sly wink that Pippin gave Phoebe, and the alacrity with which the child responded.

"Oh, yes, Pippin. Will you tell me stories too, about when uncle was a little boy, with his brothers, and all the naughty things he did?"

"Reckon I could be persuaded," Pippin said, holding out her hand and blithely ignoring Lucian.

"Hurrah!" Phoebe exclaimed and ran to Lucian to kiss his cheek. "Good night, Papa, good night, Mama."

She kissed Matilda too and rushed from the room with Pippin as fast as they could manage.

"I get the distinct feeling I am being managed," he said bitterly.

Matilda smiled. "Don't be cross. This is Phoebe's dream come true, and Pippin is an old romantic."

Lucian snorted. "Romantic? Giving me leave to debauch an innocent young lady is not romantic."

"But she's not giving you leave, Lucian," Matilda said softly. "I am."

His breath caught, and the first faint touch of colour she'd seen in his face all day marked his cheeks. He closed his eyes, but not before Matilda saw them darken with longing.

"No." The hand that rested on the table clenched. "I'll sleep in a chair. On the floor, if it comes to it. God alone knows what damage I'll have done to your reputation when this debacle is over. I'll be damned if I'll ruin you in truth."

Matilda reached out and covered his hand, easing her fingers between his and unclenching his fist. "I can't turn back now, Lucian. We have this time together, this strange little theatrical we are acting out. Let us at least make the most of it. Give me something to remember you by, my love."

"Like a bastard?" he demanded, his voice hard and cold.

Matilda withdrew her hand.

"I'm going to bed," she said, her voice unsteady. "At the very least you need to rest that shoulder, or you'll be in terrible pain tomorrow, and I don't doubt the rest of us will suffer for it too. It is up to you whether you wish to make these days we have been granted ones of misery and regret, or whether they will be memories we can cherish in years to come. I will not beg, Lucian. You will do as you think best."

***

Lucian closed his eyes as Matilda walked out of the room. When a pretty maid poked her head around and batted her eyelids at him to ask if Mr Bennet required anything else... *anything* at all, he curtly ordered a bottle of brandy and demanded he not be disturbed again. His shoulder was throbbing like the devil himself was poking at it with his blasted pitchfork, he was tired and irritable, and the moment Matilda had said Pippin was not giving him leave to debauch her but she herself was, all that had disappeared and the only throbbing he was aware of was much farther south. He groaned and put his head in his hands. He was despicable and Matilda was doing her damndest to encourage him, confound her.

Utterly wretched, he stared at the bottle of brandy and contemplated getting foxed and sleeping in the carriage, but knew he could not face the reproach in Matilda's eyes in the morning. He had to go up the stairs and into their room, and he knew damn well that she would not lie down and go to sleep without a murmur, though she certainly did not need to beg him. Hell, she didn't need to open her mouth or so much as look in his direction. He'd do anything she wanted, *anything,* but the thought of taking her innocence and then marrying another woman was so obscene it made him want to do something violent and destructive, or crawl into a dark hole and weep.

Though it was inadvisable, his thoughts drifted back to the morning they'd spent in his bed. He remembered the heady scent of her, orange blossom and something uniquely feminine and utterly her. He closed his eyes and remembered the silk of her skin and the warm, taut nub of her nipple as he'd taken it in his mouth. Before he knew what he was doing he was on his feet, climbing the stairs, his heart hammering in his chest.

He did not have to take her innocence, said the devil on his shoulder. It was possible to bring them both pleasure without stealing her virtue, and he knew all the ways. He could show her, he could give her the memories she'd asked for, memories that would be all he had in the frozen landscape of the future that beckoned him. They could have this much. No one would know, she would still be a virgin, would still bleed when her husband....

Lucian stopped halfway up the stairs as pain lanced through his heart like a dagger had struck, up to the hilt. He leaned upon the wall to brace himself against the impact, looking down, almost puzzled when there was no sign of a blade, not a trace of blood when the wound had to be mortal, sucking the life from him.

Matilda would not be his. No matter what happened between them, she would one day belong to another man. He would marry a well-bred lady who didn't give a damn for him past his title and his wealth, and the only woman he'd ever love would be lost to him. The thought was like dying. He *would* die. Not all at once. He would sire his heirs and see Phoebe married to a man who would cherish her as he ought… but every day a little more of him would wither and die without Matilda's love to sustain him, until there was nothing left.

Lucian drew in an unsteady breath. *Don't think of it.* He knew how to do that. He'd had plenty of practise. The pain was buried down deep and covered over in ice, freezing it and locking it away like he had always done with anything that was too painful to endure. But that was the trouble with Matilda, and with Phoebe too. They were warm and alive. They had thawed his heart and made him feel things, things that he could not afford, could not have.

He took another step, then another, moving forward because he could not go back. He was Montagu and he would endure. Matilda would survive the loss of him and, whilst he would not survive the loss of her, he would cast himself in ice and go through the motions of living until his title and Phoebe were safe.

Tonight, though, tonight and all the nights they had of this crackbrained scheme, those belonged to them both, and he would not waste them.

Chapter 15

Sir,

*I have the information you sought, though I do
not think it will please you any. I have tracked
Mr Barrington down and may inform you that
he is established in rooms in a small village
outside of Loughborough. I followed him and
took note of everyone he spoke to as you asked
me to. He has met twice now with a man who
could be nothing but a villain. On investigation
I discover that he is known as Flash Jack and is
a highwayman of some notoriety. Shortly after
the meeting I discovered that this man
immediately set off with three others of equal
disrepute and the destination of Matlock Bath
in mind. I believe he means to do Lord Montagu
harm.*

**—Excerpt of a letter to Mr Gabriel Knight
from an informant.**

6th May 1815. The White Hart, St Albans.

Matilda readied herself for bed and tried her hardest not to
listen out for every creak of the floorboards that might announce
Lucian's appearance. The White Hart was an ancient building,
close to four hundred years old, and the blasted place groaned and
protested every time anyone so much as breathed heavily.

So, naturally, she was a complete basket case.

She'd washed and changed into one of her own nightgowns. She saw no reason why she ought not. Her disguise—such as it was—was for public consumption. No one would know Mrs Bennet had a taste for lavish bed wear... not that it was in any way provocative. She had not packed to visit Dern with the idea of seducing Lucian in mind. A pity, as she might have been better prepared if she had. Still, the gown was a very fine cotton lawn and trimmed with delicate lace scallops around the neckline and sleeves. Matilda had let down her hair and now sat at the dressing table, brushing it out.

Her heart leapt to her throat as she heard the door open and the hum of background noise from the busy inn grow louder as Lucian stepped through. He closed the door, muting the sound once more, and leaned against it, staring at her, his expression unreadable.

Matilda swallowed and willed herself not to drop the heavy silver-backed hairbrush. With great care, she set it down on the dressing table and clasped her hands in her lap to stop them trembling.

"You ought to have locked the door," he said, his tone gruff. "It's not safe in a place like this."

"I was waiting for you," she replied, relieved her voice did not quaver.

Lucian didn't reply, but there was something hot and agitated blazing in his eyes that made her pulse flutter.

He would not sleep in the chair tonight.

She watched as he dragged his gaze from her. It appeared to be an effort, which was reassuring. Instead, he looked around the tiny room and, though he did not react, she knew he was displeased with what he saw. It was small and cramped, and no doubt a great deal less luxurious than what he was used to. A muscle in his jaw ticked.

"It's the best Mr Bennet can afford," she said lightly. "And Mrs Bennet is well pleased with it. The bed is comfortable."

It was. It looked to be as old as the inn, too, and was heavily carved. Lucian moved to it and stood staring down at the dark red coverlet, one elegant hand curving around one of the ornate posts.

"You ought not be here at all, Matilda, but at the very least it ought to be the best room. You ought to be treated like a queen, not—"

"Stop it," she said, her voice firm and somewhat impatient. "Little I care for such fripperies. I've told you before. I do not lack for money, and I do not need or want you to buy me things. Do you think a bigger room and better furnishings could make me love you anymore than I do, could make being with you mean more than it does?"

He didn't reply, but his shoulders were stiff with tension. Matilda got to her feet and walked to stand behind him. She slid her arms about his waist and rested her head on his back. His hands covered hers, holding on tight.

"I do not want to feel shame for taking you to my bed," he said, and the aching emotion she heard in his words, the anger that grew harsher as he spoke, made her eyes prickle. "I want to stand beside you and let everyone know you are mine, that I love you and that I am loved, and I *cannot,* and it is killing me."

"I know," she said, wanting to weep but trying to be strong for him. Crying would change nothing. "But we are not the first lovers torn apart by circumstances, and we won't be the last. We shall fight this battle with your uncle, and this time you will win, and you and those you care for will be safe from harm. Until then, we will have these days together, and that must be enough. Whether or not we spend those days in a carriage, a cramped little room in an inn, or a hole in the ground matters not a whit, so long as we are together."

He turned and took her face between his hands, stroking her skin with his thumbs, his silver eyes glinting.

"My love," he said, staring down at her.

Matilda smiled. "Yes. Always."

He bent his head and put his lips to hers, a delicate brush of his mouth that was a prelude to another featherlike caress, and another. Matilda sighed and touched her tongue to his lips. It was like dropping a lit taper upon spilled brandy.

He pulled her into his arms, holding her tight and kissing her harder, deeper, plundering her mouth with something close to desperation. Far from being daunted, Matilda's heart soared and she clung to him, twining her limbs around him like honeysuckle scrambling up a trellis.

His hands slid down her sides to cup her bottom, pressing her closer against him, kneading the plump flesh until he reached down and lifted her up. Matilda tore her mouth from his with a cry of surprise, wrapping her legs about him.

"Your shoulder!" she protested in alarm.

"Damn my shoulder," he cursed, carrying her to the bed.

He set her carefully on the mattress. Matilda moved back and lay herself down and he watched until she settled, before climbing over her. His knees pressed into the layers of bedding beside her thighs and he stared down, watching her, his usually cold eyes full of heat and longing.

"You are so beautiful," he said, so solemnly that Matilda could only swallow hard as emotion rose in her throat. "Not just on the surface. Your goodness, your kindness, shines from you. It is like staring at the sun. Even after I have looked away, it is still imprinted on my mind, upon my soul. You have changed me, Matilda, and I wish that you had not, for I want so many things that I had believed to be nothing more than fairy stories. You have made me wish for impossible things, and knowing I can't have them is so much worse than believing they did not exist at all."

"It is better to have loved and lost…." She blinked hard and tried to smile, to take away the anguish in his eyes.

"No it isn't!" he said fiercely. "I keep trying to believe it, but it isn't."

"No," she agreed, her voice quavering. "It isn't, and yet I don't regret it. I will never regret it." She reached up and tugged at his coat. "Take it off."

Lucian closed his eyes and gave a huff of laughter. When he opened them again, he had composed himself, and he looked down at her with a wry smile.

"You are forever demanding I take my clothes off."

"I know," Matilda replied with a heavy sigh. "I just can't help myself. I am not only in love with you, but wild with lust. Can you bear it?"

"I shall do my best," he said gravely, and struggled out of his coat.

Matilda helped him as best she could, tugging at the sleeves and then unbuttoning his waistcoat and pushing it off his shoulders. She fought with his cravat and finally loosened it, before sliding it free. He cursed and muttered, trying to get the shirt over his head without jostling his injury, but at last his top half was bare and she drank him in. The wound on his shoulder was uncovered now, and healing well, though it was still pink and angry against his fair skin. The sight of it made her heart clench with fear at how close she had been to losing him, and she looked away, preferring to enjoy the view of his impressive physique.

"Oh, Lucian," she said, running her hands over his chest. "I wish we could be naked all the time. I can never get enough of looking at you."

"If you keep looking at me like that, I won't be responsible for the consequences," he murmured, his voice so low it sent shivers coursing over her skin.

"Oh, good," she said happily.

He chuckled and tugged at her nightgown. "My turn. Take it off."

"Oh, but I wasn't finished," Matilda protested, pulling at the waistband of his trousers.

"Too bad. Off," he commanded, and Matilda squeaked and wriggled as he yanked at the nightgown, pulling it up and over her head and flinging it to the floor.

He stilled, staring down at her, his fierce gaze devouring her. There was nothing of the icy marquess present here now. He was all ablaze and she could feel the heat radiating from his body as though an inferno burned beneath his skin. He traced the curve of one breast with a tentative fingertip, his breath catching as though he'd dared to reach for something forbidden.

Matilda held her breath, shivers running over her as her body caught fire. She wanted to grab hold of him and draw him down to her, into her, to never let him go. Instead she held herself still, allowing him to touch her at his leisure. His thumb traced a circle around her nipple, a lazy, caressing movement that made her arch like a cat seeking further attention from the hand that stroked it.

"Lucian," she said, her breath coming faster as both hands stroked and touched with something close to reverence. She reached her arms up to him, wanting him to come to her, wanting his body against hers, his mouth on her.

"Yes?" he said, amusement glinting in the silver of his gaze. "Is there something you want, my love?"

"Yes," she said, turning her head to the side, closing her eyes against the jolt of pleasure as he lightly pinched her nipples. The sensation shot through her, tugging at her core, making the place between her legs throb and clamour for attention. She arched her hips, but he sat astride her thighs and offered her no relief.

His hands slid down her torso and, for one blissful moment, she thought he would touch her there, would seek out the intimate place he had found before and send her off into glittering ecstasy with his clever fingers. He did not, and Matilda huffed and pouted.

"What's the trouble, darling girl? Won't you tell me?"

She opened her eyes and glared at him reproachfully.

"You *know* what the trouble is," she accused him.

"I do?"

He tried to look innocent and failed by a mile. He looked like a fallen angel. He had the body and face of an angel, at any rate, but devilry burned in his eyes.

"Yes. Yes, you do! Oh, Lucian, *please*," she begged him, writhing beneath his touch as his hands continued to caress her breasts, teasing the hard peaks that were sending shock waves of sensation rolling through her when he so much as brushed against them now.

"I'll do anything you want, Matilda. Only ask it of me. Command me."

"Touch me," she demanded, beyond being embarrassed now. "Touch me like you did before, in your bed."

"You mean here?" he asked, shifting back a little and trailing a lazy finger through the curls between her legs.

"Yes. Yes." Matilda nodded, wanton and eager.

"Like this?" Slowly, so, *so* slowly, he teased a fingertip along the seam of her sex.

Matilda gasped, spreading her legs as far as she could between the cage of his thighs, silently demanding more.

"Do you remember the dinner at Mrs Manning's?" he asked, tormenting her with barely there touches designed to send her wild with frustration.

"What?" Matilda snapped, bewildered by the question as her patience frayed. He wanted to make conversation *now*? "The one where you pretended I'd agreed to go to Green Park with you, when I'd done nothing of the sort?"

"That's the one," he murmured, still trailing his finger too lightly over her sex, just enough to make her tremble and quiver beneath his touch. "The one where I touched your hand and you fell to pieces."

"Oh, you devil!" she cried, laughing yet half mad with exasperation. "*Yes*! Yes, I remember."

"Do you know what I was thinking then?"

"No." Matilda closed her eyes and prayed for endurance.

Her body was nothing but nerve endings, every one of them standing on end, oversensitive and on edge with anticipation, her focus entirely concentrated on the too gentle brush of his finger between her thighs.

"I was thinking of you, like this, with your beautiful body open to me. I was quite desperate. All I could think of was tasting you. I wanted my mouth on you so badly I could not have stood up without everyone in the room knowing just what you'd done to me. It was excruciating."

Matilda's eyes flicked open and she stared up at him in astonishment.

"You were as cold as ice," she accused him. "You didn't so much as bat an eyelid."

His lips quirked. "Appearances can be deceptive, my love. I was never more out of control in my life. I only thanked God there were a great many courses so I could govern my unruly libido in time."

Matilda stared at him disbelievingly. "You wanted…?"

"To taste you." His eyes glittered with desire. "Here."

He illustrated his meaning by sliding his finger in between the delicate folds to the slick heat beneath, and Matilda exclaimed, her hips jerking as pleasure jolted through her.

"There?" she demanded, raising her head to stare at him, once she had wit enough to speak again. "You mean you were thinking about your mouth… *there*?"

"Yes," he agreed, a wicked smile tugging at his lips and giving her a tantalising glimpse of those elusive dimples. "I was suffering a world of discomfort for it, too."

"Oh good Lord," she said, as her head flopped back to the mattress.

"I have wanted it very badly, Matilda, and for such a long time. May I? Please?"

Matilda nodded weakly. A small part of her wanted to ask if that was *normal,* in the circumstances, but a much larger part of her didn't give a tinker's cuss if it was or not.

She was vaguely aware of Lucian moving off the bed, of him kneeling between her legs. He tugged her towards the edge of the mattress, spreading her wider until she felt exposed and vulnerable and then… and then she didn't care about anything else. She cried out as his mouth covered her, hot and wet and sinful, and her body convulsed at once, heat and pleasure surging through her in a heady wave as she arched and trembled beneath him. The climax left her breathless and gasping.

He laughed, blowing a fluttering stream of air over her until she shivered. His hot breath felt like a cool breeze against her burning flesh, and he nuzzled the delicate skin at the apex of her thighs.

"So sweet, my beautiful Matilda. Sweeter than honey. I knew you would be, and I think you can do that again."

He set out to prove it until Matilda was nothing more than sensation and quivering flesh. Her world had narrowed and constricted to the place where his mouth and tongue kissed and lapped and tormented, over and over again. Just as she thought he could not possibly wring another ounce of pleasure from her trembling body, he would start again until she was helpless and moaning, abandoned to his touch, shamelessly crying out his name and begging for more.

When at last he stopped, pressing a tender kiss to her thigh, she was too dazed to even notice for a moment. She was giddy and muddled, uncertain of anything besides the gentle buzz of pleasure simmering through her veins still. Movement in the room made her eyes open, though, and she focused hazily until she realised that Lucian had finally divested himself of his boots, and everything else.

Her breath caught and suddenly she was perfectly wide awake.

He climbed onto the bed on the far side of her and lounged back against the pillows, his silver grey eyes glinting. He'd crooked his good arm behind his head and looked quite at ease, if you did not notice the rapid rise and fall of his chest. Matilda scrambled up and turned around to see him, pushing her hair out of her face. Greedily she drank him in, the long, elegant limbs and the taut, sculpted muscle all gilded perfection in the lamplight. The warm glow shimmered over him, casting him in gold.

"For God's sake, touch me," he said, betraying his insouciant posture as his voice rasped with impatience.

"With pleasure," Matilda replied, daring to move closer.

She knelt beside him and laid her hand on his ankle, drawing her palm up over his leg, feeling the rasp of hair as she moved higher, sliding over his knee, over his thigh. Her attention snagged on the most masculine part of him and could not be diverted. He was everywhere in proportion, beautifully wrought, and Matilda felt her breath catch.

His member twitched under her hot gaze, and Matilda smiled. It seemed to beckon her, to beg for her notice. Remembering how wickedly he'd tormented her, she decided she could take her time. He wasn't going anywhere. So, she traced a fingertip along the surprisingly delicate skin where his thigh met his torso, and then trailed it back down again. She tangled her fingers in the coarse hair at the base of his shaft and tugged at it gently before tracing a pattern over his belly. His stomach muscles twitched and leapt beneath her touch, and she grinned.

"Matilda," he said.

Her name was a harsh rasp of sound, a plea, and she looked up to find his heavy-lidded eyes dark with wanting. She held his gaze and bent her head to press a kiss to his belly.

He groaned and closed his eyes.

"Wicked girl."

She smiled against his skin and dared to trail her tongue around his belly button, as it seemed silly not to. Shivers cascaded over his body and she felt a surge of satisfaction that her instincts had been correct. What now, though? She wanted to touch him, to see if the smooth skin of his sex was as silky as it looked, but she felt suddenly uncertain. He had asked first, after all.

"What should I do?"

His eyes flickered open, hot and gleaming like quicksilver.

"Whatever you want," he said urgently. "Only for the love of God, put your hands on me, or your mouth. I don't care. Just touch me, *please*."

Her mouth? Goodness.

Deciding she was not quite brave enough for that yet, she reached out her hand instead. He was burning hot beneath her touch and impossibly hard, though his skin was so fine it slid like the most delicate of silk. He hissed out a breath as her fingers trailed over him and she snatched them away in shock, wondering if she'd done something wrong.

"*Don't stop*," he gritted out, sounding just as impatient and fractious as she'd been earlier.

She looked up to discover he'd flung his arm over his eyes. Tension radiated from him, his muscles taut and defined as he held himself still.

Matilda returned to her exploration, stroking the burning shaft gently, inexpertly touching and caressing.

"I don't know what I'm doing," she admitted cheerfully, gaining a choked laugh in response.

"I know," he said, the words ragged and breathless. "Doesn't seem to matter. Oh, God...."

He groaned, his hips canting upwards, seeking more.

"Harder," he commanded. "Like this."

Lucian reached down, curling her fingers about him, guiding her movements.

She did as he instructed, pleased with the results as his breathing sped. He cursed and sat up, watching her now, his silver eyes burning. Moisture glistened at the rosy head, making her hand slick, the slide and caress easier and faster.

"Damn it, that's..., Oh, hell, I... I can't...." he muttered, and suddenly Matilda was flat on her back.

Lucian settled between her legs and, for one heady moment, she believed he would make love to her properly, make her his in the one, irrevocable way she longed for. He did not, but instead slid his erection over her sex in a slow, sinuous movement. Matilda gasped at the intimacy of it, her own arousal surging back to life in an instant. She turned her face into his neck, nuzzling his skin, feeling his pulse as something wild and trapped as it beat frantically beneath her lips. It reached a crescendo and his body grew taut.

"Oh, Christ."

He groaned, his breath hot as he moved over her, his shaft caressing her and making her gasp and writhe beneath him. She brought her legs up, cradling him between her thighs and he made a harsh sound, his body spasming. The hot splash of his seed was a shock as it spilled upon her belly. She closed her eyes against the sting of regret, knowing he was protecting her.

In this moment, she did not want the care he took. She would have given anything to have taken him inside her, to have taken his seed within her and have kept his child with her as she could not keep him. She blinked, willing the tears not to fall, but she could not hold them back this time and they scalded her eyes, impossible to halt.

"Matilda," he said, his voice anguished. "Oh, God. I'm sorry. My love, I'm so sorry. I ought never—"

"Don't," she said fiercely, holding onto him when he would have left her, would have wrapped himself in guilt and regret and loathed himself for what he had done. "I am only weeping because I am greedy for more, not for anything you have done. Don't make it worse by feeling guilty for giving me as much as you could."

"It is not enough," he said, his voice angry. "Not good enough. I bring you shame where there ought only to be joy."

"I am not ashamed," she said, wanting to shake him. "There is no shame in loving you. I have had practise enough at living with others' opinions of me. They are *their* opinions, not my own. It is my own voice I heed now, and I see nothing wrong in what we have done, and I won't have you feel guilt for it. I won't bear the burden of your guilt either, Lucian, so stop it, now."

She could not stop him leaving the bed though. He kissed her forehead and pulled out of her embrace. Matilda watched as he poured water from the pitcher on the washstand into the bowl and turned away from her, cleaning himself up. Reaching for a clean cloth, he returned to the bed and tenderly wiped her clean too, removing all trace of himself from her body.

"Come back to bed, Lucian," she urged him, sliding under the bedcovers. She was cold now, missing the heat of his body and needing him to return to her.

He did not reply, keeping his back to her, taking the time to rinse out the used cloths and set them aside. He leaned upon the washstand, his head bowed, shoulders set.

"Lucian."

He took a deep breath and turned, returning to the bed. He did not look at her, but got in and put his arm about her as she snuggled into his side.

"Don't be cross," she said, an anxious, panicked sensation growing in her chest.

"I'm not cross."

"Well, don't be whatever you are," she retorted. "Don't spoil it."

He sighed and reached out, pinching out the candle on the nightstand before sliding down the bed. He pulled her closer, pressing a kiss to her forehead.

"Go to sleep, my love. We have another long day tomorrow."

"I don't want to sleep," she protested, though in truth she could hardly keep her eyes open. He was so warm, and the bed was comfortable, and it had been a long and tiring day.

"Yes, you do," he said, his hand stroking up and down her spine, soothing her as he might a fractious child.

"But I don't want to miss you."

It was a faint, whiny complaint, and his reply was soft and amused.

"Dream of me, then," he said. "As I shall dream of you."

***

Lucian did not dream of Matilda, for he did not sleep, but she filled his thoughts all the same. He closed his eyes, forcing the pain in his throbbing shoulder from his mind and instead reliving the past hours, marvelling at how easily she had stripped him of control. It had been the hardest thing to deny himself, to not breach that fragile barrier and make her his own. Even now, his soul howled with the pain of denial, not just because he had wanted her physically beyond anything he'd ever known, but because he hungered to be close to her, to show her how it could be between them. Instead, she had shown him. Her touch had been sweet and loving, and clumsy with inexperience, and he'd been utterly disarmed. No skilled lover had ever wrung such a response from him with such startling speed, and her touch seemed to have scoured his mind of the past. It was as though no one had ever come before her, for nothing else had ever meant so much.

Everything.

It had been everything, and not nearly enough. He'd been too aware of the fragility of the moment, of the sense that he must hold tight and remember every single exquisite second and never let it go, and then she had cried and he'd wanted to weep too at the raw feeling in his chest, at the weight of guilt, at the unfairness of it.

He had always known that physical pleasure and love were separate things, but he had not appreciated the power of the two combined. How could he bear it? How could he bear not having this again, forever? He calculated the time it would take to get to Matlock Bath, and return, and the handful of days and nights mocked him when set against the eternity of days and nights that would come after. He sought the ice he always reached for, the comforting weight of duty and honour. These things he had clung to all these years. They had given him purpose and the will to survive, at least until Thomas had died... and then he had discovered the existence of his little niece.

Phoebe had given him a new purpose, alongside a growing fear: the fear of failing her as he had her father. But Phoebe would grow, and she would marry and leave him alone, leave him with his duty and his honour to support him. With Matilda warm against his body, the tantalising feminine scent of her filling his head, duty and honour seemed diminished, their substance changed, made frail and brittle from exposure to the powerful light of her love. He feared they would no longer sustain him once she was gone, that they would not be strong enough to make him endure.

No. That could not be. If he did not have his duty to his family, his name, his honour, he would not survive the future. So, he resurrected the ice, forcing his feelings down, burying them deep in the frozen tundra of his soul, but they burned inside him, hot and resentful, melting his resolve.

Chapter 16

Come at once! Matilda is in trouble and we must help her.

—Excerpt of a letter from Lady Helena Knight, copied to each of the Peculiar Ladies.

6th May 1815. Midnight. A meeting of the Peculiar Ladies. Beverwyck, London.

"What the devil is this about?" Nate demanded of Helena as he thrust his hat and coat at Jenkins, the butler. "What on earth did you mean by sending such a missive? Poor Alice has been fretting herself to death all the way here, not to mention the fact we were forced to travel with Leo in the dead of night."

As he spoke, Alice handed baby Leo, who was sleeping peacefully, into the arms of his nanny.

Helena swallowed, not taking offence at the man's fury as she knew it stemmed from fear of what trouble his sister was in. She wondered how on earth he would take the news that Matilda was not only in grave danger, but had likely become Lord Montagu's lover. Well, one explosion at a time.

"I'm so sorry," she said, embracing Alice, who looked extremely well, despite the anxiety in her eyes and the fraught nature of their journey. "I'm afraid it couldn't be helped. Do come through, and Gabe and I will explain everything."

She showed the two latecomers into the huge drawing room and Nate stopped in his tracks as he saw the assembled company.

Prue sat in a chair by the fireplace, with the duke standing behind her. Aashini and her husband, Lord Cavendish, mirrored their stance on the other side. On the sofas, set at right angles to the fireplace, sat Harriet and Bonnie—with their husbands, Jasper and Jerome—then Minerva and Inigo, and Jemima and Solo.

Nate turned to stare at Helena as Gabe came and stood beside her, sliding a reassuring arm about her waist.

"I think you'd best tell me at once," he said, his expression grim.

Helena looked to Gabe, who smiled at her as everyone sat down. Gabe remained standing, keeping hold of Helena's hand as she sat and gathered herself for the coming storm. Helena opened her mouth to speak when the door opened once more, and her uncle came in. He paused, his eyebrows going up as he saw everyone.

"Goodness, I had no idea we were having a party," he said with a smile.

"Not a party, Uncle Charles," Helena said with regret. "But I think you'd best come in. This involves you too."

"Oh?" The old man looked puzzled but came in as he was bid and sat down.

"Firstly," Helena said, wondering how on earth she would explain this, "you must promise me to listen to this to the end and not make assumptions. I know you will find much of it hard to believe, but I swear to you, it is *all* true."

"It is," Gabe said, his voice firm and his gaze settling on her Uncle Charles. "Though I'm afraid some of you will not wish to believe it."

He nodded at Helena, who took a deep breath and began.

"Mr Theodore Barrington, Lord Montagu's uncle, is a villain. He has been doing his best to murder Lord Montagu since the marquess was a little boy, and he is—at least in part—responsible for the death of Montagu's younger brother, Thomas. A few days ago, he sent men after Lord Montagu to murder him on his way to Derbyshire. Montagu is travelling to the dreadful mills which he bought from Mr Burton, who is every bit as wicked as was recently reported. The marquess did not slander him, and Montagu is not mad, but he is in grave danger, and…." Helena took a deep breath, grateful for her husband's warm grip on her hand. "And Matilda is with him."

***

7th May 1815. The White Hart, St Albans.

Matilda sighed and buried deeper under the covers. The unfamiliar scent of bergamot and a warm male body enveloped her, and she opened her eyes to the new and intriguing experience of waking beside Lucian. She looked up, blinking even in the dim morning light filtering through the curtains, to discover she was being observed.

"Good morning," she said, a little shy now, uncertain of what to expect of him, or what he expected of her.

He smiled, though his eyes were shadowed, and she wondered if he'd slept at all.

She reached up and touched his face, still astonished that she could. He turned into her touch, kissing her palm. *You're mine,* she didn't say. *You belong to me.* Her unspoken words shone in his eyes though, and that was enough.

"I suppose we have to get up." Her pronouncement was reluctant, spoken on a sigh.

"I suppose we do," he said, and the echo of her feelings was in his voice too.

The real world would intrude on this little idyll the way it always did, not that it had ever gone away. Daylight was creeping into the room past the thin curtains, too bright and insistent, and she could hear the noise of the inn as a dull murmur of sound, the rumble of carts and the call of voices on the street below, the everyday clatter and hum of a day already well underway. Matilda was assailed with the sudden, desperate need to make it go away, to turn back the clock and bring back the night and let them live it all over again. She would not waste hours of it in sleep this time, she would persuade him to love her as she longed for him to do, and she would not regret it. She reached for him, pressing close and curling her fingers about his shaft, finding his body primed for her and delighting in the deep tortured groan of pleasure she wrung from him.

"No, love. There's not time," he protested, reaching to grab her wrist and stop her. "We have to go down for breakfast. It's late and we need to be on our way."

Matilda batted his hand away. "I'm not hungry. We'll make time."

She bent down and ran her tongue over his nipple and he shivered. Pleased with that, she did it again, trailing her mouth and tongue across his chest. His arousal was hot in her hand, throbbing now, and her confidence grew. He gave a shaky sigh and then shook his head.

"Matilda, we… we can't," he said and then groaned as she ignored him. "You must not…. Oh, yes, like that…. No… *No*. We *must* get up… Oh God…."

It was intriguing, this newfound power over his body. She was in no danger of believing herself a femme fatale, or thinking herself a skilled lover, but she suspected enthusiasm counted for something. Certainly, he seemed very responsive to her touch if the tormented sounds he made were anything to go on.

"We have to get up?" she queried innocently, firming her grip on him and watching as he threw his head back upon the pillow.

"Yes," he said, though he shook his head and laughed.

"Shall I stop?"

"No! Ah, Matilda, do as you wish with me. I am weak, putty in your hands. I give in. Oh, my God, you will drive me insane."

Matilda laughed too, delighted by his capitulation, and determined to make every second of it count.

***

Somehow they made it downstairs. Phoebe leapt up from the table as they approached, flinging her arms about Matilda first and then Lucian.

"Good morning, Mama!" she said, beaming at Matilda before dancing over to Lucian. "And good morning, Papa! Isn't it a lovely morning?"

"It is," Matilda agreed, hoping her blush was not too pronounced as she guided Phoebe back to the table.

They ate a quick breakfast and were soon fastening bonnets and hustling outside to the carriage. Belatedly, Matilda realised why there had been so much noise and bustle this morning. It was market day, and the scene before them filled with the rumble of carts and the indignant calls of livestock as cows and sheep were herded towards St Peter's Street. Everywhere she looked, the roads were thronged with people, the air heavy with a ripe combination of cheese and hot food, manure and unwashed bodies. As they pushed through to the waiting carriage, Matilda was jostled by a man carrying a tray of fragrant meat pies. She sucked in a breath as the corner of the deep wooden tray struck her elbow and the arctic glare Lucian turned upon the fellow had him blanching and hurrying away.

"Are you hurt?" he asked, taking her arm gently.

"No, it's fine," she said, giving him a reassuring smile.

He drew her closer into his side.

"Montagu!"

Lucian turned and then went very still. Matilda could not see who had hailed him and was about to ask when Lucian put a hand to her back.

"In the carriage. *Now*."

Before she could protest, he'd swept Phoebe up into his arms and had herded them both inside. She glimpsed Denton moving Pippin and Mrs Frant on with equal urgency to the carriage behind theirs and heard Lucian shout at the driver to move out.

He climbed in after them and reached beneath the seat, taking out a heavy wooden box. Matilda gasped as he opened it to reveal two gleaming pistols.

"What on earth is the matter?" she asked, pulling Phoebe into her side. "Who was it that called you?"

"I don't know," he said, his expression grim. "I could see no one, but I don't expect they wished to be seen, nor that I would recognise them if I had. They just wanted to confirm their suspicions and fool that I am, I obliged them."

Matilda's heart gave a flutter of anxiety and she told herself not to panic. "Perhaps it was someone who knew you and you could not see them."

Lucian shook his head. "I never doubted my uncle had a variety of unsavoury characters in hand to watch this route for any travellers matching my description. They just wanted to make sure."

He fixed his gaze to the world beyond the window as the carriage moved slowly through the crowds. His hand remained upon the pistol on the seat beside him, his tension palpable.

"*Idiot!*" he cursed under his breath.

"Lucian, you cannot blame yourself for turning at the sound of your name. It has been yours for decades and it is a natural reaction."

He snorted.

"Perhaps, but I can blame myself for bringing you with me. How I ever let you talk me into this madness…." He shook his head. "No. That is unfair. I needed little enough persuading. I wanted you with me. It was pure selfishness, and now I have put you both in danger."

"Nonsense," Matilda retorted. "If we'd been left behind, we would have been targets too. Your uncle would have known he could manipulate you if either one of us was in danger."

"And you would not have been in danger!" he snapped. "I'm a marquess for the love of God. Do you not think I could have hired an army of men to keep you both safe? But no, instead I brought you with me on this hare-brained adventure, and now—"

"And now, someone has figured out who you are, and we must be on our guard," Matilda said, keeping her voice soothing even as her heart was beating a rapid tattoo in her chest. "We must make haste and lose them, that is all."

"That's no good." Phoebe shook her head, staring at her uncle, her little face grave and thoughtful. "We could not be certain we'd lost them. We would not know if we were safe or not. So, we ought to trap them, confront them. Then we'd know exactly where they were."

"I'm afraid that sounds rather dangerous," Matilda said with a placating smile, taking Phoebe's hand.

"No." They both looked up as Lucian stared at Phoebe, frowning. "She's right."

Phoebe beamed and jumped up and down in her seat.

"Shall we trick them, Papa? And then tie them up and throw them in the river? A pity we're not at sea, we could make them walk the plank," she added, clearly beside herself that Lucian approved of her mad scheme.

"What a bloodthirsty creature you are," he observed mildly, though his expression was still grim. "And I'm not your papa, sweetheart, much as I wish otherwise."

Phoebe frowned, but Matilda did not have time to consider her feelings for the moment, too alarmed by what on earth Lucian was considering.

"Lucian," she said, praying he was not serious. "You cannot possibly think that is a good idea. Surely, if we make haste...."

He shook his head. "No. They'll look for a quiet place to ambush us or murder us in our beds. No, this needs meeting head on."

"But—"

"Let me think, love," he said, sounding distracted as he returned his attention to watching the world outside.

Matilda could do nothing but hold her tongue for the moment and hope to goodness she could make him think again.

***

"This is insanity," Matilda said, for at least the fifth time. "We don't even know if they are following us."

Lucian held her hand, one arm about her waist as he guided her over the steep ground that led down to the river's edge.

"They're following us," he said, not needing to see the men his uncle had sent to know that much.

"But, Lucian, you don't know how many there are, or what they have in mind."

Lucian thought he had a pretty fair idea of what they had in mind, and all of those ideas ended up with him dead. The other thing he knew was that these villains were likely nothing more than cutthroats, paid to do a job. Therefore, they owed no allegiance to Theodore past wanting to collect their money. Money which his uncle would struggle to obtain, since Lucian had a stranglehold on his finances and Mr Burton, who had been financing Theodore's vendetta, had troubles of his own. Lucian might be travelling in disguise—and might be furious with himself for allowing his desire to keep Matilda and Phoebe close to override good sense—but he had no problem with securing appropriate funds. What's more, he *was* Montagu, no matter his uncle's ambitions, and these devils knew it.

He guided Matilda and Phoebe down the steep bank that led to the River Ouse and under the dark, dank arches of Stratford Bridge. They'd changed horses as Stony Stratford, less than a mile back, and though there had been no sign of pursuit, Lucian could feel their presence like a storm on the horizon.

"I will not hide here whilst you put yourself in danger," Matilda objected, folding her arms and glaring about the gloomy environs beneath the bridge with disgust.

"You will do as you are told," Lucian retorted, wishing just this once that Matilda was not quite so stubborn and brave. He had adored that about her from the beginning, and that she would stand up to him and tear him off a strip without batting an eyelid. Right now, though, he heartily wished it were not the case. "You will keep Phoebe safe," he added, hoping that would call to her maternal instincts if nothing else.

Matilda narrowed her eyes at him. "If I'm to protect Phoebe, why have you given her the pistol?" she demanded with indignation.

"Because you've never fired a pistol in your life as you freely admitted, and Phoebe is quite adept."

His heart ached at the pride in Phoebe's eyes, and he felt a surge of relief at having taught the girl such things. Instinct and his own experiences had told him she might need such skills, even as he'd wanted to keep her innocence intact and her view of the world untainted. Sometimes innocence had too high a price, though, as Thomas had discovered. So Phoebe had been prepared for a world that could be cruel and even dangerous, whilst he'd done his best not to taint her view of it too badly.

He crouched down now, his eyes fixed on the blue-grey gaze of his little niece. "Tell me what you will do."

Phoebe put her chin up, her face pale but determined. "I will raise the pistol and tell them clearly and firmly to *go away* or I will shoot them. I'll look them in the eyes and speak out loud and not be afraid."

Lucian nodded, his throat feeling suddenly restricted.

"And?" he prompted.

"And I won't lower the pistol even if they go, and I'll keep my guard up, for they might return."

"And?"

"And if I feel threatened, I won't hesitate. I will shoot whoever seems to be in charge."

"And?"

"And then I'll run like the devil is at my heels."

Lucian pulled her into his arms and hugged her tightly. He closed his eyes and promised himself that he would make his uncle pay for all of it. Theodore would pay for having benighted his life all these years, for the harm he'd done Thomas. For all of it.

"Will Pippin and Mrs Frant be all right?" Phoebe asked, her voice quiet.

Lucian nodded. "Yes, sweetheart. These men are not interested in them. They'd have noticed if I'd left you or Matilda behind, but Pippin and Mrs Frant are safer back at the village, though I might not be when we go back for them. Pippin was fit to be tied."

"She was terribly cross," Phoebe agreed, and put her arms about his neck. "I love you. You will be careful, won't you?"

"I promise," he said gravely. "But if anything bad happens, Miss Hunt will look after you. I have made her your guardian."

"Nothing bad will happen," Phoebe said, her mouth compressing into a firm line. "I'll shoot anyone who tries to hurt you."

Lucian raised his hand and pointed a finger at her. "You... will stay here out of sight and not make a peep, young lady, or highwaymen and cutthroats will be the least of your problems. I'll have your word of honour, Phoebe."

A mutinous expression crossed Phoebe's face and Lucian glowered at her.

"Phoebe," he said, his voice low and filled with warning.

She huffed, furious.

"Very well, I'll stay here and be quiet like a good little coward whilst you go and get yourself shot," she muttered, folding her arms and glaring back at him. "Word of honour."

Lucian let out a breath and kissed her.

"I love you, Bee. Keep yourself and Matilda safe for me." He turned to Matilda, who was looking just as annoyed as Phoebe. "Please, love, make sure she stays out of sight."

Matilda glared at him.

"I suppose you expect me to promise too?" she said tartly, folding her arms. Her eyes glittered in the dim light under the bridge.

"You must, love. I have to know she will be safe if anything happens to me. If my uncle got his hands on her...."

His voice quavered and he trailed off, unable to complete that thought.

Matilda's expression changed at once and she flung her arms about his neck. "I promise. Oh, of course, I promise. Only you must promise me not to do anything foolish. Please, my love."

"I am in no hurry to allow my uncle his victory, I assure you. Do have a little faith in me," he added with reproach.

"Very well." Matilda nodded and stepped away from him, moving to Phoebe and laying her hands on the girl's shoulders. "We shall do as you've asked."

Lucian nodded, satisfied, and then looked around as he heard Denton hailing him.

"Someone is coming." He hesitated at speaking out before Phoebe, but the child was no fool. "I love you both," he said, and then turned and left them.

Chapter 17

*It grieves me to ask such a favour of you,
indeed; I find it mortifying in the extreme, but I
am running out of options. Montagu has frozen
my accounts and any line of credit, and I find
myself somewhat embarrassed.*

*May I be so crass as to ask if you might lend me
some funds until I can remedy the situation?*

**—Excerpt of a letter from Mr Theodore
Barrington to Charles Adolphus, Baron
Fitzwalter.**

**7th May 1815. Stratford Bridge. Stony Stratford.
Buckinghamshire.**

To the casual observer the carriage had been damaged and was
immoveable, blocking the far side of the bridge. The horses had
been unhitched and were contentedly cropping grass at the side of
the road whilst Denton made a show of rummaging through a tool
chest stashed under the driver's box. Their driver, and the driver of
the carriage they'd left behind in the village, were both ducked
down behind the bridge. All were armed.

Lucian sat in the carriage, waiting. They would hardly expect
a marquess to dirty his hands with manual labour, no matter what
manner of man he was disguised as.

His hands were steady on the pistol as he heard the horses approach. Four, by the sounds of it, which gave them even odds. He heard a coarse voice yell at Denton to leg it and he'd come to no harm, and prayed the man remembered to play his part and get to cover. The door swung open and a large, ruddy faced villain filled the opening. A spotted red cravat was tied about his face, and on seeing Lucian, he tugged it down. He was a huge brute with a broken nose and pockmarked skin and the odours of stale sweat, liquor, and smoke permeated the carriage. His bloodshot blue eyes swung to the pistol Lucian held and he grinned, showing a row of tombstone teeth in various stages of decay.

"Well, good day to you an' all, lord," he said, apparently undaunted by the sight that had greeted him. Naturally, he too held a pistol.

"Good day," Lucian said, not batting an eyelid. "I take it you have come to murder me on my uncle's behalf and collect your reward?"

"That I have, your grace," the chap said, quite amicably.

Lucian returned a withering look. "'My lord' is sufficient, I am a marquess, not a duke. I do hope this does not diminish your comrades' estimation of your talents, as the title is less elevated than you imagined."

"Ah, no, bless you, lord. Everyone knows Montagu is a wicked devil. You is as good as any duke by my reckoning. Better, even."

"How reassuring," Lucian replied dryly. "But before you put a period to my life, I wonder if we might have a little chat?"

The fellow sighed and pushed back his tricorn hat with the barrel of his pistol, returning a regretful expression. "Well, that would be right nice, but murdering a peer is a perilous business, and I'd rather get the messy part of the job done and get clear, if it's all the same to you."

"Well, as it is my life in the balance, it is not all the same to me," Lucian said, crossing one leg over the other and sitting back against the squabs, apparently quite at his ease. "And as you say, murdering a peer of the realm is a perilous undertaking. I promise you you'll never sleep sound again. You see, my solicitor knows to publish a deal of exceedingly unpleasant material if I were ever to die in suspicious circumstances. Which means many equally unpleasant men would be most displeased if I were to meet an *untimely* end. So, you see, it would not just bring you the inevitable difficulty of dodging the noose for having murdered a peer. Not only would justice need to be done quickly to set an example, but those men whose dirty secrets had been published to the world would likely want to seek retribution for the trouble that had befallen them." Lucian gave him the benefit of a cool smile. "You do take my meaning?"

A glimmer of doubt flickered in the bloodshot eyes, and his would be assassin rubbed at his jaw, his expression thoughtful.

"They do say 'ow you is a dangerous fellow to cross," he replied, his tone considering.

"I'm afraid that's true," Lucian said. "And I must also assure you I would by far rather shoot you before I die, than go peacefully. I've never been in the least biddable, I'm afraid. However, I have a proposal for you I believe you will find worth your while, should you decide to stay for that little chat after all?"

"Oh, aye?"

Lucian held his gaze. He'd had too many decades practise of hiding his own feelings to betray any glimmer of doubt or anxiety. This fellow would see nothing beyond the facade, just Montagu at his most icy and disdainful.

"I beg you to consider the facts, sir. I *am* the Marquess of Montagu and as such I control the purse strings of my entire family. Including my uncle. As I severely curtailed his spending some years ago, and recently crippled the man who has been financing his little schemes in the meantime, where do you think he'll find the money to pay you?"

"You reckon he'd bilk me?" the fellow said, his head rearing back in disgust, his indignation genuine.

"I'm afraid he will have no option. He's not got a feather to fly with."

"Well, damn me, if the old gentleman hasn't taken old Flash for a fool," he said, shaking his head and then turning back to Lucian with narrowed eyes. "'Ere, how do I know you're not telling me some Banbury story?"

Lucian shrugged. "You know who I am. You say you have heard of me by reputation. What do your instincts tell you? I suspect a man in your profession has learned to listen to them."

"Cold as ice, just like they said," the fellow murmured with obvious admiration as he considered this.

Lucian held his tongue for a moment, trying to remember where he'd heard the fellow's sobriquet before and noting the large ruby glinting in one ear. It was pretty and incongruous on such a villainous character and, no doubt, the means by which the fellow had earned his name.

"Might you be Flash Jack, by any chance?" he asked, frowning.

The big brute brightened, grinning broadly. "Aye, lord. You've heard of me too, eh?"

Lucian nodded. "I once met a friend of yours. At least, he spoke of you being in the same, er… line of work. Galloping Johnson, I believe he went by. We did a little business together, though it was years ago."

Flash Jack's eyes grew wide. "Old Johnny? Lord, yes, he told me once about a right fancy toff he'd worked for. A deep one, he said, and not to be crossed if you knew what was good for you.

'Ere, you don't mean to say…. You're not the cove what saved Johnny from the noose?"

"Actually I am," Lucian replied with a cool nod and an inward rush of relief, suddenly certain he was back on solid ground. "I was indebted to him for information he'd brought me, and he was a thief, not a murderer. I saw no reason for him to hang, so I stepped in."

Lucian waited whilst Flash Jack gave him a hard stare. He returned the man's gaze placidly.

"Reckon I will have that little chat, lord," the fellow said, and climbed into the carriage.

***

"What the devil is going on up there?" Matilda fretted, pacing back and forth.

She felt sick with fear and her heart was thudding too fast. It had been ages since the horsemen had thundered onto the bridge and since then there had not been a peep out of anyone. To her intense relief there had been no shots fired, no clash of swords or shouts of pain but… what on earth was happening?

"Perhaps we should go and see," Phoebe said, peering around the side of the bridge.

Matilda grabbed hold of her coat and hauled her back again.

"No. We promised we would stay put," she said, though the indignation of hiding down here was gnawing at her insides.

"Like good little girls," Phoebe retorted in disgust, folding her arms.

Matilda looked at the child and shook her head. "Your uncle had better survive, for I'm not sure I have the stamina to see you come out to society."

Phoebe shrugged. "He always says it's society that needs to be prepared for my come out, not me prepared for society."

Matilda smiled despite everything. "I believe he is correct."

They both turned with a gasp as footsteps sounded outside the bridge and Phoebe swung the gun up, holding it in both hands.

"Miss Hunt, Miss Barrington… it's Denton."

"Oh, thank heavens," Matilda said with a sigh of relief.

Phoebe did not lower the pistol though. The man himself appeared, peering cautiously around the corner of the bridge.

"Now then, Miss Barrington, everyone is quite safe. You can put the pistol down."

"Are you sure?" Phoebe asked suspiciously, not budging an inch. "Where is my uncle, then?"

"His lordship is making arrangements with a Mr Flash Jack, miss, and begs you to come and meet your new travelling companions."

***

Matilda stared disbelievingly as she saw Lucian lounging against the side of the bridge, deep in conversation with a large man who looked like a flesh and blood representation of every highwayman sketch she'd ever seen. She hurried to Lucian, who held out his hand to her before Phoebe barrelled into him.

"Hello, Bee," he said, lifting the little girl up and kissing her. "I'm glad you didn't shoot Denton."

She giggled as he set her down again and shook her head before giving Flash Jack a furious glare.

"Don't be silly, but why didn't you shoot this man?" She pointed at the fellow who held his hands up in a gesture of surrender.

"Ah, now don't be like that, missy. Old Flash Jack wouldna done you no 'arm. I don't hold wiv hurtin' lasses."

"But you would have killed my uncle," Phoebe said, scowling at him ferociously.

The villain just shrugged and gave a mournful shake of his head. "Ah, that were business, little princess. Nothin' personal, but now your uncle has done me the honour of giving me employment, so we're all fair and square, ain't we, lord?"

"Indeed," Lucian said gravely, though there was a glimmer of mischief in his eyes that Matilda had not seen before.

It reminded her suddenly of the boy in the portrait Mrs Frant had shown her on her first visit to Dern.

"I have been looking for just such a fellow as Jack for some time, and it so happens he is desirous of retiring from life on the er... *high toby*."

Matilda stared at Lucian in patent disbelief. He looked smug, and rather pleased with himself at having not only met a notorious highwayman but taken him into his employ.

"Ah, well," the big brute said sadly. "What wiv poor old George Lyon going to the nubbing cheat last month, and me getting no younger.... 'Tis too perilous for little reward, not like in the good old days. Reckon the time of the highwayman 'as gone the way of all good things. I'm in no hurry to climb the three trees wiv a ladder, and I have a fancy to roost in a proper pad at night, so it's about time I did an honest day's work for a change."

Matilda stared between the rather terrifying ruffian and Lucian with bewilderment. Phoebe took her hand.

"One of his friends, George Lyon, was hanged in April for holding up the Liverpool mail coach," she explained kindly. "Flash Jack says he'd rather not hang, and he's tired of sleeping in rough places, so he'll work for uncle instead."

Lucian sighed and shook his head as he stared at his niece. "I have a dreadful feeling I've taken being honest with you way too far, you young scapegrace. I also forbid you—again— to mimic the grooms, nor read the papers when I'm not looking."

"Oh, but, Uncle," Phoebe said in delight, eyeing Flash Jack with fascination now. "He's a real life highwayman. Isn't it marvellous?"

From the glittering look in Lucian's eyes, Matilda rather believed he did think it was marvellous.

Flash Jack seemed to swell visibly in the light of Phoebe's admiration.

"Ah, well, little lady. Not no longer. Now, old Jackie will keep you and his lordship, and the pretty lady here, out of trouble," he said, casting a rather warm and approving glance upon Matilda.

"Indeed," Lucian replied, drawing Matilda closer to him and turning to see that the horses had been put back in harness. "And now we must be on our way. I'm afraid we shan't make Market Harborough before dark if we don't make haste."

Matilda allowed him to hustle them back to the carriage and forced herself to still her tongue long enough for them to get moving.

"One of Jack's men will take John Coachman back to Stony Stratford to fetch Mrs Frant and Pippin. So we'll meet up with them in Northampton before heading onto Market Harborough." Lucian said with perfect calm, as though he made deals with highwaymen as a matter of course.

Perhaps he did, for all she knew.

Matilda stared at him. "Lucian Barrington, if you don't explain yourself this instant, I shall hit you. How the devil do you know that fellow isn't just biding his time, waiting to murder you?"

"Because I saved Galloping Johnson from the scragging post," he said with perfect gravity. "There is honour among thieves, love."

And then he burst out laughing.

Matilda stared him with mingled astonishment and outrage. "I don't see that there is anything the least bit funny about it," she protested, folding her arms. "That awful man was sent here to kill you!"

"Oh, but it was nothing personal," Lucian replied with just a slight twitch of his lips.

Matilda threw up her hands.

"Uncle," Phoebe said, a little frown tugging at her smooth brow. "Where and when was Mr Flash going to meet with Great-Uncle Theodore to collect his money?"

"What a clever girl you are," Lucian said, regarding his niece with a combination of approval and deep apprehension. "I fear for your future husband, I truly do. The poor devil will never have a moment's peace. I know I haven't."

Phoebe preened as Matilda looked between the two of them.

"What do you mean— Oh, no!" she said, shaking her head at Lucian and folding her arms as her heart raced. "Oh, dear me, no. You can't mean it."

"But my uncle is so eager for proof of my demise, love," Lucian said, his eyes twinkling, and it was not mischief that shone there now. Now it was the gleam one saw on the edge of a blade in the moment before it struck with deadly precision. "I do think we ought to provide it. Don't you?"

***

They made the Three Swans in Market Harborough just as the last rays of sunlight were sinking beneath the horizon. To Matilda's intense disappointment, only two rooms were available. As the day had been fraught with tension on all sides, she could hardly complain at Lucian's decision of giving one room to the ladies, and for him to share the remaining room with Denton. Still, she was bitterly discontent. They had so few nights together that losing even one of them seemed a heavy blow. Neither were they to have a moment alone, as they had arrived so late that dinner was served almost at once and everyone hurried off to bed immediately after.

They at least had the good fortune of securing the largest room, which had two good-sized beds. So, Matilda shared with Phoebe, and Mrs Frant and Pippin shared the other.

Though she was exhausted after the trials of the day, Matilda did not immediately fall asleep. Phoebe had snuggled into her, her soft curls tickling Matilda's chin, one little arm flung about her waist. Matilda hugged the child tightly and allowed herself the foolish indulgence of an impossible dream, of a future where she could stay with Lucian and they could give Phoebe the parents she longed for. A place where the real world never interfered. Her eyes prickled with the impossibility of it and she scolded herself for a fool.

Instead, she turned her attention to the events of the day, how very bold Phoebe was, and how her daring plan had not been dismissed by Lucian, but executed. He never treated the girl with condescension, always listened and valued her opinion. What a marvellous father he would be. Cursing herself, Matilda tried again to turn her mind to other things, and worried instead about the night when Flash Jack was due to meet Theodore Barrington at High Tor on the Heights of Abraham.

A confrontation between Lucian and his uncle seemed to her to be a recipe for disaster. It could only ever end in bloodshed and, whilst Lucian may well prevail, he did not need that stain upon his soul nor the taint that such a scandal would leave upon his reputation. At the very least she must be with him, he must not be alone when he faced that wicked man, and she swore that he would not be. No matter the cost.

Chapter 18

*We are having the most marvellous adventure
and are now travelling with a real
Highwayman. Though he is a villain and says
himself he ought to have been choked by a
hempen quinsy by now – he means hanged of
course – he has given his word of honour to keep
us safe. His honour seems as precious to him as
it is to my uncle, so I believe him. Flash Jack –
Jackie, he says I may call him – has also
promised to teach me how to pick a lock, though
I made him swear not to tell Uncle Monty. I
would never tell my uncle a lie, but I don't see
why I should tell him about things <u>before</u> I do
them.*

**—Excerpt of an entry by Miss Phoebe
Barrington to her diary.**

8th May 1815, on the road to Matlock Bath.

Matilda spent the entire day plagued by a dreadful sense of
unease. They would arrive at Matlock Bath that night and Lucian
would meet with the press at Liddon Mill the following morning.
She stared at the countryside beyond the window as the journey
progressed and the scenery became ever more dramatic.
Leicestershire, Mount Sorrel and Loughborough came and went
and the wide expanse of the River Trent, glittering in the afternoon

sun. The weather closed in as they reached Derby, and by the time they arrived at the Old Bath Hotel the skies were dark and forbidding as evening settled over Matlock Bath like a heavy wool cloak.

Phoebe, who had been in high spirits all day, had finally given in and was sleeping with her head in Matilda's lap. Matilda smiled down at her. In sleep, Phoebe's usual mischievous expression was replaced by a peaceful one, as innocent as an angel. She reached out and tucked a stray curl behind the girl's ear and stroked her satiny cheek. Saying goodbye to this funny child would break her heart as much as it would to turn away from her uncle.

Matilda blinked and forced herself not to think of it.

As the carriage finally rolled to a stop Matilda, looked up to find Lucian's gaze upon her, and upon the hand that protectively cupped Phoebe's head. Their eyes met and she saw something fierce and hot in the cool silver, but then a footman opened the door and Phoebe stirred, and the moment was lost.

Matilda admitted herself a little disconcerted to be shown into the hotel via a back door.

"We are incognito," Lucian reminded her gently at seeing her confusion. "And you ought not be here, but I know the manager, and we may rely upon his discretion. I have taken the entire south wing of the hotel to ensure our privacy, however."

Matilda nodded, wondering if she ought to care more for her tattered reputation. She wondered if the whole of the *ton* was abuzz by now. Word must have spread. It always did. Did the world know she was his lover? Did her friends, her brother? She waited for the burn of shame, but it did not come. There was regret for any pain or embarrassment she would bring to those she cared for, but all her friends were happily settled, and she could do them no harm now. She was as free as she would ever be to follow her heart, and so she would and, when it was over, she would travel and see how far away she could get from everything she loved most.

The Old Bath Hotel was large and luxurious, and the manager, Mr Elliot, greeted Lucian with an effusion of obsequious delight guaranteed to irritate him. Matilda watched, a little amused as Montagu surfaced, dealing coolly and efficiently with Mr Elliot, ensuring dinner would be served *as soon as it was convenient*—which the manager correctly interpreted as *at once*—and that the hot bath, which the hotel was famous for, be made available for the private use of the party should they wish it.

Dinner was excellent, but everyone was too weary to indulge in the hotel's attractions and so they were shown to their rooms. Matilda was not the least bit surprised to discover she had a room of her own, but took careful note that Lucian's bedroom was at the end of the corridor on the right. She bade him goodnight without a murmur of complaint, ordered a hot bath, and smiled a little at the suspicion in his eyes when she closed the door on him.

Matilda soaked in the large copper tub provided, the scent of orange blossom filling the room as she'd added a generous amount of her favourite bath oil to the water. Wishing once more that she had something a little more seductive to wear, she put on the lace nightgown and the wrap that went with it, slid her feet into a pair of dainty satin slippers, and brushed out her hair until it shone. She pinched her cheeks and gently bit her lips until they were rosy, and regarded her reflection with satisfaction. Well, it was certainly the best she could do in the circumstances. Snuffing all but one candle, which she took with her, Matilda cracked open her bedroom door and looked down the darkened corridor. All was quiet.

Her slippers made a soft shushing sound as she padded upon the thick carpet that led to Lucian's room. She paused for a moment outside his door, wondering if she ought to be more nervous about seducing him. No, she decided, smiling. That horse had certainly bolted. The irony of the situation did not escape her.

Lucian had been pursuing her for almost a year. The cat-and-mouse game they had played had put him firmly in the role of predator, stalking his prey. Yet now, here she was, willing to give him everything he'd wanted, and the wretched cat had turned tail. Well, it was high time she played the part of feline seducer. She'd been dubbed *The Huntress,* had she not? That wretched name had followed her, been whispered behind her back and flung in her face. It was well past time she embraced it. Better yet, it was beyond time to live up to it. She opened the door.

Lucian was sitting at the writing desk. He looked up as the door opened, his profile cast in gold by the single candle burning on the desk beside him. It was the kind of profile that ought to be stamped on a coin, the austere angles of his face, the straight nose and uncompromising line of his jaw that of a king or a Roman emperor. He turned to look at her, his expression revealing nothing, which told Matilda more than he could have guessed. It had not taken her long to realise that the less he showed—the harder he worked to hide any trace of emotion—the more deeply he felt.

"Ah," he said softly. "I thought you'd acquiesced a little too easily."

"Far too easily," she agreed, closing the door behind her.

Matilda turned back to study him: the long, elegant fingers holding the quill, the fine white shirt open at the neck, his cravat discarded, and his sleeves rolled up to show surprisingly powerful forearms. A result of all that sword play he must practice so keenly, no doubt. No one else saw him like this, without the armour he had fashioned from his impeccable clothes, lofty title, and that frigid silver glare. Far more than others of his rank, he held the world at a distance and allowed no one close, not even his equals. No one saw beyond the façade except for her and Phoebe. Even his trusted servants only caught glimpses of what they knew to be true of him, that he was kind beneath the rigid exterior, that he was not as cold as ice, but warm and loving, and that he wanted so much to protect those he loved, to keep them safe.

He set down the quill. "I won't do it, Matilda."

She did not pretend to misunderstand him. "Why not, when I want it as much as you do?"

His face darkened and he turned away from her. "Do not make me spell it out. You know as well as I do."

"Tell me, then. Tell me why I must walk away from the only man I shall ever love without knowing what it was to lie with him."

She watched his face closely, what little she could see of it, the haughty angle of a high cheekbone, the golden sweep of thick lashes cast down, the hard set of his jaw.

"Because you were not destined to be alone, Matilda. I will do everything in my power to ensure you can still marry well, have the family you long for—"

"No!" she cried out, the idea of another taking his place too impossible, too painful to contemplate.

"Yes," he said, and he spoke between clenched teeth. "I will not ruin you. I will not take what I cannot have without dishonouring us both."

"*No!*"

That one word was cried with frustration this time as she heard his cool, reasonable tone and wanted to shake him for it. She had always wanted that, she realised, to shatter his control, to make him give in to his emotions. She'd succeeded, she supposed, up to a point. Now he was drawing a line in the sand, this far and no farther, for at that point he would betray his honour. A sob rose in her throat as she realised he would not change his mind, would not give her what she wanted. He would force her to save herself for a man that would never exist, for there was no man that could take his place in her heart, in her life. Though she knew he acted for the best, though she understood his reasoning and respected it, it did not soften the blow. Regret and a bone deep sense of loss was all she could feel.

Matilda set the candle down, her hands trembling too hard to hold it steady now. The sobs racked her body, though they were silent cries, shaking her as another corner of her heart broke free, smashing to pieces. It would all be gone before this was over, but she'd known that.

"My love, please don't...."

As he came closer to her, she realised she'd gotten her wish. The facade had shattered, his expression betraying everything, laying open his heart, the tears in his eyes the mirror of her own. He pulled her into his arms, burying his face in her neck and breathing in deep.

"Don't hate me," he begged her. "Please don't. I know you should, but I cannot bear it. Let me love you the best I can, let me give you all I can allow myself, but don't make me hate myself for having loved you."

Matilda gave a choked laugh. "I could never hate you."

He took her face between his hands and looked down at her, amusement glittering in the silver.

"Little liar," he murmured. "You hated me once."

She laughed again, even as the tears streamed down her face and she shook her head, denying it. "I did not. I hated Montagu, I hated that damned title, and I hate it still, for it keeps us apart. I never hated *you*, Lucian, not from the first moment I realised who you really were."

"I am Montagu," he said, his words gentle but firm. "Don't separate us, for we are inextricably twined. Two flawed halves of a whole, and wholly in love with you, God help me."

"Yet you would see me wed another," she said, the pain of his words still raw.

"*See* it?" he repeated, his voice harsh with bitterness. "No. Not that. I should die before I saw the man who had what I could not. But you will marry, because your heart is too generous not to be kind to some poor fool who falls at your feet and begs for your hand. You'll marry and have children and, in years to come, I will be a memory that you take out from time to time and recollect like a story from a book you once read, a long, long time ago."

She wanted to rail at him for thinking her capable of that but he took her hand and held it tight, raising it to his mouth. She gasped as his lips pressed against her pulse, knowing it must flutter under the kiss like the wings of a panicked bird.

"You wanted memories," he murmured against her skin. "I shall give you something to remember."

Lucian lifted her up, sweeping her into his arms, and Matilda no longer wanted to argue the point. All she wanted was that this night should not end. She put her arms about his neck as he carried her to the bed, some distance this time as the room was large and opulent. It was not poor Mr Bennet with his modest income and the best room he could afford that held her, but the Marquess of Montagu, a powerful, wealthy man who was feared and admired in equal measure: Lucian, the man who had survived the ordeal of his childhood and kept his heart intact, and had given it to her.

He laid her down on the bed, the silver in his eyes glinting in the dim light of the room. She watched as he walked away and picked up the candle she'd brought, and then set about lighting every lamp and candelabra.

"I want to see you," he said in response to her enquiring gaze.

She ought to have blushed at that, she supposed, but she wanted to see him too. Her attention was avid as he stripped the shirt from over his head, wincing a little but moving easier that he had before.

"The wounds are healing nicely," she observed.

Lucian glanced down. "Yes."

"You'll have heroic scars to bear."

He laughed, a rather bitter sound.

"If only these little marks were the only ones." His eyes settled on her as he reached for the buttons on the fall of his trousers. "The deepest scar will be well hidden, but you will know it's there, love."

Matilda nodded. "I'll bear its twin."

Her breath hitched as he moved towards the bed, the candlelight casting him in gold. Would she have become used to this, she wondered, if they'd had a future together? Would she have been able to look upon him one day without feeling her heart pound, her breath catch in her throat? She'd never know, but suspected it was doubtful.

"I love the way you look at me," he said, as he lay down on his side, his head propped on one arm.

Matilda reached out and touched him, her fingers trailing through the scattering of golden hair on his chest.

"How do I look at you?" she asked.

He took her hand and raised it to his mouth, kissing her knuckles. "Like I'm everything you could ever want."

Matilda smiled. "That's because you are."

The smile left his eyes and he shook his head. "I'm not, but I wish that I had the chance to try."

"Don't speak of it," she begged him. "Not now. Make it go away."

She reached for him and he pulled her closer.

"I will," he promised.

He did, turning her onto her back and stripping off her nightgown and wrap before kissing every bared inch of her. He found places that made her quiver quite unexpectedly, like the sensitive skin behind her knees, the back of her neck. She discovered the astonishing pleasure of his warm tongue trailing over the curve of her bottom, loving her with exquisite tenderness, his hands and mouth seeking and caressing, bringing her to the peak over and again until she was giddy and exhausted.

"I can't, you wicked man," she protested, laughing and dazed as he returned to the tender place between her legs yet again. Surely, he couldn't command her body to respond with abandon any more than it already had. Could one die from an excess of pleasure? She must be in danger. "Lucian, I couldn't possibly!"

Yet she sighed happily as he ignored her objections.

"Yes, you can," he insisted, sliding a finger into the slick heat he'd stoked inside her and finding a tender spot that made her exclaim at the intense surge of bliss.

"Lucian!" she cried, clutching at the bedclothes as he licked gently at the delicate pearl of flesh that seemed to so fascinate him.

His finger returned to that magic place inside her and her breath caught as pleasure rippled through her yet again, bowing her body in a taut arc beneath him before the release took her, ever more powerful, racking her to her core and leaving her boneless and spent.

***

"So sleepy," Matilda murmured, her frustration at that fact apparent.

She looked up at him, battling to keep her eyes open, but Lucian chuckled and nuzzled at her neck.

"Sleep, love. I'm not going anywhere."

"No," she protested. "I won't waste another night."

"I'll wake you again in a bit, I promise. Just sleep for a little while."

Reluctantly, she closed her eyes, her breathing deep and even in moments. God, she was magnificent, so responsive to his touch, everything he had dreamed she would be and so much more, and he *had* dreamed of her.

Lucian stared down at her in wonder. He had been cataloguing every moment of this night, every soft moan of pleasure, the sound of his name cried out in ecstasy, every curve of her beautiful body, so he might remember it all when she was no longer his. She sighed in her sleep and he curved his body closer about hers as though he could protect her from harm. An ache filled his chest, so powerful it stole his breath. The worst harm that had ever befallen her, that *would* ever befall her, was because of him and he burned with sorrow and guilt because of it. He turned his face into her neck, breathing in the scent of orange blossom and fighting the swell of emotion that rose in his chest. She was so beautiful, and she loved him. How extraordinary that was. He had never expected it, never looked for it, assuming that love was not something he could ever experience for himself. He had read about it in poems and in novels with the curiosity of someone reading of a foreign land they knew they would never see with their own eyes, never expecting to find themselves there in reality. Yet here he was, and he wondered if it was a blessing or a curse.

When his parents and Philip had died, he had been cast adrift, his well-ordered world turned on its head. Until that day, he had known precisely what had been expected of them all, of Philip as the heir, and of him and of Thomas. All at once, his parents and Philip were gone, and suddenly the staff addressed him as they'd addressed his father, and all the lessons he'd heard his father give Philip became his to learn overnight. The book his father had written, detailing everything Montagu should be, became his bible, his talisman against failure, the only thing that made the ground beneath his feet feel steady.

He remembered his father's steward putting it into his hands the day he had received the news that his family was dead. His father was barely cold and Lucian, eleven years old, sat in the big leather chair in the study that had become his, reading of his duty with his stomach in a knot, trying vainly not to cry.

Montagu never showed emotion, and he was Montagu now.

That had been written among those first pages, with words like duty and honour underlined in thick black ink. Lucian had swallowed down his tears and made a vow to the dead, to himself, that he would make his father and Philip proud. He would not let them down. He would be everything Montagu ought to be. He would protect the title, his family, his brother….

Well, he had already failed his brother, and now this woman had shaken his world all over again. For this astonishing woman, he wanted to cast it all aside. He closed his eyes as he heard his father's voice: the lecture on duty, on marrying to further the interests of the title, and never for any other reason. How strange that he could remember the exact timbre of his voice, the deep resonating sound of a man used to blind obedience. Lucian did not think his sire had ever uttered the word *love*. He wasn't sure the man had even believed it existed. Certainly, he'd displayed no sign of it.

Lucian barely remembered his mother at all, past the fact that she'd been absurdly lovely, like a perfect china doll. She had always been a distant figure in their lives, austerely beautiful, fragile and untouchable. She detested noise or mess, and three small boys who were never anything but noisy and messy had held little appeal, so they seldom crossed paths. His father had been proud of her, Lucian remembered that much, like a fine piece of porcelain or a beautiful painting. He'd rarely seen them together, which made the fact they'd died together somewhat ironic.

It had been a typical aristocratic marriage, which had been considered a wild success by their kind: a marriage of power, money, and breeding that provided three healthy male heirs—for Thomas's sickly nature was a closely guarded secret. As far as the *ton* were concerned, they had been the perfect family. No wonder his father had been so damned smug, so bloody proud.

Lucian dared allow himself—as he had never allowed himself before—to imagine Matilda as the mother of his children, and had to slam the door on the image at once as too many unwieldy emotions rose inside of him. He drew in a shaky breath and forced the dream away before it could unravel what remained of his defences. No matter how he loved her, how worthy she was to be his wife, in the eyes of the world she would damage him, she would weaken the proud name that had stood for so many generations, and his father and Philip would turn in their graves.

Guilt clawed at his heart, weighing him down. Why could he not have this one thing—the only thing he had ever truly wanted—for himself?

He reached up to stroke Matilda's hair, sifting the golden strands between his fingers, and the fine scar across his wrist shone white in the candlelight. Lucian made himself look at it for the first time in almost eighteen years. He hated it, hated the proof of his weakness, feeling the familiar swell of shame. He had thought to escape his duty once before, overwhelmed by loneliness and the burden of responsibility. He had thought he could go through with it, but in the end he'd not been able to betray his family, his destiny, his father's wishes, even in the depths of despair. So Pippin had patched him up, and his uncle had never known that Lucian had almost done his work for him.

He would not let his uncle win, could not let his father and Philip down, could not let Thomas have died for nothing. There was no escape. The future of the title was both a noose about his neck and the thing he must live for.

Destiny.

He closed his eyes and breathed deep. Orange blossom, the musky scent of a lush female body, and something entirely unique to the woman in his arms enveloped him, chasing away desolation, for now at least. Her body's perfume was a heady combination that filled his senses and made him taut with longing.

"Matilda," he whispered, pressing his aching cock against the soft curves of her lush behind. "Matilda, wake up, love. I need you."

She sighed and turned in his arms, the flutter of her eyelids revealing a flash of blue like the glimpse of a kingfisher on a summer's day.

"Lucian," she whispered, tugging at his neck, drawing his head down for a kiss.

He took what she offered, demanding more, deepening the kiss as something like desperation stole over him. His breath caught as her hand slid down his body and curved around his arousal, already slick with his desire for her.

She broke from his mouth and kissed his jaw, trailing kisses down his neck, his chest, lingering to tease at his nipples, nipping with her teeth. He closed his eyes and let bliss steal over him, his mind growing hazy as her sweet mouth moved lower. With no other lover had he ever been anything other than in control. He'd preferred it that way until now, but with her everything was different. He spoke little to his bed partners usually, preferring deeds to words, but now he could not stop. Love words and endearments fell from his lips, and he would not have halted them if he could. She deserved to hear them, even though he had no right to speak them.

She had settled between his legs now, her warm breath fluttering over him, a heady torture she likely did not understand she was inflicting.

"Oh, God, please. Please, love," he begged her, beyond pride, desperate for her mouth on him. "I want you so much."

"Like this?" she asked, and gave him a tentative lick from root to tip.

Lucian's mind grew black and he swallowed a curse, clutching at the sheet beneath him, reacting like an innocent to that timid swipe of her tongue. The words that had fallen from his lips with such ease just moments earlier fled, leaving him stupid with shock.

"Yes," he rasped, the breath knocked from his lungs. "Oh, yes, just like… *Oh, God.*"

The decadent feel of her mouth closing over him was so overwhelming that he felt like a green boy, ready to spend at the first touch of a girl's hand.

"You like that?" she asked, the enquiry a little shy.

Lucian made a choked sound, somewhere between laughter and desperation. How did she do this to him? He'd been bored to death in recent years, the most skilled of lovers only ever bringing release, nothing more. Yet barely a touch of her mouth and he was on the brink, holding on for dear life.

"Yes," he managed, somehow dredging up the memory of what words were and how to use them. "Yes, I like that very much."

"Oh good," she said, pleased. "So do I."

Her words shot straight to his groin and the little sound of pleasure she made as she repeated the action was almost more than he could take.

"Oh God, oh God, oh, God," he muttered, praying that he could hold on. He did not want this delicious torture over before it had begun.

"You feel like hot silk here," she said conversationally, trailing a fingertip over him that made him shiver. "And I like the way you taste."

Lucian groaned and flung his arm over his eyes, clinging to sanity by a thread. The need to turn her onto her back and lose himself inside her was so powerful he could have wept with frustration and regret at the slightest provocation.

She returned her mouth to him, inexpertly but with growing confidence. Lucian concentrated on breathing, on holding tight to the forbidden, exquisite pleasure of this night that was to be as fleeting as a sunrise, the beauty of it imperfectly remembered, never living up to the stunning reality when it was brought to mind again.

"I want you inside me, Lucian."

The plea in her voice undid his control, what little of it remained, and he reached for her, pulling her into his arms, plundering her mouth. He rolled her onto her back, moving swiftly between her legs. She opened to him at once, welcoming him into the cradle of her body. Their bodies moved on instinct, ready to fit flawlessly together and he stilled, poised to slide inside, into the perfection he knew awaited him.

"Lucian," she begged, and he heard the plea in her voice, heard the urgent demands of his own flesh as he buried his face in her neck and breathed, steadying himself. "It's all right, please, I want this."

He closed his eyes, wanting to rage and curse as he shook his head, loathing himself for denying her anything at all when he wanted to give her everything. Yet this would not be giving but taking, and he could not, *could not* dishonour her so thoroughly, could not risk leaving her with child, and he did not have nearly enough control to promise he wouldn't let that happen.

She made a sound halfway between a laugh and a sob. "Damn you, Lucian, and your blasted honour."

"Yes," he agreed, utterly wretched. He turned onto his back, releasing her and more than a little surprised when she shifted close again. "I'm so sorry."

The words sounded hollow, pathetic, and he had never hated himself more.

"I know," she said, regret and forgiveness in her voice.

She moved over him, her hair tickling his chest as she pressed kisses to his skin, and his breath caught as she slid her body intimately against his arousal. He watched as she sat up, her hair a tumble of golden curls about her beautiful face, her blue eyes staring down at him with such love he felt his heart would burst. She bent and pressed her mouth to his and he gripped her hips, taking control, wanting her to take her pleasure with him.

She sighed and closed her eyes. He watched, imprinting the sight on his mind as she rocked against him until she cried out, clutching at his shoulders, and he could hold back no longer. He pulled her down to him and they clung together, shipwrecked in the storm until it tore them apart for good.

Chapter 19

Dearest Ruth,

I don't know whether you will be fortunate enough to intercept this message on your journey to London, but if you do, please come at once to Matlock Bath instead. Matilda is there and she will need us all.

In haste, with much love,

—Excerpt of a letter from Mrs Bonnie Cadogan to Mrs Ruth Anderson.

9th May 1815, The Old Bath Hotel, Matlock Bath, Derbyshire.

"I wish you could come too," Phoebe said with a sigh.

"So do I," Matilda replied. "I have wanted very much to visit the mills and see everything your uncle has been doing to improve them. But you must tell me all about it, so fetch your bonnet and gloves and get ready. You don't want to keep him waiting."

Matilda watched the little girl run off, looking up a moment later as Lucian came into the room. He stole her breath away as he always did, impeccably dressed and empirically handsome, he exuded power like no other man she'd ever known. She smiled at him as he came forward and took her hand, bowing over it and kissing her fingers, a courtly gesture that made her smile.

"Good morning, my love."

"You said that already," she observed, daring to remind him of how he'd woken her this morning and all that had followed.

"So I did," he said, the warmth in his eyes bringing an answering spark of heat deep in her belly.

"You're taking Phoebe with you," she remarked, tearing her eyes from him before the temptation to throw herself into his arms and disarrange his perfect cravat became too overwhelming.

"You disapprove?"

"No," she said, frowning a little. "At least, I don't think so, but... if it is a very dreadful place...."

Lucian nodded, understanding at once, as she'd known he would. "It is no longer the hellish place it once was, but it is not a comfortable place to be either, and so Phoebe must see it. We live gilded lives and it is dangerous to believe anything other than luck separates us from them. Phoebe must appreciate the privilege to which she has been born, and the responsibilities that come with it. It is no more fair that I cannot marry the woman I love than that they live the way they do, but it is the world we have been born to."

Matilda stared at him, a little surprised even after everything she had learned about him. "You believe it is nothing more than luck that stands between you and a beggar on the streets?"

He shrugged. "Luck, circumstance, whatever you wish to call it. An accident of birth, of fate."

He laughed as her mouth fell open, and she closed it with a snap.

"I have heard no one of your rank speak so, have heard no one who did not believe their blood, their breeding made them superior."

A derisive snort was his first response, and she saw the glimmer of Montagu in his eyes, haughty and aristocratic.

"Naturally, class yields advantages, a superior education being only a part of it. My blood is bluer than most anyone outside the royal family, but who decided I was born to be Lucian Barrington, and what sleight of hand might have seen me raised in a workhouse? I don't pretend to understand whether that be the hand of God, fate, biology…." He made a dismissive gesture, the heavy gold signet ring he wore on his little finger glinting. "But we all have two eyes, two hands, two feet, a heart, and all the other component parts that make us the same."

"I always believed you so high in the instep," Matilda said, shaking her head. "All the talk about the Barrington superiority, about breeding and power, but it never came from you, did it? You inherited it all."

He shrugged. "I was raised to believe it."

"Yet you don't."

"No more than you do," he countered. "You treated all your friends with the same kindness, the same extraordinary loyalty, no matter who they were or the circumstances of their birth."

"I had a good name once," Matilda said, her tone thoughtful. "One the *ton* welcomed, and it disappeared in the blink of an eye. Yet, I had not changed in the least. It is all a fabrication, these rules we have made for ourselves that entrap all of us one way or another. We should do well to throw them all aside."

"Would that I were that powerful. I would do it. I would change the world for you if I could," he said, such longing in his voice her heart ached. So, she smiled, trying to lighten the mood.

"Yes, I believe you would. What an extraordinary fellow you are."

Lucian chuckled, following her lead before their words led their emotions astray.

"Finally she realises," he said with a sigh, followed by a quirk of his lips that gave her a tantalising glimpse of one of those elusive dimples.

She laughed, wishing she could make him smile more often, that it wasn't such a fleeting pleasure, wishing she could chase away the loneliness and the burden of responsibility for good, not just for the matter of days that remained to them. His wretched aunt's ball was no doubt being planned with military precision. The nineteenth, she had said. That left ten days before Lucian announced his betrothal. Matilda wondered if he had already made his choice, and bit her tongue against the desire to torture herself further by asking.

Phoebe ran back into the room, neat and pretty in a simple dark blue spencer that matched her uncle's coat, and a plain bonnet with a blue ribbon.

"How handsome you both look together," Matilda said, steadying a sudden quaver in her voice as she noted the resemblance between them. It was not only in the way they looked, though the high cheekbones and fair complexions were certainly cut from the same pattern book, but in the tilt of their heads, a careless gesture of their hands, a grace and elegance in the way they moved that was inherently natural and could not be learned.

"We should look a matching set if you were with us," Phoebe observed, her smile falling as Matilda had to look away to blink back tears.

"Come, sweetheart," Lucian said, his voice soft. "We'd best go. We shall see you this afternoon, Matilda."

Matilda took a breath and composed herself, nodding and returning a smile that felt false and uncomfortable. "So you shall, and I expect to hear all about it."

Phoebe ran to her and kissed her cheek before hurrying from the room. Lucian stared at Matilda for a long moment but did not come closer, and she knew he did not trust himself any more than she trusted herself not to cling to his lapels and not let him out of her sight ever again.

"Goodbye," she said, hoping to make it easier for him.

He gave her a slight bow, the glimmer of a smile at his lips, and then he was gone.

***

Lucian suppressed a shiver as the carriage conveyed them closer to Liddon Mill. He did not believe in magic or ghosts, yet he felt the weight of all the wickedness done here as the mill came into view. Despite himself, he drew Phoebe closer and took her hand in his. She went willingly and he thought perhaps she sensed it too, though he had not told her the details of what had gone on here. Some truths were too vile for a child's ears, and he would protect her where he could.

She would not know, as he knew, of the abominations that had taken place here. It seemed impossible to credit, as the tranquil beauty of their surroundings was breathtaking.

The delightfully named Water-Cum-Jolly Dale ought to have been a place where children would run and play and laugh, but that had never happened here, though Lucian was striving to change that. These children had been stolen from London, orphans every one, and abandoned to their fates here by the 'Guardians of the Poor.'

Lucian's stomach had turned as he'd learned the story, how with the promise of learning a trade, Mr Burton had taken children on as indentured apprentices. The workhouses he'd taken them from had been happy as he'd paid for the children, and the children believed they would be taught a useful trade and so signed away their lives, though they could neither read nor write. For this, Lucian had discovered they'd endured hazardous work, rising at five am and working for fifteen hours Monday to Friday, and sixteen on Saturday, when an hour would be spent cleaning the dangerous machinery. They were starving and exhausted, so mutilations and fatal accidents had become commonplace, with illness and epidemics rife. The bodies were then taken away under cover of darkness and buried in unmarked graves. He'd done what he could, creating a memorial for those vanished in the night but it was a pitiful compensation for too many lost lives. Those poor devils that had survived Burton's barbaric regime had been turned off when they reached their late teens and returned to the tender mercies of the poorhouse. After all, there was a ready supply of little orphans, who were cheaper to feed and easier to control than their adult counterparts.

The corporal punishments for even the slightest misdemeanours were cruel and vicious, and had made Lucian sick when he had heard of them. It had been the hardest thing not to cut Mr Burton into tiny pieces when he'd had the chance, not to mete out his own justice, knowing whose hand had directed such treatment. If not for the risk of his uncle finding a way of using the crime against him, he would have.

Lucian took a deep breath as the carriage finally rocked to a halt and turned to look down at Phoebe. "Are you ready, sweetheart?"

Phoebe nodded, her little face solemn, and Lucian squeezed her hand.

"Then we'd best begin."

***

Matilda set her book to one side as she heard the door swing open. Lucian came in, holding Phoebe's hand, and one look at their faces told her everything she needed to know. She held her arms out to Phoebe and the little girl ran into them.

"Are you all right?" Matilda asked gently.

"I am," Phoebe said, sounding a little shaken. "But I hope that Uncle hurt that wicked man very badly. Very badly indeed."

Matilda hugged her.

"I believe he did," she replied, uncertain if that were the right thing to say to a small girl, but aware of Phoebe's sigh of relief at her words, at a little of the tension easing from her slender frame.

"We will put it right, won't we?" Phoebe said, looking to Lucian for confirmation. "It's already much improved, but Uncle will build new houses for the workers and make the conditions inside safer for them, and with better pay."

"Yes, love," Lucian said. "We shall do all of that, I promise."

"Would you like to take your bonnet and gloves off now?" Matilda asked, releasing Phoebe at last and tugging at the ribbons of the bonnet as Phoebe nodded.

"Yes, thank you, and I think I'd like to see Pippin."

Matilda nodded, smiling, aware that Pippin also provided excellent hugs. "Run along, then."

She waited until the door had closed and got to her feet, moving towards Lucian. "Do you need a hug too?"

He gave an unsteady laugh and nodded. "I do."

She held out her arms to him and he moved into them, resting his head upon hers with a sigh. "There will be no doubt of the story now. It will publish in every major paper all over the country, and Burton will be prosecuted for his part in it. God, Matilda, if ever a place was haunted…."

He shook his head as if trying to rid himself of the little ghosts.

"You will make it right," she said, believing in him. "And you will allow the ghosts to rest in peace."

"Such faith you have in me," he said in wonder, touching a finger to her cheek. "Like Phoebe, believing I can make everything right."

She returned a wistful smile. "Perhaps not everything, but this."

He nodded and held her tight until a knock sounded at the door. With a regretful sigh, he let her go and put some distance between them.

"Come."

To Matilda's surprise, Flash Jack walked in, looking about the lavish hotel room with his eyes almost on stalks. She wondered what he would make of Dern Palace when he saw it. He clutched his battered tricorn hat in his hands, silver rings glinting on his meaty fingers.

"The meetin' is all set up like you asked, lord," Jack said. "The fellow is holed up in some little cottage up on the heights, so there's no chance of him running into yon newspapermen. I got my fellows watchin' him close, though, just in case."

Lucian nodded. "You'll meet him tonight?"

"Aye, six o'clock, afore it's full dark. So, there's the matter of proof. I used that shirt like you said," he added, reaching into one of the capacious pockets of his greatcoat and hauling out a fine linen shirt, soaked in dried blood.

Matilda exclaimed with shock as Jack put out a hand to calm her.

"Oh, don't fret, lady. 'Tis nowt but pig's blood but on his lordship's own fine linen, to reassure the old man he was proper cut up. And you said you'd give me your signet an' all, lord."

Lucian nodded, giving Jack the benefit of one of his iciest glares. "I did, and I will expect it returned to me promptly, or our association will be a short one, as will your life expectancy."

Jack returned a reproachful stare, his haggard face settling as close to innocent affront as it was capable of attaining. "Ah, now, lord. I've sworn fealty an' I meant it."

"It's *my* lord," Lucian said coolly, tugging off the heavy gold signet with difficulty. "I am a marquess, not God Almighty, though you may not appreciate the difference if you renege on our arrangement."

Jack's mouth quirked.

"Aye, lord," he said gravely.

Lucian sighed and tossed the ring to him. Jack caught it deftly in a hand the size of a ham hock and tucked it into an inside pocket.

"Sure you don't want me just to cut his throat and be done with it?" he asked Lucian, a wicked glint in his eyes. "I owe it him, for bilking me, like."

"A tempting offer," Lucian replied dryly. "But I decided many years ago I would not allow him to make me in his own image. I will not change my opinion at this late stage of the game."

"The game?" Jack repeated, one dark eyebrow lifting.

"The game," Lucian agreed, his expression grim. "And a dangerous one at that. Do not underestimate my uncle and believe him to be the pleasant old man he appears to be. And he will appear so, I assure you, even though you know he ordered my throat cut. He believes you and your men are the only witnesses to his nephew's murder, the only ones who can implicate him. He will kill you without a second thought. Do not turn your back on him, or give him the opportunity."

"Ah, lord, preachin' to the choir, you be. Though I appreciate the concern. I'll be back soon enough, with yer famble cheat an' all my word on it."

He spat in his hand and held it out to Lucian, who looked at it with mingled disgust and outrage.

"Right," Jack said, wiping his palm hurriedly on his trousers. "I'll bid ye adieu."

Matilda watched as the big man hurried from the room and turned her gaze upon Lucian.

"Famble cheat?" she enquired with interest.

Lucian grinned at her, that mischievous look firmly back in his eyes. "I believe it is a cant expression for a ring."

"Ah," Matilda said, nodding her understanding. "The things one learns in your company, Lucian Barrington. I can hardly credit it."

***

The three of them had just finished dinner when Flash Jack returned.

"Show him in," Lucian said blithely to the rather incensed hotel manager, who had just left off protesting at having such a villain wandering in and out of his fine establishment.

Mr Elliot's jaw was rigid and determined until Lucian settled his icy gaze upon the man. After an uncomfortable moment, the manager blanched, bowed, and hurried out. Jack strode in a few moments later with a face like thunder.

"Bleedin' cheap-arsed scaly cove," Jack fumed as he approached the table. "Reckoned to give me twenty yellow boys instead of fifty for snabbling you, lord. As if I'd stick me neck in a noose for such a paltry return. I ought to have put him to bed with a mattock and tucked him in with a spade, the blackguard, but I did like you bid me, though it pained me sommat fierce."

"Mind your tongue, you old rogue," Lucian said mildly, pouring out a glass of wine and handing it to Jack, who brightened perceptibly.

"Beggin' your pardon, missus," he said to Matilda, belatedly swiping his hat from his head before turning to Phoebe and grinning. "Princess."

Matilda nodded and hid a smile.

"Good evening, Jack," Phoebe said. "We did warn you Uncle Theodore would cheat you. He's a very bad man."

"Aye," Jack said sourly. "You can't trust no one these days," he added without even a trace of irony.

Matilda caught Lucian's eyes though and saw the glimmer of amusement there.

"My ring?" Lucian said, holding out his hand.

"Oh, aye, the blighter wanted to keep that an' all, but I weren't havin' it, not when I was thirty guineas light on the deal." Jack's expression was one of righteous indignation as he fumbled about in his coat pocket and retrieved the signet ring, handing it back to Lucian.

"You've done well, thank you, Jack," Lucian replied, sliding the ring back on. "You will be rewarded as promised. Did you have any trouble?"

Jack shook his head. "No, but it was just like you said. Creepy old bast— devil he is, once you know. Like butter wouldn't melt in his mouth, but I know there was a pretty couple of barking irons under the table and he'd 'ave used 'em too, if I'd given him the chance. Old Jack's too canny, though, and we got away sharpish without giving him a chance at us."

"What did you tell him?"

"Just like you said, lord." Jack took an appreciative swallow of the wine. "Ah, that's nice, that is," he said, smacking his lips.

"Jack," Lucian pressed.

"Yes, lord, sorry. I told him I was gonna get cleaned up and come and visit the pretty lady what had been with you when I, er…." He paused, frowning as he looked towards Matilda and Phoebe.

"When you cut Uncle's throat?" Phoebe said helpfully.

"Aye," Jack replied, his face clearing. "Told him we had some business to settle, what with her not wantin' anyone to know she'd been with you and get caught up in some nasty scandal, and me wanting to keep me neck out of a noose. Told him we'd made a deal, but not what it was."

"Do you think he swallowed it?"

"Oh, aye. I left one of the boys there and he'll run ahead once the cove is on the move, but he'll be here tonight. Reckon he knows the lady has figured he was behind it, and he'll want to silence her."

Lucian nodded. "Very well. You will inform me the moment he arrives. I find I cannot wait to see the look on his face when he sees me rise, like Lazarus, from the dead. In the meantime, take Miss Hunt and Miss Barrington to their rooms and guard them with your life. My uncle is to get nowhere near them, do you hear me?"

"Aye, lord."

"No."

They both looked up as Matilda shook her head.

"No, Lucian, this won't do. Your uncle is bound to come armed, and you've already been shot once this month. Let us not risk another bullet, please."

"I should say not," said a voice from the doorway as Pippin came in. "I'll not want all the bother of patching you up again, my lord."

She walked up to the table, pursing her lips in displeasure as she looked Jack over. Jack returned the favour, though he didn't look the least bit displeased. His dark eyes twinkled appreciatively.

Lucian shook his head. "My uncle is expecting to deal with you, Matilda. He'll believe he can frighten you into silence with tales of scandal. When he realises his mistake, and that I am very much alive, he will be furious, but he will not shoot me in full view of the hotel staff and guests, for he will hang for it. So, we will have a little chat, and Jack and his men will escort him to the nearest docks, where I will have him returned under armed guard to India, and this time he will not be treated as kindly as before. He will not be coming back."

To Matilda's surprise, Jack gave her a reassuring smile.

"Don't you fret, lady. His lordship is right. The old devil can't do nowt in public and my men will guard him, don't you worry none."

Pippin made a scathing sound of disagreement, and Matilda frowned, equally unhappy at the arrangement and about to say so when raised voices sounded outside the door.

Lucian glared at Jack, who shook his head.

"It ain't your uncle. My men would have warned us," he protested.

Jack was right, and Matilda gave a startled cry of surprise as the door flew open and her brother appeared, followed in quick succession by... by *everybody*, apparently.

"Good heavens, Nate!" she exclaimed, getting to her feet. "What are you doing here?"

Nate advanced on the table, ignoring her completely and stalking towards Lucian, who stood slowly, his face expressionless.

"Bastard," Nate growled, his tone one of white rage. "Name your seconds."

"Nate!" Matilda shouted, pushing between the two men in the instant before Nate made a grab for Lucian's cravat. "Stop this at once!"

There was something of a scuffle as her brother was restrained between the Earl of St Clair and Gabriel Knight, and Matilda stared about her in astonishment.

"What is the meaning of this?" she demanded, uncertain whether to be touched or outraged at their interference.

"We've come to take you home, Tilda," Nate said, yanking his arms out of the men's hold. "Your reputation has been shredded by this bastard, and all the vile stories circulating the *ton*."

"That is *not* why we came," Alice said, glaring at her husband, running to Matilda and taking her hand. "We came to be with you, Matilda, because… oh, because we think you will need us. Nate is right, love. The stories are just awful, though Helena has assured us they are not true," she added, giving Lucian a doubtful glance.

"How could you?"

Matilda looked around to see Prue's husband, the duke, had addressed Lucian, though Prue was not beside him. Lucian was very still, his expression as cold and hard as she had ever seen it. He looked to Phoebe, who had gone to stand with Pippin and held out his hand. She ran to him and took it before he turned back to Bedwin.

"I would like my niece returned to her room before I am subjected to an interrogation."

"Oh, *now* you consider your niece, and wish to observe the proprieties?" Bedwin said with obvious loathing.

How dare he.

Matilda felt a furious protective rage overwhelm her tongue.

"Excuse me, your grace," she said, surprising herself with the force of her anger. "If you will forgive me for observing it, but this is none of your damned business. You don't have the first idea what is going on, and I am a grown woman. I make my own decisions. I do not need you, or you, Nate," she added, turning to glare at her brother, "to speak for me. Lucian did not ask me to come with him, any more than he asked me to follow him to Dern. Indeed, he has tried very hard to make me go away. *I* refused. *My* decision, and whilst I am beyond touched that all of you have come all this way… I do not need or want to be rescued."

"What hold do you have on her, you bastard?" Nate said in fury, as Jasper and Mr Knight grabbed hold of him again.

"Don't you talk to him like that!" Phoebe yelled, letting go of Lucian's hand and running to kick Nate hard in the shin. "Uncle Monty loves her, and she loves him."

Nate yelled, as much in shock as pain, Matilda thought, and Phoebe promptly burst into tears.

"Oh, Phoebe, love," Matilda said, her heart breaking as the little girl ran back to Lucian, who swept her up in his arms and held her tight, soothing her tears.

She turned on her brother in fury. "Nate, how could you?"

Nate glared at her, opened-mouthed.

"She kicked me!" he said indignantly.

"You insulted her uncle," Matilda retorted, folding her arms.

"Matilda."

Matilda looked around at the sound of the quiet voice and smiled with relief as Aashini stepped forward, flanked by her husband, Lord Cavendish, and her grandmother, Dharani. Matilda ran into the arms that were held open to her and had to work hard not to cry as Aashini hugged her tight.

"You look well, despite all of this," Aashini observed, her beautiful face calm as she let her go, holding Matilda at arm's length. "Are you?"

Matilda nodded. "I am. Thank you. But we do not have time for explanations. Aashini, you know what it is to fight a man who has wronged you, and Lucian is doing the same. We believe his uncle is a dangerous man and he's on his way here, and… and…. Oh, lord, it's all terribly complicated but, if you would just do as I ask, I think perhaps we can make things right."

"Then we will do as you ask," Aashini said simply. "Oh, but Dharani wishes to meet the wise woman that travels with you. And do not ask me how she knows of her, for she will not tell me."

"Pippin?" Matilda replied, surprised, glancing over at the woman in question, who was helping Lucian comfort Phoebe. "Of course, but later, there is no time now. Mr Barrington will be here soon."

Aashini nodded.

"If we do as you ask, will you come home with us, Matilda?" Nate said, looking as though he was fighting to keep his voice even. "If you come now, we might silence the worst of the gossip, if we all stick together."

"No."

"Yes."

Matilda swung around as Lucian's answer overlaid her own.

"No!" she said, her voice firm. "Ten days, Lucian. There are still ten days...."

"No, love," he said, shaking his head, though the calm tenor of his voice and his emotionless expression did not fool her. "Your brother is right. You ought not be here. I ought never to have allowed it, no matter what you or I wanted. We must now do everything we can to save you from this mess. I won't have you ruined."

Nate snorted in disgust, but held his tongue as Matilda shot a sharp-edged glare at him, clenching her jaw against all she wanted to say. She would not argue this now, before everyone. She still could not believe that nearly all her friends were here. Only Prue, who was too heavily pregnant for such a journey, and Ruth and Kitty seemed to be missing. A quick rap at the door was punctuated by the appearance of the narrow, pointed features of one of Flash Jack's men.

"He's on his way, Flash," the fellow called out.

"Right ho."

Belatedly everyone turned their attention to Jack, their eyes on stalks.

"Who the devil is this?" Nate demanded.

Despite everything, Matilda could not resist introducing them. "Nate, this is Flash Jack. Jack, my brother Nathaniel Hunter."

Jack's eyes lit up.

"Him what owns *Hunter's*?" he asked with obvious awe.

"Matilda?" Nate said faintly, clearly beyond astonished at her and the Marquess of Montagu keeping such company. "What the hell have you been up to?"

"You must forgive me," Lucian said coolly, setting Phoebe down, though he kept hold of her hand, his icy gaze settling on Nate. "But this must wait until later. Mr Hunt, if you wish to call me out, that is your right, but you must get in line. My uncle is about to discover I'm not as dead as he had hoped, and I'm afraid he will be rather disappointed. If you will excuse me."

"Lucian, no!" Matilda exclaimed, running to him. "Listen to me. You need witnesses. You need to get your uncle to confess to his crimes."

Lucian snorted. "He's not a fool, love. He never has been, more's the pity."

"No, but if he doesn't know anyone is listening, he won't be so careful," she said impatiently. "Have someone tell him I will meet him in the assembly rooms, and then you meet him there, if you must take my place. There are curtained balconies that overlook the floor. If a duke, an earl, a viscount, and all of us could confirm we had heard his confession…."

"He's not done anything, though, Matilda," Lucian said in frustration. "I'm still alive."

"But he paid to have you murdered! Flash Jack could testify to that."

Jack promptly turned as white as a milk pudding and shook his head.

"Don't worry, Jack," Lucian said, smiling a little. "I would not ask it of you."

"I would!" Matilda said furiously. "We could say we asked Jack to pretend to agree to it, not that he ever had any intention of going through with it. We could say he was already in your employ. You saved Galloping whatever his name was from the gallows, did you not?" Matilda turned to Jack and glared at him. "You owe him!"

Jack shifted from foot to foot, one large hand rubbing the back of his neck uneasily.

"What the devil is going on?" the earl's brother, Jerome, grumbled, clearly dissatisfied by the explanation so far. "Are you saying Theo Barrington paid this villain to murder Montagu?"

"Yes!" Matilda said furiously.

Everyone stared at Jack with wide-eyed alarm and Matilda watched, a little surprised as colour rose in Jack's cheeks.

"It were only business," he protested. "Nothin' personal."

"Oh, well, that's all right, then," the earl drawled, earning himself an elbow in the ribs from Harriet.

"Jack!" Matilda shouted, on the verge of stamping her foot.

"All right!" the fellow bellowed back at her. "All right, but only if you promise me, word of honour, I'll not get me neck stretched for me troubles."

"I swear it, Jack," Lucian said, holding out his hand.

Jack stared at it in surprise as the shock of the gesture rippled through the room. The nobility did *not* shake hands with anyone unless they were of equal rank. Montagu certainly didn't. *Ever.* It was a gesture of commitment, and even Jack seemed to realise it.

He took Lucian's hand, and the deal was made.

"And now I must go," Lucian said. "If you will excuse me." He took Phoebe over to Matilda, his silver eyes meeting hers. "Look after her for me."

Matilda heard the meaning in his words. Look after her, not just for now, but if anything goes wrong. Her heart clenched.

"You know I will."

He nodded, a look in his eyes that spoke more than anything he might have said before the present company.

"The assembly rooms, Lucian."

Lucian sighed, his lips quirking.

"Yes, love," he said obediently. "Jack, keep them safe."

"Aye, lord," Jack said, his expression grave.

Matilda waited until the door closed. "We must get to the balconies over the assembly rooms."

Jack shook his head. "They can go. I'm supposed to take you back to your room."

Matilda returned a scathing look.

"No," she replied succinctly, pleased to discover Pippin at her side, looking equally determined. "Perhaps you should take Phoebe up to her room, though," Matilda added, feeling wretched at the fury in the little girl's eyes.

"No!" Phoebe said, folding her arms. "I hid when Mr Burton came, I won't hide again. I'll be safe with all of you. Jack will look after me, won't you, Jack?"

The big man sighed and nodded. "Reckon it's more than my life's worth if I don't, princess."

"There, see?" she said, her wide, grey-blue eyes hopeful.

"She knows what manner of man her great-uncle is," Pippin said, taking Phoebe's hand. "I think she ought to come, if this big lummox swears to look after her."

"I'll look after all three of you," Jack said, puffing out his chest a little.

Pippin gave a huff, which suggested she'd like to see him try to protect her, before striding for the door.

"I've a few words for Theodore Barrington myself," she muttered. "Once his lordship has said his part."

"Save some for me," Dharani chimed in, gaining a measuring look from Pippin, who studied the tiny Indian woman with interest. "I cannot stand a bully."

"Nor I," Pippin replied, giving an approving nod. "Especially ones as would hurt a child."

"Ah, a kindred spirit. We shall right some wrongs, shall we not?"

Dharani's dark eyes flashed with anticipation and Pippin smiled in return, something like recognition flaring in her expression. All the hairs on the back of Matilda's neck stood on end. Pippin offered Dharani her arm, and the old lady took it.

"You heard of me?"

Dharani nodded. "We spent some time in Sussex when Aashini was a child. I heard whispers, rumours of the wise woman of Dern Palace."

Pippin's lips twitched. "And that interested you."

Dharani grinned.

"Come along, everyone," Matilda said, hustling them out, having no time to analyse the strange prickling sensation tripping down her spine as they hurried to the stairs that led to the upper floors of the assembly rooms.

Chapter 20

Dearest Harriet,

I hope this letter arrives before I do, but I know you will forgive me if it does not, for I am hoping we might impose upon your hospitality. Luke and I have been in Stratford-upon-Avon, staying with his mother who was taken ill. The miserable old cow has recovered now, and is just as awful as ever, mores the pity.

This wretched castle seems to be cut off from the world at large, but I have this morning heard of all the horrid gossip about Montagu and poor Matilda. I don't know what on earth we can do to help, but we are coming at once.

—Excerpt of a letter from Mrs Kitty Baxter to Harriet Cadogan, Countess of St Clair.

9th May 1815, The Old Bath Hotel, Matlock Bath, Derbyshire.

Lucian bided his time for some moments after he heard his uncle enter the grand assembly room. He was just a man; he reminded himself, an increasingly elderly one at that. He was not, in truth, the monster that had stalked his dreams as a boy, as monstrous as his actions had been over the years. He was the man who had turned Lucian's life into a game of survival, a living nightmare where nothing was as it seemed, but he was flesh and blood, just an old man, and this time Lucian would not be so merciful. He would not murder the man in cold blood, for he was not cut from the same cloth, but Theodore would lose any illusion of freedom. Lucian would keep him a prisoner in the comfortable home he'd given him, and closely watched, and heaven help anyone who thought to betray Lucian's trust again. Theodore would die alone and unremarked, and Lucian would not have to think of him again.

He drew in a deep breath and opened the door, stepping through. His uncle was standing by a table where two large candelabra had been set, their golden light spilling around them, but not touching more than a fraction of the grand room.

"Good evening, Uncle."

Theodore spun around, and for a moment Lucian experienced the satisfaction of having shocked him. His eyes grew wide, the colour leaving his cheeks, and then he roared with laughter and clapped his hands together, the sound echoing about the grand hall.

"Touché! Well played, my boy, well played. Damn me, but I really thought I'd won that time. Ah well, the game continues, I see."

"No," Lucian replied. "I have no patience left with this game, and you have no cards left to play. And so you will leave."

"Ah, but I do, or did you want the world to have proof that the lovely Miss Hunt is your whore?"

Lucian stamped down the impulse to react with difficulty, knowing it was what his uncle wished for.

"You will keep your filthy mouth from ever speaking her name again, Uncle, or I shall make it so you cannot speak at all."

He spoke calmly, aware that that his threats were more potent when there was no emotion underlying them.

"No," his uncle's voice was hard, angry now. "You are not the only one who tires of this game. You are in my way, Lucian, just as your father was in my way. I am tired of waiting around. I am growing older, and one way or another I will have that bloody title, the money, and all the things you, your father, and your brothers stole from me."

Lucian stiffened as his uncle pulled a pistol from inside his coat. Despite his words to Matilda, he'd known there was a risk that Theodore was mad enough to act out of impatience and anger. He would not get away with it, but that was small comfort.

"You will hang if you kill me now. There are witnesses, people who know you are here tonight. You will be the marquess as you desire so badly, but only until the day you die, which will be sooner than I believe you are hoping for."

"I don't think so," his uncle replied, smiling, his expression so gentle and sad that Lucian's stomach turned. "They've never come for me before, after all."

Lucian paused, an unpleasant sensation climbing up his spine. "What do you mean by that?"

Theodore grinned at him, and there was the flash of evil that Lucian had always known was there, but no one else had ever believed in. Only Pippin, and eventually Denton and Mrs Frant. He studied his uncle now, noting that his clothes were crumpled, and he'd not shaved. He looked ill, in fact, his face lined with strain, his colour high.

"I admit, I did not think it would work quite so admirably," Theodore said. "I mean, I only hoped to rid myself of your father. I never dreamed to remove two from the succession in one fell swoop. Though I always regretted that your mother died too. Such a beautiful creature, she was. I had hopes of taking her on myself."

Lucian's heart crashed about in his chest, and he fought to keep his breathing even.

"No," he said, shaking his head, refusing to believe it. Theodore was just a man, an evil man, not a monster of those proportions. Not like in his dreams. "No. It was an accident, a terrible accident."

"Of course it was an accident," his uncle replied, his tone soothing, like Lucian was a boy again. "I just… helped it along a little, is all."

"No," Lucian said.

His uncle smiled, removing a fleck of lint from his crumpled coat sleeve as if he were dressed in his finery for a grand ball. "Your father never took the least notice of his staff, did he? They were nothing more than insects, scurrying little insects, ants that did his bidding. I'm not like that, though. I noticed. I notice everything."

Lucian's chest was tight, a sensation like ice water trickling through his veins. Matilda had once said he had ice in his veins, had she not?

"I noticed that his driver liked a drop of brandy more than he ought," Theodore continued, smiling. "And so I gave him a little gift. A fine bottle it was, though dosed with opium, I'm afraid. And do you remember that evening, the evening your father and mother and brother went out to dine with friends, all dressed up in their finery?"

Lucian nodded, unable to speak. He remembered. He remembered every moment in terrible detail. His mother dressed up, jewels sparkling, impossibly beautiful, and him and Thomas standing on the steps, waving them off. He had spent far too much of his childhood wondering what had happened that night, how he might have stopped it, how he might have at least saved Philip from going out to that blasted dinner. He hadn't wanted to go; he only had because Father had insisted.

"Do you remember your little brother, Thomas, that night?" Theodore continued, a sad, singsong note to his voice that nauseated Lucian.

It made him want to stop the vile story before he could hear any more, and made him want to put his hands about his uncle's throat and just... *squeeze.*

"He always loved to give the horses a sugar lump. Do you remember, Lucian?"

Lucian didn't answer, a sickening cold sensation swirling in his guts. He didn't want to hear this.

"You should have seen Thomas' face when I finally told him he'd poisoned his father's horses. I told him that a week or so before he died, I believe. He was rather upset to discover that he was responsible for all those senseless deaths, because... I wasn't even there, was I?"

"No," Lucian said again, denying it, shaking his head even as he felt the truth in the dreadful words, even as the ground was shifting beneath him, like the tide dragging the sand from under his feet. "Oh, God. You did it...."

"I did," Theodore replied amicably. "Not that you can prove it. It was someone else who put the bottle of brandy in the driver's hand, someone else who gave little Thomas the sugar lumps, but I was the spider spinning his web, guiding all the little insects that your father took no notice of until I caught the big juicy fly I wanted. Three flies, as it turned out."

"You killed my family."

"Yes," Theodore said, all trace of that cordial old man gone now, his face hard and implacable. "And now, I shall kill you. You've caused a great deal of trouble, Lucian. I never knew a boy who was so hard to put an end to. Thomas was so much easier to destroy, but you... it was like there was some golden charm protecting you."

"That's because there was."

Theo spun around, though he kept the pistol pointed at Lucian.

"Pippin," Lucian said in alarm, fighting through the shock of everything he'd just learned. "For the love of God, get out of here!"

"No, my lamb. I told you there needed to be a reckoning, and it's about time."

"Oh, it's time," said a cheerful voice with a heavy foreign accent from above.

Lucian looked up to see the curtains on the balcony had been drawn back and all of Matilda's uninvited guests were there, including Lady Cavendish's grandmother, who seemed to be the source of the comment and was looking down at them as if she was watching a fascinating theatre production.

"I think you had best put the gun down, Mr Barrington," said the commanding voice of the Duke of Bedwin. "We have all heard your confession. There is nowhere to run."

As he spoke, Jack's men appeared by the doors at either end of the assembly room, pistols glinting in the dim light from the candles. Lucian raised his hand, telling them silently to wait, not to shoot unless there was no other choice.

He saw the implacable look in his uncle's eyes and knew what he meant to do. If Theodore would die, either here or on the scaffold for murder, he may as well take Lucian with him.

"Put down the gun, Mr Barrington," Pippin said, her voice and her presence startlingly impressive for a cook.

Lucian smiled at her, remembering all the times she had looked out for him, all the small kindnesses and the hugs he had needed so badly after his parents and Philip had died... *had been murdered.*

"Go away, Pippin," he said softly. "I don't want you hurt."

Pippin snorted. "He can't hurt me, the old fool. He's not nearly clever enough for that."

"Matilda!" shouted a male voice from above.

"Lucian!"

Lucian turned once again, looking behind him this time as Matilda flew through the door, running towards him while her brother roared with helpless terror from the balcony.

Bloody hell!

"Jack, you useless bastard," Lucian shouted in fury.

"I didn't see her go," Jack called down.

He had a tight hold on Phoebe, however, thank God.

"Get Phoebe out of here!" Lucian shouted, his heart thudding uncomfortably. Good God, he'd not have Phoebe see him killed before her eyes.

"Aye, lord."

"No!" Phoebe screamed, kicking and biting and thrashing madly in the big man's grip. "No, I won't go!"

"Lucian!"

"Damn you, Matilda," he cursed as she flung herself at him. "What the devil are you thinking?"

"She's protecting you, Lucian, because she loves you," Pippin said, smiling. "Like her friends have come to protect her."

"Hell and the devil, you're all mad," he exclaimed, pushing Matilda behind him.

A low chuckle echoed around the dimly lit space. He looked up again and saw Aashini taking her grandmother's hand and the woman gesturing for Helena to take the other. Pippin stared up at her and the old woman nodded. The hairs on the back of Lucian's neck prickled.

He turned back to his uncle.

"You murdered my family. It was all you, and now they all know it. I would have let you live, but you'll hang now. Whatever happens."

"Ah, well," Theodore said with a shrug. "I'll be the marquess for the duration of the trial. The Mad Marquess has quite a ring about it, doesn't it, my boy?" He grinned, an expression that made Lucian's skin crawl. "My word, how your father would have despised the scandal, not to mention the end of our illustrious line. That's why he hated me. You know, that don't you? Because our mother was a whore. She'd gotten her heir and forgot to secure a spare before she leapt into another man's bed. Our father never said a word, naturally, didn't want a scandal, but they all treated me like I was diseased, a rotten limb that ought to have been cut off, so I cut them off instead."

"I'm sorry," Lucian said, thinking only that he ought to keep him talking. "I had no idea."

"Or what?" his uncle sneered. "You'd have been different? You'd have treated me with respect?"

"Yes," Lucian said. "I would have. We loved you, Theodore. Thomas and I loved you. That would never have changed, no matter what."

"Liar."

"No," Lucian said, shaking his head. "Upon my honour."

His uncle's face whitened, though high colour remained on his cheekbones. He looked ill, but his lips thinned into a taut line, his grip on the pistol firming. "What's done is done."

"No!" Matilda cried, her arms wrapping about Lucian's chest, over his heart, trying to protect him. "No, don't hurt him."

Lucian tugged her hands away and watched Theodore raise the pistol higher, only relieved that Phoebe and Matilda would be safe. If he died now, his uncle would hang, and Phoebe and Matilda would make a new life for themselves. He would die knowing what it was to love and be loved, and that was more than he'd ever hoped for. Matilda clutched at him, trying to protect him even now, but he held her firmly behind his back, feeling her trembling against him.

"Yes, Theo, what is done is done, and it cannot be undone," he said, his heart thudding too fast. "But you could stop now, before you make it worse."

Theodore shook his head, a febrile glint in his eyes. "No, it's too late."

"It is," Pippin agreed, something in her voice that made Lucian uneasy. "Far too late."

He glared at her, wondering now if she was trying to get him killed.

"Pippin," he said, pushing Matilda back again as she struggled to move out from behind him.

"Too late!" called Aashini's grandmother, her words echoing Pippin's, eerie somehow.

His uncle was sweating now, breathing hard as he looked between the two woman, alarmed. "What the devil are they on about?"

Lucian stared at them too, just as unnerved as his uncle at the certainty in the women's voices.

"Pippin?" he said, and Pippin just smiled at him, calm and reassuring.

"I told you she looks after you."

"Pippin," he warned, angry with her. "Don't be foolish, not now."

He jolted as Matilda gave a soft laugh, something like relief in her words. "Pippin is a wise woman."

A strange prickling sensation crackled down Lucian's spine, even though he knew it was all nonsense. Matilda spoke again, her voice louder this time, surer.

"One of her ancestors was hanged for a witch. Did you not know that, Mr Barrington?"

"Matilda, shut up, love," Lucian muttered, wishing these blasted women would get themselves to safety, but he saw something that looked very much like fear in his uncle's eyes, and wondered at it.

"You got it, didn't you?" Pippin said, a confident note in those words, such a hard edge to them that Lucian felt a little daunted himself. "All those years ago. I knew you did. I warned you not to come back again, didn't I? I told you what the price would be."

"Nonsense," Theodore said, though a hunted look flashed in his eyes.

"Got what?" Lucian asked, looking between Pippin and his uncle, who was tugging at his cravat.

"Shut up, boy!" Theodore shouted, struggling to raise the pistol again as his hand trembled.

He pulled the cravat from his throat and wiped his face with it. Lucian tugged Matilda behind him as she tried to break free once more.

"I told you, sooner or later," Pippin said, sounding incredibly smug. "Time's up. That old heart of yours is giving in, like I said it would. Only a few beats left now."

Theo staggered and clutched at the arm that held the pistol, a cry of pain leaving his throat. The gun went off, the report echoing around the vast room as screams rent the air, but the bullet had buried itself in the polished wood floor, and the pistol clattered to the ground as Theodore fell to his knees.

"You did this," he said, staring at Pippin, wide-eyed with terror.

"*Me?*" Pippin said, scoffing at the accusation. "I'm just an old woman."

"An old woman," Aashini's grandmother echoed from above, satisfaction in the words. "Just a silly old woman."

Lucian looked up, staring at the women, all hand in hand, looking down upon his uncle with fierce concentration. No. That was... ridiculous. His gaze swung back to his uncle as Theodore gasped and clutched at his chest, falling backwards, his face a rictus of agony. And then... he was still. No one moved to help him.

"He's gone," Matilda said, holding Lucian's hand tightly. "He can't hurt you anymore."

"He killed my family," he said, too numb to take anything else in. "It was him. My parents and Philip. It was all him."

"I'm so sorry, Lucian, so terribly sorry, my love."

"Uncle! Uncle Monty!"

Lucian turned as Phoebe ran at him full tilt and he swung her up into his arms, holding onto her as tight as he could, turning her away from the sight of the dead man.

"It's over, sweetheart. It's all over." His voice quavered and he breathed in deeply, inhaling the scent of her, soap and innocence and all that had been good in his life.

"Yes," she sobbed, burying her face in his neck. "The monster is gone. Pippin killed him."

"He's gone," Lucian agreed, hardly believing it himself. "But it was nothing to do with Pippin, love. His heart gave out, that's all."

Phoebe shook her head. "No. It was Pippin, with all the ladies, especially that Indian lady in the pink silk. I want to meet her. Can I go and talk to her now?"

"Not now, my lamb, perhaps in the morning. You come along now," Pippin said, as Lucian set Phoebe down. "It's late and there's been far too much excitement. Time for a nice hot bath and bed, I think, whilst the grownups sort out all the unpleasantness. You come with me and I'll have some warm milk and biscuits sent up for us. I think we've earned them."

Lucian watched, too shocked to say or do anything at all as Pippin led Phoebe away.

"His heart gave out," he repeated numbly as Matilda squeezed his hand. "I could see he was ill when he arrived. It was just his heart...."

"Yes, love," she said, giving him a placating smile. "Come away now."

Lucian went with her, suddenly exhausted. All he wanted was to go to bed and take Matilda with him, to curl his body tightly around hers and know that they were safe. For the first time since he was eleven years old, he and those he loved were safe. He wanted to sleep with Matilda in his arms, knowing that were true, and he knew he could not. He would never hold her that way again. Her brother and her friends were here. They had come for her, come like a rampaging army to save her from harm, from him. They loved her and wanted to protect her, and so did he, so he must let her go. No, not *let* her. She would not go willingly, she was too brave for that, too loving. He must make her go. His soul howled with misery at the idea, such pain in his heart he imagined he would follow his uncle to the same demise, for surely it could not endure such damage.

"What is it?"

He looked up to find Matilda studying him with concern, only then realising he had stopped moving.

Lucian shook his head, staring at her, committing her beautiful face to memory.

"I love you," he said, wanting to say more, wishing he had words enough to explain everything he wanted, everything he felt.

She moved closer and pressed a soft kiss to his mouth, tender and lingering, ignoring the furious growl from behind them. Her brother, no doubt.

"As I love you," she whispered.

Lucian nodded, accepting that, even though it was too extraordinary to be true, and made himself move on.

Chapter 21

My Lord Marquess,

I am writing to beg your forgiveness for the part I have unwittingly played in the actions of your uncle, Mr Theodore Barrington. He and I have been friends for decades, and never in my wildest dreams had I imagined him capable of such despicable acts. I am shocked and saddened and feel a burden of guilt and responsibility for all that has passed. Unhappily, I believed everything he told me of you and did not once doubt his sincerity. I cannot imagine what you have endured these past years, but if there is ever anything I can do to make amends, you may consider me your ally.

—Excerpt of a letter from Mr Charles Adolphus, Baron Fitzwalter to The Most Honourable Lucian Barrington, Marquess of Montagu.

10th May 1815, The Old Bath Hotel, Matlock Bath, Derbyshire.

"Stop looking at me like that," Nate protested, setting down his teacup with a clatter. "I'm protecting you, for heaven's sake."

Matilda glared at her brother from her position at the window, unimpressed.

263

"Well, aren't you lucky I didn't protect Alice from you, Nathanial?" she said, her voice dripping sarcasm. "How fortunate that I believed her to be a grown woman, capable of making decisions of her own, or things might have worked out a little differently for you."

"It's not the same," Nate insisted, and she heard the anger in his voice. "I wanted to marry Alice, not to ruin her."

"You would have ruined her, though," Matilda shot back, too furious to be reasonable. "If not for Lucian, but I suppose you'll forget about that, just like you'll forget how she would have been raped at Vauxhall Gardens if not for his intervention. Yet, you persist in seeing what you want to see, casting him as a villain."

"Oh, please don't argue," Alice said miserably, caught between the two siblings.

Nate had the grace to look uncomfortable, at least. He sighed. "I admit he's been maligned, and I can't imagine what kind of life he must have lived, but still, Matilda. You know how he treated you. He let the *ton* ruin you... he helped them do it."

Matilda shook her head, knowing she could not tell him about Thomas, about the circumstances of his death and how Lucian had worked to protect his brother's name. "You know nothing about it, Nate. You don't understand, and I can't explain without breaking his confidence. Why won't you just believe me when I tell you he is a good man, that he loves me?"

"If he loves you so bloody much, where is his proposal?" he demanded, slamming his fist down on the table so that the china jumped and rattled.

The thin wail of a baby crying sounded from the room next door. Alice shot her husband a look of sheer exasperation before hurrying to her son.

Matilda sighed, weary of this argument which had been raging from the moment she'd sat down to breakfast with her brother and Alice. Nate had ensured they had moved her bedroom close to their suite of rooms last night without her knowledge, and she was seething with fury. He had guarded her like a dog with a bone, and she wasn't certain she would ever forgive him. Worse yet, Lucian seemed complicit in his actions. She could feel him pulling away from her, putting distance between them, forcing her to leave him. Though she'd known it was inevitable, she had not seen it this way. She had imagined their last days together to be bittersweet, spent with each other, snatching every second of every day in each other's company, until the night of that damned ball, when he would step beyond her reach for good.

"It's a fair question," Nate said, though his voice was gentle.

Matilda stared out of the window, at the stunning countryside laid out before her. It promised to be a lovely day, the sunrise painting the sky in shades of gold, but for now an ethereal mist clung low to the ground, giving the landscape an unreal, fairy tale quality that was quite enchanting.

"It isn't a fair question, or at least it might be, for Mr Bennet or someone like him."

"Who is Mr Bennet?"

Matilda smiled and shook her head. "It doesn't matter, only that Lucian isn't Mr Bennet, he's Montagu, and unless you were bred to be Montagu, you would not understand what that means. It is not merely the expectation of a nobleman to marry well, it is laden with the burden of guilt and responsibility he feels for the dead, to honour their memories, to make them proud and fulfil the destiny they set out for their family generations ago. Especially now, after the damage his uncle has wrought to the family name."

"So, he cannot marry you," Nate said, his voice grim.

Matilda shook her head, tracing a pattern in the fogged up window pane, a witch's heart with a crooked tail. "He won't be able to keep it all quiet, and in truth I'm glad for that. People should know what he has endured, how badly they misjudged him, but now he must marry quickly, to some perfect young lady who will help him repair the damage that has been done."

"Then you must leave him, Matilda."

She did not answer, could not as the truth of his words burned in her throat. She heard him move, felt his hands on her shoulders as he turned her around to face him.

"I'm sorry, Tilda. I would do anything to save you from pain. Anything at all, but there is no escaping this. Your name is being dragged through the mud, and there is little we can do to repair it, but we must try, love. Think of Alice and Leo, if you won't consider your own future, consider how difficult it will be for them to be seen with you if you don't mitigate the damage."

"I know," she said, feeling the misery rise in a wave, swallowing her whole. "B-But…. Oh, God, N-Nate, it *hurts*. I love him s-so much and it h-hurts so badly."

She could not hold back any longer and the tears came then, ugly and too powerful to stop. She clung to her brother as sorrow threatened to pull her under.

"I know," he said, holding her tighter, and she heard his voice crack as he rocked her like she was a child. "I do know, and I'm so sorry. So terribly sorry, but there is nothing else we can do. We must go."

Matilda sobbed harder, barely noticing as the door opened.

"Oh, love."

She looked up, blinking through her tears at Ruth, who hurried towards her and held her arms open. Matilda let her brother go and fell into them, feeling more arms going about her as other women pressed closer, enclosing her in a circle as they gathered near.

"We're here, darling," Helena whispered, hugging her too. "And we'll look after you, we all will. You'll not be alone, I promise. Prue wanted to be here so much, but Bedwin wouldn't let her travel since she's so close to her date. She's waiting for you."

"And I'm certain Kitty is on her way too," Ruth added.

"But the rest of us are here now," Bonnie said, finding Matilda's hand and squeezing it tightly. "And we'll ruin anyone who says a word against you, won't we ladies?"

"We will," Jemima said, looking as if her heart was breaking.

"Absolutely," Harriet agreed, her voice muffled as she blew her nose on a large pink handkerchief.

"Indeed, we will," Aashini said, her beautiful eyes filled with sorrow as they met Matilda's.

Matilda laughed, despite everything. The pain was too overwhelming to be eased, but her friends were here with her, lending her their strength, their comfort and support, and that meant the world, that meant the difference between enduring alone, and surviving.

"I love all of you," she said, somehow forcing the words out though her throat was aching, too tight to swallow.

"As we love you, Tilda," Minerva said, tears streaming down her face. "And we'll protect you and keep you safe. We always will."

She nodded and accepted the handkerchief that Jemima pressed into her hands, wiping her eyes.

"We're coming with you," Jemima said. "Back to London. The carriages are almost ready to leave."

Matilda straightened, panic lancing through her. "So soon, but... oh, but I must go to him, I have to say goodbye, I must...."

"Oh, love," Ruth said sadly, her voice trembling. "I'm so terribly sorry, but he's gone."

Chapter 22

My dearest love,

I hope you can forgive me for leaving as I did. You must believe me a coward, and it is no more than the truth. I could not say goodbye to you, Matilda. I do not have it in me to say the words to your face and walk away. I would only need to see the tears in your eyes and my resolution would fail me, even as it fails me now.

I know what loss feels like, my darling. What it is to have the world you relied upon swept away and to be left adrift, yet I have never known pain like this. How I shall endure it, I do not know. I will wear the pain of my loss like a hair shirt, so I might always remember the joy too, the extraordinary privilege of being loved by you. Perhaps my only saving grace is that I know I was never worthy of it, though I wished to be more than anything.

If there is such a thing as another life, as Pippin insists there is, I shall find you again, and perhaps in that lifetime, we shall find a way.

I cannot imagine how I will look Phoebe in the eyes and explain this to her, or if she will ever forgive me when I cannot forgive myself. I pray she does not hate me.

There will never be another in my heart, my love, my soul grieves for all I must turn away from. I wish it were otherwise. I am yours, always.

M.

—Excerpt of a letter from The Most Honourable Lucian Barrington, Marquess of Montagu to Miss Matilda Hunt.

***

Lucian,

There is nothing I can say. Of course I forgive you, though I feel you have stolen from me the last days of happiness that I will ever have. Yet I understand how the dead weigh upon your soul, how they shape your life. Only remember that life is for the living, my love, and try to find some measure of joy. It does not soothe my heart to know you will be as wretched as I am. I love you too much to want you to feel such pain.

Live, Lucian. Live for Phoebe and for those children who you make this sacrifice for or else what was the point of it?

I sometimes wonder if you have ever contemplated your heir as anything more than an abstract idea. Have you ever considered that he will be a child, <u>your son</u>, and that you will love him as you love Phoebe, that you will want to protect him and will wish for his happiness *more than for your own? Don't bring him into the world with nothing but duty and honour as his purpose in life. Don't condemn him and all those who follow him to live as you have done. There is more. We know there is so much more.*

Goodbye, Lucian.

I will love you always.

Yours ever,

Matilda.

—Excerpt of a letter from Miss Matilda Hunt to The Most Honourable Lucian Barrington, Marquess of Montagu.

16th May 1815. Dern, Sevenoaks, Kent.

Lucian took the letter out for the tenth time that morning alone, sliding it carefully from the breast pocket of his coat. The writing had been blurred in places when it arrived and now it was near illegible. Not that it mattered. He knew it by heart. After he smoothed the rumpled paper, he traced the shape of her name with his finger.

He had known it would hurt to leave her, had known it would feel like dying, and yet he had not expected it to be as bad as it was. Each day the pain only grew worse as the realisation that another day would follow, and another, and still more, and not one of them would bring him her smile, the sound of her laughter, the scent of orange blossom and the soft press of her lips.

Lucian closed his eyes against the exquisite pain that cut through his heart, jolting as the door to the library swung open and Great-Aunt Marguerite came through without so much as knocking. He got to his feet, turning his back on her, wiping his eyes and tucking the letter away before she could make some barbed comment about sentimentality. He might just kill her if she did.

"The ball is in three days, Lucian," she said, with no preamble. "As you are incapable of deciding, it is past time I helped you to come to the point. I have chosen three girls, and I will have an answer as to which one you will take as your marchioness."

"Go away, Marguerite," he said, struggling to reach for the ice with which he was so used to freezing out that which he did not wish to feel.

The trouble was, Matilda had melted it all away, and the knack seemed to escape him now. His emotions were in turmoil, forever too close to the surface, ready to spill over, and he did not know how to make it stop.

"I will not go away. This vile gossip about Theodore, not to mention that... that *woman*...."

"*Don't.*" Lucian swung around, fists clenched, and his aunt took a step back at whatever it was she saw in his eyes. "Don't you dare speak of her."

Marguerite hesitated, but put her chin up and one by one set down three small framed pictures on his desk.

"This," she said, pointing at the first painting. "Is undoubtedly the best choice available. Lady Constance Rivenhall, daughter of the Duke of Sefton. She is an heiress, bringing fifty thousand pounds, plus the association with Sefton, and a wealth of property that is hers via her mother's line. It would be the match of the century, Lucian. Not to mention that she is young and pretty, and that she has four brothers. Good, fertile stock."

"Get out."

Marguerite froze in response to the icy command, her finger suspended over the second painting.

"Lucian," she said, though her voice was a little less certain than before.

"Get out!"

He roared the words with such fury she leapt in shock. Marguerite paled, picking up her skirts and rushing from the room with a swish of black bombazine. Lucian stopped by the desk and stared down at the paintings, at the pretty painted faces of his future bride, whichever one he wished to choose.

With an incoherent howl of rage and pain he swept his arm across the desk sending everything smashing to the floor. He stared at the destruction for a long moment, breathing hard, before turning towards the brandy decanter. The heavy crystal stopper hit the fireplace with a satisfying smash as he snatched up the decanter and strode from the room.

***

17th May 1815. Dern, Sevenoaks, Kent.

"Uncle?" Phoebe poked her uncle's shoulder uncertainly.

She knew he wasn't dead because his chest was rising and falling. It had given her a shock when he'd not come home last night. She had persuaded Denton to come with her to find him at first light and now the sun was higher. Denton was waiting with the pony and cart, as she was aware her uncle wouldn't want anyone to see him like this, and he was most certainly foxed. She had realised where he must have gone when she'd found the empty decanter in the stables last night, but it had been too dark and she knew he just wanted to be alone, so she said nothing about it and had taken the decanter back to his study. Still, she had felt a deep surge of relief to find him sat under the great oak tree on Mast Head.

When he'd taken her away from Matlock Bath without letting her even say goodbye to Matilda, Phoebe had been angry with him. For a very short while, she'd wanted to punish him, until she saw that he was being punished already. She had heard the people talk about broken hearts before, but she'd never thought you could actually see one.

You could.

"Uncle Monty, wake up. You've been out here all night."

His eyelids opened reluctantly, the silver grey of his eyes dull as he tried to focus on her.

"Bee?"

His voice was thick and scratchy, and Phoebe blinked back tears.

"Yes, it's me."

He groaned and clutched at his head.

"I'm afraid you must have a terrible headache," she said, reaching out to stroke his blond hair. "Pippin is making something to make you feel better."

He gave an incredulous bark of laughter that was not the least bit funny and made her heart hurt. She hugged him, throwing her arms about his neck.

"I'm sorry," she said. "I miss her, too. Dreadfully."

He nodded and held her tight, the scent of brandy and a damp night out of doors clinging to him. When he spoke, his voice was unsteady. "I want her back, Bee."

"I know."

He put his head in his hands, and Phoebe bit her lip. It seemed so simple to her, but she knew the rules that grown-ups lived by were not so easy to cast aside. Pippin had explained it all to her, but it still made no sense.

"He'll be my son," he said, the words slurred and not entirely clear.

"Who?" she asked, confused.

He looked up then and reached out to touch her cheek. "You mean the world to me, Bee. You know that, don't you?"

Phoebe felt her eyes prickle with tears, and she nodded. "Yes."

"I'll love him like I love you."

"Who?" she said again, not understanding.

"My son," he said, his voice fierce. "My heir."

"Oh."

His expression grew fierce and tears glittered in his eyes. "Why must he make this choice, and his son too? Why must I?"

"Uncle?" Phoebe stared at him, not quite understanding what he was asking, only that he was hurt and angry because he loved Matilda and the world would not let them be together.

He stared out into the light of a new day, the sunrise glinting in his eyes, turning the silver to gold.

"*No*," he said suddenly, the word so certain and forceful that Phoebe jumped a little. He reached out and took her hand, holding it tight. "Will you help me, Phoebe?"

"Of course," she said at once, as if that had even been a question he needed to ask. "But help with what?"

He scrubbed his hand over his face, his beard rasping beneath his palm. She had never seen him quite this dishevelled before, unshaven, dressed in his shirtsleeves, his clothes rumpled and dirty. He looked up then, his eyes focused, the sense of certainty that she had always relied upon renewed.

"Are you afraid of ghosts?"

"Yes," she admitted. "I am."

He nodded, gripping her hand. "So am I, Bee, but maybe… maybe together, we can face them."

She nodded, determined to be brave, no matter what. She'd do anything if it meant bringing Matilda back into their lives.

"We can. I know we can."

Phoebe helped to haul him to his feet and then pretended to be interested in picking flowers for Pippin as he disappeared into the undergrowth to be sick. He looked dreadful when he reappeared, but the light that had dimmed in his eyes since they'd left Matlock Bath was shining again, and Phoebe's heart gave a skip in her chest. She ran to him and took his hand, and he smiled down at her.

"Ready?" he asked softly. "We have little time, and I will need your help."

"I'm ready for anything," she said, beaming at him.

"Thank God for you, Bee," he said fiercely, picking her up and hugging her to him. "Thank God for you."

***

17th May 1815. South Audley Street, London.

"Who's a handsome boy then? Yes, you are."

Matilda smiled as she watched Prue cuddling baby Leo over the growing bulk of her own pregnancy whilst Alice looked on with an indulgent smile.

"Have another, Tilda," Bonnie urged, trying to press another of tiny little delicacies that Ruth's marvellous cook had sent around to tempt her appetite.

Matilda shook her head. "No, thank you, Bonnie. Not just now."

All of her friends had set up some kind of schedule, which meant that she was never alone. They had filled her house with the sound of their chatter, Helena playing on the pianoforte, Minerva and Harriet discussing some obscure book that made no sense at all to anyone else. Even Kitty had arrived and was bickering with Bonnie over which of them should get to eat the last *pain á la duchesse*.

Today they were all here, every one of the Peculiar Ladies that she had watched as they made friends and fell in love, discovering their own strengths and everything they were capable of along the way. If she had the energy, she might begrudge them their happiness, for she was no saint and, though she would not allow herself to become bitter, she resented that she had been denied what they had. She was too weary for resentment, though, for anything at all. A strange lethargy had settled over her like a damp wool blanket, and she did not care enough to fight free of it.

So she watched her friends, grateful for their presence but not really a part of the proceedings, of the conversations and plans for the future. She would be, she promised herself. One day she would go back to the world and remind herself that there was joy to be found, adventure even once her travels began, but not now. Not yet.

Distantly she was aware of her butler speaking to Ruth but paid it no mind until a small and familiar face was right in front of her.

Matilda blinked. "Phoebe?"

"Oh, Matilda!"

Matilda put her arms out just in time as the girl launched herself towards her, throwing her arms around her neck.

She held her tightly for a moment before letting her go. "Whatever are you doing here, my love?"

Phoebe stood straight again and smoothed out her skirts, her little face growing serious. She pursed her lips as if she was remembering just what she must say. Taking several large gilt-edged cards from the pocket of her pelisse, she handed them to Matilda.

"Those are invitations for you and all of your friends for the ball. You must come. It's very important. Uncle will make everything right, but you have to be there."

Matilda blinked at her. "What do you mean?"

"I cannot tell you any more than that," Phoebe said, her grey-blue eyes filled with anxiety, her little gloved hands twisting together. "Only you have to promise to come. He can't make it right if you don't come."

"Oh, but," Matilda protested, shaking her head. "I... I can't love. He will announce his engagement and.... No. No, I'm sorry, it's...."

She shook her head and Phoebe looked panic-stricken. The little girl stared around the assembled company until she saw Helena.

"Helena!" Phoebe ran to her and took her hands, tugging at them urgently. "She must come," she beseeched. "She simply has too. Please. *Make* her!"

Matilda shook her head at Helena, warning her not to try, but Helena was staring at Phoebe, a little frown between her eyebrows.

"She's right," Helena said, and in that moment Matilda hated her just a little.

She hated that she was happily married to the man she wanted, that nothing had kept her apart from Mr Knight, despite the inequality of their status. Helena turned to her, though, not allowing her to escape.

"It is the best way of getting it over with. We will all be there to support you, Matilda, and if Montagu can help you, he should. Besides, you have still to complete your dare."

"Oh, your dare," Kitty said, eyes wide. "I don't even know what it is."

"To do something that frightens her," Helena said, smiling a little at Matilda.

"Oh, that was one of mine," Ruth exclaimed. "Though I must admit, I was thinking more of picking up a spider or climbing a tree."

Kitty snorted and rolled her eyes. "Well, it would get the dare done, and show all those stupid gossips that the Peculiar Ladies do not bow down to their stupid ideals. We don't care for the *ton*, or for its rules; *we* shall make our own."

"Oh!" Phoebe exclaimed, clapping her hands together with delight. "Oh, what a marvellous idea. There, see Matilda, you must come."

Matilda looked around at her friends, searching for one of them to support her in saying that it was a terrible idea.

Aashini reached out and took her hand. "Sometimes, we must face what frightens us most of all before we can move on, Matilda. Once it is done, you'll know there is nothing that will break you, that you can overcome anything. And, if Montagu really has a plan to help you, should we not give him the chance? You trust him, don't you?"

"Yes," she said, though she wondered why he would put her through such an ordeal, when he knew what it would cost her.

"And we'll all be with you," Jemima added, smiling at her. "You won't be alone, Tilda."

Matilda drew in a deep breath and returned her gaze to Phoebe.

"It seems I am outnumbered," she said, trying to keep her voice light and hearing the bitterness there all the same. "You may tell Lucian I will be there."

The relief in Phoebe's eyes was dramatic, the smile that wreathed her pretty face so wide that Matilda wondered at it. Perhaps she had been arrogant in supposing she was important to the child's life, that she would be missed, for the little girl seemed thrilled to have arranged this for her uncle. Yet, Phoebe knew what this ball was for, and had hated the idea of Lucian marrying anyone else. Matilda was too tired and miserable to consider it any further, though, and gave the girl a kiss on the cheek and watched her leave.

Well, she would see Lucian once more. She would endure the stares and the gossip of all those invited who were desperate to glimpse Montagu's bride-to-be and his mistress in the same room.

Let them look. For that one night, she would hold her head up and act as though she and Lucian were nothing more than friends, as though her heart had not been torn from her chest, and if Lucian could repair her reputation, let him.

It really didn't matter either way.

***

Phoebe ran down the steps, waving at Jack in the driver's seat before she climbed into the carriage, where her uncle was waiting for her.

"Well?" he demanded, his expression taut with worry.

"She's coming!" She squealed, jumping up and down in her seat.

"Oh, thank God." He sat back and let out a harsh breath and then laughed. "Well done, Phoebe. I don't know how you did it, but thank you. Thank you so much."

"Oh, it was easy. She still has a dare to complete, like the ones her friends did, and they told her this would be the challenge."

"What was the dare?" he asked, frowning.

"To do something that frightens her."

She watched his face darken, his blond brows draw together, and she shifted, moving to sit beside him and take his hand. "It will be all right, and you're frightened too, aren't you? So it's fair."

He turned and looked at her and gave a little huff of laughter.

Emma V. Leech

"Terrified," he admitted.

"Well, there you are, then." She grinned at him, relieved as his expression eased.

"There we are, then," he said, smiling in return, and then his face fell again, and he tightened his grip on her hand.

"How was she?"

Phoebe bit her lip and shrugged.

"Like you," she said.

He nodded, falling quiet for a moment. "Bee, what if—"

She rolled her eyes and grabbed hold of the silver-topped walking stick he often carried when in town. She rapped smartly on the ceiling of the carriage, turning back to him as it moved out.

"Stop worrying," she ordered, wagging a finger at him. "You scared Great-Aunt Marguerite so badly she won't come near you again. She doesn't know a thing, and neither does anyone else. It's all worked out, you just have to do as we planned, so stop fretting about it."

He snorted and sat back, shaking his head.

"Oh, well, if you say so," he remarked, and she knew he was only being sarcastic because he was nervous.

"I do. Everything will be just fine. Better than fine," she amended sternly. "It will be perfect."

"Perfect." He nodded, holding her gaze. "Yes."

"So, now we have to see the Duchess of Bedwin."

He groaned and put his head in his hands. "Well, it was your idea," she retorted.

"I know," he muttered.

"She's still with Matilda at the moment, so that means you have time to take me to Gunter's."

Lucian snorted. "Oh, is that right?"

"I've earned it, don't you think?" She grinned as he laughed at her smug expression.

"I do. You may have enough chocolate ice to make yourself ill, with my blessing."

"Excellent. And then we shall go see the duchess."

Her uncle sighed. "Let us hope the duke is not at home when we do. Bedwin will be unbearable."

Phoebe shrugged. "You're far more unbearable when you want to be. You'll win any contest of that nature, you always do."

He grinned at her, an expression she had seen so rarely of late that her heart leapt. "Thank you, Bee. It's nice to know you have such faith in me."

"Of course," she said, hiding her smile, and beside herself with anticipation.

Chapter 23

Oh, I'm so excited I could burst!

—Excerpt of an entry by Miss Phoebe Barrington to her diary.

19th May 1815. Montagu House, St James's, London.

Lucian paced up and down the length of the library. Everyone was here, awaiting him, awaiting his announcement. Phoebe sat in the chair behind his desk in a pretty pink dress, satin slippers swinging back and forth, watching him placidly.

"Anyone would think you were nervous."

Lucian shot her a narrow-eyed glare, and she just grinned at him.

"Dreadful creature," he muttered. "You're supposed to be giving me words of encouragement."

"Pfft. You don't need those. Do you?"

He laughed a little and shook his head. "No, though I must confess to being somewhat—"

"Afraid?"

Lucian nodded and Phoebe jumped down from the chair, walking towards him.

"She loves you."

He let out a breath. "Yes."

"And you love her."

"I do."

"Well, then."

Lucian laughed and crouched down to hug his niece tightly. "Quite so, love, and you'll be watching, won't you? Cheering me on?"

"Of course!" she exclaimed. "Pippin and Mrs Frant and I are going to sneak up to the balcony and watch from up there."

There was a knock at the door, and Lucian's heart thudded hard in his chest. Despite everything, he felt sick. He straightened and went to the mirror, checking his reflection before turning back to Phoebe.

"Well?" he asked, waiting as Phoebe gazed at him critically, walking a circle about him.

"Very handsome," she declared. "She'll be so proud of you. I am."

"Thank you, Bee. I don't know what I'd do without you."

"Me either," she said with a sigh, lips quirking.

***

This had been a mistake. Nate was white-faced with rage and was being given a stern talking to by Jasper, who was trying in vain to calm him down. He'd just about stopped Matilda's brother murdering some fool who'd thought to make a sly remark about her relationship with Montagu.

"Everyone is staring at me," she said.

Aashini gave a soft laugh. "Darling, of course they are. You look incredible in that gown."

Matilda snorted and stared down at it. It was lovely. The beautiful pure white cotton gauze was embroidered with sequins and gilt thread. It was sheer and ethereal. She'd admired it once in a shop window, and Lucian had offered to buy for her—to buy it for his mistress. She had bought it for herself and had it made into the most stunning gown she'd ever seen. It had cost her a small fortune, and she'd done it for him. At the time it had been to rub it in his face, the fact that she did not need or want his money, that she could not be bought. Now, she simply wanted him to see it, because he had wanted to see her wear it, and she wanted him to remember her like this.

She sighed and turned back to Aashini.

"That is *not* why they are looking," she said bitterly.

Everyone was staring at her because they believed she was Lucian's mistress. They knew he would announce his betrothal tonight and she knew all eyes would turn to her, waiting for her reaction to the news.

Lady Constance Rivenhall was here and kept sending scathing glances over at her. Matilda was strongly tempted to scratch her pretty eyes out. No doubt she was Lucian's intended bride. Marguerite had always favoured her over the others. Her stomach roiled and she took a deep breath.

She would *not* cry.

"It's not the only reason they are looking," Aashini replied with a slight smile. "It's not the only reason they look at me either."

Matilda nodded and reached out, taking her friend's hand and gripping it tightly.

"Oh, look, there's Prue and Bedwin," Bonnie said.

Matilda turned to see the couple hurrying towards them, though hurrying was a relative term, as Prue looked like a ship in full sail, with her voluminous skirts doing little to disguise her pregnancy, magnificent and every inch a duchess as she swept through the crowd.

"Matilda!" she said urgently, her eyes alight with excitement.

"Prue, slow down, love," Bedwin muttered, steadying his wife as she gasped for breath.

"Prue, what is it?" Matilda said, a little alarmed.

"Oh, Matilda!" Prue dabbed at her eyes with a lace-edged handkerchief, and then took hold of her hands. "Darling, it will be all right...."

"The Marquess of Montagu."

Prue's words were halted as Lucian was announced, and the crowd stilled, every head craning to see him standing at the top of the stairs that led down into the vast ballroom. Matilda's breath caught, her heart speeding in her chest, so fast she feared she might do something as appalling as swoon. Aashini held her hand, gripping tightly.

"We're here, Matilda," Helena said quietly beside her.

Matilda knew they were. She could feel the presence of all her friends, their love for her giving her courage, giving her the ability to look up across the ballroom and meet those silver eyes, perhaps for the last time.

Oh God, he was magnificent, resplendent in his evening dress, the severe black-and-white a perfect foil for his austere beauty. He was staring at her as though he could not look away, and colour rose in her cheeks.

Stop it, Lucian.

Why was he staring at her so? He was supposed to be saving her, not making it worse.

Suddenly, he was moving with the grace of a panther, stalking down the stairs to the ballroom, the crowd parting before him like prey before a predator. A murmur of delighted anticipation shivered over everyone assembled as they saw where he was going, expecting a delicious scandal to unfold before them as he headed for the woman they knew to be his mistress.

"What is he doing?" Matilda demanded, clutching at Aashini's hand.

"Courage, Matilda," Prue commanded. "It will be all right."

Matilda wanted to look to her friend, to demand how she knew that, but she could not take her eyes off Lucian as he moved towards her. He looked as cool and untouchable as always, icy and remote, and yet she saw something in his eyes as he drew closer, something that had her heart skipping about in a mad dance behind her ribs. A flash and glitter of light under the glare of the chandeliers above drew her gaze to his lapel. The ruby-and-diamond witch's heart he had sent her once before sparkled against his black coat. He had told her she had bewitched him when he had sent her his gift. She had refused it and sent it back again. Why on earth was he wearing it?

Matilda had no time to consider the question, as he was standing right in front of her.

"Good evening, Miss Hunt," he said, giving her a deep and respectful bow, as the murmurs of shock and delighted fascination grew louder.

"What are you doing?" she demanded, her voice quavering.

He smiled at her and reached for the brooch at his lapel, unpinning it.

"You scolded me the last time I tried to give you this," he said, holding the little heart in the palm of his hand. "You said a gentleman would never presume to send a gift of such value and intimacy to a lady unless they were betrothed. Not if he had any respect for her."

"And I was right," she said, furious now, too conscious of the hundreds of eyes upon them, watching him ruin her for good, announcing to the world the intimacy of their relationship.

To her horror, he stepped forward and put his hands to her gown, earning a gasp from all corners of the ballroom. Matilda was too shocked to react at all, only dimly aware of Bedwin fighting to restrain her brother. With perfect calm, Lucian pinned the heart to the neckline of her dress, his gloved hands brushing her skin, making her shiver with longing. His silver eyes glinted with satisfaction as he looked back at her.

"You have my heart now, Matilda, for always, and this time I should like you to keep it."

"Lucian," Matilda began, bewildered, tears gathering in her eyes as the declaration made her heart sing even as he cast her from society for good, and then he did the most extraordinary thing.

Matilda watched, astonished, as Lucian Barrington, the Marquess of Montagu, got to one knee.

***

His hands were shaking so badly he hadn't the faintest idea how he'd pinned the bloody brooch on. When he'd seen her standing in the ballroom, proud as a queen, surrounded by those who loved her, he'd thought his heart would give out. He had always had to turn away from the things he'd wanted, to choose his duty over pleasure, over happiness. Could he really make a different choice this time? His chest had been tight with panic, with terror, for surely she could not be his, surely he had not the right to such a prize. Everyone here thought him the prize to be won, but that was because they were fools who could not see the truth.

God, she was beautiful.

The gown she wore sparkled beneath the light of hundreds of candles, making her look as if she was ablaze, a fairy queen dressed in starlight. He was certain he hadn't breathed from the moment he'd seen her, his lungs locked down as he crossed the floor. All the world was watching and, if she refused him, he would be a laughingstock, ridiculed until the end of time. Which was why he had to do it this way, why he had to give her the power when he had taken that from her all those years ago. He loved her too much to do anything less than this, a public declaration of his love and esteem before all of those who had scorned her. Let them think less of her now, the woman who had brought the Marquess of Montagu to heel, and to his knees. He would crush anyone who so much as glanced at her with anything less than respect.

He could see the hurt in her eyes as he grew closer, her confusion, and prayed she would not run from him, but stand sure and proud until he could make clear his intentions.

"You have my heart now, Matilda, for always," he said, aware that his voice trembled as much as his hands. "And this time I should like you to keep it."

"Lucian...." She broke off with a gasp as he got to one knee before her and reached for her hand.

"My love," he said, as everyone else disappeared and only she was before him, the woman who had melted the ice, who had stood beside him while he faced the monster from his childhood and all the ghosts that haunted him. "I have been dying a little more each day without you. I cannot live this way, cannot endure another day without you by my side. *Please,* Matilda, would you do me the very great honour of becoming my wife?"

Her mouth fell open, her beautiful blue eyes glittering with tears, wide with astonishment. She said nothing, just stared at him in silence, and Lucian's heart thudded unevenly as panic bloomed in his chest.

"Say yes, Matilda!" cried a little voice from the balcony above. They both looked up to see Phoebe hanging over the balustrade, waving madly. "Say yes!"

Matilda gave a startled laugh and turned back to him, her smile wide and glorious.

"Yes," she whispered, and Lucian let out a breath of relief. Louder this time, she said it again. "Yes. Yes, yes, yes!"

"Oh, thank God."

He got to his feet as a shriek of horror echoed around the ballroom, loud even over the din of excited chatter and shock. Lucian saw his aunt Marguerite fall back in a swoon with a billow of black bombazine.

"Oh, dear," Matilda said, meeting his eyes.

Lucian could only grin at her as he took her hands, holding on tight. He felt it was an expression that would not leave his face for some considerable time.

"I love you," he said, wishing they were alone, wishing he could take her in his arms and kiss her, never let her go.

"I love you too," she replied, though she looked bewildered. "Oh, but Lucian, are you sure? Your name, the title—"

Lucian shook his head.

"My son," he said, squeezing her fingers. "I won't condemn my son to the life I have led, the life my father expected of Philip. I would have him be happy, be loved. I would know how that feels too, Matilda. For always."

She made a choked sound, tears spilling over, and Lucian felt his heart squeezed with happiness. He made a gesture to the orchestra, instructing them to play.

"Might I have the pleasure of this dance, love?"

"Yes," she said, laughing and crying at once now, as he led her onto the floor. She wiped her eyes with a gloved hand, trying to compose herself. "Oh, my word, Lucian. Everyone is staring at us. They think you've run mad."

He shrugged and took her in his arms. "There is nothing new there, my love, and I don't give a damn. You and Phoebe are all I care about. The rest of the world can go to the devil."

The music swelled and he pulled her close, too close for propriety, gazing down at this extraordinary woman, knowing that all the world could see what he felt, could see how hard he had fallen, and not caring if they did. He had spent his entire life hiding his emotions, keeping himself apart, but not in this moment. He would not hide this, for it was too vast to be contained, and it burned too fiercely to be hidden under layers of ice.

"I could not bear the pain, love," he said, wishing he could take her away with him now, this instant. "I have missed you so dreadfully. I did not know what to do with myself."

"Me either," she said, gazing up at him. "I was so furious with you for leaving me as you did."

He nodded, his heart aching for the hurt he had inflicted. "I'm so sorry. I was too afraid to stay. I knew I could not tell you goodbye, so I ran. But I have come back again, Matilda, and I shall never leave you again. You are all I want, only you, and I shall do everything in my power to make you happy."

"You have," she said, laughing, the joyous sound of it making his heart light. "And I know you always will."

***

The music ended but Lucian did not let go of her. He just stood, gazing down at her, such an expression in his eyes that she could not look away.

"The dance has ended," she whispered, but he shook his head.

"It's only just begun."

She laughed again, giddy and bubbling over with happiness.

"If this is a dream, don't let me wake up."

"Never," he promised. "We'll dream it together."

Together. They would be together. He'd asked her to marry him, in front of everyone! Suddenly they were surrounded by her friends, and there was a babble of noise, laughter, and happy tears as she was hugged and embraced, and Lucian's hand was shaken. Matilda choked back a laugh as Gabriel Knight slapped Lucian on the back, and Lucian slid her a glance, amused by the friendly, masculine gesture. He would have to get used to such things as friends now. The thought made her heart light. She would make him happy. She would fill that vast palace with the sound of laughter, with their children and their friends, and the sounds of a life lived to the full.

Lucian reached for her, taking her hand and holding it tight, as if he feared she might yet escape him. Out of the corner of her eye, she saw Lady Constance Rivenhall and her mother stalking from the ballroom in disgust. She ought to feel sympathy perhaps, but… not tonight.

"Oh, Tilda!"

Matilda staggered, forced to let Lucian's hand go as Bonnie hugged her fiercely, almost toppling them both to the floor.

"That was the most romantic thing I've ever seen in my entire life," Bonnie proclaimed at the top of her lungs, pressing a hand to her heart in dramatic fashion as their friends laughed, and all the old tabbies tutted and shook their heads.

"Oh, I say, love," Jerome protested. "Steady on. I'm dreadfully romantic, too."

Bonnie snorted. "Yes, of course you are," she said, her voice soothing. "But still… Montagu of all people, down on one knee. Oh, my word, I nearly swooned."

"Me too," Kitty sighed, shaking her head. "Oh, Matilda, people will talk of this for decades. What a conquest, and the look in his eyes…! My word, he adores you."

"He does," Matilda replied, deciding she had every right to feel smug in the circumstances. "Prue!" she exclaimed, seeing her friend draw closer.

"Congratulations," Prue said, beaming.

"You knew," Matilda accused her.

Prue looked just a little sheepish and extremely pleased with herself as she nodded.

"I did, but only since yesterday afternoon, and I was sworn to secrecy. I wanted to give you a hint before he arrived, but this sweet darling was causing me some difficulty," she said, smoothing a loving hand over her belly. "And so we were late leaving."

"But how?" Matilda demanded, perplexed.

Prue drew her to one side, lowering her voice. "Montagu came to see me with an idea of how your story, his story, could be told as it ought to be. So that people would fall in love with you as he did—his words."

"You're going to write it," Matilda said, breathing the words in wonder.

Prue nodded. "Only with your blessing, Matilda, and you shall both read every word before it is printed. Of course, I shall change all the names and it won't be published as your story, but everyone will know, all the same."

Matilda stared at Prue. "He really wants that?"

"He wants people to know how you suffered, how badly misjudged you were, and how brave and strong you have been. It's rather clever, actually. I think if I do it right—which I will, naturally—it will not only repair your reputation, I think you will be the most beloved figure of the *ton*. I am a marvellous writer, after all," she added gravely, her eyes twinkling with mischief.

Matilda laughed, delighted by her, by the idea, and by Lucian for having thought of it.

"Yes, you are," she said, embracing Prue as best she could around her bump. "But won't you be a bit too busy for such things soon?"

Prue shrugged.

"Honestly, I'm too fat to do anything else at the moment, and I've been bored to tears. Your story has everything: triumph over evil, star-crossed lovers. Oh, and that scene this evening." Prue gave a contented sigh. "If I had a pen to hand I would begin at once."

Matilda laughed, well aware she was quite serious. "Well, whatever makes you happy, love. I can't wait to read it."

She looked up as Lucian approached again, his eyes alight with pleasure.

"If I could steal you away for a moment, Miss Hunt," he said, reaching for her hand. "I believe there is someone who is dying to speak to you."

"Of course," she said at once.

He made their apologies and guided her out of the ballroom and through to an elegant blue salon. The moment the door opened, there was a shriek of delight and Phoebe ran towards them.

"She said yes!" she shouted, launching herself at Lucian who swept her up and spun her around, laughing with such unabashed joy that Matilda was in danger of sobbing again.

"She did, Bee, with a little help from you."

"I was going to say yes anyway," Matilda protested, wondering if her heart could stand any more; it was already bubbling over with happiness. "I was just a little stunned."

"Well, whatever the cause, you nearly gave me heart failure," Lucian admitted, kissing Phoebe's cheek. "I was dying there, Bee."

"I know, I could tell," Phoebe said gravely, hugging his neck. "That's why I gave her a hint."

"Congratulations, my lord."

Lucian looked around to see Pippin, who had been hanging back, giving them their time together. He set Phoebe down, and she ran at once to hug Matilda, while Lucian moved towards Pippin. Matilda watched, holding Phoebe to her and feeling her throat grow tight as Lucian drew the woman into a hug.

"I have never said so in as many words, Pippin, but I don't think I would be here at all, if not for you." He looked down at her and leaned in, kissing her cheek. "Thank you. Thank you for always being there, for every little kindness, for all the hugs and the biscuits, and words of comfort. I shall never forget them, and there will always be a place for you at Dern, for the rest of your days, Pippin, for I could not be parted from you now."

"Ah, Lucian," Pippin said, dabbing at her eyes with a handkerchief as he released her. "It was my pleasure. I was proud to do it, and I'm proud to serve you, my lord."

Lucian nodded and Matilda snatched at the handkerchief that Phoebe offered her with relief.

"Pippin," he said, his voice more serious now. "There is one thing that has been bothering me. What did you send my uncle?"

Pippin's face darkened and she folded her arms. "When you sent him back to India, I had something put in his trunks. Along with a letter, warning him that his heart would tick down like an unwound clock if he ever set foot in England again."

"What, Pippin?" he demanded.

Pippin pursed her lips. "You don't believe in my nonsense, my lord, so there's no point in you knowing, now is there?"

"It was heart failure," he said stubbornly. "He always indulged too much in rich food and wine. A lifetime of such overindulgence would have taken its toll."

"Probably." Pippin shrugged, though the glint in her eyes did not tally with her reply.

Lucian turned to Matilda for confirmation and she bit her lip, uncertain of how to reply. "Well, it was odd, Lucian," she said apologetically. "Helena said they all felt the strangest sensation when they held hands. Something powerful."

"Of course it was powerful," Pippin scoffed. "They love you, Miss Hunt. Whatever you believe, my lord, Theodore knew what I had predicted. He knew he'd lost the game, and he could feel how protected you were, both of you. Perhaps the knowledge made his heart give out, perhaps it was something more…. What does it matter? He's dead, and life is for the living. For you both. Make the most of it, my dears."

Lucian laughed, shaking his head. "We will, you old witch. So don't go casting any spells on us."

Pippin winked at him. "I make no promises I've no mind to keep, my lord. Now come along, Phoebe. Miss Peabody will have my guts for garters if I don't take you up to bed now."

"Miss Peagoose," Phoebe said, grinning at her.

Pippin pursed her lips, wagging a finger at her. "I told you not to repeat that, you little devil. Come along with you."

Phoebe gave a crow of laughter and ran to kiss Lucian and then Matilda.

"This is the happiest day of my life," she announced, as Matilda had to resort to the handkerchief again.

"That it is, my lamb," Pippin said taking her hand. "While I think of it, my lord, would it be all right with you if Dharani Das were to come to visit me here tomorrow afternoon? It is my day off."

Lucian stared at her, a little frown between his eyebrows. "On the sole condition you do not cast spells in my kitchen. I do not wish eye of newt for my supper, I assure you."

Pippin returned a rather wicked smile.

"As if you'd know," she said, chuckling, and escorted Phoebe out of the room.

"That's the most terrifying thing I've ever heard," Lucian said as the door closed behind her.

Matilda laughed and ran into his arms. She pressed close as he pulled his arms tight, smiling down at her.

"My love."

"Yes," she replied, her voice quavering with happiness. "Always."

"Always," he repeated softly.

"What changed your mind?" she asked, still unable to believe it was really happening, that she would be his wife.

"I love you too much to let you go," he said simply. "And your letter made me realise that it was not only I who would suffer if I turned away from you. If I lost you, I would condemn generations to come to live without love. I read your words a hundred times at least, and each time they seemed to echo in my heart, louder and louder."

"Oh, Lucian," she said, resting her head on his chest and holding on tight.

He nuzzled her hair, breathing in the heady scent of orange blossom and the woman he loved.

"You were right," he whispered. "I had never considered my son as anything other than the next Montagu. I had not considered him as a real person, as a boy like Philip or Thomas… or like me. The thought of him living the life I have lived, or anything close to it…."

He shook his head and pulled back to look at her, his beautiful eyes grave and full of adoration.

"I want them to be loved, Matilda, to grow up in a family where they never doubt that each one of them is as valued as much as the next. I want them to know what happiness looks like, and that they are at liberty to find it."

"Then we must set a good example."

"Yes," he said, smiling at her. "We must."

And then he kissed her.

Chapter 24

My dearest Prue,

It was so lovely to see you and your beautiful daughter last week. How proud Bedwin looked too. The little dab has him wrapped about her finger already, the clever girl.

I just had to write and tell you how much I am enjoying The Eagle and the Lamb. I have cried buckets and fallen profoundly in love with the hero. For heaven's sake do not tell Jerome or he'll be dreadfully cross. All the ton is abuzz with it, not to mention the entire world. I heard the servants discussing it this morning. The kitchen maids were all a-flutter, swooning over the icy marquess whose heart was melted by the lamb. I believe there will be quite a crowd outside St George's tomorrow. It will be the wedding of the century and no mistake. The world has fallen in head over ears in love with Montagu and Matilda, and cannot wait to see their happy ending.

—Excerpt of a letter from Mrs Bonnie Cadogan to Her Grace Prunella Adolphus, Duchess of Bedwin.

19th June 1815. St George's Church, Hanover Square.

"Good Lord, this crowd is ridiculous," Nate complained, craning his neck to see the road ahead out of the window. "At this rate the eagle will not get a look at his lamb until sometime next week."

Matilda blushed a little at the reference to Prue's outrageously romantic book, which had sold in its thousands the moment the first chapters had published. It was being released in instalments and the anticipation of the happy ending in tandem with a real life wedding had caused quite a furore.

The eagle was a thinly disguised version of Lucian, and referred to the Montagu crest of an eagle with wings outstretched. Matilda had protested somewhat at being compared to a lamb. Prue, however, had assured her that the imagery was necessary to capture the audience's heart and that the lamb would be proven to have the heart of a lioness as the story progressed. She'd been correct, of course, and Matilda was overwhelmed by her newfound celebrity. Everyone wanted to know her, and in truth it was becoming a little tiresome. She longed for Dern, for the peace and tranquillity of the beautiful countryside, and for her life with Lucian to begin.

She had been bitterly disappointed when Lucian had refused to buy a special licence, determined that they should conduct the marriage just as it ought to be done. He was insistent that they would be married in the full view of the *ton*, with no hint of embarrassment or anything rushed or hidden. When he had told her he wanted the world to see how much he loved and admired her, all her arguments had evaporated. Although the month he had forced her to endure in waiting had been excruciating, she was glad that they had. Through his efforts, his public display the night of the ball, and Prue's beautiful story, her reputation had been restored to her. They had become society darlings, their presence sought at every event, their names on everyone's lips, and their likenesses in every print shop window.

Phoebe had begged for one particular image that Lucian had gone into a print shop himself and bought for her, much to the delight of the scandal sheets. It depicted him down on one knee, with Matilda falling into a swoon. Meanwhile Phoebe dangled precariously over the edge of the balustrade shouting encouragement whilst Pippin held her by the ankles. Phoebe was enchanted with the image and had immediately pasted it to the wall behind her bed.

At long last the carriage rocked to a stop outside St George's having fought its way through the crowds. The door was opened, and Nate got down, holding out his hand to her.

"We're late," he said, looking far too pleased about that. "Montagu will think you've changed your mind."

"No, he won't," Matilda retorted, giving Nate a warning glare that instructed him to be nice.

Whatever Nate might have said in reply was drowned out by the swell of cheers from the crowds gathered outside the church when they caught their first glimpse of her. People were waving prints of her and Lucian, and shouting encouragement, and Matilda laughed, shaking her head in wonder.

"They're all barking mad," her brother complained, helping her with the voluminous train on her gown as their footmen made a path through. Finally, they made it under the grand portico supported by its six Corinthian columns and to the doors of the church.

"Well, then," Nate said, as a swell of music could be heard from inside. "Last chance to change your mind."

Matilda sighed and kissed his cheek. "No, thank you, Nate. I should very much like to get married now."

"Oh, very well," her brother said with a heavy sigh. "If you insist. It's about time the fellow took you off my hands."

Matilda resisted the urge to kick him as he moved forward, and her heart thudded with excitement. She was going to marry Lucian. It was happening, and she could not wait.

***

Lucian looked at his watch for the fifth time in as many minutes. "She's late."

Gabriel gave him an amused grin and shook his head. "Bride's prerogative, isn't it?" he said mildly and then laughed. "Don't panic. The world and his wife has descended on Hanover Square this morning. The carriage will be struggling to get through."

"That ought to have been accounted for," Lucian muttered darkly, knowing he sounded like a sulky boy, but he had waited about as long as his nerves could stand. An entire month was enough for any man to endure, another five minutes and he would lose any semblance of his legendary composure for good. His best man wasn't helping particularly, seeming to take great delight in Lucian's inability to hide his nerves.

Lucian cast another surreptitious glance at his watch before slipping it back in his pocket. He looked up to see Gabe casting him a pitying smile.

"Friends are greatly overrated," he said, folding his arms.

Gabe just chuckled and handed him a small silver flask.

"We have our compensations," he assured Lucian. "I have the ring and brandy, what more could you ask for?"

Happily, Lucian did not have time to think up an appropriate retort to that. Phoebe, as ever, saved him from a rapid plunge into gloom by hitching up her skirts and running down the aisle, yelling *"she's here!"* at the top of her lungs.

Lucian let out a breath and beamed at her, ignoring the gasps and mutters of all the old dowagers who exclaimed at her dreadful behaviour.

"Thank you, Bee," he said, shooing her back to her position as Matilda's bridesmaid.

The organ began to play, the sound resonating in his ears as the congregation stood for the bride. Lucian's breath snagged in his throat. Matilda glimmered as she walked down the aisle, shafts of sunlight catching the silver thread in her gown and making it sparkle, making *her* sparkle. There were diamonds at her throat, her ears and wrists, and a heavy tiara to match: jewels that had been in their family for generations and worn by every Marchioness of Montagu on their wedding day. Lucian knew, without a doubt, that not one of those women had been loved by their marquess as he loved her. They would break the mould, the two of them together, and make their family great and powerful, though not through wealth or politics or brilliant marriages, but by living life to the full. Their success would come by finding happiness and love and joy, and all the things he realised now could not be bought or taken, but had to be given, selflessly and with your whole heart.

Suddenly, she was standing beside him and, as always when she was near, the rest of the world fell away.

"My love," he said, holding out his hand to her.

She smiled at him, her eyes alight with happiness, and held on tight.

***

"Bee, if you eat another slice of cake, you'll be sick," Lucian warned, though he was smiling at her.

Phoebe shrugged and popped another piece in her mouth.

"I don't care," she said around the cake.

Matilda hid a smile as Lucian sighed. "It's hopeless," he lamented. "No one will ever marry such a hoyden. I'll have to send her to a nunnery."

"They wouldn't have me either," Phoebe said cheerfully. "Besides, I'd escape. Flash Jack taught me how to pick a lock."

Lucian groaned. "That's it. No one will ever take her off my hands."

Phoebe snickered and climbed into his lap, heedless of her sticky fingers on his immaculate wedding clothes. "You said you couldn't part with me unless it was someone I liked very much, enough that I couldn't bear the thought of not being married to him."

"I'm sure I said no such thing," he remarked. "You're a diabolical child and you know it."

She stared up at him, batting her eyelashes shamelessly. "I love you, Papa."

Matilda's eyes burned, her heart squeezing in her chest. From the fierce glitter in Lucian's eyes, he was similarly afflicted.

"Phoebe, sweetheart," he began, but Phoebe cut in over him.

"I know you're not really my papa," she said softly. "I know it was Thomas and I shall never forget that, but I never really knew him, nor my mother either, and… and I should like so much to have a mother and father. Couldn't we pretend again, like we did before?"

Matilda reached for Lucian's hand and squeezed, and he looked to her, his beautiful eyes no longer cold, but filled with warmth and love. She nodded at him and he smiled, a full, wide smile that showed the dimples she adored all the more for how elusive they were. Though she thought perhaps they would be more familiar from now on.

"Well, Bee," he said, his voice a little thick. "Perhaps we can see about making it official, not just pretend. If… If you are certain it is what you would like?"

Phoebe stared at him, eyes wide with wonder, and then threw her arms about his neck. "Oh, yes! Oh, yes, please!"

Lucian hugged her tightly and kissed her cheek before she scrambled off his lap.

"I must tell Pippin!" she shrieked, running full tilt across the room to the door.

"You don't mind?" he asked Matilda, holding her hand tightly.

"Of course not," she said, torn between laughter and tears as how perfect the day had been. "It's a wonderful idea, and it will make her so happy."

He let out a soft huff of laughter and spoke quietly, his voice low and dark, mischief glinting in his eyes.

"Speaking of making people happy," he said, "I think I have endured quite enough. I want to be alone with my wife."

"*You've* endured enough?" she retorted indignantly. "It was your idea to wait so long."

She blushed a little as he cast her a smile that made something hot and liquid erupt deep inside her.

"Ah yes, you'd have had your wicked way with me back in Matlock Bath if I'd not protected my virtue so fiercely."

"Oh, you devil!" she whispered as her blush increased and turned her scarlet. "I can't believe you said that."

"Truly?" he replied, all innocence. "My, you are in for a shock, wife. For I have many things I want to say to you that will make you blush far harder than that."

She met his gaze and held it, recognising the challenge there.

"I should like to see you try," she said, watching his eyes grow dark as a sloe berry, the silver almost swallowed entirely.

"Should you?" he asked, leaning in, his breath fluttering against her ear.

Matilda shivered and turned back to him, returning the favour, brushing her lips against his ear as she spoke.

"I dare you...."

There was a brief, electric silence and then he stood, so fast his chair would have toppled back if Gabriel hadn't been passing and caught it.

"In a hurry, Lucie, old man?" He said, his voice warm with amusement and quite obviously a little foxed.

Lucian turned to glare at Matilda in outrage.

"I didn't!" she squeaked, realising he thought she'd told Gabe of Thomas's pet name for him. "My word, Lucian, I never told him."

Gabe snickered at Lucian's narrow-eyed glare.

"You're lucky I have more important things to consider," Lucian grumbled. "But I promise dire consequences if you ever say that aloud again."

"Yes, my lord marquess," Gabe replied, with as much insincerity as he could muster.

Lucian growled at him impatiently and took Matilda's hand, hurrying her out of the room before anyone else could waylay them.

"You like him," she said happily, while Lucian dragged her across the hallway towards the stairs, struggling to keep up as her heavy skirts weighed her down.

"He's a pain in the neck," Lucian replied succinctly. "He's rude, has almost as many enemies as I do, no respect whatsoever for my station, and insists I muddy my hands with some dreadful moneymaking scheme he's all excited about."

He turned then, his silver eyes glinting.

"Of course I like him."

Matilda laughed as they got to the top of the stairs and then squealed in shock as she was swept off her feet and into his arms.

"You're too slow," he said, smiling at her as he carried her along the corridor to the bedroom.

"It's these dratted skirts, they're so heavy."

"Then we had best dispense with them at once."

Matilda gave a happy sigh as the sounds of the wedding breakfast below grew quieter the farther they got from it. Lucian kicked the bedroom door shut behind them, and set her gently down, his hands at her waist. She looked up at him and he leaned in, pressing his forehead to hers.

"I love you, Lady Montagu."

Matilda let out a breath. "How marvellous that sounds."

"It does," he agreed. "And you are magnificent, love. I think my heart stopped when I saw you walk into that church. You looked so exquisite."

"It is a lovely gown," she said, stroking one hand over the fine silver material. "I knew I had to have it the moment I saw it. It's the colour of your eyes."

He frowned a little, shaking his head. "My eyes are grey."

Matilda laughed, finding herself laughing harder still at the perplexed expression he was giving her.

"They're grey," he insisted.

"N-no, my love," she said, shaking her head helplessly. "I promise you, they are not, and I am your wife now, so you must agree with me."

"Oh, is that how it works?"

"It is," she said gravely. "And I seem to remember you have a dare to complete."

"So I do," he said, and all at once her skin was alive with anticipation. "Then I had better get to work. Turn around."

He took his time, undoing every button and hook with what seemed to Matilda to be excessive care.

"Oh, do hurry," she complained.

Lucian only laughed and shook his head. "No, my wicked darling. This time, you are mine. Mine to do with as I please, there is no escape for you. I will make you beg for me, love."

"I'll beg now, if you like," she said, frustrated already, but he only chuckled again, a dark sound that shivered over her skin like a caress.

Finally her chemise slid to the floor with a soft flutter, to join the puddle of silver fabric at her ankles. She was naked but for her stockings and the silver ribbons that held them in place. Lucian walked a circle around her, his eyes glinting as he looked her over.

"Lucian," she said breathlessly, desperate for him to touch her.

"What, love?" he asked, a now familiar quirk to his lips that made her pulse thunder. "Is there something you want?"

She huffed out a breath. "You just want to make me say it."

"Of course I do," he said. "I want to hear what you want me to do to you. I want to know that you want it, that you want me."

"I don't think there's much doubt of that," she said, feeling the truth of her words as heat pooled inside her.

He stepped closer, not quite touching her, his lips ghosting over hers in a teasing caress. "You don't?"

Matilda shook her head.

"Show me then, show me your desire."

Matilda saw the challenge in his eyes and felt the answering blush colour her skin, blooming all over her.

"Such a pretty colour," he murmured, chasing it from her cheeks, down her neck, to the peak of one nipple with a fingertip.

Matilda shivered.

"Show me," he whispered, moving to stand behind her, his soft command tickling her neck and he pressed a kiss to her nape.

Gathering her courage, she reached for his hand and put it flat against her stomach, and then drew it slowly down, guiding him between her legs. She heard his slow exhale as his fingers slid through the soft curls, to find the wet heat beneath.

"You do want me." The words were smug, spoken against her skin and sending goosebumps rushing over her. "Very badly."

"Yes," she agreed, leaning back against him as his fingers found the source of her pleasure and circled the little nub of flesh with expert caresses.

She closed her eyes, her head falling back against his shoulder as he kissed her neck.

"Do you remember your friend Prue's Christmas ball?" he asked her, and Matilda struggled to open her eyes, to consider the question as his clever fingers commanded her body to succumb to the pleasure of his touch.

"Mmmmm," was all she could manage by way of reply, and he chuckled.

"I took you for a walk about the house. I intended to seduce you that night, may God forgive me. I was so desperate for you, out of my mind with jealousy whenever you danced with another man."

She laughed at that. "You could have fooled me."

"No, I couldn't. You knew it soon enough, once we were trapped behind those curtains. And you loved it, didn't you, my wicked angel?"

He pressed closer and the hard length of him burned hot against her even through his clothes. Just like that night, when she had felt the evidence of his desire for her for the first time.

The blush burned her cheeks. She was unable to deny it. She had loved it. The sounds of another couple's lovemaking and Lucian's arm about her waist, holding her close, trapping them in the darkness, had been the most erotic thing she'd ever known. Not that she'd had much experience of such things, though she suspected that was about to change.

"Answer the question, Matilda."

"Yes," she said, as one lazy hand caressed her breast, tweaking the nipple until she gasped, the other still occupied between her thighs, slowly driving her out of her mind. "I loved it."

"You wanted me too," he murmured. "You told me no, but you didn't want me to stop. Did you?"

She shook her head, but that did not satisfy him.

"Tell me."

"No," she said, the word breathless as desire made her giddy, her knees weak. "I wanted you to touch me."

"How? How did you want it?"

"Like this. I wanted your hands, your mouth, I wanted you to touch me, to make me cry out with pleasure like the woman on the other side of the curtains."

He groaned and slid a finger inside of her. Matilda cried out as the pleasure of it broke over her, her body clenching around him as he drove her higher. Helpless in the crisis' wake, she was relieved when Lucian swept her up before her knees gave out entirely. He carried her to the bed, laying her down.

Matilda collapsed against the soft counterpane, her body pliant, limbs cast wide in abandon. How wanton she must appear, not that she cared... until she saw the look in his eyes, the hunger there. Then she cared, and she loved it.

"You were jealous," she said happily, gazing up at him as he slowly stripped off his coat, casting it aside, and his long, elegant fingers undid the buttons on his waistcoat.

"I was. Madly jealous," he agreed, his voice dark.

"You wanted me."

"More than I have ever wanted anything. I thought I would die when you told me no."

"Did you think of that night often?" she asked, feeling the curve of a decadent smile move over her lips.

He laughed then, low and wicked. "Oh, that pleases you, my lady. Yes. Yes, I thought of it often, though in my dreams you never denied me. Such depraved things you did. You gave me everything I asked, and more."

"Then I shall make it up to you," she said, opening her legs wider, a shameless invitation.

His hands stilled, his gaze riveted upon her, his breathing harsh.

"Yes," he said. "You will."

A thrill of excitement shivered over her. She watched as he rid himself of the rest of his clothes, taking his time, deliberately, the beast.

"Lucian."

She spoke his name like a plea, a complaint, an urge for him to hurry. He ignored it, moving closer to the bed, his cravat held loosely in one hand, the other reaching out to draw lazy circles over her skin, until she shivered.

"Please," she said.

"I love you."

She sighed and stretched, feeling the pleasure of his words like a caress. "I know. Show me."

"I will," he promised. "Do you trust me?"

"Of course."

He smiled and moved onto the bed. "You can say no to me, Matilda. At any time. Do not be afraid to do so."

"I'm not," she said, a little puzzled by his words, unable to comprehend what she might say no to. There was nothing she wanted to deny him.

He laughed then. "No, that is true enough, I think. You've never been shy of denying me what I want in the past."

"What do you want, Lucian?" she asked, intrigued at the heat in his eyes at her question. He leaned down and brushed his lips over hers.

"Everything," he murmured. "But for now, I should like to blindfold you."

Matilda's eyebrows rose. "Why?"

"Because I want to see you that way, because it is erotic. If one sense is denied you, the others become heightened."

"They do?" She was intrigued, only too eager as he nodded. "Yes, then. I should like you to."

Matilda shivered as he drew the soft cloth over her eyes and the world went dark. There was nothing then, nothing else but the feel of his hands upon her, gentle and caressing, touching her so carefully, making her heart and soul sing with the knowledge that she was loved. She cried out as his mouth joined the assault on her senses, and he was right, of course. The darkness was freeing and she let her inhibitions fall away, writhing with abandon beneath him, asking him for what she wanted—*more*, and *more* and *don't stop*—until she was quaking with the force of yet another climax, clutching at the bedcovers and crying out his name.

She was gasping, wrung out, when the blindfold was carefully drawn away and she blinked in the dim light.

"So beautiful," he murmured, nipping at her ear, nuzzling her neck until she shivered. "And all mine."

"Yes," she said, a little astonished at the way her body responded at once as he moved over her, taking his place between her thighs, sliding his arousal over the slick flesh that still throbbed with pleasure. "Oh, yes, Lucian, please."

"Tell me what you want," he whispered. "Like you did before. Ask me."

She looked up at him, wrapping her arms about his neck and drawing his mouth down to hers for a lingering kiss. "And if I do, will you deny me?"

He laughed at that, shaking his head. "I'll never deny you anything again, my love. I would give you the world if you asked me for it."

"I just want you, Lucian. All of you. I need you, inside me."

He made a harsh sound and responded at once, pushing into her. Matilda stilled at the sudden invasion. The sense of fullness she had wanted so badly was more than she had expected. A little too much. He stopped at once.

"Matilda?" His voice was taut, filled with concern.

"Yes. Don't stop."

"Relax," he murmured, exhaling with relief, distracting her with a kiss that stole what little remained of her mind, and then he was thrusting deeper and it was delicious.

She sighed and wrapped her legs about his hips, urging him deeper still, wanting more. He groaned with pleasure and the sound thrilled through her.

"Yes," she said, clutching at his shoulders, sliding one hand into the warm silk of his hair.

He sighed and ducked his head, closing his mouth over her breast, suckling until she cried out, the pleasure close to unbearable. She laughed with the joy of it and he looked up, his eyes alight with happiness.

"I'm sorry. I probably ought not laugh at such a time," she managed, smiling anyway.

He shook his head.

"I love to hear you laugh, to hear your pleasure. I want to make you happy, always." His breath caught as she tilted her hips, seeking her own pleasure and exclaimed at the same time he did. "Oh, God, love."

He moved again, repeating the angle for her to hit the spot she had discovered and Matilda saw stars.

"Oh!" she cried. "Oh, that makes me happy. Do it again."

Lucian chuckled.

"Here?" he asked, holding her in place and nudging against the place that made her gasp. "Ah, yes."

Matilda could not laugh, too enraptured, too committed to chasing sensation as they clung together until his body grew taut and he shuddered in her arms, calling her name and holding her close. His pleasure in her was entrancing, the hot spill of his seed inside her enough to tumble her over the edge with him and leave her gasping and dazed in his arms.

"Oh," she said, once she could speak again, once words were remembered and she could bring the right ones to mind. "At last."

She felt his shoulders quivering under her hands as he laughed, helpless with relief and love and happiness.

"At last," he echoed, rolling onto his back and taking her with him. "At last. Thank God."

Epilogue

Dear diary,

It has been the best day ever in the world!

I know I have written that before, but each time it is true. Today was my birthday and I have friends. They came to celebrate with me, and we had cake and presents, and Mother arranged parlour games. We played blind man's bluff and snap dragon and it was marvellous. Tomorrow the grown-ups are coming and there will be more cake and more presents and Papa says I am quite dreadful and horribly spoiled. He smiles when he says it, though, so I know he doesn't mean it. He smiles all the time now.

—Excerpt of an entry by Miss Phoebe Barrington to her diary.

7th February 1816. Dern, Sevenoaks, Kent.

Seven months later…

Gabe gave a yell of triumph as the snowball hit Lucian smack in the head, knocking his hat off.

"Oh, good shot!" Helena cried, clapping enthusiastically.

Matilda snorted with laughter, earning herself a reproachful glare from her husband.

"Think that's funny, do you?" he demanded, scooping up a large handful of snow.

"No," she said, holding her hands out and backing up, correctly interpreting the look in his eyes, which were dancing with mischief. "No, Lucian, don't you—"

She shrieked, hitching up her skirts as her husband pursued her.

"Don't you dare!" she shouted again, dodging behind a tree.

"Get her, Papa!" Phoebe yelled in delight, then screaming as Bonnie stuffed a snowball down the back of her neck. "Oh, you'll regret that!"

Bonnie darted away, skirts hiked up to her knees, shrieking with laughter.

Matilda pressed on into the undergrowth, the sound of their friends enjoying the snow fading until nothing but the snap of twigs and the crunch of snow was heard. She stilled, leaning breathless against a tree as Lucian stalked toward her.

"Now you're in trouble," he said with satisfaction, brandishing the ball of snow.

Matilda shook her head, grinning. "I'm not. I shall make a deal with you."

"A deal?" he said, silver eyes glinting. "What kind of deal?"

"The kind that stops you stuffing that snowball down my neck," she said, laughing.

"Intriguing," he replied, moving closer. "What did you have in mind?"

"A kiss. A kiss for the snowball."

He snorted and shook his head. "I can have a kiss whenever I like. My wife is very obliging, you know."

"She is?" she asked, raising an eyebrow at him.

"Oh, yes," he murmured, stalking closer. "Very. She'll give me anything I want."

He leaned one gloved hand on the tree beside her head, the one holding the snowball raised on her other side.

"Why would she do that?" Matilda asked, her lips twitching.

"Because she wants it too." He spoke the words so close she shivered, leaning down and pressing a kiss to the sensitive skin beneath her ear. "She's insatiable."

"So are you," Matilda retorted, and then she looked up at him, a little anxious at the truth of her words.

"What?" he said at once, instantly aware of the change in her mood. He dropped the snowball, taking her into his arms. "What's wrong?"

Matilda shook her head and laughed. "N-Nothing is wrong."

"Then why do you look so worried?" he asked, his eyes full of concern, searching hers. "Is it the baby?"

Matilda stared at him, her mouth falling open.

"You know!" she exclaimed in astonishment. "I hardly dared believe it myself, and... Oh, drat you, Lucian. I wanted to surprise you."

He laughed and pulled her closer against him, cradling her head against his chest. "I can count, love. We spend every night together, and it's been sometime since you told me you were indisposed."

Matilda blushed, as aware as he was that she would never tell him she was indisposed if it were possible. "Well. You might have pretended. I was so looking forward to telling you."

"Were you?" he asked, his beautiful eyes troubled. "Then why did you look so worried?"

Matilda pouted and then gave a huff of frustration. "Because I shall be *indisposed* for some time, and fat too, and you won't want me anymore."

She was well aware of the whiny note to her words and looked up, a little affronted all the same to find Lucian struggling to keep a straight face.

"Don't you dare laugh at me," she scolded him.

He shook his head, making a heroic effort to rearrange his face.

"I'm not," he managed, though his voice quavered a little. "But really, love. How could you be so addle-pated? Not want you, indeed. Are you mad?"

She looked up at him, the knot of worry that had kept her awake the past few nights falling away.

"Are you sure?"

He smiled and moved to her side, so he could lay his hand over her belly, to the place where his child had taken root.

"I've never been surer of anything in my life. I love you, both of you, so much. So, you may get as fat as you like, and I shall still find new ways to make you cry my name to the rafters and frighten the ghosts, no matter how ungainly you become."

Matilda snorted and buried her face in his coat. "I'm not that loud."

"You are," he murmured, nipping at her ear. "And I love it."

"Papa!"

They turned to see Phoebe running towards them, her face pink with the cold, her golden ringlets all a tumble.

"It's time for cake," she said, staring at them in frustration. "Oh, do come along. Everyone is waiting for you."

Lucian looked back at her. "Can we tell her?" he asked softly.

Matilda nodded, adding. "But only if she can keep a secret."

Phoebe eyes grew wide and she hurried closer, tugging at Lucian's coat. "I can. I can. Oh, you know I can, Papa. Do tell me."

Lucian grinned and got to his knees in the snow.

"I have one last present for you today, Bee, but it won't arrive for…." He looked up to Matilda. "A little over six months?"

Matilda harrumphed, rolling her eyes at him, but nodded.

Phoebe stared at him, then at Matilda and back again.

"A baby!" she shrieked, throwing her arms about Lucian's neck so hard he almost fell over backwards.

"Hush," he said, pressing a finger to her lips. "A secret for a little longer, Bee."

Phoebe returned a sheepish grin and then danced on the spot.

"A brother or sister," she squeaked quietly.

"Yes," Lucian said, and Matilda heard the emotion in his voice. "Though nothing will change. You know that, don't you? I could never love you less, no matter how many brothers and sisters come along."

Phoebe gave a snort of laughter as though that were obvious.

"I know that," she said, kissing his cheek and sounding a little exasperated. "How could you love me any less? I'm adorable."

With a wicked laugh, she gave Lucian a little push, sending him sprawling back into the snow before she ran away, giggling madly, skirts flying as she went.

"Hurry up, I want my cake," she yelled over her shoulder.

Lucian looked up from the snow with a rueful grin. "Heaven help us."

He got up, and Matilda helped him brush the snow from his clothes.

"Well, we'd best go and have cake," she said, taking his hand, but he stilled her, his expression growing serious.

"There's something I must tell you about Phoebe. I meant to before, only…." He laughed. "Only there never seems to be a moment for anything serious. Every day has been too full, too extraordinary to speak of such things, but I need you to know about her, about her heritage."

Matilda held his hand tightly, sensing his tension. "She's illegitimate," she said.

Lucian nodded.

Once, the notion of the Marquess of Montagu bringing a bastard child into his home would have been extraordinary, but she knew him now. She knew his revulsion at the idea was not for the babe itself, but for those who would be so thoughtless as to create a child who must bear the burden of such a cross, in a world that could be cruel.

"Does she know?"

He nodded. "Though she knows too that I have done everything I can to bury the truth. She knows she must never speak of it."

"She's strong and brave and she knows she is loved, Lucian. Whatever the future holds, she will face it head on."

"She will," he agreed. "When I received my brother's letter, the one he wrote before he died, he said he'd not known about her. He had lost himself to the darkness by then, and was rarely in one place for long. The child's mother had been too ashamed to contact me, a fact for which I hold myself entirely responsible. If I had been more approachable—"

Matilda kissed his cheek. "You were not to know, Lucian, and you had your own troubles to bear."

He smiled and hugged her close to him. "By the time Thomas discovered he had a child, the mother had died. She had never recovered fully from the birth and she contracted influenza. Thomas left Phoebe in the care of the girl's grandparents. Good people, but too old to cope with a lively little girl. He begged me to see to her future, to see she had everything she needed."

He took a breath and Matilda waited, knowing he would tell her the rest.

"I went to see her, believing I would find a good family to raise her, and settle enough money upon her that she should want for nothing."

"But it didn't work out that way did it?" she asked gently.

Lucian shook his head. "I walked into the room to see my niece for the first time. She was just a baby, toddling about, all blond curls and pink cheeks. The moment she saw me, she ran to me and raised her arms. *Up,* she said." And he laughed at the memory, his voice thick as he spoke again. "There she was, this tiny girl with this imperious little voice, and my brother's eyes gazing up at me. I was done for. I could deny her nothing. She's had me wrapped about her thumb ever since."

"And so you took her home."

He nodded. "This is her home, and now I am her father, and between us we will see she is safe and happy and wants for nothing. Any man that wishes to marry her, when she is of age, must be worthy of her, must prove he deserves her."

Matilda laughed and put her arm through his as they made their way back to the house for Phoebe's birthday and the delicious cake Pippin had made for her.

"We will do all of that, my love," she agreed. "But I cannot help but feel that Phoebe will the one to judge his worth. In truth, I pity the man that falls in love with her. He will have quite a battle on his hands to prove himself. After all," she said, looking up at him with adoration. "He has a very high standard to live up to."

The End.

Almost…

If you would like to see just who is worthy of Phoebe's hand, and just how hard the poor devil must prove himself, don't miss the last exciting instalment of Girls Who Dare – To Dance until Dawn

And if you are as sad as I am to say goodbye to the Peculiar Ladies, who have become my dearest friends as I hope they are yours too, don't despair. For all our happy couples have been prolific in producing a wonderful cast of offspring, so don't miss my new series, and a whole new set of Daring Daughters, as well as a chance to catch up with old friends.

Look out for "Dare to be Wicked" and pre-order your copy soon!

Girls who dare– *Inside every wallflower is the beating heart of a lioness, a passionate individual willing to risk all for their dream, if only they can find the courage to begin. When these overlooked girls make a pact to change their lives, anything can happen.*

Twelve girls. Twelve dares in a hat. Who will dare to risk it all?

Next and final in the series

To Dance Until Dawn
Girls Who Dare, Book 12

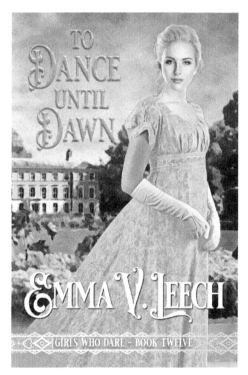

Pre Order your copy here: To

To Dance until Dawn

Want more Emma?

If you enjoyed this book, please support this indie author and take a moment to leave a few words in a review. *Thank you!*

To be kept informed of special offers and free deals (which I do regularly) follow me on *https://www.bookbub.com/authors/emma-v-leech*

To find out more and to get news and sneak peeks of the first chapter of upcoming works, go to my website and sign up for the newsletter.

http://www.emmavleech.com/

Come and join the fans in my Facebook group for news, info and exciting discussion...

Emma's Book Club

Or Follow me here......

http://viewauthor.at/EmmaVLeechAmazon

Emma's Twitter page

About Me!

I started this incredible journey way back in 2010 with The Key to Erebus but didn't summon the courage to hit publish until October 2012. For anyone who's done it, you'll know publishing your first title is a terribly scary thing! I still get butterflies on the morning a new title releases but the terror has subsided at least. Now I just live in dread of the day my daughters are old enough to read them.

The horror! (On both sides I suspect.)

2017 marked the year that I made my first foray into Historical Romance and the world of the Regency Romance, and my word what a year! I was delighted by the response to this series and can't wait to add more titles. Paranormal Romance readers need not despair however as there is much more to come there too. Writing has become an addiction and as soon as one book is over I'm hugely excited to start the next so you can expect plenty more in the future.

As many of my works reflect I am greatly influenced by the beautiful French countryside in which I live. I've been here in the South West for the past twenty years though I was born and raised in England. My three gorgeous girls are all bilingual and the youngest who is only six, is showing signs of following in my footsteps after producing *The Lonely Princess* all by herself.

I'm told book two is coming soon ...

She's keeping me on my toes, so I'd better get cracking!

KEEP READING TO DISCOVER MY OTHER BOOKS!

Other Works by Emma V. Leech

(For those of you who have read The French Fae Legend series, please remember that chronologically The Heart of Arima precedes The Dark Prince)

Girls Who Dare

To Dare a Duke

To Steal A Kiss

To Break the Rules

To Follow her Heart

To Wager with Love

To Dance with a Devil

To Winter at Wildsyde

To Experiment with Desire

To Bed the Baron

To Ride with the Knight

To Hunt the Hunter

Matilda and Montagu, the story so far

To Dance until Dawn (August 14, 2020)

Rogues & Gentlemen

The Rogue

The Earl's Temptation

Scandal's Daughter

The Devil May Care

Nearly Ruining Mr. Russell

One Wicked Winter

To Tame a Savage Heart

Persuading Patience

The Last Man in London

Flaming June

Charity and the Devil

A Slight Indiscretion

The Corinthian Duke

The Blackest of Hearts

Duke and Duplicity

The Scent of Scandal

The Rogue and The Earl's Temptation Box set

Melting Miss Wynter

The Winter Bride (A R&G Novella)

The Regency Romance Mysteries

Dying for a Duke

A Dog in a Doublet

The Rum and the Fox

The French Vampire Legend

The Key to Erebus

The Heart of Arima

The Fires of Tartarus

The Boxset (The Key to Erebus, The Heart of Arima)

The Son of Darkness (October 31, 2020)

The French Fae Legend

The Dark Prince

The Dark Heart

The Dark Deceit

The Darkest Night

Short Stories: A Dark Collection.

Stand Alone

The Book Lover (a paranormal novella)

Audio Books!

Don't have time to read but still need your romance fix? The wait is over…

By popular demand, get your favourite Emma V Leech Regency Romance books on audio at Audible as performed by the incomparable Philip Battley and Gerard Marzilli. Several titles available and more added each month!

Click the links to choose your favourite and start listening now.

Rogues & Gentlemen

The Rogue

The Earl's Tempation

Scandal's Daughter

The Devil May Care

Nearly Ruining Mr Russell

One Wicked Winter

To Tame a Savage Heart

Persuading Patience

The Last Man in London

Flaming June

The Winter Bride, a novella

Girls Who Dare

To Dare a Duke

To Steal A Kiss

To Break the Rules

To Follow her Heart (coming soon)

The Regency Romance Mysteries

Dying for a Duke

A Dog in a Doublet (coming soon)

The French Vampire Legend

The Key to Erebus (coming soon)

Also check out Emma's regency romance series, Rogues & Gentlemen. Available now!

The Rogue
Rogues & Gentlemen Book 1

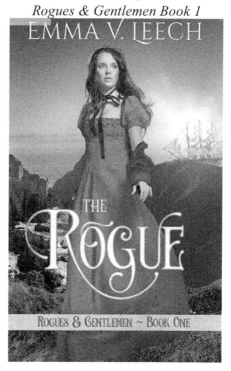

1815

Along the wild and untamed coast of Cornwall, smuggling is not only a way of life, but a means of survival.

Henrietta Morton knows well to look the other way when the free trading 'gentlemen' are at work. Yet when a notorious pirate, known as The Rogue, bursts in on her in the village shop, she takes things one step further.

Bewitched by a pair of wicked blue eyes, in a moment of insanity she hides the handsome fugitive from the local Militia. Her reward is a kiss that she just cannot forget. But in his haste to escape with his life, her pirate drops a letter, inadvertently giving

Henri incriminating information about the man she just helped free.

When her father gives her hand in marriage to a wealthy and villainous nobleman in return for the payment of his debts, Henri becomes desperate.

Blackmailing a pirate may be her only hope for freedom.

Read for free on Kindle Unlimited

The Rogue

Interested in a Regency Romance with a twist?

Dying for a Duke

The Regency Romance Mysteries Book 1

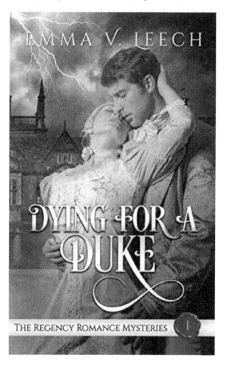

Straight-laced, imperious and morally rigid, Benedict Rutland - the darkly handsome Earl of Rothay - gained his title too young. Responsible for a large family of younger siblings that his frivolous parents have brought to bankruptcy, his youth was spent clawing back the family fortunes.

Now a man in his prime and financially secure he is betrothed to a strict, sensible and cool-headed woman who will never upset the balance of his life or disturb his emotions ...

But then Miss Skeffington-Fox arrives.

Brought up solely by her rake of a step-father, Benedict is scandalised by everything about the dashing Miss.

But as family members in line for the dukedom begin to die at an alarming rate, all fingers point at Benedict, and Miss Skeffington-Fox may be the only one who can save him.

FREE to read on Amazon Kindle Unlimited. Dying for a Duke

Lose yourself in Emma's paranormal world with The French Vampire Legend series…..

The Key to Erebus
The French Vampire Legend Book 1

The truth can kill you.

Taken away as a small child, from a life where vampires, the Fae, and other mythical creatures are real and treacherous, the beautiful young witch, Jéhenne Corbeaux is totally unprepared when she returns to rural France to live with her eccentric Grandmother.

Thrown headlong into a world she knows nothing about she seeks to learn the truth about herself, uncovering secrets more shocking than anything she could ever have imagined and finding that she is by no means powerless to protect the ones she loves.

Despite her Gran's dire warnings, she is inexorably drawn to the dark and terrifying figure of Corvus, an ancient vampire and master of the vast Albinus family.

Jéhenne is about to find her answers and discover that, not only is Corvus far more dangerous than she could ever imagine, but that he holds much more than the key to her heart …

FREE to read on Kindle Unlimited The Key to Erebus

Check out Emma's exciting fantasy series with hailed by Kirkus Reviews as "An enchanting fantasy with a likable heroine, romantic intrigue, and clever narrative flourishes."

The Dark Prince
The French Fae Legend Book 1

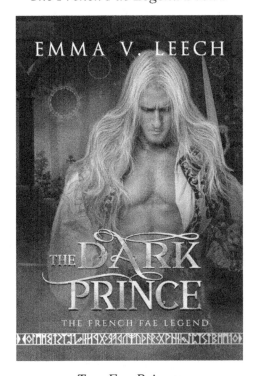

Two Fae Princes
One Human Woman
And a world ready to tear them all apart

Laen Braed is Prince of the Dark fae, with a temper and reputation to match his black eyes, and a heart that despises the human race. When he is sent back through the forbidden gates between realms to retrieve an ancient fae artefact, he returns home with far more than he bargained for.

Corin Albrecht, the most powerful Elven Prince ever born. His golden eyes are rumoured to be a gift from the gods, and destiny is calling him. With a love for the human world that runs deep, his friendship with Laen is being torn apart by his prejudices.

Océane De Beauvoir is an artist and bookbinder who has always relied on her lively imagination to get her through an unhappy and uneventful life. A jewelled dagger put on display at a nearby museum hits the headlines with speculation of another race, the Fae. But the discovery also inspires Océane to create an extraordinary piece of art that cannot be confined to the pages of a book.

With two powerful men vying for her attention and their friendship stretched to the breaking point, the only question that remains...who is truly The Dark Prince.

The man of your dreams is coming...or is it your nightmares he visits? Find out in Book One of The French Fae Legend.

Available now to read for FREE on Kindle Unlimited.

The Dark Prince

Acknowledgements

The vile Mr Burton is, sadly, loosely based on a real person and Liddon Mill on a real place. The story Lucian uncovered is one that existed at Litton Mill and is heart wrenching to read about. "A Memoir of Robert Blincoe, an orphan boy; sent to endure the horrors of a cotton mill," makes uncomfortable reading.

***

Thanks, of course, to my wonderful editor Kezia Cole.

To Victoria Cooper for all your hard work, amazing artwork and above all your unending patience!!! Thank you so much. You are amazing!

To my BFF, PA, personal cheerleader and bringer of chocolate, Varsi Appel, for moral support, confidence boosting and for reading my work more times than I have. I love you loads!

A huge thank you to all of Emma's Book Club members! You guys are the best!

I'm always so happy to hear from you so do email or message me :)

emmavleech@orange.fr

To my husband Pat and my family ... For always being proud of me.

Made in the USA
Monee, IL
09 May 2021